My Lady Deceiver

a&b

My Lady Deceiver

FREDA LIGHTFOOT

Allison & Busby Limited
13 Charlotte Mews
London W1T 4EJ
www.allisonandbusby.com

First published in Great Britain by Allison & Busby in 2012.

Copyright © 2012 by FREDA LIGHTFOOT

A CIP catalogue record for this book is available from
the British Library.

First Edition

ISBN 978-0-7490-1128-4

Typeset in 11.25/16.5 pt Sabon by
Allison & Busby Ltd.

Paper used in this publication is from sustainably managed sources.
All of the wood used is procured from legal sources and is fully traceable.
The producing mill uses schemes such as ISO 14001
to monitor environmental impact.

Printed and bound by
CPI Group (UK) Ltd, Croydon, CR0 4YY

My Lady Deceiver

Chapter One

1905

It was the shudder of the ship's engines slowing to a dull rhythmic beat which gave the weary passengers the first indication that they had survived. Packed as they were in an odorous pit where they'd languished for three long weeks of this perilous voyage, even the sickest traveller roused from their stupor sufficiently to whisper a quiet prayer of thanks.

'Is it over at last? Are we there?' they asked each other in stunned disbelief. Shouts were heard overhead, the sounds of men calling out instructions to each other, chains rattling and ropes being flung about.

Glancing into her mother's pale face, Rose let out a sigh of relief as she hugged her tight. 'We've landed, Mam. We're in America at last.' How they had longed for this moment, thinking that it might never come. In the strange, eerie silence that followed when the engines ceased their rumbling at last came the raucous squawk of a lone gull wheeling high above in a blue sky which they, as steerage passengers, could scarcely glimpse.

A great cheer went up and, as one, people began to scramble to their feet, to gather their children about them, to collect their precious belongings which they'd guarded for so long. Rose too set about thrusting bags and bundles into the arms of her siblings. 'You carry the heaviest bag, Micky. And Mary, you take this smaller one, and mind you keep tight hold of little Clara's hand. You know what a flibbertigibbet she is. If she doesn't behave, toss her overboard,' she said, plonking a kiss on the child's brow to show she was only teasing. 'Mam will mind the twins and the bedding, while I carry the rest of our stuff.'

Each person was allowed one piece of luggage or bundle. Choosing what to take with them to their new life might have proved to be a difficult decision, were it not for the fact that they'd had few possessions to begin with. Even so, the little ones couldn't carry much, so the task was largely left to Micky, Mam and herself.

Rose was already filling her arms with bundles of clothing, hefting the other brown suitcase, her excitement and the breath required to carry out this task such that she succumbed to a sudden fit of coughing.

Annie Belsfield rested a careworn hand on her daughter's cheek. 'Take care; that chill is worsening, if anything. We're not in America yet, girl, and we don't want no setbacks.'

Rose instantly sobered. They all knew they still had to

face the much feared inspection, which would begin the moment they stepped onto Ellis Island.

'Here, let me take that. It's too heavy for a slip of a thing like you.' A familiar voice at her side, and the heavy suitcase was wrested from her grasp.

'I can manage,' Rose protested, determined to do her bit. 'We're all supposed to carry our own.'

'But why should you when you've me hanging around with nought to do but help?'

She looked up into the young man's grinning face, round as a moon in the dim light with a smattering of freckles on nose and forehead, and, as her oldest friend, dearly familiar. Stocky and robust with a tousle of red hair, Joe was always at her side when most needed, like an elder brother. Rose trusted him absolutely, so relinquished the precious suitcase into his capable hands, together with some of her hard-won independence and pride.

'Just don't start your bossing, all right?'

Joe grinned. 'If I do boss you at times, it's only because I know what's best for you.'

Rose gave him a quelling glance from beneath thick brown lashes, pursing rosy lips tightly against a sharp response, as this wasn't the moment for one of their squabbles.

At heart she was a rather shy and unassuming girl, despite having lived all of her twenty years in a common lodging house on Fishponds Road in Bristol. Thin and underfed she may be, but also capable and uncomplaining, well used to coping with difficulties, particularly since the death of their father. He'd been in the Rifle Brigade, killed in action in South Africa in the Boer War. Following his death, and with six children to care for, Rose and her mother had grown even closer, but the family had suffered near starvation, dependent as they were upon poor relief.

Then quite out of the blue her mother's sister had sent them the money to join her in America. It felt like a gift from the gods, the answer to their prayers. They'd needed to pay six pounds and six shillings each for Mam and Rose, half price for each of the remaining five children. Which left them with the barest minimum to begin their new life. They could but hope it would be enough.

Joe, when he'd heard of their plan, had asked to come along as well, since he had no family of his own.

'How would you manage without me?' he'd teased, when Rose had expressed surprise over this decision. She'd guessed it was more likely the reverse since she was only too aware that Joe Colbert was sweet on her, which troubled her at times.

The battle over the suitcase turned out to be premature as it was some hours before the steerage passengers were even allowed out on deck. First and second class were naturally given priority, subjected to a superficial medical, and allowed to go on their way without too much hassle. The sick were being taken for a more intense physical examination at the quarantine facility on Staten Island.

Tension mounted, emotions running high by the time they eventually clattered up the stairs to emerge blinking into the bright sunshine, gazing in wonder at this new, much longed-for land. Everyone was dressed in their best clothes, waiting with exemplary patience for their turn to

10

disembark. They shared disturbing stories of those who had failed in their dream and been sent back home, like a faulty parcel. Many filled the long hours by practising what they might say in response to the dreaded questions, testing and advising each other. Others remained grimly silent, clinging on to the ship's rails and their few belongings with equal tenacity.

Like Rose and her family these people had staked everything they owned on this enterprise. Many had left behind loved ones they might never see again, while gladly turning their backs on poverty, unemployment, congested living conditions and miserable oppression.

In America they hoped for a better future, free education for their children, a free vote, low taxes, high wages, and an end perhaps to religious repression or compulsory military service. Liberty and justice for all. Not to mention a more forgiving climate. But they never stopped speculating on the fear of not achieving that dream, of being turned away at the gate. What might they be asked? they worried. What would be expected of them? It was essential they give the right answers, as well as be in good health.

Rose had succumbed to a chill during the last few days of the journey, coupled with a dry chesty cough that simply wouldn't budge. Many had suffered worse, falling prey to a mysterious shipboard fever. Far too many children, together with the dreams and hopes of their grieving mothers, had been slipped into the deep blue ocean. Rose had daily sent up a silent prayer that their own family would remain healthy and strong.

The ship had come to a halt at a pier close to the Brooklyn Bridge. Both the East and the Hudson River appeared to be packed with ships, some lined up on the New Jersey side, the rest anchored by the New York piers.

'Bringing immigrants to New York must be big business,' Rose speculated. 'Disembarking could take hours at this rate.'

'Aye, we could mebbe be here for a day or more,' Joe cheerfully agreed. 'Depends on where we are in the queue. Not that I mind waiting as it means I can stay with you a bit longer. Course, I could always come and settle near this aunt of yours, then I'd still be close by. Makes no odds to me where I live.'

'You might not like where Aunt Cassie lives, or be able to find a job. You have to go where the work is, Joe. What about your dream to work in a grand hotel? I don't want you making any sacrifices on my account.'

He moved a step closer, slipping an arm about her slender waist. 'I'd sacrifice anything for you, Rosie, you know I would.'

Rose rewarded his devotion with a patient smile, but chose to say nothing, not wishing to encourage him in this fancy he had for her. His attachment seemed to have grown daily throughout the voyage, and she wasn't entirely comfortable to find him forever at her side. Joe was a good friend, nothing more, so far as she was concerned. Besides, there was far too much to be done when they finally landed for her to even think of romance. It would be up to her to find employment as quickly as possible to help Mam provide for the younger ones. Micky too, at fourteen, could work, but the rest were too young as yet to earn their keep.

Gently disengaging herself from his hold, she went to slip her arm into her mother's and hug her close. 'Don't worry, Mam, Aunt Cassie will be waiting, and everything will be fine, I'm sure of it.' But as Rose again fell to coughing, she marvelled at the confidence in her own voice, quite at odds with the fear that was gnawing her insides.

At length, the steerage passengers were shepherded on to the ferries which were to transport them to Ellis Island for the examination. A great cheer went up as they sailed past the Statue of Liberty, a sight that would live with them for ever. The voices around her were now a jabber of different languages: Italian, German, Hungarian, Slovakian, Polish, all talking at once, mixed in with sobbing and prayers of thanks, the result of highly strung nerves and fearful trepidation.

What if they were rejected? What would they do then?

And there it was at last: a two-storey brick building with a stately tower at each corner and a myriad of windows looking out like hooded eyes over the bay. The reception centre claimed to be able to handle ten thousand immigrants in a day, and to Rose's bemused eyes there looked to be that many crowded on the patch of land in front of its open doors. Two ferries, each loaded with immigrants, were already lined up along the wharves. One began to draw away as their own took its place. Then the gangplank thumped down, and they stepped out into the unknown.

* * *

It was an hour later and they hadn't moved more than a few feet from where the ferry had deposited them. Clara tugged hard at her sister's hand. 'I'm hot, Rosie, and hungry. Can I have something to eat? Can I have a drink, please?'

'I'm sorry, sweetie, but we don't have anything to give you, not till we find Aunt Cassie.'

'Is she here now?' The little girl's face brightened as she looked eagerly about her. But, small as she was, Clara found it impossible to see around the crush of people that hemmed her in. And the shouted orders and instructions of the uniformed officials sounded so very frightening to her young ears that she began to cry.

Rose lifted the four-year-old into her arms for a hug. 'It's all right, you'll see, Aunt Cassie will have something nice ready for your tea, I'm sure. Dry your eyes now, and be a good girl for Mam.'

She had to admit to feeling every bit as hot, tired and hungry as her little sister. Like her mother, Rose was wearing several layers of clothing, that being the safest and easiest way to carry them. She felt a bit stupid knowing how ugly and ridiculous she must appear, but everyone was doing the same. The Eastern Europeans looked even stranger in their brightly coloured babushkas, laced bodices and swirling petticoats. The men wore odd little hats and fur coats, their faces running with sweat. Balanced on their head, or tucked under an arm, might be a small box, sack, carpet bag or rolled-up bundle. Some were carrying feather bolsters or household utensils. Being so heavily laden only added to everyone's weariness and shortened tempers still further.

A babble of tongues in every language and dialect filled the air as people shouted and argued with each other above the din. The line of exhausted immigrants inched slowly forward, shepherded into groups of thirty or so, according to the manifest of the ship that had brought them, the number plain to see on the label each of them wore pinned to their hat or lapel.

'Leave your luggage here on the ground floor,' ordered a stentorian voice. Once again Rose resisted.

'We'll keep tight hold of them, ta very much.'

'You'll do as you're told, miss, if you know what's good for you.'

'Do hush, Rose,' gasped Annie in dismay. 'This isn't the moment for one of your stubborn moods. Can't you see, everyone is being told the same thing.'

A kindly woman standing behind them in the queue gently patted Rose's shoulder. 'It will be quite safe, dearie. You pick them up later after you've passed through the inspection. And when you go up them stairs, mind you walk proper, and don't hold the kiddies' hands.' With a jerk of her chin she indicated a wooden staircase leading up to the next floor where two stern-faced officials waited. 'Children have to prove they aren't disabled. Make sure none of 'em limp, or are short of breath, or they'll be hauled out of line for a health check. These stairs are not called "the six-second exam" for nothing.'

Rose put a hanky to her mouth to stifle another threatened fit of coughing, terror filling her heart at the prospect of losing one of her brothers and sisters.

Bravely, Annie smiled at her children as they gazed

anxiously up at her, a worried look clouding her own eyes at this well-meant advice. 'Remember you must all be on your best behaviour. They won't let naughty children or bad boys into America, you can be quite certain on that score,' she sternly warned them. 'So keep your back straight, your chin up, and no matter how tired or hot and hungry you might feel, see that you all look bright and alert and healthy. Otherwise they might think you feeble-minded and send you back home. Do you understand?'

Small heads nodded with earnest solemnity.

'And smile. It can do no harm to look happy at the prospect of coming to this fine land.'

Rose took a breath. Never, in all her life, had she felt less like smiling.

As wary of offending their beloved mother as the stern-looking officials, the children reached the top of the staircase without incident. A woman in front of them was less fortunate. She suddenly became aware that instead of three children clinging to her skirts, there were now only two. One child had been pulled out of line and her plaintive cries of terror could still be heard as he was carried briskly away. The woman was near hysterical, gabbling in some foreign tongue, with no husband at her side to protect her.

'He's probably waiting for her at the gate, as Aunt Cassie is,' Mam told Rose, sympathy warm in her voice. 'And now one of her children has no doubt been found to be carrying a contagious disease.'

Annie patted the woman's arm in an effort to comfort

her but she ran off in search of the missing infant, clutching the other two tightly by the hand.

The Belsfield children, having safely reached the top of the staircase, gazed about them in wonder. Their astonished gaze took in a high-ceilinged hall bigger than anything they'd seen in their young lives, bigger even than the church they attended every Sunday back home in Bristol. It was railed off into rows, along which they were being herded like sheep or cattle, and where they were to endure yet another long wait.

Everyone else must wait too, save for those who seemed picked out for special treatment. Women in wide stylish hats, admittedly a little battered after the long voyage but obviously bought in Paris or London, were dealt with first. There were men who carried silk umbrellas or ivory-topped walking canes, who likewise passed through quickly to their freedom because of their smart attire.

The Belsfield family were not so fortunate. After a while they became so weary they sat on the hard wooden floor, glad to rest their tired limbs. Little Clara was quietly weeping again and the twin boys were becoming increasingly fractious and argumentative. Mary was doing her utmost to keep them amused with a piece of string and a game of cat's cradle, but the ploy wasn't working as they started to surreptitiously punch and kick each other in their hunger and frustration.

From somewhere in the crowd ahead came the strains of an accordion. Rose at once leapt to her feet and started an impromptu little jig which set her brothers and sisters giggling, such a happy sound that it warmed her heart.

'Come on, dance. Be happy. We're nearly in America.'

Laughing out loud, they joined in the jig, Joe too, for as usual he was sticking close by the Belsfield family. Taking Rose in his arms he whirled her around till she was giddy and had to urge him to stop.

'I just need to hold you in my arms,' he whispered urgently in her ear. 'Why don't you marry me, Rosie, then we could set out on this adventure together. We could help each other in this strange new land.'

She pushed him away, brown eyes flashing. 'You mind your cheek, Joe Colbert. If it's a woman you're looking for to do your cooking and cleaning, you can look elsewhere. I have other plans for my life.'

'What plans?'

She didn't have any, not yet. Getting to America had taken all Rose's energy. Plans for her own life could come later, once she had work and money coming in. 'To help look after Mam and the kids, of course.'

'You're young and single, and need to make your own life. But a woman alone in this land could soon run into trouble. I'd take care of you, Rosie love. I'd be a good husband to you. You know how I feel about you.'

'Aye, I do, but I'm not seeking a husband right now, ta very much.' Rose was thankful the music was still playing, the children still dancing, so they couldn't hear this half-whispered proposal. Inside, she was quietly fuming. How dare he choose this fragile moment, when they were all tense and anxious, to again put forward this daft idea of his.

'But you do like me, I know you do.'

'Course I like you, but that's not the same thing as

wanting to marry you.' How many times had she asked him to step back and allow her some breathing space? He was too pushy by half. 'Leave it, Joe. Let's just be friends for now, shall we?'

And grabbing the children's hands she again danced and jigged till they were all gasping for breath from the heat and exertion and obliged to sit down again to rest, Rose punishing Joe by sitting with her back to him.

But the boost to their spirits soon dissipated and the children started moaning and fidgeting once more, Annie doing her utmost to console her tired offspring. 'It doesn't matter how long we have to wait, as long as we meet dear Aunt Cassie at the end of it all.' She handed them each a last biscuit which she'd kept for just such a moment as this, when everyone was at their lowest, smiling at their joyous delight as they munched on the hard ship's biscuit.

Rose declined hers, handing it over to Micky as she was nervous of setting off her dry cough again. Besides, she was too busy anxiously watching the doctor who stood at the end of their line to have any appetite. Dressed in a blue uniform, he was rigorously examining every man, woman and child who shuffled before him, presumably checking for physical or mental defects.

'He's looking for lice and ringworm,' Annie said, following her daughter's gaze. 'At least my children are all clean and free of such pests. Just don't you dare cough, girl, as you pass by.'

'I won't, I promise.'

The doctor unbuttoned a young woman's coat to run

his hands over her belly in such an intimate way that Rose was shocked. 'What's he doing now?'

'Checking to see if she's pregnant, I shouldn't wonder,' Annie said. 'They won't want the expense of looking after an orphan should the mother not survive the birth.'

Rose shivered. It all seemed so much worse than she'd imagined or feared. Puzzling chalk marks were drawn onto backs, people pulled out of line and sent off somewhere, perhaps for further examinations.

'He's written *L* for lameness on that old man's back,' Joe said. 'Poor soul. He only tripped a little on the top step, but it was enough to condemn him.'

'*Wo ist meine Frau?*' cried one man in despair, his wife having vanished from his side.

One youth was pulled from the line. He looked strong and fit, quite clearly the main breadwinner of the family, but something was chalked on his back and he too was taken away, amid howls of distress.

Joe muttered under his breath, 'Let no one say that landing on the shores of the land of the free is either easy or pleasant. Look out, now it's our turn.'

'Be respectful,' Annie warned her children. 'And smile.'

By a miracle it was soon over and they were through, grinning at each other in relief, having passed the physical exam with flying colours. And Rose had not coughed once. She felt so proud of herself she was positively perky. All that was left now were a few questions to answer, largely a repeat of what they'd been asked at the start of the voyage, and they'd be home and dry.

The Belsfield family stood before the inspectors, bright-

20

eyed and determined to put on their best show. 'Did you pay for your own passage?' they were asked.

'My sister sent me the money,' Annie politely replied.

'Do you have tickets through to your final destination?'

'We have the money to buy tickets.'

'How much money do you have?'

Annie showed her purse containing twenty-five dollars, which proved to be a satisfactory sum.

'Where are you going? Where will you live?'

'With my sister, the children's aunt.'

'Who is she? Where does she live?' And so the questions continued. Name, age, sex, marital status, nationality, occupation, last residence, destination in America, whether they could read and write. Question after question, Rose filled with admiration for the way her mother remained calm throughout, which gave her the courage to face a similar interrogation.

'Are you under contract, expressed or implied, to perform labour in the US?' Rose was asked. They'd been warned that a 'yes' to this was apparently wrong, since the law forbade contract labour. A 'no' could result in further questioning in order to prove they wouldn't be a drain on the state. Rose said, 'I intend to find work in the US.' The inspector nodded and put a tick on his form.

Then came the expected questions about whether they'd ever been in prison, suffered from any deformities or illnesses, been charged with prostitution, or ever supported by charity.

Annie wisely made no mention of the poor relief she'd received, claiming to be a war widow, which was true, in possession of a small income, which, strictly speaking, was not.

The children were asked to put blocks into the right shaped holes, to prove they weren't feeble-minded, and then it was all over.

'Is that it? Are we done?' Rose asked, a wave of relief and what she could only describe as excitement washing over her. She could even tolerate Joe continuing to make cow's eyes at her if only they could pass safely out of this terrifying great hall and into her aunt's waiting arms.

But she'd reckoned without the dreaded eye test, the most feared examination of all. This was the test for trachoma, an inflammatory coating of the eyes which caused blindness. Annie subjected herself to the test first, keeping her back to the children so they couldn't see what was happening. Each child was then examined in turn, and under stern instructions from their mother, managed not to cry. Rose came last.

She stepped forward with some trepidation while doing her best to show the same bravery exhibited by her mother and siblings.

'Put your head back, girl,' the doctor brusquely instructed, frowning at her.

She did as she was told, then to her horror he began to roll back her upper lid with what appeared to be a button hook. Never had she known such excruciating pain. She wanted to scream and run, but daren't move a muscle in case that caused the instrument to do real damage to her eye. The pain was unendurable and Rose couldn't help but let out a little whimper. The whole process was repeated with the other eye, the doctor peering so closely she could smell his breath. It stank of tobacco and something stale that was deeply repellent.

Rose was all too aware that her eyes were indeed somewhat red-rimmed, due to her recent cold. She was wondering whether to explain this to the doctor when he suddenly turned her about, chalked something on her back, then she was being led away and pushed into a wire holding area with a dozen other people.

Startled by this turn of events, she turned to a woman sobbing pitifully beside her. 'What's happening? What is this place? It looks like some sort of cage. What is it for? Are we to be examined again?'

But the woman was shaking her head in great distress. 'No, this is to keep us all together until they can put us back on board.'

Back on board!

Rose stared at the woman in shocked disbelief. She could hear her mother calling to her, screaming as she was physically restrained by two officials from running to her daughter. Rose saw Joe quickly rescue Annie from this rough treatment to fold her mother safely in his own arms, his horrified gaze seeming to burn into hers. Micky stood paralysed with shock while Mary wailed like a banshee. The smaller children all burst into noisy tears at witnessing such a distressing scene, without understanding any of what was going on.

But Rose understood perfectly. In that instant she realised she'd been rejected. She would not be entering America to start a new life after all, but sent back to England on the very next ship. Alone.

Chapter Two

Bryce Tregowan glanced at the mantel clock and smothered a sigh. It would be an hour or more before he could tactfully withdraw, no doubt following several rubbers of bridge, a piano recital, or whatever other cultural delight Mama considered suitable to entertain her guests this evening. The room was abuzz with conversation, footmen refilling half-empty wine glasses, maids dressed in their best black bombazine with white starched aprons, constantly replacing empty plates with full ones. How he loathed these long drawn-out dinner parties. He had no quarrel with Mrs Pascoe's excellent turbot, or the haunch of mutton, roast pheasant and cheeseboard that had followed, although he'd happily left the meringues à la crème to the ladies. But he was bored rigid by the idle gossip that characterised these functions. Generally this revolved around who would be holding the next soirée or card party, the latest scandalous affair, engagement or marriage, or more entertaining still, what everyone thought of the vicar's sermon.

Even now Bryce was finding great difficulty concentrating on the animated chatter of the lady on his right, whose name had already shockingly slipped his mind. Smiling and nodding he watched her mouth move, speaking words that failed to penetrate as his mind was busily engaged elsewhere. He was contemplating an appointment with his solicitor on the morrow when he would put forward his plan of acquiring a chandler's business in nearby Fowey. Bryce was intrigued by the prospect, believing it long past time he took control of his own future. He did note that his companion's lips were thin and rather prissy, not at all the kind of mouth he would wish to kiss, and her hair a most unnatural shade of red.

'Will you be going up to town for the new season?' she asked, intruding upon his thoughts.

'I fear I have pressing business matters to attend to,' Bryce apologised.

She made a little moue with the pursed lips. 'We shall be going up as soon as Easter is over. Mama insists I be properly presented. What a bore if you aren't going to be around,' she simpered. 'May I dare to hope you might come up later? I'm quite looking forward to all the dances and parties, but I swear I'm nervous that I shan't know a soul, and it would be so good to see a familiar face.'

Bryce managed to smile and offer some platitude or other, but once again his attention drifted elsewhere as she carried on talking.

As he had now reached the ripe old age of twenty-three, dearest Mama was constantly presenting him with possible candidates for matrimony. But if Bryce dreamt of a woman likely to capture his heart it would be someone with a natural warmth and gentleness, not this prattling scatterbrain, although he certainly had no plans at present of even looking. Being blessed with a mother who seemed to make a career out of matrimony had rather turned him against it.

'What on earth do you call this?' As if on cue her strident tones rang out in a room that had suddenly gone ominously silent. 'I quite clearly ordered a muscat. Take this bottle back and change it at once.'

Stifling a groan, Bryce studiously closed his ears as his mother proceeded to harangue Rowell, the butler, the poor man having inadvertently brought the wrong dessert wine. She was ever a stickler for following the niceties of etiquette to the letter, if only to prove her own role in society. Penver Court, his stepfather's fine Queen Anne mansion, seemed to be bursting at the seams with maids and footmen; a constantly changing tribe of servants forever under a fellow's feet, opening doors you didn't want opening, telling him what he should, or more likely should not, be doing, wearing or eating. And he dreaded to think how this merry band was all paid for.

A light voice, filled with teasing banter, whispered in his ear. 'I do so admire the way Aunt Lydia makes everyone scurry to do her bidding, as if she were a duchess and not simply the second wife of a baronet?'

'She can be quite formidable, that is true,' Bryce sorrowfully agreed before grinning good-naturedly at his cousin. 'And do you wish to emulate her success, Gwenna, on this, your second season? A pity you didn't take on the first, but perhaps you are saving yourself for my brother?'

26

Tossing her golden curls, she lifted a rather plump chin in defiance. 'I may well consider him. You know that I love you both, with all my heart, and would marry either one of you handsome Tregowan brothers. But I need to consider that the name is not truly your own, and Jago has no hope of inheriting the title.'

'Ah, I do see there can be no true value in an adopted name, however well connected, without a title attached to it.' He gave an exaggerated sigh, one hand pressed to his chest. 'Then I must prepare my heart to be broken.'

Gwenna frowned. 'If you are making fun of me, that is most unkind. Jago may be well known for his cruel wit, but I thought better of you, Bryce.'

'I dare say you could manage to overlook my brother's personal flaws if he were able to offer compensation in a more substantial currency? Such matters as wealth and land most likely weigh large in your list of attributes required in a husband?'

'No woman worth her salt would marry a pauper.'

'Heaven forfend,' Bryce dryly remarked. 'The value of hard cash can never be underestimated. It has ever been prevalent in my mother's mind when considering a new husband, and certainly her reasoning behind insisting we take Sir Ralph's name. Remind me, this particular marriage has lasted now for how long?' He shook his head in despair as he watched Lady Tregowan bring Gladys the maid running with a snap of her fingers, and begin to berate the poor girl for not removing the cruet and bread basket. 'Is it ten years? I forget.'

'Twelve. You were eleven and Jago thirteen. And I was seven, looking upon you both as my heroes since dear

Aunt Lydia took me under her wing, a poor little orphan with little memory of my own parents.'

Bryce looked at her askance. 'Poor little orphan? Perhaps you should not play that sympathy card too often, dearest, since your late papa left you very comfortably provided for, if sadly unprotected. Too much, perhaps, for a young gel who must watch out for fortune-hunters.'

Gwenna's blue eyes glittered. 'One can never have too much. If I did not "take", as you call it, in my first season, it was because I had not yet found a man worthy of me. I intend to marry well, the richest husband I can find. Money should marry money.'

'Which is where this conversation began, I believe, with your wish to emulate Mama.'

'You should be proud of her for having risen so high. Was she not suffering from the ignominies of a scandalous divorce when she married Sir Ralph?'

'I will admit that my mother does possess a strange fascination for changing husbands rather too frequently, although that particular one was a rogue of the first quarter. Fortunately, most of her marriages have proved profitable, so considered a success in her terms,' Bryce added with a touch of droll humour. Less successful so far as himself and his brother were concerned, bringing a lack of permanence to their young lives, and a feeling that they really couldn't depend upon anyone but themselves. Although perhaps he'd coped better than Jago, for whom a constantly changing father figure had done no good at all.

Gwenna gave a dreamy little smile. 'What an exciting time that was when we all settled here, to live at Penver Court.'

Bryce was frowning, not quite sharing this viewpoint. He recalled a tension in the air between the newly-weds from the start, a sense that each had not attained quite what they'd hoped for from the match, although his mother had certainly enjoyed playing the titled lady. 'Unsurprisingly, this latest union did not receive the same unalloyed joy from the baronet's own son, resulting in an estrangement that has lasted to this day, as you well know.'

'Foolish young man,' Gwenna snapped, very much imitating her aunt's sharp tone, as she did her manners and behaviour in many other ways, Bryce had often noticed. Now she dropped her voice still lower. 'Is it true that Sir Ralph has written to his son in recent months, begging him to come home?'

Bryce sighed. He felt only pity for the portly, bewhiskered old man seated beside his mother, his faded grey eyes glazed as if in some world of his own. Big-boned, with a bulbous nose and bald pate, it was certainly not Sir Ralph's appearance which had persuaded his ambitious mother to marry a man a good twenty years older than herself. 'I really couldn't say, but why should he not? A man deserves to have his family about him.'

'Ah, but the inheritance – I don't mean the title, or even the house, which I know will automatically go to the son, but much of the land was to be divided between the pair of you, was it not? And a sizeable sum in hard cash? Now Aunt Lydia is fearful you will have your noses pushed out, were the son to return.'

The frown had changed to a dangerous scowl, Bryce's tone turning hard and condemning. 'It is no fault of mine if my mother suffers from such false delusions. I have no wish to raid the family silver and fully intend to make my own way in the world, as is only right and proper. I would go so far as to say that Mama's entry into the upper classes has done us few favours. What we have gained in security we have surely lost in freedom. Jago may enjoy playing the role of landed gentleman, I prefer to depend upon my own skills to forge a future for myself. I am certainly not expecting handouts from a stepfather who misguidedly fell for my mother's rapacious charms.'

'I meant no offence,' Gwenna huffed, her lovely blue eyes widening in faux innocence. 'I'm concerned for you both, that is all.'

Bryce managed a wry smile. More likely she was thinking of her own ambitions, rather than theirs. 'You have always demonstrated a salacious appetite for gossip, Gwenna, which is most unbecoming, and unworthy of you. Do not, I beg you, imitate Mama in every degree. It would be wise to exercise a little more control and think for yourself now and again, if that is possible.'

'How dare you!'

'I dare because you are as near to a little sister as you could possibly be, and very dear to me.'

Blue eyes glittering, Gwenna pressed herself close against his broad shoulder so that her breasts swelled above the neck of her gown, full and white. 'Ah, but I am not your sister, am I? Only a cousin, and a distant one at that. Do not feign indifference to me, Bryce Tregowan, for I see how you ache to have me.'

Bryce allowed a long moment to pass before he answered. 'I am a normal, red-blooded male, so if you present

30

yourself to me in a mode of dishabille, am I not entitled to look?' Deliberately staring at her décolletage.

'And wouldn't you just love to touch?' she breathed, slipping a hand beneath the tablecloth to caress his thigh.

Bryce calmly removed it. 'I wouldn't recommend you nurse any romantic dreams on my account.'

'Damn you! I wouldn't have you as a husband if you were handed to me on a platter.'

'Ah, but I reckon you would,' he said, chuckling softly. 'As the elder, Jago may in theory be the better bet, but money slips through his fingers as swiftly as the cards he slickly deals at the gaming table each evening. I am much more likely to bring home the bacon, and keep it hanging in the chimney breast. And for all he may excite you, Gwenna, you are not such a romantic nincompoop that you don't value property higher than love, as you have just made very clear.'

Blushing furiously, Gwenna flounced from him, and digging her spoon into her dessert sent shards of meringue flying.

Inwardly amused at her discomfiture, Bryce picked up his glass of wine to take an appreciative sip. Discussions with his charming cousin nearly always ended in an argument between them. But then she was almost as much a chameleon as his brother, never the same two days together. One moment all sweetness and bonhomie, the next a veritable termagant, a real little hellcat. Certainly they did not spoil a pair, as the saying goes, although they'd no doubt tear each other apart were they to ever make a match of it.

But what if it were true and Sir Ralph had indeed written to his son seeking a rapprochement? How would his mother react were the prodigal son to return home? Now that would put the cat among the pigeons. The second Lady Tregowan had rather set her heart on exploiting all that Penver Court and its substantial estate had to offer. She fully intended to enjoy the fruits of her labour over the length of this, her – what was it – third marriage? No, her fourth, including the elopement at seventeen.

And how would his brother react to such news?

Bryce was startled out of his reverie by a loud, sonorous snore. Sir Ralph's eyes had drooped almost closed, now he jerked upright in his seat, woken by the volume of his own snorts. The ladies looked shocked and deeply embarrassed, while the gentlemen smirked with amusement. Lady Tregowan simply pretended to be both deaf and blind, as was generally the case when confronted with anything remotely unpleasant.

Bryce leant across the table to gently tap his stepfather's hand. 'Sir, would you care for your usual glass of port? Shall we ask the ladies to retire?'

'That is my prerogative to decide,' his mother snapped.

He smiled at her. 'Then pray hasten to do so, Mama. I fear your husband will fall asleep shortly otherwise.'

Instead, he promptly fell off his chair to lie jerking on the floor in what could only be a seizure. His wife screamed, and pandemonium broke out as the entire company flapped and fussed about, some ladies fainting while the servants stood apparently frozen with shock. Only Bryce had the wit to rush to the old man's aid.

'Will someone please call the doctor,' he cried. '*Now*!'

Rose couldn't believe what was happening to her. Only yesterday she'd been excitedly anticipating a new life in

America, now she was back on board ship about to sail to England. She thought she'd never forget the look of complete horror on her mother's face when she was pulled out of line and shoved into that cage. They'd had to drag poor Annie away screaming, but they'd both known there was nothing to be done. The dream was over. Dead in the water. The fear that she might never see her mother, or her brothers and sisters, ever again was a pain so crippling it seemed to tear her heart in two. Rose doubted it would ever go away. Fear pounded through her, drummed in her ears, a hollow beat of terror. She felt sick, as if she might throw up at any moment, although the ship hadn't left the dockside yet.

She'd spent the previous night in the detention room, together with a motley collection of other rejected souls. There'd been one group of women, all garishly painted and attired, marking them out at a glance as what her mother would call 'ladies of the night'. There were other more respectable women who had come to meet a prospective husband but found no eager young man waiting at the gate, as promised. Lone females were unacceptable in the New World. Who knew what they might get up to?

Many fortune-seekers, entrepreneurs and adventurers were also turned away, some of them perhaps bankrupts fleeing the heavy arm of the law in their own land, others honest, upright citizens, but for one reason or another, possibly mistakenly, as in Rose's case, they'd been marked as suffering from some physical infirmity. They were to be sent back to the pit of despair from whence they came, or to the bottom of the sea for all America cared.

One young man was to be deported because his pocket

had been picked and the inspectors believed he would become a charge upon the state. The loss of just ten dollars had made the difference between the success or failure of his dream, possibly even life or death.

Rose heard an inspector suggest to one pretty young girl that he'd see she was allowed in if she went with him to a certain nearby hotel. She declined, which Rose thought very noble and honourable of her, wondering if she could have been as brave if faced with such a choice.

Now the steamship company, who were obliged to take the rejects back free of charge, would provide them with only such leftover food as the crew didn't want, or else wasn't fit to be eaten by anyone. If the crossing to America had been tough, Rose fully expected the return journey to be a thousand times worse.

Wrapping her arms about herself, she sank her head to her bent knees in abject misery. Perversely, the day after the examination her eyes had cleared and appeared reasonably bright, almost normal. But it was too late. The officials had only laughed when she'd begged to be checked again by a doctor, telling her the government hospitals were already full of more worthy cases, that they must enforce the law strictly. Nothing could be done.

The upset caused by that little dispute set off her coughing again, and they'd marked her down as consumptive as well.

What she would do in England without a home, without a job, without her beloved family, Rose couldn't even begin to think. Would she simply be abandoned on the dockside at Bristol? Then what should she do? Where could she go? How would she find food? And when she arrived she'd be viewed not only as a pauper, but with a stigma attached for having been rejected by America.

Tears rolled down her cheeks, splashed onto her clenched hands, her chest tight with pain.

She knew only too well what happened to young girls with no means of support. Bristol was no different in that respect to any other city. There would be only one way for her to earn a crust, and it wouldn't be either honest or pleasant. Her stomach curdled at the prospect, and, as she heard the rumble of the anchor chain being pulled up, she began to weep all the more.

'Hey, what's all this? It's not like our Rose to wallow in self-pity?'

'I don't believe it. Joe!' Leaping to her feet she hugged her old friend in surprise and delight. Then pushing him from her she gazed at him in disbelief. 'I'm not dreaming, am I? It is really you?'

He laughed. 'Aye, it's really me, and it feels more like a nightmare to me than a dream.'

'So they rejected you too?'

'They didn't, actually. I gave my cash to your mum and pretended I didn't have any.'

'Oh, Joe, what a thing to do. Mam had no right to accept.'

He grinned at her. 'She protested, of course, at least at first. But when I explained I meant to go home with you she soon changed her tune, was quite grateful, in fact, and sends her love. But then, I couldn't let you be packed off back to England on yer own, now could I? Wouldn't have been right. So here I am.'

'I don't know what to say, how to thank you.'

He flicked one wicked eyebrow. 'I could think of a way.

Still, all in good time, eh? How are you, girl, feeling any better? See, I've fetched you a hunk of bread.'

Whether it was the sight of the food, her highly strung state or the sudden lurch of the ship, but by way of response Rose threw up all over Joe's best boots.

Gwenna lay beneath the apple tree in the far orchard beyond the walled garden, her skirts rucked up, her bodice unbuttoned so that her small breasts spilt out, happily content that no one could see her as they were some safe distance from the house. It was a lovely May afternoon, the sun warm on her bare skin, and there was nowhere she'd rather be than here with Jago, lying in the sweet-smelling long grass. She was deeply aware of how enticing, how beautiful she must look, her body plump and soft, her slender arms wrapped about his neck. She was willing to yield him anything – well, almost anything – that he wanted. Much as she might insist to Bryce that she meant to catch herself the richest husband she could find, she had her heart set on a quarry much closer to home. 'Oh, please don't stop,' she whimpered, as he drew away slightly. 'I love it when you kiss me.'

No one could kiss like Jago. He seemed to take complete possession of her, devouring her with his mouth and tongue, as if to prove she belonged entirely to him. Which indeed she would, if Gwenna had her way, title or no title.

He traced a trail of burning sweetness along the curve of one breast. 'I was hoping you might be feeling a bit more generous today, ready to offer something more substantial than mere kisses,' he murmured, and sliding one nipple into his mouth began to lick and suckle it, making her groan with pleasure.

Very carefully, paying full attention to what his mouth, and his busy fingers beneath her skirt, were doing, smiling at her soft moans, Jago shifted his weight gently onto her. She was moving instinctively against him, that timeless rhythm which augured well for his next move. He began to swiftly unbutton his linen trousers.

Gwenna was alert in a second. 'Oh, Jago, you mustn't. You know I daren't go too far,' she gasped, a giddiness creeping over her, robbing her of resistance. Valiantly, she fought the weakness. 'Not unless there was some sort of understanding between us?' She cast him a sideways glance from beneath golden lashes, which caused him to laugh out loud.

'And what sort of understanding would that be, dear girl?' he chortled, sliding one hand over her bare thigh, making her squeal in delighted protest. 'You know full well how I feel about you, how much I ache to make you mine.'

She listened, entranced, silently praying he meant what she hoped, loving the way he scattered tender kisses over her eyes, her mouth, her bare throat. He must love her enough to marry her, mustn't he, if he was so rampant for her? Yet as always with Jago, there was room for doubt. His next words served to confirm this.

'But marriage right now is out of the question while the old man lies sick. It wouldn't be proper, now would it? We couldn't possibly consider any sort of celebration, not until he's well again.'

Although his reasoning was sound, in her heart Gwenna knew this was yet another of Jago's many excuses. There'd been any number over the last couple of years. That she was too young, that he was not yet ready to take on the responsibility of a wife, that he must be sure of coming into his inheritance. This was but another. Oh, but as he skimmed the tip of his tongue around the curl of her ear lobe, she couldn't find the strength to push him away, to challenge or scold him. He knew exactly how to please her, how to reduce her to a shivering wreck. And didn't *she* want to please *him*?

'What if Sir Ralph doesn't ever get well?' she whispered, desperately wanting him to say that he would then marry her, like a shot. Instead, he laughed, told her she talked far too much and gave her one of those kisses that set her head spinning, his tongue dancing with hers so that she could hardly breathe, let alone think.

'Don't you find me beautiful?' she managed, while he struggled with the laces of her stays.

'Deliciously so.'

'And exciting?'

She could feel the hard swell of his manhood pressing against her, only the thinness of her pleated skirts between them. Daringly she caressed the bulge through the bunched fabric, curious to know how it felt, and was shocked by its size. On a grunt of impatience he suddenly pushed her skirts right up to her waist, leaving her half naked to his gaze. 'Stop this silly game, Gwenna, you know how much I want you. How many times do I have to tell you that I love you?'

'But you haven't ever actually . . .' she began, and then gasped as she felt his cock slide inside her. Oh, what had she done? Why had she let things go this far? But then the glory of having him pushing and thrusting inside her, claiming her for his own, caused her heart to soar with joy. He would have to marry her now.

Chapter Three

The sickness continued for the rest of that day as the ship set sail, although there was nothing left in Rose's stomach, which made the retching all the more painful. Her head pounded, and as if being sick wasn't bad enough, the cough too got worse. At least it was quiet in this corner of steerage, save for the muffled sound of sobbing every now and then, and fewer people fighting for space. There was no dancing or singing on this journey. No merry jigs or the tinny sound of a harmonica or accordion. The steerage passengers being returned to starvation and oblivion did not have the spirit left to brighten the long lonely hours of endless days at sea with joyful merriment. The good fellowship and joking of the earlier crossing were gone, and with it all hope.

These were a people in despair, folk who had lost not only a dream but also the loved ones they'd travelled with to achieve it. They had been cast out, forgotten and unwanted by the authorities. It was a bitter pill to swallow. They were all to be returned to Slovakia or Russia, Liverpool or Bristol, back to the starvation or oppression they thought they'd escaped, to all the reasons they had left, and worse, this time they would be alone.

Some played cards, others drank vodka, a great deal of vodka, and gin. But many simply sat slumped in abject despair, as distraught and terrified of what was to happen to them as was Rose.

She could hear a group of Italians quarrelling, a woman sobbing out a lullaby to her lifeless child.

'Christ is risen, Christ is risen,' someone whispered, and Rose shivered in her bed. Would she ever rise again? There were times when she very much doubted it.

The barriers of class were as rigid on board ship as in the more normal strata of society, yet somehow here it seemed more callous, more artificial and offensive in this closed community. First- and second-class passengers could loll about on deck, have their maid bring them a soft steamer rug. They could lean over the ship's rails and marvel at the rippling blue sea, or stroll about the deck to enjoy the spring sunshine. They also liked to hang over the barriers and look down upon the misery of those in steerage below, those taking the air in the tiny square of space allotted for exercise. It was almost as if they were watching animals pace back and forth in their cage in a zoo. Some would even call out or make ribald jokes, which always roused Joe's anger.

'Them toffs in the cabins above think themselves proper

lords and ladies, while we're the peasants to be jeered at.'

'I'm sure they aren't all like that. I've heard some show real concern, even throw down food,' Rose said, wishing someone would toss down something tasty for her too. The ache of hunger in her belly was not helping her recovery. Her longing for something other than stale water and salty fish was becoming almost an obsession. How she longed for the sharp sweetness of an orange, for a sip of weak ale, or even a cup of hot tea, a drink she'd admittedly tasted only once in her entire life. Mostly she dreamt of her mother's stews and how Annie had always kept the stock pot bubbling, no matter how poor they were.

Joe dismissed her comments as sheer fantasy. 'None of that lot gives a toss about us. They can breathe pure air, sleep on spotless linen, be served delicious food by courteous waiters. And the crew on board act as if they were the flipping police, ordering us about, keeping us locked up down here and making sure nowt good comes our way. It would cost twenty dollars to buy you a cabin, love, and if I had such riches I'd get you one, like a shot.'

'I know you would, Joe.'

'What I wouldn't do to give you a good life, Rosie. I'd kill for you, I would really.'

She laughed. 'You talk a lot of daft nonsense, Joe Colbert. Always did. Now see if you can find me some of that stringy beef or soggy bread. Anything will do.'

Joe went off, still bitterly complaining. 'Not even soap or hot water to help us keep clean, or a decent place to relieve ourselves. We might as well be animals. Is it any wonder you're sick?'

'Please don't worry, I'm fine . . .' And as if to disprove her own optimism, Rose promptly threw up again.

The next morning she woke with a fever. Rose lay on her bunk feeling as if she was burning up, barely able to move, quite unable to sleep or eat. She wouldn't even have troubled to take so much as a drink of water had it not been for Joe pressing it upon her. Numb with agony, aching in every muscle, one minute burning up, the next shivering with cold, she had never felt more ill in all her life.

'Come on, love, you must eat. At least drink something,' Joe urged her, offering Rose a sip of water and yet another hunk of dry bread.

Rose shook her head, quite unable to even attempt to eat it, knowing it would near choke her. 'No thanks,' she murmured. Her voice was weak, cracking with the effort of speaking, her face flushed, mouth and throat swollen and dry as parchment.

Undeterred, Joe helped her to sit up. 'At least try a little, or you'll never get better. Look, I'll soften the bread in the water, will that help?'

The stale water made the bread taste even more foul, and what sustenance could there be in dry bread and water? But she didn't say as much, and dutifully sucked on it. It wasn't Joe's fault there was no decent food. The poor boy was doing his best. The water did help clear her throat and she made a huge effort to speak. 'Help me out of bed,' she croaked. 'If I could smell the sea, catch a glimpse of a blue sky, I might feel better.'

Joe was at once all concern. 'I'm not sure that's a good idea.' There was little breathing space below deck, although more than on the outward journey. On the crossing out, with over eight hundred passengers packed into the hold like cattle, finding your way through the crush to take a walk on deck had been impossible. There was equally little hope of breathing clean air below, particularly in rough weather when the hatches were down.

'I have to do something. I feel like I'm fading away down here, the stench alone is enough to make me nauseous.'

Joe slipped an arm under her and lifted her from the bunk, then half carried Rose towards the small space in the centre of the steerage area where they could look up at the sky, cloudy today, with only a few patches of blue in sight. 'Wrap your shawl about you, there's a stiff breeze. We don't want this nasty dose of flu turning into pneumonia.'

With great care and patience he walked her slowly to and fro, back and forth in the narrow space. Others were doing the same, anything for a little fresh air and exercise. But after a few turns, Rose's legs began to wobble.

'Let me sit down for a minute, I've come over all queer again.' Almost at once her knees gave way and she sank to the floor.

'Hey, you down there. You, boy, the one helping that poor girl, can you hear me?'

Rose looked up into the face of an angel. Not one

dressed in white with wings and a halo, but a young woman hanging over the rail above. She appeared to be waving a pink parasol at them, no doubt its more usual purpose that of protecting her pale, translucent skin from the sun. Her gown was blue, brighter than the sky, with matching ribbons blowing from the tiny hat perched on a head of light-brown hair. 'Are you all right, child? You don't look at all well.'

Joe answered for her, since Rose could not have found voice at that precise moment. 'Course she isn't well. How can she be well when she's suffering from the influenza, not to mention being half starved.'

'Good heavens, are you saying she's hungry? Why is she? Isn't there enough food on board? Don't they feed you properly down there?'

'Not that I've noticed.'

'Then bring her up here at once.'

'Sorry, ma'am, we're not allowed on your part of the deck.'

'Then you must help her up the stairs and I'll fetch her some food. Go on, don't just stand there gawping.'

Joe did as he was told. Rose protested that she couldn't possibly climb the stairs, that her legs were too shaky, her head pounded, in fact her entire body was wracked with pain. But Joe gently bullied her up the wooden steps, supporting her in his arms, knowing this might be her last chance of survival. She'd die for sure, if something wasn't done to save her soon.

By the time they reached the top, Rose was utterly exhausted. She managed no more than a couple of steps across the slippy boards towards the lady in the bright-blue dress, before collapsing. Her last sight before darkness closed in was the pink parasol bowling along the deck in the wind.

Rose had little recollection of the days following but was afterwards told that her fever broke on the third day. Only then did she begin to make a slow and steady recovery, one that would have been impossible had she not been rescued by a guardian angel, from what felt very like purgatory into this beautifully appointed first-class cabin.

She was fed hot beef tea and chicken broth, which slipped deliciously down her sore throat without the least difficulty. Day by day, Rose could actually feel the strength flowing back into her limbs. And she hadn't coughed for twenty-four hours or more.

'You've been so kind,' she said on the fifth day when she was at last allowed out of bed. Rose was sitting on deck in a steamer chair with her feet up and her knees covered by a soft rug, just as if she were one of the toffs instead of a reject from Ellis Island. It was hard to get her head round this sudden change in her circumstances. 'I really don't know how to thank you,' she shyly offered.

'Don't be silly, it was the least I could do. I couldn't possibly leave you to starve, poor lamb. I've spoken quite sharply to the captain about the conditions in steerage, and am optimistic that improvements will be made. I insisted on taking a look myself and it really was quite atrocious.'

'Oh, ma'am, that was ever so brave of you.'

'Fiddlesticks! Now drink your tea while it is hot, Rose, and we can enjoy a nice chat. Your friend Joe told me your name. I hope you don't mind my informality in using it?'

'Course not, it's me name, isn't it?'

'Would you believe that I too bear that name, or one very similar? Mine is Rosalind. Isn't that fun?'

Rose smiled. 'Yours is much prettier than mine.' And posher, she thought. Then she was staring more closely at her companion, taking her in properly for the first time, almost forgetting to sip her tea. The young woman laughed.

'Ah, you've noticed. As you see, I am to produce any time soon. My baby is due in three weeks or so. I expect you are too young to have any children. How old are you, Rose? Seventeen? Eighteen?'

'Just turned twenty, s'matter of fact. What were you thinking of, ma'am? You shouldn't be sailing on a ship in your condition.'

A shadow darkened the other woman's face. 'I dare say you're right, but I was anxious to get away, and wasn't able to leave sooner as I had certain matters to attend to: an apartment and various possessions to dispose of in New York for one thing. It was all rather sad as I'd lived there for almost a decade. And then it takes such a long time to receive a reply to one's correspondence, does it not?' She gave a determined little smile, but her sadness took the shine from it. 'You see, my husband died of consumption some months ago.'

'Oh, ma'am.' Rose was overwhelmed with sorrow, recognising only too well the pain in the other woman's face. 'That is so sad, so tragic.'

'Robert never even knew that I was pregnant. He would have been so thrilled. We'd been trying for a child for quite a few years, you see.' She fell silent for a long moment while she struggled to regain control of her emotions. 'However, on the bright side, when I wrote to inform his father of his son's demise, he invited me to his home in Cornwall. The pair hadn't spoken in years, having suffered an estrangement over some family trouble. I don't think Robert approved of his new stepmother, for whatever reason.' She gave a wry smile. 'I dare say it is difficult to see one's mother replaced. Now I'm going to meet my father-in-law for the first time. I've never even been to England, having been brought up in Canada, admittedly of British parents, so it will all be new to me. I'm looking forward to seeing the old country at last, having heard so much about it from them. And at least my child will have a grandfather, poor mite. Family is so important, do you not think? Oh, but I am forgetting, what of your own family, Rose? What happened to them? Are they still below in steerage?'

Rose shook her head, then it all came pouring out. Her father's death in the war, the money from Aunt Cassie which had brought a rebirth of hope to them all, the excitement of the journey out to America, and its disastrous end, so far as Rose was concerned. Rosalind listened without interrupting once, and when her tale was told and Rose was wiping the tears from her eyes with the flat of her hands, she took hold of them to give them a warm squeeze.

'Then we are both alone in the world. You realise this

was *meant* for us to meet like this. This is what they mean by fate. I wonder, therefore, if you are not in too much of a hurry to return to your friend below, loyal and devoted as he obviously is, whether you would be willing to stay on as my maid? I am so very clumsy and easily tired these days, and my own maid refused absolutely to sail with me. The minute she felt the ship move beneath her, she fled, poor girl. So I am bereft of assistance.'

Rose's heart leapt at the prospect of not having to return to steerage, and of being offered a job. It felt very like salvation, with a kernel of new hope that her future might not be so bleak after all. Although she did feel a slight prick of disloyalty towards poor Joe. Still, Miss Rosalind had said she'd insisted on improvements in steerage, so maybe things were better for him now.

'Ooh, ma'am, I'd be honoured.'

'Excellent! We have both suffered loss. Now we can be companions for each other. When my child is born, you shall help me to care for him or her. You will be safe now, Rose, as I know I shall be safe with you. And you must call me Rosalind, not ma'am or madam. Our friendship, even our shared name, is a gift from God.' And smiling sweetly, she kissed Rose on each cheek. 'We shall neither of us be lonely any longer. I certainly won't, not now that I have you for a friend.' Two days later Rosalind went into labour.

It was long and difficult, not helped by a storm at sea with the ship pitching and tossing like a cork in a bath, with huge waves rolling across the decks and running into the cabins soaking everything and everyone in its wake. The mother-to-be was exhausted, both from the toils of her labour and the violent seasickness she suffered, her cries lost in the roar of the wind. Rose constantly wiped her face with a cool damp cloth, clung to her hands when the pains threatened to overwhelm her, offering what she could by way of comfort and solace, for all it felt like a futile exercise. The doctor called in regularly to check on her progress, but could never stay long as he had many other passengers suffering from broken limbs, and the most dreadful *mal de mer*.

Fortunately he was present when the baby finally decided to make his appearance, and was able to deliver Rosalind a fine son.

'He's perfect, absolutely perfect.' She wept with joy, as did Rose.

The ship's doctor checked him over and declared the child healthy. The mother, however, was not faring quite so well. 'You must take particular care of her,' he instructed Rose. 'She's slightly feverish, and this storm doesn't help one bit,' he added, clinging fast to the rails at the edge of the bed.

'Can't you give her something to stop the bleeding?'

'All new mothers bleed,' he said, contempt in his tone and in the scathing glance he cast over her rumpled figure. He couldn't for the life of him imagine why such a refined lady would drag this waif out of steerage to tend her.

'Not this much. My mam never did, although she lost a couple of babies after me.' Rose wanted him to know she was not as ignorant in these matters as he might think.

'Your mother was of a different breed entirely,' he

scornfully remarked. 'Now, I do have other patients to attend to, if you please. Keep the patient warm and dry, the baby too. Even you can manage that, I'm sure.'

Rose guarded her tongue and agreed that she probably could.

'Take no notice of him,' Rosalind said kindly, after he'd gone. 'A snob of the first quarter, obviously. Oh, but isn't my darling son adorable? I shall name him Robert, after his father. You'll find a nightgown and shawl for him in my luggage, Rose.'

Rose made sure the baby was warmly swaddled, folding a napkin around his little bottom. Then she half emptied one of her new mistress's many small trunks, and tucked him safely inside on top of a bed of clothes. She left the lid open, of course, so that it served as a crib, lodged securely between two chairs, all dry and warm.

Keeping his mother in a similar condition proved to be almost impossible. The storm was beginning to calm down a little by this time, but everything in the cabin, for all it was spacious, with the finest linen and accoutrements, was soaked. Waves washed in under the door, and water seeped through the cracks around the porthole, running down the wall. Nothing seemed to be quite as waterproof as it should be. She was also running out of fresh bedding and towels, as the bleeding continued unabated. Rose had tried kneading her stomach, as she'd seen the midwife do with her mam, but was obliged to stop when the poor lady complained it hurt too much, and began retching. As if giving birth were not enough, she was still suffering from the *mal de mer* like the rest of the passengers.

Rose had reached the point of despair when, quite out of the blue, Joe stuck his head around the door. 'Ah, there you are. Found you at last!'

'How did you get up here?' Rose cried, not sure whether to scold him for his recklessness at venturing into first class, or give him a big hug. But she felt in sore need of a friend right now.

'I took a chance to sneak up and see how you were getting on. I heard you'd recovered but as I hadn't seen you in an age, and in view of the storm, I wanted to be sure you were all right.'

Rose rolled her eyes. 'Stop fretting over me. It's poor Miss Rosalind you should feel sorry for. The doctor's useless, everything is soaked, she's been dreadfully seasick and her labour dragged on so long she's exhausted and a bit feverish. I'm really frightened for her, Joe.'

'I'll see what I can do,' he said, and instantly disappeared to return minutes later with two dry blankets, a pile of clean sheets and several fresh towels.

'Oh, bless you. Where did you find those?'

'Ask no questions and I'll tell no lies,' Joe said with a huge wink.

Rose was mortified. 'You mean you stole them?'

'I *borrowed* them. Do you want to keep her warm, or not?'

Biting her lip Rose quickly changed the sheets, then tucking the blankets around her mistress, told herself that surely Miss Rosalind's need was greater. When she was done, she turned to Joe, a new briskness in her tone. 'Since you're here, you might as well make yourself useful. Keep an eye on her, and the baby, while I go and fetch her a cup of hot soup. She needs her strength keeping up, but you aren't allowed in the dining room. You shouldn't be in here either, by rights, but if you keep your head down, no one will see you. I'll be back in ten minutes at most.'

It took far longer. Deciding against venturing into the first-class dining room, Rose went instead to the kitchen, or galley as they called it on board ship, where she became engaged in an argument with the ship's cook in her efforts to convince him that she was indeed Miss Rosalind's maid. Admittedly, her appearance did not help, her clothes being rumpled and threadbare, but this didn't seem the moment to be discussing a proper uniform with her new employer. Having finally convinced the fellow of her identity by threatening him with the ship's doctor, she carried the soup back to the cabin, taking great care not to spill a precious drop.

'Thanks for staying. How is she now?'

'Asleep, and I'd say growing weaker by the minute,' Joe said, looking concerned. 'The baby's a grand little chap.'

'You'd best get back, before anyone catches you up here.'

Gathering her small face between his broad hands, he kissed her full on the lips.

'Here, what do you think you're doing?' Outraged, Rose cuffed him away, although not too firmly. He was still her very good friend, after all, always there when she needed him, as he'd proved to her just now. 'Don't you take no liberties with me, Joe Colbert.'

'When I look into those chocolate-brown eyes of yours,

Rosie, I can't seem to help meself. I could eat you all up, I could really.'

'Get away with you, before I report you for harassment, not to mention trespassing into first class.'

Chuckling softly and totally unmoved by her threats, he cheekily kissed her again, then fled.

'Is he your beau, Rose?' asked the voice from the bed.

'No, he's not! He's a cheeky tyke, that's what he is.'

Rosalind smiled, not believing her outraged protest, and managed about half the soup, insisting Rose finish the rest herself. But when she'd heard the trouble her new maid had suffered in securing it, she realised something had to be done.

'Of course you need better clothes. There must be something suitable amongst my luggage, just help yourself. Why didn't I think of that?'

'You've had more important matters on your mind,' scolded Rose, handing over the baby to be fed as he started to stir and whimper.

'He's a miracle baby, don't you think?' Rosalind asked, her eyes soft with love as she put him to her breast.

'He's beautiful,' Rose agreed, then sat on the edge of the bed to watch entranced as he fastened his tiny mouth around Rosalind's nipple and eagerly began to suckle. 'Look at the strength of that, and him no more than a few hours old.'

'I'd rather given up hope of having a baby, we'd tried for so long.' There were tears in her eyes as Rosalind went on. 'I'm almost thirty now, quite old, I suppose, for a first-time mother. Robert, my husband, was forty-six, considerably older than me although far too young to die.' She gave Rose a bleak look. 'What I fear most is this little chap becoming an orphan.'

'Oh, don't say such a thing. Don't even think it,' Rose protested, appalled.

'But I must, I'm his mother. Now that he's here, I have to make provision.' She smiled down upon him, letting his tiny hand curl about her little finger. 'There's something I haven't told you about who my son might one day be. Little Robbie here is no less than the grandson of a baronet.'

'Oh, my giddy aunt.' Rose was shocked, gazing at the baby in wonder. 'You mean he'll have a title, and a coronet or something?'

Rosalind laughed. 'Something of the sort, yes, so you see how important it is that were anything to happen to me, he needs to be taken to my husband's family. Will you do that for me, Rose? Will you care for him and take him to England and his grandfather? I know it's a lot to ask but there is no one else.'

Rose was dumbfounded. 'You're going to be fine. You said you were looking forward to seeing England, and you've helped me over my fever, so I'll help you over yours.'

'But mine is a different sort of fever,' Rosalind quietly reminded her. Even talking was tiring her, yet she was determined to say her piece. She took a moment to gather her breath. 'And not easily resolved on board ship, particularly in these conditions. Your young man was right, I am growing weaker. I need to know that my child will be safe, were the worst to happen.'

As Rose looked into her new mistress's pale face, so gaunt and drawn following her ordeal, and from losing far too much blood, she saw the wisdom of what she was suggesting. She knew from personal experience that not all women were as hale and hearty as her own mam, who gave birth rather like shelling peas. This lady was finely bred, and far more fragile. The doctor was right in that respect at least. 'Oh, ma'am, what can I say . . . ?'

'Just say you'll see him safely home to Cornwall, to his grandfather Sir Ralph Tregowan at Penver Court. I'm sure he will offer you gainful employment in return.'

Rose had to lean closer to hear the whispered words, and answered as softly. 'Course I will. You don't need to ask, although I'm sure it won't ever be necessary. Except that the ship's captain, or the doctor, might not allow it. They see me as a steerage passenger, nothing more.'

'Oh, of course they do. You're right, Rose. My mind is growing muddled. It's the wind hammering away. Thank goodness one of us can still think clearly. Fetch the steward. And paper. Pen.' Her breathing seemed to be growing more ragged, each breath she took harder to grasp, more shallow, the final rattle not far away. 'We must set this out all legal and proper.'

The steward was called, the paper written and duly signed and witnessed, final details agreed. And not a moment too soon. By dawn, Rosalind was dead.

Chapter Four

Rose stood on the busy quay, the pink parasol held over the baby in her arms, keeping the noonday sun off his tiny head. It had a secondary purpose, its presence meant to identify her to whoever had been sent to meet Rosalind from the ship.

'The mistress assured me someone would be here to collect her, and she particularly mentioned I must show the parasol,' Rose explained to Joe, who stood by her side, as usual, looking faintly stunned at seeing her in this outfit. 'Miss Rosalind had never met her husband's family and this is the way they'll know who she is. I am to see little Robbie safely to his grandfather's house, and then present the document we all signed, by way of introduction. I'm hoping he'll let me stay on, as the baby's nursemaid.'

'And what about me?' Joe grumbled.

Rose gave him a teasing little smile. 'Not that it's any of my concern where you go, or what you do, Joe Colbert, but

Rosalind did suggest it might be a good idea for you to act as escort, and mebbe ask for a job at Penver Court yourself.' Rose giggled. 'And you can help carry this lot,' indicating the several pieces of luggage clustered about her feet.

'I'd live in a midden, Rosie, if I can only be with you. You know I would.'

Rose scowled crossly at him. 'If you come with me, you have to stop all this lovesick nonsense, it's becoming embarrassing. No more wearing your heart on your sleeve, is that clear?'

'I'll try.'

'You'll do more than try. No more argument, right? If you don't agree then I won't let you come at all.'

Joe shuffled his boots on the cobbles, wishing he could think of something clever and witty to say, or that he was handsome and rich. But, lost for a way to press his suit further, he felt obliged to agree. He certainly couldn't risk losing her. 'All right, I promise. But how do you know we can trust this Tregowan family?'

Rose looked at him askance. 'Why would we not be able to trust them? Sir Ralph is a gentleman, titled and rich.'

'Aye, my point exactly. And nobody gets that way by being nice to folk, not in my experience, so why would he care about us, or that babby?' He indicated Robbie sleeping peacefully in Rose's arms.

'This child is his grandson, so of course he will care.'

Grabbing hold of her arm, Joe pulled Rose away from the hurly-burly and crush of departing passengers to stand behind a stack of crates where they could be a bit more private while able to still keep an eye on the baggage.

'What I mean to say is, why would they bother to offer us employment, and what happens to us if they don't? I don't know about you but I don't fancy going back to the life of starvation we had before we set off to America. We're in an even worse position now than we were then. We've no job, no money, nowhere to live, and without even your mam and brothers and sisters for company.'

Tears flooded her eyes. 'Oh, don't remind me of losing them, not right now, Joe, I can't bear it.'

'I know it was sad – tragic, in fact – what happened to you, Rosie, which is why we have to think carefully how we're going to survive. I've no wish to depend on begging for me daily crust, or to share it with the rats down by the waterfront, which is where we'll likely end up. I'd like a roof over my head, ta very much, and a way to earn an honest shilling.'

'Me too; I know what happens to girls down on the waterfront. Anyway, I'm sure we'll find Sir Ralph helpful.'

'Then you've more faith in human nature than I have. Think of the opportunity you hold in your arms here to make something of your life,' he said, jerking his chin in the direction of the baby. 'You say the Tregowan family have never met this Rosalind, that she's never even visited England.'

'That's what she told me. She was brought up in Canada, and there was some estrangement between her husband and his father. Why, what has that got to do with little Robbie?'

'It has everything to do with him. No one in England, in Cornwall, has any idea what this Rosalind looks like. You could easily pass yourself off as the baby's mother.

You could be a real lady, then you'd never be homeless or starving again. You'd live a life in the lap of luxury.'

Rose's jaw dropped open, utterly shocked by this suggestion. 'Oh, Joe, what a wicked idea. I could never do such a thing.'

'Why not?' Grabbing her by the shoulders he gave her a gentle little shake. 'Think, girl, once you tell them who you really are, they'll say this babby is your little bastard. Why would they believe some yarn about a woman dying in childbirth? What proof do have?'

'I have the paper we all signed.'

'They could easily accuse you of forging that in order to pass your bastard off as a possible future baronet. Besides, even if they believe the tale, maybe they won't want this baby. Sir Ralph fell out with his own son, after all. What if he rejects little Robbie, and us, what then?'

She was staring at him appalled, distressed by what he was saying. 'Perhaps you should have more faith in people, Joe Colbert,' Rose chided.

'And happen you should have less and not be so naive. They owe us nowt. They've no obligation to offer us work, money or anything, not unless Sir Ralph is prepared to accept this child as his grandson. And that's very much open to question.'

'Ah, there you are, at last. You must be Rosalind, I assume. I've been looking everywhere for that blasted pink parasol. I'd almost given you up for lost.'

Startled by the sudden appearance of a good-looking stranger at her elbow, and flustered by his use of Rosalind's name, Rose was momentarily overwhelmed. Joe's warning was still whirling in her head, and, hampered by her customary debilitating shyness, she couldn't think how to respond. Her mind was a complete blank as she gazed up into his handsome face.

'We've never met but I'm Bryce Tregowan, Sir Ralph's stepson, at your service,' he said, removing a rather sporty peaked cap as he introduced himself. 'And this is your luggage, I presume? Gracious, Rosalind, I didn't expect quite so much.'

He was tall and broad-shouldered, dark hair rumpled as a consequence of the hat he'd politely doffed, yet his tone was anything but polite, sounding rather brusque and impatient. Dry-mouthed, Rose gathered her courage.

'Pleased to meet you, I'm sure, but I'm not . . . I mean, I expected a servant or chauffeur, not an actual family member to come and collect us,' Rose managed, thinking how deliciously good-looking he was, even as she struggled to decide how best to deal with this unexpected encounter. A fellow servant of her own class would have been much easier to deal with.

His suit was of the finest tweed, worn over a canary-yellow waistcoat, a cream and green silk cravat at this throat. Even as she was speaking he took a watch from his pocket and gave it a cursory glance. He certainly seemed to be more concerned with the time, not to mention the quantity of luggage, than showing any proper interest in her. He hadn't even asked if she'd enjoyed a safe passage. For some reason this irritated her, bringing her thoughts back to Joe's fears. Were they justified?

Twin furrows appeared between his dark brow as he glowered down at the cluster of bags. 'There does seem to be rather a lot,' he complained again, scanning the array of trunks and boxes, and then his gaze fell upon the child. 'Good lord, is that an infant in your arms?'

'Yes, it is. Actually, this is—'

'I heard about the death of your husband, but nothing was said about any child,' he interrupted. 'Is it yours? Drat, silly question. I do apologise, Rosalind. I'm rather at sixes and sevens this morning.'

Thrown completely off balance, Bryce was thinking of what his brother's reaction would be to this startling piece of news, not to mention that of their dear mama. The pair had been alarmed enough to discover a letter from his daughter-in-law among Sir Ralph's papers, announcing this visit. They were also tellingly relieved to learn of the death of his son. But the presence of a child put a whole new complexion on the matter. Embroiled in his own thoughts, Bryce paid even less heed to the woman he presumed to be the child's mother.

Seeming to collect himself, he continued, 'We were only recently made aware of your impending visit, and that Robert had died.' He cleared his throat, as if having difficulty in finding the right words. 'May I offer my sincere condolences on your loss.'

Rose found herself politely thanking him while privately thinking he didn't sound in the least bit sincere, simply parroting the words as a duty. If anything, he sounded even more cold and unfriendly. Was the baby hers indeed? What cheek! Perhaps his arrogance was the reason she had still failed to point out his mistake in taking her for Rosalind, or else it was her sudden fear for the child.

Holding little Robbie possessively close, she exchanged a quick troubled glance with Joe. Something wasn't right here, but she couldn't quite put her finger on what it was.

Intercepting the glance, Bryce half turned. 'Ah, and who might this be? Your new beau perhaps?' He glanced again at the baby, the train of his thoughts plain to see.

Rose was struck speechless, quite unable to believe the sheer effrontery of the question. Even if this man didn't know exactly when her husband had died, to imply that Rosalind would have replaced him with another lover so quickly, and got pregnant by him already, was deeply offensive. Perhaps Joe had a point about this family, after all, if they presumed always to think the worst. How dare this man cast such a slur upon that gentle lady's reputation?

She opened her mouth to say as much, but at that moment Joe stepped hastily forward, giving the slightest of head bows.

'I am Joseph, My Lady's manservant, if you please, sir. You would not expect Her Ladyship to travel without proper protection, would you, sir?' he very reasonably pointed out, extending a hand to Rose, as if she were as much of a delicate flower as her name suggested.

'Ah, no, of course not. I beg your pardon, Rosalind, I wasn't thinking.' He inclined a half head bow towards her, as if that made everything fine and dandy.

Rose was glaring at Joe in shocked fury, horrified by what he had just done. Should she deny it? Should she come out with it right now and say exactly who she was? But if she did, it would be tantamount to accusing Joe of being at best a liar, at worst a fraudster. And what would this man do to him then? Call the customs officials, or the police? They'd already been thrown out of one country, could they be evicted from their own homeland as well? Oh, what on earth had possessed Joe to say such a thing! Now they were in a proper pickle.

But of course, she knew the reason. Hadn't he made his resolve only too clear that he had no intention of bedding down with the rats, or begging for his daily crust? Mercy me, this was all going badly wrong.

'Where would you wish me to deposit the luggage?' Joe was respectfully enquiring.

'Hmm, the problem is that my Electric Phaeton is only a two-seater. I wasn't expecting to carry two passengers, or three counting the child, let alone all this baggage. I'll call a cab to take you to the station,' he continued, calm as you please. 'It's a long journey down to Cornwall and you'll be more comfortable, in any case, making it by train. Will that suit, Rosalind?'

'Actually, my name is Rose, and—' she began.

'I'm sure it makes no odds to me what you prefer to call yourself,' he snapped, his tone sharp with impatience. 'We can settle such minor details later. In the meantime I must press ahead with all speed in the motor. Family matters needing attention, I'm afraid.' The sooner he imparted this news to his mother, the better, and make some attempt to calm her resulting fury before the lady in question arrived. 'I can at least relieve you of the luggage.'

Rose felt rather as if she'd been smacked in the face. This man had travelled goodness knows how many miles, all the way up to Bristol to meet them, and was now going to dump them on a train to make their own way. How dare he! He didn't even have the courtesy to pause long enough to listen to what she had to say.

Less than half an hour later she and Joe, along with Robbie and one piece of luggage for the baby's requirements, had been put into a railway carriage and told to disembark at St Austell Station.

'Someone will come to collect you, though probably not myself,' he told them, rather vaguely, then he was slamming shut the carriage door and striding away without even troubling to say goodbye.

Lydia Tregowan stood staring down at her sick husband as he lay inert in his bed, and struggled to keep herself from laughing out loud. Could the moment she'd so longed for be here at last? Twelve years she had waited, twelve long, boring, excruciatingly dull years. Sir Ralph Tregowan had been old the day she'd married him, both in years and in his demeanour. As she was so much younger than he, by some twenty years or more, she'd made it very plain from the start that she expected to maintain certain standards.

'I am accustomed to attending balls, dinner parties and theatre during the season and would wish to continue to do so,' she had told him, feeling it essential they agree proper terms from the outset. 'And I like to winter in Biarritz, having done so for several years now.' Lydia certainly had no intention of burying herself in deepest Cornwall for the entire year, however delightful Penver Court and the estate might be. She'd never noticed any shortage of offers from rich men in search of an attractive wife, and one was as good as another so far as she was concerned. If this match didn't take, she had other fish to fry.

But he had taken her, and accepted her terms with alacrity, which was most gratifying. She believed the Tregowan family to be very rich indeed, also in possession of a title, and she'd really rather fancied herself as Lady Tregowan.

Sir Ralph had readily agreed to rent her a house in London, and even when he declined to join her there, due to some perceived illness or pressing matters on his estate, he had made no protest about her own continued jaunts up to town. His absence was a great relief to her as Lydia found his lovemaking odious in the extreme. She really could not endure his physical presence in her bedroom, let alone in her bed, and used every subtle ploy she could think of to avoid it. She also considered that he kept too tight a rein on her purse strings, paying her an insultingly small allowance which obliged her to delve too deeply into her own carefully hoarded funds. When these restrictions became both stifling and irritating, she did not hesitate to deny him access to her boudoir entirely.

Lydia saw this as just punishment for his reneging on their agreed terms. 'Why will you not grant me a proper allowance?' she'd railed at him, on countless occasions.

'Why will you not be a proper wife to me?' had been his infuriating rejoinder.

Had she not been so very certain of her own attractive charms, Lydia might have begun to wonder if Sir Ralph had married her for her own fortune, carefully garnered through several productive marriages. Besides, the Tregowan family owned hundreds of acres, several farms and an entire village in Cornwall. The man was simply mean.

Fortunately, her husband's ill health had grown worse over the years, which meant that he had become increasingly dependent upon her to oversee much of the management of Penver Court. Once she'd disposed of the odious man who had acted as his steward for over twenty years, that is. Bartlett had been the most awkward, difficult man she had ever met, and she'd felt no compunction over dismissing him on accusations of fraud. Whether or not these were entirely true was quite beside the point. The fellow had to go. Lydia was always determined to have her own way.

Glancing again at the prostrate figure on the bed, she curled up her nose at the unpleasant odours. An all-pervading air of sickness, and something worse, permeated the room. Had he voided his bowels yet again? Where was that dratted nurse? She gave the bell pull a firm tug before crossing to open the window, wafting in some very welcome fresh air, even if it was against all the rules of the sickroom.

The door opened, yet it was not the nurse who entered, but her younger son. Lydia hurried across to kiss him on each cheek. 'Jago, my dear, thank goodness. Have you seen Nurse Fenton? She is never around when needed.'

'It is twelve noon, so I dare say she will be taking dinner in the kitchen.'

'Then tell her to stop feeding her face and return to her duties, at once.'

Ignoring her request, Jago went to stand beside the bed, gazing down upon the man who had initially welcomed him into his family, even allowing him to take his name. The smile he gave his mother did not reach his frost-grey eyes. 'That is a most attractive taffeta gown you are wearing this morning, Mama, if somewhat gloomy. Would you call it navy blue or black? Anyone would think you were about to enter into mourning.'

'I rather thought I might be,' Lydia said, with a small smile.

'Has there been any sign of life yet?'

'None. Doctor Bevan believes he has slipped into some kind of coma, from which he may, or may not, wake.'

Mother and son looked at each other, sharing the same thought. 'And what if he doesn't – wake, that is?' Jago asked at length, in his characteristically soft drawl.

Lydia came to put her arms about him and rest her cheek against the hard plains of his chest. She could hear his heart beating, which always excited her. It had had that effect upon her ever since she'd first held Jago in her arms as a newborn baby. 'The doctor says he could well remain in this comatose state for months, if not years.'

'Years?' Jerking free of her cloying hold, he stared at her, appalled.

'Indeed, that's what he said. Years. Or else poor Sir Ralph could suffer another relapse and die tomorrow. It is hard to say which is the most likely,' Lydia explained as she carefully adjusted her husband's pillows.

'In the meantime you must continue to play the good wife?'

She smiled, although the pale-blue eyes remained cold and calculating. 'Indeed I must. Haven't I always spoilt him, not least by providing him with his favourite food?'

Jago snorted with ironic laughter. 'So much so that he quickly became too heavy to ride out on his horse around the grounds, which meant he wasn't able to keep quite as close an eye on the estate as he should, or on his wife for that matter. What a neat trick that was, Mama. And I seem to recall you kept him well supplied with the finest brandy and port.'

She was laughing with him now, even as she stroked the dark curls from his handsome face; a quiet, satisfied chuckle of amusement at her own cleverness. 'I also made certain that he slept well every night with the aid of my herbal sleeping potions, particularly when his dyspepsia was troubling him. Oh, indeed I was, and in fact still am, the most diligent and caring of wives, as is only right and proper when tending a decrepit old husband.'

He kissed the tip of her pert nose. 'And, once you'd successfully alienated him from his only son, you very cleverly milked the estate of thousands without your decrepit old husband even being aware of it. And why not? Don't you deserve suitable recompense in view of how miserly he was?'

Lydia's smile of self-satisfaction quickly faded. 'The problem now, Jago, is that land is no longer the rich source of wealth it once was, and as a consequence Sir Ralph insists he has less liquid capital than he previously enjoyed. I battled with that offensive little man, that Bartlett fellow, ordering him to cut down on repairs, but even though I'm now rid of him we still have the problem of finding tenants willing to pay a decent rent. It's extremely difficult, what with farming in the sorry state it is.'

'Don't worry your lovely head about all of that. You can safely leave recalcitrant tenants to me.'

'I know I can, my darling, but the holding out at Lanlivery has been standing empty for three months or more. It is quite unacceptable.'

'If we fail to find a tenant, then we must sell it. We surely have plenty more farms on the estate.'

'Sir Ralph would never agree, and we'd need his signature.'

Jago smirked in disbelief. 'I cannot recall you ever being fazed by the inconvenience of acquiring a correct signature in the past, Mama? Besides, I doubt there will be cause to worry about money for much longer.'

They both looked down at the paralysed figure, as if suddenly recalling his presence, half afraid he might actually be able to see them or hear what they were saying.

'I did it for the sake of my boys. Never for myself, you understand? I have to consider their needs,' Lydia told the corpse-like form, just in case he could.

'Of course you did, Mother dear,' Jago said, slipping an arm about her tightly corseted waist and giving her an affectionate squeeze.

Lydia's face was expressionless as she continued to gaze upon her husband. But when she lifted it to meet that of her son's, it burnt with the fervour of her need. 'It would seem that the end of our purgatory might well be in sight.'

'We must make sure that it is,' Jago quietly agreed. And as he bent to kiss her rouged cheek, Lydia turned her face at the last second so that his kiss landed quite close to her smiling mouth. The pair of them were always in such perfect accord.

Chapter Five

At any other time, this being her first ride on a steam train, Rose would have been filled with excitement. It was nowhere near as thrilling as embarking on a ship to America with her family, but an adventure all the same. Yet in the circumstances she could take no pleasure in it. She was boiling up inside. Rose could hardly speak, her anger with Joe was so great. The tension between them seemed to grow as the miles slipped by, and they studiously avoided each other's eye.

'What were you thinking of, to come out with that remark?' she challenged him at last, the words bursting out of her as the train chugged steadily along.

'Don't start shouting at me. We agreed that neither of us wanted to end up starving or worse, in some godforsaken hole on Bristol waterfront.'

'We did *not* agree,' Rose vociferously argued, causing

heads to turn so that she was obliged to drop her voice to a hissing whisper. 'You were ranting on about not trusting the Tregowans, but *I* have every faith in them.'

'So why didn't you tell him straight out who you were?'

'I tried.'

'Not hard enough.'

'He arrogantly interrupted me, that's when he noticed me at all. I did mean to say who I was right at the start, but he so put my back up I couldn't seem to get the words out. But then I didn't expect you to barge in and say what you did.'

Joe grinned at her, his green-brown eyes twinkling with admiration. 'You could easily be a lady, looking so elegant in that fine blue gown. You look a proper society beauty, Rosie, you do really. He clearly took you for one.'

'Stop that!' Rose's cheeks flushed bright crimson. 'I was only doing what I was told. Rosalind insisted I make use of her clothes, and the parasol for identification purposes. Like I say, I meant to introduce myself right away. I only hesitated because you put a doubt in my mind, and I promised I'd see the baby safely into the right hands, and that's what I mean to do. But once you'd addressed me as "My Lady" and "Her Ladyship", how could I deny it without leaving you open to accusations of fraud or deception? Can't you see what you've done, Joe? You've ruined everything.'

'No, actually, I don't see it that way at all. Bryce Tregowan could easily have snatched the child and left us standing there. How would you have felt about that?'

Rose gathered Robbie protectively close, rocking him

gently at this frightening thought. 'Why would he do such a thing? Anyway, you insisted that the Tregowan family wouldn't want him. You can't have it both ways. And how on earth do we get out of this muddle now, tell me that?'

Joe put his mouth close to her ear so that there was no risk of anyone in the carriage overhearing a word he said. 'We play our cards carefully, that's what we do. We keep them very close to our chest. We watch the Tregowan family. We listen and observe. Once we're satisfied that they want the babby, that they are willing and able to offer him a good home, plus a job as his nursemaid for you, and a place for me, then you can come clean and own up. You did promise your beloved Rosalind that you'd act as guardian to her son, so why shouldn't you check them out first, before simply handing him over?'

Rose thought about this for a while as the train rumbled on, turning the argument over in her mind, for it did make a certain sense. 'But they'll think we're after money or something.'

'How can they if we don't take any? Anyway, if they keep us, we won't need money, will we? For now, anyway.' Joe could see she was weakening. If he could just persuade her not to spill the beans, he could see a whole new future opening up for them both.

'I'd never be able to carry it off, pretending to be a proper lady when I'm not.'

'Course you could, and it wouldn't be for long, only a day or two, no more, just till we're sure Robbie is safe.' It would be far longer if Joe had his way, but one step at a time.

Rose sighed, fidgeting on the wooden seat, which was far from comfortable. But the rhythm of the engine was soothing her, exhaustion from the long voyage finally setting in. The sway of the carriage was so much less bothersome on the stomach than an ocean-going ship, particularly one caught up in a storm. She thought sadly of Rosalind's final hours with overwhelming seasickness adding to her misery, poor lady. Rose thought of her own misery in steerage, of the ache of hunger deep in her belly, with which she was painfully familiar. She remembered the ladies of the night who had waited with her in the holding pen, and how she could easily become one if she and Joe didn't find employment soon.

Because of Rosalind's kindness, Rose meant to make absolutely certain that she did right by her friend and take the baby to his grandfather. But not for a moment had she imagined things would turn out like this, finding herself embroiled in a lie. There was a real danger of them being considered fraudsters, yet Rose was anxious to ensure that Robbie was indeed wanted, and would be safe with the Tregowans. As Joe said, they had turned away his own father.

She cuddled the baby and kissed his brow, gazing in wonder at the way his fair lashes fanned each plump cheek, his little mouth contentedly pursed in sleep. He was such a good little thing, no trouble at all. She loved him dearly already. You only had to look at him to fall instantly under his spell. And Rose still nursed a fervent hope that she'd be taken on as his nursemaid. Wouldn't that be grand?

But it had not been an auspicious start. Her mind kept replaying what Bryce Tregowan had said, or rather what he had not said. He hadn't offered one word of welcome, not even a 'delighted you could come', or 'happy to meet you'. He must be the rudest man she'd ever met. Did he really imagine that a woman of Rosalind Tregowan's quality would arrive from America with only one piece of luggage? The foolish man probably never gave the matter a moment's thought. Then to go on and accuse her of having a lover was utterly despicable. Was he quite without common sense or decency? It was perfectly clear that the sight of the baby had thrown him completely. Now why was that? she wondered.

'So what did you think of him, then, this Bryce Tregowan?' she asked Joe, quietly marvelling at the views of the sea, and the way the waves splashed over the railway track without seeming to hinder the train.

'Pompous idiot!'

Rose giggled. 'My thoughts entirely. What is it about the upper classes that makes them so arrogant and pretentious? Who does he think he is to cast such aspersions upon a respectable lady?'

'And he could at least have provided us with a meal before abandoning us,' Joe complained, rubbing his aching belly. 'I don't know about you but I'm fair starved.'

Rose sighed. 'Me too, but it's not his fault that we're hungry, is it? Or that we're not who he thinks we are, with not a penny to our name to buy a crust of bread. I dread to think what the rest of the family will be like.'

They both fell silent then, wrapped in their own

74

private thoughts, and each quietly nursing a gnawing hunger. Food had proved hard to come by after Rosalind's death as Rose had been far too nervous to enter the first-class dining room, preferring to beg the ship's cook for a few scraps now and then, as well as milk for the baby. Thankfully, he'd taken pity on her, but poor Joe had naturally remained in steerage. Now she was more worried than she admitted. Bryce Tregowan's behaviour had been odd, to say the least. And there was no getting away from it, Joe rushing in like that and pretending to be her manservant had complicated matters considerably.

'The minute we're satisfied all is well, we make it clear who we were really are, agreed?'

'Agreed!'

Lulled by the train she rested her head on his shoulder, and minutes later she was fast asleep.

This time when they reached their destination they were met by a chauffeur who scurried about opening doors for her, as if she really were a lady, while ignoring Joe completely.

The drive through the Cornish countryside was deliciously pleasant on this sunny afternoon in late May, with the scent of new grass and blossom in the air. Yet it was nerve-wracking too. While Joe rode up front with the driver, Rose sat back on the leather cushions, revelling in this unexpected luxury. Perhaps if she really were Rosalind, here to meet her late husband's family for the first time, she'd still be feeling a certain degree of nervousness at the prospect.

Sternly reminding herself that this was not the case, Rose

occupied the few miles of the journey carefully practising in her mind how to approach this most sensitive situation. She'd changed the baby's napkin on the train, so that he would be fresh and sweet-smelling when he met his new family. Surely a baby could win the coldest heart, so she truly did not share Joe's doubts that the family wouldn't welcome him. How could they not fall in love with him, as she had done?

Rosalind had been most reassuring that her father-in-law was anxious to heal the breach, passing off the family dispute with a philosophical smile. 'You needn't fear. Sir Ralph has a reputation for being the kindest of men, which makes it all the more sad that he and Robert, his only son, became estranged, a situation they both afterwards regretted. But his reply to my request for assistance came swiftly, and with real compassion. He did not hesitate to offer me a home and a warm welcome at Penver Court.'

Rosalind had apparently chosen to say nothing of the coming child at that stage of their correspondence, in case anything should go wrong. She explained to Rose that as Sir Ralph had already lost a son, she'd no wish to raise false hopes until the baby was safely delivered.

So if Rosalind had been happy to make her home with a father-in-law she'd never met, in a country she'd never even seen, Rose saw no reason why the old man would not be overjoyed to welcome this grandson in her place, particularly as the poor little mite was now an orphan. Although this stepmother might have a different view of the matter, Rose worried.

Refreshed from her sleep on the train, she was convinced that she would soon be able to explain away Joe's foolish remark at the docks as a bit of brashness on his part. She'd politely assure the family that she hadn't corrected this folly because as the boy's guardian she needed to be sure that all was well before handing him over. And Mr Bryce Tregowan had not made things easy for her with his cold, unfriendly manner, not least by accusing Joe of being her lover.

Rose decided she would then go on to explain how she'd nursed dear Rosalind in her final hours, and how she had plenty of experience with babies, being the eldest of a large family. She was quietly optimistic that everything would go smoothly, at least until the moment the carriage turned in between two tall gateposts and started down the longest drive she'd ever seen in her life. There must surely be a palace at the end of it, she thought, caught by a sudden attack of nerves. Not that she'd ever seen a palace, or visited such a posh house before, let alone ridden in a fine carriage, so how could she be any judge? But her heart seemed to turn over with fear the moment she was faced with the reality of all her hopes.

'Be brave,' she softly chided herself. 'You've faced worse challenges than this, Rose Belsfield, and survived.'

For a moment Rose ached to be with her own family, wherever they were in America. She prayed they were now safely with Aunt Cassie. Oh, but how she longed to rest her head on her mother's breast and be told all would be well; to see Micky, and Mary, the twins, and silly Clara again. How she missed them. And what was she even doing here, in the middle of Cornwall, taking the orphan child of a perfect stranger to a family she'd never even met?

Edging forward in her seat, eager for her first view of

Penver Court, the sight that met her eyes when the carriage drew to a halt in a clatter of horses' hooves on gravel was a coffin. It was being carried across the courtyard, a trail of mourners following in its wake.

'We'd best sit and wait till they pass, if you don't mind, My Lady,' said the driver, coming to stand by the carriage window. 'Or maybe you'd like to join them in the family pew to pay your last respects to our dear departed lord?'

In that moment of horror Rose realised that she had arrived too late. Sir Ralph Tregowan, with his generous heart and anxiety to heal the wounds of a family rift, never would meet his new grandson. As well as dealing with Joe's foolish remark, she now had a worse problem to face. She would no doubt have to put forward her case to the arrogant Bryce Tregowan instead.

Rose was too shy and nervous to join this unknown family in their private pew close to the altar, instead choosing to remain at the back of the small chapel and view proceedings from a safe distance. She could see, however, that they were only too aware of her presence. The younger of the two women turned at once to look at her, then bent her head to whisper to the older woman, who must be the stepmother Rosalind had mentioned. She too swung about to cast a withering glance in Rose's direction, the curled feather in her pert little hat seeming to quiver with disapproval in a most disconcerting manner. The man seated beside her likewise glowered when prompted to also look her way by the two ladies. Rose recognised Bryce Tregowan instantly, but he seemed to be studiously avoiding her eye.

They must know who she was, or who they thought she was. Could none of them find it in themselves to offer a polite smile?

The rest of the sparse congregation appeared to comprise the housekeeper and butler, plus various servants, and possibly a few tenant farmers in their best funereal attire. They too were staring at her, as if she had grown two heads. Or else they were looking at the child.

Darling Robbie was thankfully still sleeping peacefully through all of this unwelcome attention, despite the grinding squeaks and chords of an ancient organ, although Rose doubted this state of bliss could continue for very much longer. It was rapidly approaching his time for a feed.

For the first time Rose longed for Joe's presence, but he had gone off with the groom to find her luggage. Infuriating, pushy and self-opinionated he may be, yet she could have done with some friendly support right now. Straightening her spine, Rose held fast to her failing courage. She must accept their interest as perfectly natural. Since they'd never met her, possibly weren't even aware of her existence until recently, it was only to be expected that they would be curious. She had a good deal of explaining to do, whether or not she went along with Joe's plan, but she'd judge the right moment to relate her tale. And Rose fully intended to do so with tact and care, breaking the news of dear Rosalind's death gently. In the meantime she must put on a good face and exercise patience.

After the short service the coffin-bearers shouldered their burden once more to carry Sir Ralph to his final resting place in the small private graveyard. Rose stood in respectful silence as everyone fell into line and trooped out behind the coffin. She noted that not a single family member so much as glanced her way as they passed by. It felt almost as if they had snubbed her, which caused a shiver to ripple down her spine. Even Bryce Tregowan refused to acknowledge her presence, but kept his cold gaze fixed rigidly ahead. Yet she really mustn't overreact. This odd behaviour might be the Tregowan family's way of maintaining dignity, but there was little sign of real grief. Not a tear shed between them. Maybe toffs reacted differently to ordinary mortals on such occasions, she decided.

Rose dutifully tacked onto the end of the line, and made sure she stood some way back as they all gathered at the graveside, family on one side, servants and tenants on the other.

But watching Sir Ralph's coffin being lowered into the ground was really quite upsetting, as it reminded her of his daughter-in-law's body being committed to the deep only a few short weeks ago. She brushed away a tear from her cold cheek, not wishing to presume to weep over a man she'd never met, yet her heart was filled with sadness that this tiny baby should lose so many family members so quickly. Not only orphaned, but losing someone who might well have become a devoted grandfather. She could weep with the pain of it, for all these people were strangers to her, she really could.

Robbie chose this precise moment to let out a hiccup, and then a loud wail. All eyes swivelled in her direction, their accusing gaze condemning her for allowing the child to disturb such a poignant moment. Quickly lifting the baby to her shoulder, Rose rubbed his back, hoping to quiet him as she hastily backed away. But Robbie was by now in full-throated roar, having woken to find his tummy empty. And he wanted it filled *now*!

'I'm so sorry,' she mumbled, hurrying away as quickly as she could, half running across the grass in the direction of the house. She had no idea where the kitchens were, or where Joe had taken the baby's luggage, but somehow or other she must find Robbie's bottle and feed him. There would be time enough to meet the family later.

'Excuse me, ma'am.' A breathless voice came from behind. Rose turned to find a young girl hurrying to join her. 'I'll take the baby if you like, see he's fed and changed.'

Rose was reluctant to hand Robbie over. 'I can manage, thank you, if you'll just point me in the direction of the kitchen.'

The young woman smiled. 'I'll do better than that, I'll take you. It's a maze of rooms and corridors inside that house. Tilly's the name, ma'am, short for Mathilda, although only me mam uses me Sunday name, as I call it, and generally when I'm in trouble.'

'Then I'd be glad of your help, Tilly. Please call me Rose.'

'Ooh, no, milady, that wouldn't be proper. How old is he, the little one? He looks very young.'

'Not quite a month.'

'Goodness, what a little star to have kept quiet for so long. Let's find him some grub, shall we?'

With Tilly's help Robbie was soon contentedly settled with his bottle, and Rose thought she might use this opportunity to find out a bit more about the Tregowan family. 'Have you worked here long?' she asked the girl.

'About seven years, since I was twelve.'

'Are they good people to work for?'

Tilly half turned away to fuss over putting little Robbie's nappy to soak, not quite meeting Rose's eye as she carefully answered. 'So long as my wages come in regular and I can send some home to me mam, I've no complaints. There are plenty worse.'

'What about Lady Tregowan – she's Sir Ralph's second wife, I believe?'

'Aye, and she nursed him well in his last years. She dotes on her boys, as she calls them, particularly Jago, the elder of the two. But she's a stickler for rules and how things should be done. Runs this place with an iron hand, as they say, so we have to mind our *p*'s and *q*'s, do things proper or we soon know about it. My trouble is I'm a bit ham-fisted and clumsy, and not much good with rules.' Tilly smiled, as if at the folly of her own failings. 'But then I didn't have Her Ladyship's fine upbringing. She went to the very best academy for the daughters of gentlemen, was finished on the Continent and presented at court, since her father made a deal of money in banking.'

'Enough to buy his daughters rich husbands?' Rose smiled, but Tilly was beginning to look embarrassed, so she quickly apologised. 'Sorry, I shouldn't be asking you these questions. I don't mean to encourage you to gossip about your employers, only I'm feeling a bit new and strange.' Lifting the baby, Rose put him to her shoulder to bring up his wind.

Tilly rushed to fetch a towel to protect her gown. There

was an eagerness now in her expression. 'I expect it does feel a bit odd, milady, this being your first day an' all. Everyone was thrilled to hear you were coming. You're just what this place needs: new blood, and young blood at that. It'll be grand to have a new Lady Tregowan.'

Rose was stunned. Talking to Tilly, a girl almost her own age, she'd temporarily forgotten her agreement with Joe to maintain the deception, at least for a while. 'Oh, that's not the way of it at all,' she began, then hastily changed the subject before she said something she shouldn't. 'What about your own family? Do they live nearby?'

Her gaze still fastened on the baby, Tilly didn't immediately answer. 'Could I hold him for a minute, milady? I love babies, having any number of brothers and sisters younger than me. I lose count of 'em, I do really.'

They both laughed as Robbie furiously protested over the loss of his bottle as Rose shifted him gently onto the other girl's lap. Once he was settled and suckling well, she was unable to resist adding, 'I come from a large family myself.'

'Really? Then we have something in common, milady.' Tilly smiled.

More than you might imagine, Rose thought, although didn't say as much. She longed to talk about her family, to tell this friendly girl the full story, but realised it would be dangerous to embroil herself in too much discussion about herself to a kitchen maid. She hadn't even met the Tregowan family yet, let alone observed them or judged whether they'd be good carers for Robbie, as Joe had suggested. And judging by the sour looks she'd encountered in the chapel, she was beginning to think that his argument might well be valid. Oh, if only she could make up her mind what was the best thing to do.

'I miss mine terribly,' Rose volunteered. 'Do you see them much, your brothers and sisters?'

'Every other Sunday. That's my day off, and they don't live too far away. My parents have a smallholding in Polruan.' A shadow crossed her face, which Rose was quick to spot.

'Is there a problem? Is someone unwell?'

'Oh, no, nothing like that, milady.'

'What then? What is troubling you, Tilly?'

'It's not my place to say.'

It was obvious to Rose that something was seriously worrying her new friend, and if using her alleged status was the way to get out of her whatever it was, then maybe she should take the risk. 'You can tell me in complete confidence. Perhaps I can help?'

The frown was instantly wiped away with bright new hope. 'Ooh, that'd be grand. Do you reckon you might be able to do something, milady?'

Rose now experienced a sinking sensation in her chest. What was she thinking of, promising to help? She had no power to influence matters here, being little more than a servant herself, an impostor even. The thought startled her, as if she'd never seen herself in that light before. 'I don't know whether I can or not, but I'd certainly like to try.'

Tilly shuffled forward slightly in her seat, her gaze still resting fondly on the baby in her arms, but seemingly anxious that her next words not be overheard by anyone although they were quite alone in the kitchen. 'They've been given notice to quit,' she whispered in hushed tones.

'Sorry, I don't understand.'

'My family is about to be evicted. The rent kept going up and up till Mam and Dad couldn't pay it anymore. So now they're in arrears and have to leave.' There were tears in the girl's eyes, which she quickly brushed away with her arm, since both hands were fully occupied with the baby.

'Oh, my goodness, Tilly, that's dreadful! Do they have somewhere else to go?' Rose knew all about eviction. Her own family had suffered a similar fate following the death of her father. They'd all been forced to sleep out on the street for three long cold nights until they'd found accommodation in a flea-riddled hostel.

Tilly was shaking her head, the tears running down her cheeks unchecked. 'The next two eldest are in service, like me, but there are still nine children at home, the youngest only two. Dad's at his wits' end. He's a proud man, and a hard worker, happy to pay a proper rent, but with prices being what they are it's just not possible to find any more money. Mam weaves baskets, takes in washing and does what she can to help Dad on the land, ready to turn her hand to anything, as are the older girls. The young children pick stones from fields for hours on end, getting paid pennies for the back-breaking task. Dad has asked for time to pay, hoping to catch up with arrears as soon as things start to improve, but Mr Jago has given them until the end of this quarter to pay up or get out.'

'Oh, Tilly, I don't know what to say.'

'They'll end up on poor relief, or be split up and put in the workhouse.' The other girl was sobbing now, and thrusting the baby back into Rose's arms, she ran to the sink to splash her face with cold water. Moments later she returned to stand before her, once more calm and quite her old self. 'My humble apologies, Your Ladyship. I shouldn't be troubling you with all this, especially on your first day.'

'I'm glad you did. I want to understand what's going on here.' Why did it matter? a voice asked at the back of her head. What was all this to do with her? Because if she stayed, albeit as a servant herself, the more Rose understood about how Penver Court operated, the better. Most important of all, there was little Robbie to think of. What kind of a home had she brought him to? Here was surely more evidence that Joe was right to advise caution.

Bobbing a little curtsey, Tilly continued, 'Begging your pardon, milady, but they'll all be in the drawing room now, where Mrs Pascoe has laid out the funeral repast. The little one will be quite safe with me if you'd like to join them.' She laid the now sleeping baby in a cradle that had appeared, seemingly out of nowhere, and gently began to rock him.

'I'm most grateful for your help, Tilly, and I've so enjoyed our little talk. Perhaps you could find someone to show me the way?'

A footman was called, and the young man led Rose along a bewildering labyrinth of corridors until finally he opened the door of the drawing room to reveal an alarming number of people within. Rose almost shrank from entering, wishing the floor could open and swallow her up. Was that sympathy in the eye of the young footman? she wondered, as she cast him a frightened glance. Drawing a breath to steady the frantic beating of her heart, she stepped into the fray rather as Daniel might have walked into the lion's den.

Chapter Six

The silence was deafening. To her complete horror Rose realised that everyone had stopped talking to turn and stare at her. She gained a vague impression of a spacious, luxuriously appointed room in tasteful greens, yellow and gold, caught a glimpse of a pink marble fireplace, of silk-lined walls hung with an intimidating array of family portraits. Never had Rose seen such a room in all her life, the entire scene dazzlingly illuminated by a huge chandelier. It was a world apart from the dingy and overcrowded hovels she had experienced in the past. Her instinct was to turn tail and run, yet she felt frozen to the spot as a bewildering blur of faces swirled before her frightened gaze. It was like being caught in a living nightmare. Nobody moved, nobody spoke, and Rose had not the first idea what to do next.

'Ah, Rosalind, there you are.' Bryce Tregowan crossed

the width of an expensive Persian rug in a few swift strides, negotiating the crowd with elegant ease. Then taking her by the elbow he led her across to an unsmiling woman who stood, sherry glass in hand, framed by a wide bay window with a view of the gardens beyond. Her composure was rigid and unsmiling, and not in the least encouraging. 'Allow me to introduce my mother, Lady Tregowan.'

Without thinking, Rose bobbed a little curtsey and Bryce laughed out loud. 'There's really no need to stand on ceremony, Rosalind. Ah, I was forgetting. Mama, allow me to introduce you to Sir Ralph's daughter-in-law Rosalind, who prefers to be called Rose.'

A pair of cold blue eyes considered her with stern disapproval. They appeared to be the only mark of colour in her entire appearance, bolero, lace blouse and fluted taffeta skirt being one of unrelieved black from neck to toe. Even her hair was almost black, a shining coil of glossy tresses, atop which was perched a hat with an equally mournful ostrich feather curled about the brim.

'I trust you have given your nursemaid a sound ticking off?'

'I-I beg your pardon?'

'You clearly have no control over your staff, let alone that child. I cannot imagine what possessed you to take the infant into such an unsuitable atmosphere. You should dismiss the woman forthwith.'

Rose had been expecting a polite enquiry about her journey, her health, or possibly a question about Rosalind's late husband, or more likely why she had kept quiet about the baby. She'd carefully prepared an answer to each, willing to follow Joe's plan and hold off from telling her tale for a little while, till she'd had time to look the family over, as he had suggested. But this question was so unexpected it threw her completely off balance. It almost made her want to giggle. But then the Tregowan family seemed to make a habit of catching one unawares. 'Actually, I don't have a nursemaid.'

'*You don't have a nursemaid!*' The resonant tones rang out so loud that anyone who had quietly returned to their social chit-chat paused again to listen in to the conversation. 'Are you completely without common sense? You'll be telling me next that you feed the babe yourself.'

This was ridiculous. She had to come clean and tell the truth at once. 'Goodness, no. I couldn't possibly do such a thing, since I—'

'Since you are a lady. I'm vastly relieved to hear that you have some degree of pride.' Tilting her head to one side, the dowager scanned Rose with a deprecating glance. 'You would be wise to remember that the Tregowans do have certain standards to maintain. Perhaps it is because you have spent so many years in America, where I expect things are done rather differently. But it is not considered proper in this country to take a child into a funeral service.'

'I-I do beg your pardon, My Lady, but as I had only just arrived, there really didn't seem any alternative. I-I wasn't thinking.'

'A sad state of affairs which was all too apparent,' Lady Tregowan sharply responded. 'But you cannot simply turn up, quite out of the blue, and expect us to provide you with servants, or special treatment, because you've at last graced us with your presence.'

Rose was appalled by the direction this conversation was going. It was almost as if the woman was determined to start an argument. It was so disappointing, particularly when she'd taken such care to mind her p's and q's, as Tilly had warned her they must all do. Clearly she had already blotted her copybook. Could it really be because she'd taken the baby into the little chapel, or was there some deeper reason? Rose could almost feel everyone's gaze pricking the back of her neck, which was growing hotter by the second. She made a polite attempt to apologise. 'I wasn't expecting any special treatment, only a child is welcome everywhere, don't you think, My Lady?'

'Not at a funeral! Dear me, whatever next? Nor, in truth, do you have any right yourself to intrude upon what is, after all, a private occasion. You can hardly call yourself one of the family.'

Bryce stepped hastily forward to interrupt at this point, noisily clearing his throat. 'As a matter of fact she is, Mother. Don't forget that she is Robert's wife . . . er . . . widow, and Sir Ralph's daughter-in-law. Therefore, she has every right to be present at his funeral.'

The woman silenced her son with a freezing glare before continuing her attack. 'You are younger than I expected, quite a bit younger, in fact.'

'I'm older than I look,' Rose quickly responded, startled by the question as she recalled how Rosalind had indeed been a good few years older than herself.

'How long were you married to Robert, exactly?'

Panic hit her as Rose tried to remember the details and do some quick mental arithmetic. Rosalind had claimed they'd tried for a child for quite a few years, but did she ever mention how long she'd been married? Rose couldn't quite remember. Oh, why hadn't she considered this problem before? She could feel her cheeks growing warm with guilt beneath the dowager's scrutinising gaze. And then she recalled Rosalind's pain at her husband's death. 'Nowhere near long enough,' she answered with a sad smile.

'I dare say, but I rather assumed he married shortly after he left home, which was almost twelve years ago, or was it a more recent event?' she persisted.

There was something about the way Lady Tregowan was examining her, the curl of disdain to her upper lip, that caused Rose to bridle. But why was she being so high and mighty? Rose was dressed in one of Rosalind's fine gowns, after all, so there was really no reason why the woman should look down her aristocratic nose with such contempt. She answered without thinking. 'We married only recently.' At once a dark pit opened before her as Rose saw the trap she'd fallen into. In her irritation at the woman's condescending attitude, and her desire to defend dear Rosalind who had saved her life, she'd told a lie. What on earth had possessed her? *Now you've made it worse*, screamed the voice in her head.

Bryce laughed as he patted his mother's hand. 'Now don't start barracking her the moment she has arrived, Mama,' he teased good-naturedly. 'The poor girl hasn't even unpacked yet. Do at least give her the chance to settle in.'

The pale-blue eyes regarded Rose with cold distaste. 'Didn't you say something about her bringing a lover? He will be the young man eating his head off in my kitchen, will he?'

'Joe is most definitely *not* my lover, as I believe I made very clear to your son when he first accused me of it.' Rose drew herself up to her full height as she fixed Bryce Tregowan with a furious glare. 'If anyone tells you different, then they are mistaken. But I'll not stay here to be insulted, no matter how grand you might all think you are.' She made a move to go, and then paused to look wildly about her at the curious faces, confused and uncertain what she should do, or where she should go.

She could, of course, tell them the truth of it right now, give it to them straight that she wasn't the young Lady Rosalind Tregowan at all, but plain little Rosie Belsfield, recently rejected by officials at Ellis Island. Her heart turned over at the recollection of that terrifying ordeal, of being torn from her mother's arms and sent away from her brothers and sisters, callously deported to fend for herself as best she may. Rose was deeply afraid of being rejected yet again, of being left to starve and sleep under a hedge somewhere, of being forced to sell her body in order to survive. Joe had got her into this mess, and now she'd made matters worse with that stupid lie. But why was this woman, and her son, being so horrible before they even properly knew her?

Worries about her own fate, however, paled into insignificance at the prospect of losing little Robbie. Rose instinctively knew that for the sake of his own safety she could never risk taking the baby with her, nor could she leave him here with this heartless, sour-faced harridan. It really didn't bear thinking about.

'That was my mistake, all a foolish misunderstanding,' Bryce Tregowan was saying as he drew her gently back to the window embrasure. 'I wouldn't recommend you make any hasty decisions, Rosalind.'

She looked up into his eyes, a deep charcoal grey, and felt a little wobble in her tummy. Why was he suddenly being so kind? This unexpected change in behaviour was almost more troubling than his inexplicable antipathy to her when first they'd met.

As Rose turned these troubling matters over in her head, Lady Tregowan was lifting her pince-nez to consider her more closely. 'Which part of America did you say you came from? You don't sound particularly American.'

Rose had been doing her utmost to sound her vowels in the correct way and properly enunciate her words, as the toffs did. She'd thought she was doing rather well, but now grew strangely anxious. 'I'm not,' she said, then remembering what Rosalind had told her, quickly explained. 'I no doubt sound a bit odd because I was brought up in Canada, although my parents were British. I feel I am too, and proud to be so, same as you . . .'

Her Ladyship gave a caustic little smile. 'Dear me, no, there is no comparison. I see precious little evidence of any proper moral compass thus far in your behaviour. No wonder dear Sir Ralph came to be so at odds with his son. The poor boy clearly possessed a reprehensible taste in women. Where did he find you, in the gutter?'

Rose's mouth actually fell open with shock. But the

woman was not done with her yet, as her fellow guests were agog to hear as the cutting tones of their hostess clearly rang out.

'That obstinate husband of yours ignored this entire family for a decade or more. As for yourself, how very opportune that you should marry the poor boy presumably not long before he died of consumption, and yet managed to produce a child with commendable speed. Now you turn up here, declaring yourself homeless, in perfect time for Sir Ralph's funeral. An astonishing coincidence, and I do not believe in coincidences.'

On these barbed words, the dowager Lady Tregowan turned on her heel and stalked away, head high.

Rose could scarcely believe what had just occurred, could hardly breathe for the fury that raged through her, largely on Rosalind's behalf, but also partly from embarrassment at having landed herself in this hot water.

'I must apologise for my mother,' Bryce hastened to say. 'I'm afraid she is not the easiest of women to get along with.'

Rose stared at him in blank incomprehension. For a moment she could almost believe him to be sincere. There was something about the way he looked directly into her eyes that sent delightful little ripples of pleasure cascading through her. She almost wanted to lay her cheek against his broad chest and confess all, if only to feel his arms come about her and hold her close. Yet this was the same arrogant man who had assumed Joe to be her lover, and had no doubt repeated this mistaken supposition to his mother. She straightened her spine with dignity. 'It is not for you to apologise on her behalf, although an apology on your own account might be called for. What gives either of you the right to insult me? You know nothing at all about me.'

Bryce Tregowan looked contrite, as well he might. 'You have every right to be annoyed. But may I suggest that the best way of dealing with my mother is to ignore her barbs. It only encourages her if you overreact.'

'Overreact! You don't think I have the right to defend myself against such charges?' But it was not herself the woman was insulting, but Rosalind. What was it she said? '*Where did he find you, in the gutter?*' Dowager or no, how dare she cast such a slur upon dear Rosalind's character?

'You have every right, all I am saying is there's little point in allowing my mother to upset you. It will only make matters worse.'

His expression was so patient, so pragmatic, and so filled with sound common sense that Rose could hardly refute this very reasonable argument. But she felt deeply offended, as if she personally had been attacked. Still too stunned to know how best to deal with the situation, she watched in silence as Lady Tregowan paused to talk to a portly gentleman. Gathering Her Ladyship's hands in his he put them to his lips, obviously offering her his condolences.

The dowager accepted his offer of a handkerchief to dab at each eye, mopping up invisible tears, purely to play on his sympathy, in Rose's opinion. She'd shown no sign of grief at the funeral, nor had she appeared in the least devastated by the death of her husband. The woman was a vindictive old witch, that's what she was. There was no doubt in Rose's mind that the tears were entirely false.

Then the pair turned, seemingly with one accord, to glance back at her. Rose went quite cold. What was she saying now? What lies was she telling this man? Oh, why was it all going so badly wrong? She shouldn't have listened to Joe, but come right out with who she really was back there at Bristol docks. Now things were going from bad to worse. She had to put an end to this mess right now.

In some distress Rose again turned to Bryce Tregowan. 'May I speak with you a moment, in private?'

He offered what might pass for a sympathetic smile. 'As I said, dealing with my mother is not easy, but whatever you wish to say on the matter will have to wait. That is Mr Wrayworth, the family solicitor, and he is about to read the will.'

The reason for Lady Tregowan's coldness soon became all too apparent as the solicitor began to read out Sir Ralph's last will and testament. The guests had quietly departed while family, and other members of the household, assembled in what was obviously Sir Ralph's study, judging by the shelves of books and wide mahogany desk behind which the portly solicitor settled himself. Rose took a seat at the far end of the room, well away from them all, although it afforded her an excellent view of everyone present.

There was the weeping widow seated ramrod straight in her chair, occasionally casting menacing glances in Rose's direction. Beside her sat a young woman, slightly plump with bright golden hair and startlingly blue eyes, an expression of self-satisfied complacency on her pretty face.

Rose had heard Bryce Tregowan address her as Gwenna. His sister perhaps, or his fiancée? She felt a strange pang of disappointment at the thought she might be the latter, so much so that she had to sternly reprimand herself.

And there was Bryce himself. She studiously avoided his glances in her direction, as only to look at him confused her. At the docks he had been quite brusque and unfriendly, strangely cold and unfeeling. But there had been moments during that dreadful scene in the drawing room when Rose had felt something very like sympathy emanating from him, almost as if he were on her side.

On the chair next to him lounged a young man Rose now knew to be his brother Jago. Tall and rangy, long legs sprawled out, he was not so well set as Bryce, nor his shoulders quite so broad, and with an untidy shock of greasy brown hair. He was not unhandsome, yet there was a certain sneer to the twist of the mouth set in an angular face, the nose long and bony. Rose disliked him on sight.

Behind the circle of chairs, upon which the family were seated, stood the servants, save for Tilly, of course, who was still minding Robbie. The small bequests were dealt with first, listing pensions, gifts of money and personal items which were graciously accepted before the servants all trooped out again and the solicitor came to the most important part of the will.

'In view of this unexpected and delightful good news of a male heir, the title will naturally pass automatically to Sir Ralph's grandson, together with the entire estate. This comprises Penver Court itself, the grounds and garden, home farm and several tenant farms, plus a considerable bequest to go with it.' Mr Wrayworth looked across at Rose as he said this. 'Would you tell us the child's name, dear lady?'

Stunned to find herself directly addressed, Rose cleared her throat. 'Robert, named after his father.'

'Most suitable!' The solicitor made a note on his papers, looking pleased.

Rose was struggling to take in the import of what had just been announced. It was true, then, little Robbie was now a baronet. Nor had Sir Ralph forgotten his daughter-in-law, providing Rosalind with a generous allowance, which, to her dismay, Rose realised would now go to her. She was on her feet in a second.

'I cannot accept it. Robbie has every right to the title and whatever goes with it, but not me. I don't want a penny of Sir Ralph's money.'

The solicitor cleared his throat. 'You are quite at liberty not to accept it, of course, dear lady, although it was your father-in-law's wish that you be properly provided for.'

Rose wanted to say that Sir Ralph wasn't her father-in-law, that he was no relation at all, but everyone was glaring at her, her mouth had gone dry and she could feel her knees start to shake. In that instant she recognised her own vulnerability. Rose dreaded what the family's reaction might be if she spoke up now and confessed the truth. They would quite justly accuse her of deceiving them, even of fraud. Fear was gnawing at her insides, making her feel quite sick. They might even call the police and have her locked up in jail. Oh, what had she done! She'd made a bad mistake allowing Joe to talk her into keeping quiet, and then by failing to cope with Lady Tregowan's inquisitive questions. She really was in deep trouble.

It was Bryce who gently suggested that she sit down, as the assembled company continued to stare at her with a mix of disbelief and disdain. 'This isn't the moment to decide, Rose. Take the time to consider, and we can discuss it later.'

He sounded so very much in command that there seemed nothing else for it but to obey. In any case, her knees had quite given way. Rose sat, hands pressed together in her lap, biting her lower lip to keep herself from speaking out. She could still feel his eyes upon her, noted a slight pucker between his brow, as if he was puzzled by her refusal and striving to understand. Had he, like his mother, assumed her to be a fortune-hunter? What a terrible indictment upon dear Rosalind, an innocent young woman if ever there was one.

Rose certainly had no wish to accept the bequest that had fallen into her lap, having wanted only to see Rosalind's baby put into safe hands, and perhaps find employment for herself.

Oh, but her situation was now quite impossible. She faced penury on the one hand, possibly even a term in prison, or a life of deception on the other. And how much longer could she keep up this charade? She couldn't do it, she really couldn't. She would only enmesh herself further in a web of lies. There was nothing for it but to leave. If she and Joe were to avoid arrest, they would have to make a run for it. Yet if they did, who would be a mother to little Robbie?

Sick with misery, Rose only half listened to the remainder of the will, most of it going quite over her head, although she gained the impression from the fidgeting and murmurings of the assembled company that all was not quite as it should be, or what they had hoped for.

Quite startling her out of her self-obsessed thoughts, Lady Tregowan's voice boomed out. 'This is utterly outrageous! How dare he disinherit his own sons?'

Mr Wrayworth appeared deeply embarrassed, his flabby jowls turning quite crimson. 'That is not at all the case, My Lady. Sir Ralph believed that the provision he has made for Bryce and Jago, who are in fact *your* sons and not *his*, to be perfectly adequate. He expressed a hope that a modest annual allowance would help and encourage them both to make their own way in the world, as is only right and proper.' It was naming this sum which had brought forth Lady Tregowan's fury.

'My late husband has been mean and miserly with his money ever since I married him. He has never – I repeat, *never* – properly provided for me! On the contrary, he has broken all the terms of our nuptial agreement.'

Reaching over, Bryce patted her hand. 'Calm yourself, Mama, I am more than content. As you know, I'm in the process of buying a chandler's business in Fowey. I didn't ask for his money, and can manage perfectly well without it.'

Jago was on his feet in an instant, hovering menacingly over his brother. 'That's all very well for you, but what about me? I'm the eldest, and it is my *right*! Besides, *I* don't have a pot of savings stashed away.'

'And whose fault is that, might I ask?' Bryce challenged him.

'Sir Ralph promised that we would inherit a sizeable piece of land each, and a sum of money to go with it.

He *promised*! And what do I get? A pitiful allowance! Mother is right, he's reneged on his word.'

'It is an absolute outrage!' Lady Tregowan cried. 'My husband had no right to do this. He was probably out of his mind, not himself at all. Or else influenced by certain persons writing him begging letters.' Here she cast a venomous glance in Rose's direction. 'I shall most certainly challenge the will.'

The solicitor looked seriously disturbed by such a prospect. 'I would advise caution in that respect, My Lady. It is an expensive process to go to law, with no guarantee of success. And Sir Ralph was at pains to point out, when he made this will some years ago, that he regretted the estrangement with his only son, Robert. Had he known the young man's whereabouts, he would have made every effort to heal the breach. Since learning of his son's death, only recently, he made his wishes clear that he would not consider making a new will until after he had met his daughter-in-law. I rather think he was hoping she might still provide him with a much-longed-for grandchild, as, most gratifyingly, has proved to be the case.' Mr Wrayworth smiled again at Rose, acknowledging her with a little head bow.

Rose flushed.

The row which erupted following this seemingly innocuous remark was utterly horrifying. Voices were raised in furious argument, arms waved, fists punched the air or hammered on the desk. And all the while the embattled solicitor did his utmost to placate them, with absolutely no effect. Noticing a door behind her, Rose slipped through it and quietly made her escape.

Chapter Seven

Rose's immediate thought as she ran from the study was to check on baby Robbie. It must, in any case, be almost time for his next feed. Being slightly premature, and so small, he liked his feeds to be little and often. After that she must talk to Joe. They really couldn't go on with this deception. It was far too dangerous. What the answer to their problem might be Rose hadn't the least idea, but one must be found, and quickly. She could almost feel some sympathy for Lady Tregowan over the loss of her expectations. As stepsons of the baronet, she had clearly hoped that her sons would inherit the property and estate, if not the title. Why else would she insist they take his name? But now, despite having devoted years of her life to an old man, his money, house and title were to go to an unknown baby who had appeared quite out of the blue. It must be most vexing for her.

And as things had turned out, it was proving to be an even greater problem for Rose.

'How did it go?' Joe's voice in her ear brought her whirling about.

'Oh, thank goodness, there you are! It was dreadful, quite dreadful. We can't do this to them. I can't pretend to be what I'm not. It's wrong, it's criminal. Lady Tregowan blames me for her sons being deprived of their inheritance. Were she to learn the truth, that I am not Rosalind, she would call the constabulary, I swear she would. Then you and I both would find ourselves in clink.'

'Hush now, calm yourself, Rosie. It's not so bad as all that.'

'But it *is*, I tell you. It's awful! I can't think how we're going to get out of this mess.' Rose started to weep, couldn't seem to stop babbling. She rushed on with her explanation, telling Joe about her cold reception at the funeral and the wake following, then giving him a summary of the will, so far as she could remember it.

Unfortunately, Joe didn't seem to be listening. He was patting her hands, urging her to keep her voice down, then pulling her along the corridor and out through a side door into the garden. Rose was almost surprised to find that the sun was still shining, that it was a perfectly normal spring afternoon. Yet how could it be when her life was in turmoil, her entire world falling apart? Only when they were hidden behind a large rhododendron bush did Joe take the time to answer her questions.

'As I understand it, those two are only stepsons so have no right to inherit anything. And unless we tell her, how will Lady Tregowan ever discover the truth?'

'But it would be a *lie*!' Rose groaned. 'And I can't live a lie. It's wrong, don't you see? I'm not going to argue with you about this, Joe, I've made up my mind. I shall speak to Bryce Tregowan just as soon as he comes out of that meeting.'

Panic crossed Joe's face at this suggestion. 'No, you mustn't do that. Think what you're saying, what you're risking. You said yourself they might call the police.'

'The only other alternative is to run for it. We could go tonight, when they're all asleep, then no one would see us go.'

'And what would they think tomorrow when they realised that Lady Rosalind Tregowan had gone, apparently run off with her manservant? They wouldn't necessarily assume that you'd gone willingly. They might think I'd abducted you, might demand a ransom because of that money you've inherited. Then what would happen to me if they set up a hue and cry and a search party caught up with us? They'd lock me up and throw away the key, that's what.'

Rose put her hands to her face in horror. 'Oh, my goodness, I never thought of that. Oh, Joe, the deeper we look into this mess, the more trouble we're in. What are we going to do? There is no solution, none that I can see.'

'Aye, there is – you stick with our story,' he urged, his tone harsh. 'You carry on being Sir Ralph's daughter-in-law, for now, until we can work something out. And look on the bright side – at least you'll be with little Robbie.'

Rose's expression was bleak as she nodded. But deep in her heart she was certain that there must be a better way out of this mess, if only she could think what it might be.

Having agreed with Joe that they'd speak again about this problem, once they'd had time to think things over more carefully, Rose made her way to the kitchen to collect Robbie. She hadn't gone more than a few yards along the garden path, however, when she was confronted by Lady Tregowan herself, a very angry Lady Tregowan, her younger son by her side.

'I suppose you think you've won.'

'I-I don't know what you mean.' The very sight of this woman turned Rose into a gibbering wreck. Bryce was looking as disinterested as ever, and every bit as handsome. 'None of this – the will and all that – has anything to do with me,' Rose protested.

'It has everything to do with you. Had you not written your begging letters to Sir Ralph, he would have surrendered to common sense and left a proper inheritance to my boys, who have both been better sons to him than his own.'

'I didn't write any begging letters. When I-I wrote informing him of his son's death, Sir Ralph offered me a home without being asked.' It seemed entirely wrong to be telling Rosalind's story as if it were her own. Rose consoled herself with the thought that she was defending her friend, as well as protecting her precious offspring.

Lady Tregowan took a step closer, nostrils flaring as she met Rose almost eye to eye. Her skin was perfect, Rose couldn't help but notice, but then she was still a beautiful woman for all she must be well into her forties.

'Let me make it very clear that the "family" will never leave Penver Court. You will not rob us of our home, nor *ever* gain control of this estate, not in my lifetime.'

Bryce gave a low growl deep in his throat. 'Mama, do not say such things. There is really no need for you to be quite so overprotective. We can manage perfectly well without—'

'Shut up!' Dismissing her son with an irritable flap of her hand, she relentlessly continued. 'The old baronet may be dead, but whether you are the mother of the next, or he's just some bastard you've foisted on us, has yet to be proved. I very much doubt a dying man capable of getting himself a son.'

Rose gasped, feeling a great surge of anger at this slight upon little Robbie. 'How dare you suggest such a thing! He most certainly *is* the baronet, and not . . . what you say he is.' She couldn't bring herself to use that dreadful word. Sadly, Rose now realised there was serious danger of Rosalind's child being written off as the impostor, rather than herself. Which was unthinkable. And all because of Joe's foolishness.

'I think we should be a little more circumspect in our language, Mama,' Bryce gently scolded her. 'Although I accept that everything must be gone into most thoroughly, I'm sure we can safely leave all of that to old Wrayworth. In any case, you might see a family resemblance. The child may have Robert's long nose,' he quipped, as if attempting to lighten the growing tension between the two women.

'I very much doubt it.' Crimson lips twisted with contempt. 'I am not so gullible as stupid Robert. No doubt he accepted the boy out of desperation, thinking it would put him back in his father's favour.'

Rose gasped. 'He did not! He didn't even know that sh— that a baby was on the way before he tragically died.'

'How very fortunate. Thereby sparing you any difficult explanations.' Lady Tregowan laughed, a bitter sound that held no humour in it.

'Robert *is* his father, I swear it!' But I am not his mother, Rose silently added, biting down hard on her lower lip to prevent the words from escaping. She was all too aware of Bryce Tregowan's narrowed gaze upon her, of doubt in those burning charcoal eyes, and something else she couldn't quite put a name to.

'You'll rue the day you came here seeking an easy fortune, girl. Mark my words. I will do all in my power to foil your little scheme.' And with that parting shot, Lady Tregowan walked away, head held high.

I don't have a little scheme, Rose longed to say. Oh, but Joe did, and this woman's attitude towards her had only made it more difficult to confess the truth. 'I really will not be interrogated in this way,' she said instead, in what she hoped was a suitably haughty manner, as she desperately tried to guess how Rosalind herself would have reacted to such an accusation.

Watching Lydia stalk proudly up wide stone steps, the door opened for her by a waiting footman, Bryce said, 'I won't attempt to apologise again for my mother's attitude because she does have a point, however badly expressed. I rather think we do have the right to ask questions. I'd like to hear more of this Canadian upbringing of yours. Where were you born, for instance? Town or country?'

The tone was mild but the expression in his charcoal gaze was keen.

Rose wasn't entirely sure where Canada was. Presumably somewhere near America, and cold? That was the sum total of her knowledge. But then schooling had not featured greatly in her life on Fishponds Road, and she'd missed much of what little was available by having to mind her brothers and sisters while her mother worked. She'd learnt the three R's, how to sew and darn a sock, but not much more. And she knew even less about Rosalind's childhood. Yet to make something up would only enmesh her in further lies. 'I was born in a city, and come from a large family,' Rose said, deciding to stick close to the truth. 'But I really don't see my upbringing is any business of yours.'

'Ah, now there I must disagree, and take my mother's side. It is asking a great deal of us for you to simply turn up, out of the blue, and not expect us to be curious about you. You say you and Robert married only recently. How recent was that exactly? What kind of a wedding was it? And why did he not inform his father?'

Rose had no answers to give. She had no idea whether Robert had invited his father to his wedding, or when it had taken place. Rosalind had talked a little about her marriage but Rose had paid no attention to the details, not realising she would ever find herself in this impossible situation. 'H-he wasn't speaking to Sir Ralph at the time, and it was a very simple wedding, in New York.' Oh no, now she'd committed herself to yet more detail.

'New York? So when did you leave Canada? And where did you say you lived as a child?'

Yet again Rose fell silent as she desperately tried to recall the map their teacher used to show them, the parts of the British Empire all shown in red. Sadly, she couldn't bring Canada to mind, nor the name of a single town in all of that vast country. And she was having great difficulty understanding Bryce Tregowan's attitude towards her, surprisingly supportive while his mother was attacking her, now bombarding her with questions.

'Was it Toronto?'

Rose grabbed at the suggestion with relief. 'Yes, Toronto. My parents moved to New York a few years ago where I met Robert. We fell in love and married. What is the mystery about that?'

'Perhaps you have a marriage certificate, to prove what you say?'

'Of course!' Rose briskly retorted, hoping against hope there was such a document among Rosalind's possessions, although the date of it might present problems. 'Once I have unpacked, assuming I am ever shown to a room and allowed the time to settle in, that is, I shall be delighted to find it for you.' She was relieved to see that Bryce looked instantly discomfited by this criticism.

'How very remiss of us. I will take you to your room myself.'

'Please don't bother; I have to collect the baby from Tilly. Your maid, at least, is helpful and most welcoming, and has calmly and efficiently taken Robbie to her heart. The Tregowan family might do well to learn some better manners from their own servants.'

This parting shot was a little below the belt, but Rose had been seriously unnerved by this barrage of questions. With a deep sense of relief she turned on her heel and headed for the kitchen, although not without a fast-beating heart and some trepidation in her troubled soul.

Less than half an hour later Rose found herself settling into the nursery wing on the east side of the house. The bedroom allotted to her was quite simple, with a narrow bed and shabby green curtains that had seen better days, probably once used by the family's nanny. But Robbie would be close by in the room next door, and there was also a small parlour for her private use, perhaps once occupied by the governess.

'It just needs a bit of a clean through before you use it, but then this isn't the finest suite of rooms in the house,' Tilly apologised. 'It does benefit from being some distance from the west wing where the rest of the family reside, so you'll have some privacy.'

Rose did not doubt for one moment that Lady Tregowan had deliberately chosen to accommodate her in the worst possible rooms she could find, a decision only justified by them being the nursery suite. 'This will do fine, Tilly. I am more than content.' By comparison with the filthy, rat-infested, overcrowded hovel she'd shared with her entire family on Fishponds Road, this stark bedroom felt like a palace.

'You should see our quarters,' Tilly went on, as she hooked back the curtains in an attempt to let more light into the room.

'Really, why, what's wrong with them?'

Tilly actually blushed. 'Aw, nothing, milady. I shouldn't have spoken out of turn. I'll leave you to settle in. Should you need anything, you've only to call.' She indicated the bell pull that hung beside the small Victorian black fire grate, then, with a warm smile and bobbing a hasty curtsey, quickly withdrew.

'Now, what was that all about?' Rose murmured to herself, making a mental note to visit Tilly's room at the first opportunity. Right now, she had enough problems of her own to deal with. And jiggling the baby in her arms, she looked about her in bewilderment.

Rose walked to the window, set high in the roof, to gaze down upon the wide lawns and rose gardens far below, the twin rows of beech trees that lined the long drive down which she'd recently travelled with hope and optimism in her heart. The sight made her feel almost like a prisoner, and it crossed Rose's troubled mind that she could make no escape from this window.

She'd also noticed, as Tilly had brought her up the stairs and along a narrow landing, that these led directly from the back hall right by the kitchen, laundry and utility areas of the house, where surely servants would be busy at most hours of the day, and even through the night.

'There is an exit from the nursery wing that leads to the main staircase for you to reach the dining room, but the back way is the shortest route, milady, if you're ever carrying heavy bags,' Tilly had explained.

Which made perfect sense, as a nanny or nursemaid would use the back stairs for the most part, wouldn't they? But Rose's idea of slipping away with Joe under cover of darkness now appeared to be fraught with difficulties.

Most of her belongings had already been unpacked by Gladys, one of the maids, and Rose stared in wonder at the row of gowns, skirts, jackets and blouses, in every hue and for every occasion, that now hung in the armoire. Fortunate as it may be that she and Rosalind were of a size, and her clothes would no doubt fit her, it seemed entirely improper that she, humble Rosie Belsfield, should wear them. This wasn't at all what Rosalind had intended when she'd suggested Rose dress in her clothes, which was for identification purposes only. She'd offered her a chance of employment, not to take over her identity. How could it have come to this?

Joe, of course, was the answer to that question. He was the one who had landed them both in this mess.

And how they would ever get out of it was quite beyond Rose's imaginings, but she most certainly meant to try. Her thoughts were interrupted by a knock on the door.

'Come in, it's not locked,' she called, setting the sleeping baby down in his crib. What a sweetie he was. She loved him dearly already. All that truly mattered was that she do what was best for Robbie.

'I beg your pardon for intruding, but I thought I should properly introduce myself.'

Rose smiled, reaching out a hand to offer her guest a seat. 'It's Gwenna, isn't it? Do come in.' Rose thought the girl lovely, if with a decided pout to her full lips. 'How kind of you to call. Are you content to remain here in the bedroom while we talk? The room that is to be my personal parlour hasn't been prepared yet, or so Tilly informs me.'

'This won't take long,' Gwenna said, flouncing out her skirts as she made herself comfortable on the only chair, leaving Rose to sit on the dressing stool. 'I thought it best to call and make my situation clear from the start.'

'Oh?' Rose frowned, not quite sure what was meant by this.

'I must say you are exceedingly fortunate to have been left so much money in the will. Poor Jago is devastated at having been so callously ignored.'

'I'm sorry about that, obviously, but it was not of my making. I never even met Sir Ralph . . . er . . . my father-in-law.' What a strange way to introduce oneself by going instantly on the attack.

'Jago is so sweet,' Gwenna continued, as if Rose had not interrupted. 'But he is a proud man and does not care to be passed over. Penver Court means everything to him.'

'I'm sure it does. I can only sympathise,' Rose agreed, wondering where this might be leading, and deciding to say as little as possible.

The other girl was sitting up very straight in the chair, hands neatly clasped on her lap. 'You may not know this, but Jago and I are practically engaged. We would have been already had not Sir Ralph died and the family plunged into mourning. Jago is a most handsome man, as I'm sure you'll admit.'

'Indeed,' Rose said, thinking entirely the opposite, but then they did say that beauty lay in the eyes of the beholder.

'He has the reputation of being something of a ladies' man, but it's not true,' she insisted, rather vehemently. 'Naturally, because of his good looks he is very attractive to women, and finds such attention flattering.'

'I am sure he will make a most devoted fiancé.'

The baby-blue eyes sparked with annoyance. 'I mean that I would not take it kindly were he encouraged to stray by others with more to offer than myself.'

Rose looked at her blankly for a moment. 'I'm not sure I quite follow . . .'

Gwenna bounced up most inelegantly from her seat to look down upon Rose with derision on her pretty face. 'I think you do. You are reasonably pretty, although no beauty, admittedly. However, with money and position, far more than I possess despite being well provided for by my late parents, Jago might well find you attractive.'

'Goodness, I think you are worrying unduly. Let me assure you, Gwenna, that encouraging Jago is the last thing on my mind, even were he not affianced to your good self.'

'Almost affianced.'

'As you say.' Rose stood and held out a hand to her, only just managing not to laugh out loud. The girl was making the fellow out to be easily led astray by wicked women, of which she apparently was one. 'I fully respect your situation, and would not for the world seek to intrude upon such a close relationship.'

'You will keep well away from him?'

'I will, of course.' Most thankfully, Rose thought, wondering if the poor lovestruck creature realised what a fool she was making of herself. Had she, for instance, laid down similar rules to her would-be fiancé? 'I do hope,' Rose continued, 'that you and I will become firm friends.'

There was the very slightest pause before Gwenna answered. 'That rather depends upon how you behave.'

Now what had brought that on, I wonder? Rose thought, after her visitor had swept away in a rustle of taffeta. 'The girl must be utterly besotted.' As if she cared a hoot about Jago Tregowan. Didn't she have enough on her plate?

Rose went to check on Robbie, fast asleep and entirely oblivious of his destiny or the precarious situation they were now in. He gave a little sigh, a milky bubble forming between his pouting lips, and Rose smiled.

'I'll do everything I can to keep you safe, my lovely. I promise.'

Didn't she owe it to him, and to his dear mother, to see that he was properly protected? No matter what problems might arise from finding the necessary documentary proof of Rosalind's marriage, she really couldn't allow this darling child to be branded illegitimate simply to save her own skin.

Chapter Eight

After only three days at Penver Court, Rose had quite made up her mind to leave. There'd been numerous occasions when she'd been tempted to speak up, determined to reveal all, but either her mouth would run dry, someone would interrupt, or an incident would occur which left her more deeply entrenched than ever. She'd endured yet more interrogations from Lady Tregowan, usually over dinner or lunch, which quite dampened Rose's normally healthy appetite, and she felt she could take no more.

The dowager's probing always left her feeling confused. Rose had desperately sought suitable answers to the simplest of questions, such as the names of Rosalind's parents; when they'd moved out to Canada; and if she'd been given dancing lessons as a girl. She'd been obliged to fabricate yet more stories to fit what few facts she knew, even to describing an elegant outfit she apparently wore for her supposedly simple wedding in New York. All of which only added to the web of lies into which Rose was enmeshing herself. How would she ever remember them all? The possibility of getting something wrong filled her with terror. This really had to stop.

And learning how to behave in such elevated company was proving to be an almost impossible challenge. The smallest action was fraught with danger, Lady Tregowan watching her every move, eagle-eyed. Even as she helped herself to marmalade, on the second morning at breakfast, Rose heard the dowager click her tongue in annoyance as she carelessly dipped her knife into the pot.

'Surely you were taught to use a spoon for that task? See, here it is, hanging from the stand. Goodness, I know you come from America where everything is different, but did your mother teach you no table manners?'

Horrified by her own blunder, due largely to ignorance of the niceties of upper-class etiquette, in her clumsy efforts to put things right Rose dropped the knife, which clattered on to the table leaving smears of marmalade all over the pristine white cloth. She heard a soft chuckle, quickly stifled. Was Bryce laughing at her? Did he take pleasure out of seeing her embarrass herself? Oh, this was quite intolerable. Marmalade jars at Fishponds Road didn't come with their own stand, let alone a silver spoon to hang upon it, assuming they were ever fortunate to have any, that is.

'Weren't you properly finished? Which school did you attend?' Lydia Tregowan was asking, a frown of disapproval marring her cold features.

'I-I went to an academy for young ladies,' Rose fabricated, remembering what Tilly had told her about Lady Tregowan herself. 'Although we did like to break rules,' she added, in the hope this would let her off the hook.

'There will be no rules of etiquette broken in this house,' she was sternly informed.

What mistakes would she make next? There was so much Rose didn't know about society living, she'd be sure to make a mess of everything. She felt deeply embarrassed whenever a servant hurried over to lift the cover of a dish for her, unfold her napkin on to her lap, or hand her the toast rack, as one was doing now.

'I can manage, thank you,' she gabbled, snatching up the rack just before he reached it. Only to earn herself another chilling rebuke from Lady Tregowan.

'Thomas is only doing his job. And he is certainly paid enough for it.'

One glance at the footman's face told Rose the exact opposite was the case. For all the young man's efforts to remain implacable, the resentment in his hooded eyes was plain to see. The sight of that bitter expression for some reason reminded Rose of Tilly's comment about her room, and her own offer to help protect Tilly's family from eviction. She really must find out more about that matter, but now wasn't perhaps the moment to ask. 'He needn't trouble on my account. In any case, I'm not hungry this morning, and I really should see to Robbie.'

But as she made to get to her feet, Lydia irritably waved her to be seated again. 'Breakfast isn't over yet. You will leave when I say you may.' Just as if she were a small child at school. Sighing rather dramatically, the dowager continued, 'I dare say we should appoint a proper nanny for that child, if he is not to grow up completely uncivilised. Where is he now, by the way?'

'With Tilly. She's very good with him. Perhaps she could be his nursemaid,' Rose tentatively suggested.

Dark eyebrows raised in shocked disapproval. 'Tilly is a kitchen maid. I very much doubt she possesses the necessary skills to deal properly with children.'

'Oh, but she does,' Rose protested. 'She comes from a large family with lots of brothers and sisters, so is most familiar with caring for babies. And she already loves Robbie dearly.'

'Being one of a ragbag of siblings does not qualify a person for the heavy responsibility of caring for a Tregowan child, not in my view. But I concede that Tilly may well have to do for the moment. If you are to stay, which very much depends upon your providing proof of the brat's parentage, we will then make more suitable arrangements for his care. I look forward to seeing whatever documents you can provide.'

The brat indeed! Flushed with anger that she could so describe little Robbie, Rose began searching through Rosalind's baggage. Among her possessions there was a trunk full of books, a sewing basket and embroidery ring, personal knick-knacks, and a writing slope which fitted easily upon a lady's lap while she attended to her correspondence.

With considerable misgivings, and fast-beating heart,

Rose began to search through the papers. They contained bundles of what must be love letters tied up with pink ribbon. She carefully set these to one side, not wishing to intrude, considering them private to Rosalind.

And then she found the document Rosalind had signed, entrusting guardianship of her son to Rose, her new friend. It all seemed perfectly reasonable and above board. There was her own signature, and that of dear Rosalind, and the steward's as witness.

No one must discover this if her deceit was not to be revealed, and she and Joe were to avoid prison, at least until she'd found some way to explain their story. Finding a tin box in the writing slope, she tipped out the ink pot and pen, and in their place tucked the document. Glancing about, Rose frantically searched for a place to hide it. She tried the top of the wardrobe, but that was too obvious as the maids would certainly find it when they dusted. Perhaps under the mattress? But what if they turned it over? It was while she was on her hands and knees beside the bed that she found the very place. Right underneath, far from general view, Rose noticed a slight looseness in a floorboard. With a little effort and the help of a spoon, she managed to prise it open far enough to slip the tin box inside.

'There, now it will be perfectly safe. No one will think to search under the bed.'

But she still needed Rosalind's marriage certificate. Beneath a wad of papers and letters she finally found what she was looking for: a leather folder in which was Robert's will, and the marriage certificate. Rose sat down to read them both very carefully.

It was a perfectly straightforward will in which Robert left everything to his darling wife. The licence proved that a marriage had indeed taken place between Rosalind Besnard and Robert Tregowan in June 1896. A moment's thought told Rose she herself would have been eleven years old at the time. Oh dear, this wouldn't do at all. Quickly folding the document away, she hid that too in the tin box under the floorboard. In what other way, then, could she prove Rosalind's marriage, and that her son was legitimate? Rose picked up the bundle of love letters, and, choosing one at random, opened it with some trepidation as she felt this to be a violation of Rosalind's privacy.

Quickly scanning the contents she saw that nothing here offered the proof she needed as he always addressed Rosalind as *My darling girl*. She tried the next, and the one after that. She was in tears by the time she opened the last. His love for Rosalind shone out from every page. How tragic that Robert should die so young, and just when he was to become a father.

And then she found what she was looking for.

'*My darling girl*,' he began, as usual, but then corrected himself. '*Or more accurately, my beloved wife. Even now I can hardly believe my good fortune that you agreed to make me the happiest man alive. Those wonderful years we have had together, in which I felt privileged to be your loving husband, I shall treasure in whatever life comes next. I can hardly bear the thought of being parted from you but please do not grieve too much when I am gone. If you should feel sad, remember the joy our marriage brought us, and rejoice.*

Many are not so fortunate. I do not leave you willingly but with love in my heart for ever. I am yours into eternity, my darling Rosalind, my beloved and devoted wife.'

Lady Tregowan did not shed a single tear as she read this heart-rending letter. She humphed and puffed, before walking over to the bell pull and instructing the footman who answered to call the family solicitor at once.

'We need Wrayworth's opinion on this,' she informed Rose, who simply nodded, again stifling an urge to bob a curtsey, so much in awe was she of this formidable, beautiful woman.

This morning, Lydia's gown was a deep azure blue, which perfectly accentuated her dark hair and pale blue-grey eyes. The hourglass figure was proudly defined by a black leather belt, no doubt worn over a tightly laced corset, resulting in the smallest waist imaginable, a fashionably pouched bosom above. Rose wondered how she managed to breathe, let alone eat.

The solicitor arrived within the hour, of course, no doubt having driven at great speed in his motor from the nearby village of Penver, as always when summoned by the Tregowan family. Rose hid a smile as Lydia offered him a mere two fingers rather than her hand, as if that was all he deserved by way of a salutation, him being so far below her in status.

Mr Wrayworth read the letter and instantly declared himself completely satisfied with the validity of the marriage.

'Satisfied? How can that be?' Lady Tregowan demanded, pale eyes sparkling with anger. 'We have no marriage certificate.'

'Nevertheless, it is perfectly clear that the couple were indeed married. A man does not tell lies about his marital status on his death bed. Most tragic!' He returned the letter to Rose with whispered words of condolence.

'But where is proof of that child's birth?' Lydia insisted, obviously feeling herself ignored.

Rose nervously cleared her throat. This was the one question she'd most dreaded. 'I don't have any, I'm afraid, since he was born prematurely on board ship.' Rose was perfectly certain that the guilt she felt over what she *wasn't* telling them about that incident must be written plain on her face.

Once again Mr Wrayworth proved to be her salvation. 'I'm sure such a document can easily be obtained, once we have registered the young man's birth. Will you allow me to carry out that small task for you?' he asked, gently patting Rose's hand.

Lady Tregowan swiftly intervened, her tone crisp. 'I believe we should allow a little time to pass first, to be absolutely certain the child is who this girl claims him to be.'

The solicitor looked quite shocked. 'I'm sure I have no doubts at all on that score, My Lady. Why, I remember Master Robert well, and the child undoubtedly has the look of his father. We must honour his memory by doing our best for his son.' He then went on to suggest that young Robbie's name should be put down on the waiting list of the best local preparatory school without delay.

'Absolute poppycock,' Lydia demurred.

Wrayworth looked concerned. 'I would highly recommend it, dear lady. The best places are soon taken up.'

'Very well,' she grudgingly accepted, lips tight with fury at being bested. 'But there is absolutely no reason why it need be local,' she snapped. 'He can board, and start at five. The sooner, the better.'

'That is a possibility, naturally, although perhaps seven or eight would be a more suitable age. Then he must go on to Marlborough, which his father attended,' Wrayworth asserted. 'The boy will need tutoring in foreign languages, mathematics, history, and, of course, Latin.'

Rose could only listen, bemused, as these long-term plans were made for the child's future. 'Robbie is barely more than a month old,' she dared to remind them, as the pair became embroiled in a barbed dispute over what pocket money was right for a young boy.

'One cannot begin too soon with children,' Lady Tregowan said. 'Particularly where manners and proper behaviour are concerned. We cannot have the brat screaming the place down the whole time.'

'My Lady!' Wrayworth gently scolded, clearly shocked by her language, and Rose was astonished to see Lydia actually blush.

It was, however, agreed that a nanny would be appointed as soon as a suitable candidate could be found. In the meantime, Tilly might continue to act as nursemaid. As Lady Tregowan moved on to discussing estate matters, Rose was summarily dismissed. She escaped with a sigh of relief, thinking with no small degree of triumph that she had crossed the biggest hurdle, thanks to Mr Wrayworth. Little Robbie would surely be safe now.

* * *

'The question is, Tilly, are you willing to take on the task?' Rose asked, when she'd informed the young woman of Lady Tregowan's decision. She'd gone straight to the housemaid, who was working in the laundry, where she stood at a huge stone sink, elbows deep in hot soapsuds, washing Robbie's nappies. The little boy himself was fast asleep nearby in the bassinet. 'He's a very good baby but once he starts teething, and toddling, he might prove to be more of a handful. You would largely be responsible for his care, as I may not always be . . . available . . . due to . . . other responsibilities and duties.'

Feeling that she'd done all she could for Robbie, Rose had swiftly come to the conclusion that she must find Joe and insist they leave, no matter what the difficulties, before things got any worse. They must go before any more lies were told, or she made an unforgivable blunder. Rose was determined not to tolerate any arguments or any further delays this time.

Tilly's brown eyes were glowing. 'Ooh, milady, I wouldn't mind that at all. I'd love taking care of him, I would really. I'd be proper made up.'

'It might only be until a proper nanny is appointed,' Rose warned.

Perhaps she could leave a note explaining everything, she thought, chewing on her lip as she worried over the possible repercussions of such an action. On second thoughts, that might result in the family setting the police on their trail. Safer to keep up the charade. Then again, she could leave a note saying she'd willingly run off with Joe, which should protect him from any charges of abduction. Let them think what they liked about the state of her morals, she simply couldn't go on living a lie. Oh, what a dreadful muddle!

'Aye, but I could happen carry on, as his nursemaid, after that. Nanny would need help. She couldn't possibly manage on her own.'

'That might well be possible,' Rose agreed. Having two women to mind one baby seemed somewhat excessive, but then she hadn't the first idea how things were done in the households of the aristocracy. Picking the baby up, Rose hugged him to her breast. His soft skin smelt of talcum powder, soap and baby milk, and her heart seemed to turn over as his blue eyes lit up at the sight of her.

She could not deny that she'd find it utterly heartbreaking to leave him, but it was foolish to imagine the child wouldn't be better cared for here in this lovely Queen Anne house, with a proper nanny and an education which would make him into the fine gentleman he was born to be. Rose certainly couldn't risk taking him on the road with her. Who knew where or when she might find another job? How could she care for a baby as well as coping with her own survival?

Besides, this was Robbie's home. He belonged here. She was the interloper, an impostor, the one practising a deceit. And it must stop.

She kissed his cheek. 'Hello, my precious boy, and how are you?' An image of his mother saying very much the same thing moments before she died brought a rush of tears to her eyes. A baby needed a mother, not simply a nanny and a nursemaid, however well qualified or caring. Oh, but she daren't risk taking on the role. She'd been through all of that already. It wouldn't be right. It would be a lie. In a panic and blur of emotion, Rose quickly thrust the baby back into the bassinet where he gurgled happily and kicked his feet.

Blinded by tears she turned to go. 'Sorry, but I can't stay. I have to find Joe. Do you know where he might be?'

Tilly was frowning, puzzled by the little emotional scene she'd witnessed and wondering what the Tregowans had done to upset her new mistress. 'He'll be in the stable at this time of a morning, I should think. Shall I have him fetched?'

'No need, I shall go and find him myself. Thank you, Tilly.' Rose almost ran from the room, tears of despair now rolling down her cheeks. Oh, how could she possibly bear to part with him?

Rose searched for Joe in the stables, then out in the paddock where he sometimes exercised the horses. A young stable lad approached, bobbing his head by way of respect. 'If you're looking for Joe, milady, he's taken Lady Tregowan and Miss Gwenna into town shopping. Can I help?'

Rose was disappointed but smiled at the boy. 'No, thank you. It can wait.' It could, but not for long, she thought.

She instantly made up her mind to enjoy what would probably be her last day with Robbie. She would take him for a picnic on the beach. Of course, he was far too young to paddle or play with sand pies, but it would be good to have him to herself for one last time. Rose could remember visiting a beach only once in her life. She'd been quite small, still an only child, her mother pregnant with Micky. Her father had taken the three of them to Weston-super-Mare for a day out as a treat one Easter time. He'd bought her a little tin bucket and spade and shown her how to make sand pies. They'd built a sandcastle together and stuck little paper flags on the top. Then her mother had set out a raised pork pie and little biscuits on a blue check cloth, which had no doubt taken her days to save up for, and hours to prepare. The memory was a golden bubble in her head, her parents' beloved faces at the centre of it.

After that the babies had come thick and fast, not all of them surviving, and money had become tighter than ever. Then her father had gone away to war and she'd never seen him again.

But she wouldn't think sad thoughts, not today. She would collect Robbie from Tilly, prepare a bottle for him and a few sandwiches for herself perhaps, then take the day off to explore the headland and the beach. It would give her some precious time to think, to be sure that this important decision she'd made to leave was the right one. Not that she had any doubts on the matter. What her father and mother would think of all these lies she'd told she really didn't care to imagine.

As soon as she entered the kitchen Rose was brought up short by the sight of Tilly, who was standing in the middle of the floor, almost wringing her hands she looked so upset. Rose's heart skipped a beat as she glanced quickly about the room. 'What's wrong? Where's Robbie?'

'I tried to stop him. I said the baby needed his nap.' Tilly was almost weeping in her distress.

'Stop who?' Rose ran to the other girl and gave her a little shake. 'Tilly, what has happened to Robbie?'

The door suddenly flew open and a whole tribe of kitchen maids came in, all chattering and laughing. Each was heavily loaded, carrying a tray of dirty breakfast dishes, buckets and mops, coal scuttle, or dustpan and brush. They barely glanced at the two distraught women, too relieved to deposit the dirty dishes in the line of stone sinks in the pantry, or put away their cleaning materials and enjoy a bite of breakfast themselves where they could keep on with their merry gossiping.

Tilly dropped her voice to an urgent whisper. 'Master Jago has taken him. Like I say, I tried to stop him, but he said a breath of fresh air would most likely do the child good. What could I do? He's the master here, or acts as such.'

'Oh, my goodness. Which way did he go?'

'He went up through the copse. I reckon he might be going over the headland,' Tilly sobbed. Rose was running out of the door long before she'd finished giving directions.

She ran with the wind on her heels, fear spurring her on, oblivious to the stitch in her side, to the branches that snatched at her skirts as she raced through a copse of sycamore and silver birch, tripping over stones and roots in her anxiety to climb the steep hill as quickly as possible. She hadn't the first idea where she was going, simply hoping this was the right way. Fortunately, when she burst out from the far side of the woods, Rose found herself on a green sward of headland that sloped down to an azure sea. Her legs felt like jelly and her heart a lead weight in her breast. She drew painful gulps of air into her lungs as the morning sun blazed in a bright-blue sky, half blinding her with its glory.

And then she saw him.

Jago was standing only a few feet away from the edge

of the cliff, with his back to her, a bundle in his arms which must surely be Robbie. Rose wanted to run and snatch the baby from him, yet instinctively knew that such a hysterical reaction would only make matters worse. Reminding herself that she was supposed to be the young Lady Tregowan, and therefore had no reason to be intimidated by this man, she took a steadying breath and walked gracefully towards him.

'How very kind of you to take Robbie for a walk,' she said, managing a small smile. 'Although I really must procure him a perambulator. I don't suppose you have one tucked away in one of the many attics at Penver Court, have you?' She was gabbling, as pleasantly as possible, fists clenched into the sides of her skirt in an effort to force herself to remain calm.

Jago turned to her with a sardonic smile. 'I thought it was time I became acquainted with my rival, the child who has robbed me of a fortune.'

Rose heard a small gasp from behind, and realised that Tilly must have followed her, and was now fearfully hanging back, panting from her exertion of climbing the hill so quickly. Rose too was still struggling to catch her breath, although the pain in her chest had a more emotional rather than a physical cause. Ignoring the young maid, she kept her smile firmly in place as she held out her hands for the baby. 'You must take any complaints on that score to Sir Ralph's solicitor. This child is not to blame. He may be a baronet but he's only a baby. May I have him, please?'

For a moment Jago did not move, then he took a step closer to the edge, the tumble of rocky granite that fell away into the sea mere inches from his feet causing Rose to come over all sick and giddy as she thought of what might happen if his foot slipped. At that moment Robbie woke with a start, and began to whimper.

'Babies are so vulnerable, are they not?' Jago mildly remarked, in that deceptively soft voice of his. 'Anything could happen to this little chap. He could become sick, fall asleep in his cot and be smothered by his pillow, choke on his food, anything.' He smiled with blithe indifference at Rose, who was listening with growing dismay to these words. What was he suggesting? Were these veiled threats?

She was aware of Robbie's cries rising in pitch, of Tilly standing close by with her hands over her mouth. Sending the maid a warning look to stay back, Rose edged a step or two closer.

'Don't come any nearer,' Jago warned. His eyes, she noticed, were aglow with a fanatic's greed. Then he lifted the baby high in his arms, as if making an offering to some ancient god. Rose let out a little cry of fear, but Jago only laughed.

'Look at him. He's no bigger than a cat or a rabbit, a rat even, and barely more valuable. What does this scrap want with a fortune? My need is so much greater than his. Babies are easy to come by and even easier to dispose of.'

'Give him to me now, please. *Now*, I say!' Rose's voice was hushed, yet had never sounded more firm, more angry.

Again he gave that hollow laugh. 'And what if I should refuse? What if my hands were to accidentally slip and I dropped him? What then?' He glanced down at the swirling waves that licked and crashed against the dark rocks far below.

Red-hot fury roared through her veins, even as she gave a little sob of terror. 'Don't you dare play malicious games with *my* child.'

'Or what? What could you do, exactly? You're powerless against me.' The arrogance in his face was terrible to behold, the curl to his upper lip sharpening his nose to a knife-edge, and the cruel glint in those strangely pale blue-grey eyes chillingly detached. He made a sudden lunge, which almost stopped Rose's heart, before tossing the now screaming baby carelessly into her arms.

Long after he'd gone, Rose remained where she was in complete shock, holding the crying baby tight in her arms. Tilly was hugging both Rose and Robbie, having come to her at once with a sob of relief. The pair stood like this for some long moments, both quietly weeping, united in their concern for the child.

At length, Tilly spoke, a quiet fury in her voice. 'He's a bastard of the first quarter, that man, and I don't care if that is a rude word, and not my place to say it.'

Rose said, 'You won't hear any argument from me on that score,' and the two girls, very similar in age, and in status too, truth to tell, smiled tentatively at each other over the baby's head.

Tilly had risked her job with such a reckless remark, yet formed an unbreakable friendship instead. 'Come on, let's get this little chap his bottle and somewhere warm and safe to settle him for his afternoon nap.'

Rose had quite lost her appetite for a day on the beach and returned to spend it quietly in the suite of rooms in the east-wing tower which now felt like a haven of peace, and not a prison at all. It was here, as she sat watching Robbie contentedly sleep, safely swaddled in his bassinet, that she recalled her own words to Jago. 'Don't you dare play malicious games with *my* child.' In that terrifying moment she had felt that Robbie was indeed hers. Some primal instinct had committed Rose to him, heart and soul. And had the worst happened and Jago carried out that terrible threat and dropped him over the cliff, not even his own mother would have grieved for him more than she.

The incident had changed her view entirely by revealing the depth of her own true feelings. In some strange way Rose knew that *she* was Robbie's mother now, the only mother this child would ever know. She could never abandon him. Never! Nor could she leave, not without putting his precious life in danger, as would clearly be the case with the likes of Jago Tregowan around.

Rose couldn't begin to contemplate the problems that would ensue from this new decision, but then her heart was always wiser than her head. Were she to speak out and tell the truth about her identity, Lady Tregowan would not only send her packing or have her arrested for fraud, but little Robbie's life would be put at serious risk. And hadn't she promised his real mother that she'd protect and guard him with her life? More fervently than ever, she meant to do exactly that. From now on Rose would be little Robbie's guardian in very truth, just as Rosalind had begged her to be, if not quite in the way she had expected.

Chapter Nine

Rose woke the following morning after a troubled night with very little sleep, which was hardly surprising following the dreadful fright she'd experienced on the cliff top. Her mind, however, was quite made up to put her new plan into action. With or without Lady Tregowan's permission, she had decided to invite Tilly to move into the nursery wing. There was a spare bedroom, and having her close by would not only be far more sensible if the girl was to act as his nursemaid, at least until a suitable nanny was hired, but also an added protection for Robbie.

Finding that Tilly had already taken Robbie for his morning feed, without giving it a second thought Rose clattered down the backstairs and walked straight into the kitchen. The entire staff froze in horror at the sight of her. Mrs Pascoe was the first to come to her senses.

'Lady Tregowan, was you wanting something?'

The title always startled her. 'Oh . . . oh, yes please. I was looking for Tilly.'

'She ain't here just now, milady. I do believe she's taken his lordship out for an airing after his feed. Shall I tell her as what you'd like a word, when she's a minute?'

Rose could see that she'd made a gaffe. The Dowager Lady Tregowan would never come into the kitchen unannounced, which could easily be interpreted as checking up on the staff. And it was a mistake dear Rosalind would never have made either. What a fool she was. 'I do beg your pardon for intruding,' Rose said, in the carefully enunciated tones she had rapidly been obliged to acquire since she'd arrived at Penver Court. 'I'll catch her later,' and she fled, embarrassingly aware of the collected sigh of relief at her hasty departure.

Catching sight of Gladys who chanced to appear in the back hall at precisely that moment, and remembering Tilly's comment about her room, an idea came to her. Having made this mistake, Rose felt the need to justify it.

'Ah, Gladys, would you mind showing me to Tilly's room.'

The girl looked as if she couldn't quite believe what she was hearing. 'Begging your pardon, milady, did you say Tilly's room?'

'Yes, please. I mean to surprise her, and you can help. Please lead on, if you wouldn't mind.'

Whether she minded or not, Gladys was fully aware she was in no position to refuse, even if it did get her into even more trouble with Cook for being late back. Very reluctantly, and at the slowest pace she could reasonably manage, hoping against hope that Tilly herself might appear out of nowhere and relieve her of this embarrassment, she led the new Lady Tregowan up a winding staircase and along numerous gloomy landings to where the maids' quarters were situated.

Coming at last to a door, she turned to Rose. 'This is the maids' room, milady. Are you sure you wouldn't prefer to wait until she comes back from wherever she is?'

'No, no, I'd really like to surprise her. You could help me move her things up to the nursery wing. Would you do that, Gladys?'

Gladys bobbed a curtsey, knowing when she was beaten, and pushed open the door.

Inside were six beds, all narrow and crammed quite close together with nothing but a chair beside each. Apart from these essentials, the only other piece of furniture in the room was a table upon which stood a jug and basin. At intervals around the walls were hooks where the maids' spare uniforms, coats and a variety of other garments were hung. A tattered green paper blind blotted out what little light found its way through the forest of roofs and chimneys to this attic room high in the eaves.

Gladys cleared her throat. 'She don't have much stuff, ma'am. None of us have, as there's nowhere to keep it. We've not much room like.'

'I can see that.' Rose herself had slept in worse places, but this wasn't a hovel on Fishponds Road, this was a grand house owned by a titled gent, a baronet no less. Sir Ralph clearly didn't believe in providing many comforts for his staff, or maybe the blame for this more likely lay with his second wife. She fingered a blanket on the first bed, thin and patched and unlikely to offer much warmth to the occupant.

She looked about her. 'Is there any form of heating, Gladys, or light for that matter? I can't see any lamps.'

'No, ma'am, 'ceptin we do get half a candle each week, there being no electricity in this part of the house.'

Rose looked at her in astonishment. 'Half a candle *each*, you mean?' It seemed precious little.

Gladys gave a little embarrassed cough. 'No, ma'am, half a candle per room per week.'

'Good gracious me, you must be in the dark much of the time.'

'We do have to be most careful with it, that's true, but candles cost money, as Mrs Quintrell, the housekeeper, do regularly point out to us.'

Rose decided she must tread carefully here. Besides, she'd seen enough. 'Which are Tilly's things? I shall take them with me now.' The girl would not spend another night in this place.

Gladys ran around collecting up her friend's belongings, pitifully few as she had warned, and mostly comprising a spare uniform and underwear, and a Bible. Rose took them from her. 'It's all right, I can manage these myself, and I'll find my own way back. Thank you for your help, Gladys.' At the door she paused to glance back at the troubled maid, who was clearly already dreading repercussions from her betters. 'And I'll see what I can do about the candles, maybe even an extra blanket each, without mentioning your name, of course.'

'Ooh, thank you, milady, I'd be ever so grateful.' Relief brought a flush to the poor girl's cheeks.

Tilly's response to this intrusion was, however, entirely different. White to the lips she stood before Rose, fists clenched tight into her skirts. 'Begging your pardon, milady, but I never asked to be moved, nor for you to root through my things and fetch 'em for me.'

'No, Tilly, that was my decision, I wanted to surprise you.' Rose was beginning to quite enjoy playing the grand lady, particularly if it brought with it a little power to help people.

'Gladys had no right to show you where we sleep. And it'll do her no good at all if it gets about that she showed you round.'

'Don't worry, Tilly, no one will be any the wiser. I promised her my absolute discretion, and at least the other maids will have a little more space now with one less in that small room. I also mean to try and negotiate more candles for them, and hopefully blankets too.'

'From Mrs Quintrell? You'll be lucky!' Then seeing she may have overstepped the mark, she instantly attempted to rectify her error. 'What I meant was—'

'I know what you meant, Tilly. I promise I shall do my best, without mentioning Gladys's name, or yours. But there is absolutely no reason why the housemaids should live in such penury, not in my humble opinion.'

Instead of tackling the housekeeper, whose reputation for sternness was clearly renowned, Rose went instead to the butler. He was surely the man in overall charge.

His response, however, was not encouraging. 'I have had no complaint from Lady Tregowan,' he informed Rose, rather brusquely.

'It is not the dowager who is asking for these changes, but me. I'm sure we can afford more candles for the servants, if only that they might have the opportunity when they retire to read their Bibles.' Rose thought this a good ploy to win him round, and it certainly seemed to sway him a little.

'The problem has been mentioned to me by certain members of staff, I will admit.'

'And what did you do about it, Mr Rowell?'

He looked at her in some surprise, not accustomed to being granted the benefit of a 'Mr' before his name. 'I put the matter to the housekeeper, Mrs Quintrell, and she said that what she didn't have she couldn't provide, so I spoke to Lady Tregowan directly.'

'And what was Her Ladyship's response to the request?' Had it not seemed entirely unbelievable, Rose might have thought she detected a crimson tide of embarrassment rising in the butler's throat at this question, although he was far too set in the traditions of the household to admit such an embarrassment.

'It was found that no changes were necessary.'

Rose fell silent, uncertain how to negotiate around this impasse. At length she said, 'Would you have any objection, Mr Rowell, if I were to make representations on the servants' behalf to the dowager myself?'

A mix of gratitude and astonishment shone from the man's eyes. 'I would not dream to comment, milady. But were such a representation to bear fruit, I am sure the staff would be most appreciative.'

'I'm not sure that I quite understand the purpose of this request,' was the response Rose received when she approached Lady Tregowan with the polite suggestion that the servants be allowed more candles.

'The purpose is to allow them to have sufficient light in their rooms when they retire, so that they might see to undress, and to read their Bibles.' Rose couldn't quite believe her own courage in speaking up, but she had the unsettling feeling that the servants weren't being treated correctly, and something should be done.

'How ridiculous! One doesn't need a candle in order to take off one's clothes and get into bed, and most of them can't even read, so why waste money on lighting? And if I might say so, you should not allow yourself to be fed such nonsense by Tilly.'

'It wasn't Tilly, I do assure you.'

'Then who was it? I find it astonishing that any maid in my employment would risk their job by telling such tales.'

'It was merely my own observation when I chanced to be passing by,' Rose hastened to add, anxious now for both Gladys and Tilly. The last thing she wanted was for either of these girls to lose their job.

'Passing by? How very strange. May I suggest, then, that you keep to your own part of the house in future. The welfare of my servants is really none of your concern.'

And that, it seemed, was an end of the matter. At least for now.

* * *

'So, what do you think of the new Lady Tregowan, then?' Mrs Pascoe paused in the delicate task of crimping her Cornish pasties as she waited for Tilly's response.

'I like her.'

'I thought as how you might, particularly since you get to help mind the child. And I know how fond you are of little 'uns. But will anything change, that's what I want to know? What difference can she make, young maid like she?'

'She's young, I know, and a bit overwhelmed by everything.' Tilly was determined to steadfastly defend her new mistress. 'She's finding it a bit hard to adjust to our British ways, and don't forget she's still grieving for her husband. But I'm sure she'll do her best. Look how she tried to get us more candles, admittedly with no success, but she did at least try, even though she's only been in the house five minutes.'

'And you're nice and comfy now, up there in the nursery wing.'

'I didn't ask for special treatment, that was all her doing, carried my stuff up an' all. She hasn't forgotten the candles either. She suggested we report any accidents the maids might have, seeing as how they have to cope in darkness much of the time.'

Mrs Pascoe looked thoughtful at this. 'Has a clever head on her shoulders, then.'

Tilly looked pleased. 'Aye, she's nobody's fool. And she's offered to help my parents.'

'And what might she be able to do for them, I wonder?' Having prepared the pasties to her satisfaction and set the tray in the oven to bake, Cook dusted flour from her hands and sank into a chair with a weary sigh. Her feet were playing up something shocking today, not to mention her back. 'Will she save them from eviction, do you reckon, or provide them with other accommodation?'

Tilly concentrated on cutting out more pastry circles for the second batch of pasties, aware of the eyes of the other servants upon her as they went about their chores, supposedly minding their own business. But there was precious little privacy in this kitchen. 'She's promised to pay them a visit and consider the matter.'

'Ah, promises,' Mrs Pascoe mumbled, nodding sagely, so that her white mob cap flopped back and forth atop the round knob of grey hair to which it was pinned. 'Promises are like wishes – they soon vanish in the mist when faced with harsh reality. Once she realises it's Mr Jago what calls the shots round here, I can't see her volunteering to stand up to that bully.'

Tilly instantly protested. 'She has far more spunk than you give her credit for. Like I say, she faced up to Lady T, didn't she? And all over a few candles. She understood the importance for us to have light – to write our letters home, if nothing else. Those of us what can read, that is, or who help those what can't. I reckon she's been through some tough times herself.'

The cook laughed out loud. 'How do you work that out? Admittedly she's recently widowed, but she's rich, quite pretty, married well, and her son is a baronet. How hard can that be?'

'I don't know, but there's something about her . . .'

Tilly was frowning, struggling to explain. 'She's not in the least bit uppity. She doesn't lord it over me but acts more like a friend. And there's a deep sadness about her, a sort of helplessness at the core of her that has nothing to do with grief. It's as if she's afraid, though of what, I can't imagine. As you say, she's landed on her feet good and proper here, with her husband's inheritance falling nicely into her lap.'

Not budging from her chair, the cook started to spoon out portions of her special steak, onion and turnip mix onto the next batch of pastry circles. 'Hmm, mebbe it's dawned on her that she faces an uphill battle to hold on to that inheritance. The old cow won't let go of the reins too easily.'

Some of the kitchen maids giggled at this use of Mrs Pascoe's favourite word to describe Lady Tregowan. The cook knocked on the table with one fat knuckle. 'Hey, you lot, get on with that washing-up and stop your earwigging.' Then leaning closer to Tilly, for whom she'd always had a soft spot, she carefully dropped her voice. 'Does she suspect, I wonder, half of what went on here? Does your new mistress ever talk about why that husband of hers was rebuffed and sent packing by his own father?'

Tilly blinked. 'I'm not sure what you mean, Cook. Wasn't it because he didn't approve of Sir Ralph marrying again?'

Mrs Pascoe rested one plump finger against her full lips as warning for Tilly to keep her voice down. There was nothing she liked better than a bit of gossip, but she'd no wish to broadcast it. In a hushed whisper she went on,

'That was the official story, to be sure. But there was much more to it than that. The poor young man was stitched up good and proper.'

Goggle-eyed, this was all news to Tilly, but then the family quarrel had happened before her time. She leant closer to whisper, 'Stitched up by whom, and in what way?'

'By the old cow, who else? She accused—'

'Ah, Tilly, there you are. I've been looking everywhere for you.'

Tilly smothered a groan of disappointment as Mrs Pascoe was cut off midsentence. 'Joe, I wasn't expecting to see you in here so soon. It's not time for dinner yet awhile. It's barely eleven o'clock. What was it you wanted? Oh, there isn't something wrong with little Robbie, is there?' She jumped to her feet, a sudden panic in her voice.

'No, no, Ro—er, Lady Tregowan is about to take him for a walk in that perambulator you found in the attic the other day, so she won't need you for a while, Tilly. But she's wanting to know when your next afternoon off is, and if she may come with you to see your parents?'

Tilly turned back to the cook with a triumphant smile. 'There you are, didn't I say she'd help? Thank you, Joe. Please tell Her Ladyship that I'll be going next Sunday, before lunch, and I'd be honoured if she was to accompany me.'

'Right, I'll tell her.'

The two women watched as Joe dashed off, evidently in a great hurry to obey his mistress. 'He's very cosy with the new Lady T, don't you reckon?' Mrs Pascoe thoughtfully remarked.

'Hmm, mebbe,' Tilly said, frowning. 'But then he's worked for her quite a while, apparently.'

'Do you reckon there could be any truth in that story about him being her lover?'

Whatever it was she'd been gossiping about with Cook now slipped right out of her head as Tilly considered this new worry. It was certainly true that she'd seen Joe deep in conversation with his young mistress on at least two occasions. Now why was that? she wondered.

It was the following morning and Joe was enjoying breakfast in the kitchen, taking his time as he savoured each delicious mouthful of Mrs Pascoe's excellent porridge and the leftover bacon and sausage that had come back from the dining room. It was a far cry from those bleak, hungry weeks in steerage when they'd had to make do with dry bread and salt fish. He'd fallen on his feet good and proper here, with regular food in his belly, a comfy bed to sleep in, a clean uniform to wear, and the opportunity to drive one of the newfangled motors as well as a horse-drawn carriage. Joe certainly had no intention of losing this position just because Rose suffered the occasional prick of conscience. She always was too soft-hearted for her own good, was little Rosie.

Tilly appeared at his elbow to warm up his mug of tea and drop a third sausage on to his plate. 'I thought you might be hungry as you were up so early. I hope you're settling in all right?'

'Aye, thanks.' He beamed at her, admiring the way her full breasts nicely filled out the bib of her apron, and wondering if he could span her tiny waist with his two hands. He'd like to do more than that with his hands, given half a chance. Of course, his heart belonged entirely to Rose and always would, but there was nothing to stop a chap enjoying a little light dalliance as well, was there? She was a looker was Tilly. 'How could I not be, when I'm being waited on hand, foot and finger by the prettiest girl I've ever clapped eyes on in me life.'

Tilly blushed, most becomingly. 'Get away with you, Joe Colbert. My mam warned me about men like you. Proper charmer, you are. Well, I wasn't brought in with the morning milk. I expect you say that to all the girls, particularly when there's some gain to yourself, like that extra sausage.'

Joe's hazel eyes glinted with mischief as he tucked into it with gusto. 'So what can I do for you in return? I'm ready to oblige in any way I can.'

'I'm sure you are.' Tilly sat on the chair beside him, and, propping her chin in her hand, studied this newcomer with her frank, open gaze. Everyone else had eaten and gone about their business, so they were quite alone in the kitchen, Joe tending to come in a bit later for his grub since he had to see to the horses first. Despite her cool response towards him, she rather liked his tousled red hair and cheeky smile. 'So tell me, how long have you worked for Her Ladyship?'

Joe looked blank for a moment, happily engaged in tracing the slender line of her throat and the way little brown curls sprang out from beneath her cap, his mind on more intimate matters. 'Ah, you mean Ro— er, Lady

Rosalind? To be honest, she never really called herself that in . . . er . . . in America, her late husband not being on speaking terms with his father an' all. Besides, he wasn't a lord then, was he, before Sir Ralph died?' Joe could only hope he'd got this right, as he really knew very little about how titles, or the aristocracy, operated.

'You've worked for her a while, then. How long have you been in America?'

He pretended to consider, as if it was hard to recall such details. 'Five years, mebbe more.'

'And you've been with her all of that time? Must have become quite chummy, then.'

Persistent little blighter, our Tilly. Her cheeks were rosy from having just come in from hanging out the laundry, he noticed. She smelt of summer breezes and lavender, which stirred his senses in a most exciting way. 'Not quite so long as that,' he hedged, not wanting to be pinned down.

'I saw you talking with her the other day, down by the shrubbery. It seemed to be quite an intense conversation, so you must know her well.'

By heck, he'd have to watch this one. Still, it was flattering that she took such an interest in him, so long as that was the only reason for her curiosity. 'Aye, well, she ain't stuffy about servants having opinions,' Joe fabricated by way of explanation, then judged it wise to change the subject. 'How about you? Have you been at Penver Court long?'

'Oh, years and years, since I was a girl,' Tilly replied.

'You're still a girl, and a lovely one at that,' Joe teased, bending closer so that he could taste the warmth of sweet breath from her rosy lips. A startled look came into her eyes and those same lips trembled slightly. So she was not entirely indifferent to him, then? Joe put his knife and fork carefully together, as he'd been taught to do as a boy by Rosie's mother, and slowly got to his feet. 'Maybe we could take a walk later, just you and me. You could show me round the village or summat. Not been there yet.'

'I don't get time off for gallivanting,' Tilly protested, though not too firmly.

'Well then, a five-minute stroll around the kitchen garden, mebbe, while the family is at dinner, surely wouldn't come amiss.'

Tilly laughed. 'Shows how much you know. It's all hands to the pump when we're serving.' Picking up his plate she flounced over to the sink. 'And don't think you can win me round with your soft flattery.'

'Wouldn't dream of it.'

'I'm immune to such tricks.'

'Course you are.' Joe chuckled, then creeping up behind her, popped a kiss on the bare arch of her neck as she leant over the sink.

'You cheeky monkey!' Turning swiftly, she flicked soapsuds at him, but Joe was already running for cover. He was, however, pleased to note that she was laughing as much as he.

Chapter Ten

Tilly usually begged a lift with one of the carriers who went to visit his old mother in Fowey, which was just across the river from Polruan, where her own family lived. Rose, however, insisted on taking the carriage. Where was the point, she thought, in living in a fine house if she couldn't take advantage of its benefits? Besides, her attitude towards the Tregowan family, Jago in particular, had changed dramatically since that dreadful day on the headland. In future she was determined not to allow herself to be intimidated by any of them, and, of course, she and Tilly had a pact never to leave little Robbie unguarded for a moment, nor ever allow Jago to take him out again.

Lady Tregowan, however, was most disapproving of her plan. 'Where is it you wish to go in the carriage exactly?' she asked, as if such a request was quite outrageous.

Rose cleared her throat, battling to hide the curl of

nervousness she felt deep inside, while resolving not to explain what she had in mind. 'I thought . . . that is, Tilly and I rather fancy a trip to Fowey. To show Robbie the boats.'

'Don't be foolish. What interest can a baby have in boats? Besides, I'm not even sure that the carriage is available. I may need it myself later.'

Bryce laughed. 'You've just said that you intend to have a lie down to ease your aching head.'

'I've decided a breath of fresh air will do it more good,' Lydia snapped.

'Then walk, Mama. Or take the governess cart, and allow Rose and Tilly to enjoy their outing. Rose isn't a prisoner here and has as much right to the carriage as your good self.'

Lady Tregowan's mouth actually fell open at this display of rebellion from her younger son, but before she managed to find her voice, Bryce was on his feet.

'As a matter of fact, I need to visit Fowey myself. Would you have any objections to my accompanying you, Rose?'

'N-no, of course not.' Stunned by his offer, but touched by his support, Rose cast him a glance of fervent gratitude, then beat a hasty retreat before his mother found some other reason for preventing the trip.

Ten minutes later, with the baby in his bassinet beside her on the seat and Bryce sitting opposite, they were soon turning out through the main gates, and happily bowling along narrow country lanes between high Cornish hedges. Tilly had opted to sit up front with John, the driver, as she considered this more appropriate.

Rose settled back against the cushions, rather pleased with this small success, yet feeling oddly shy at finding herself alone with Bryce Tregowan. Oh, but how wonderful it was to escape that claustrophobic house, grand as it was, and to be out and about at last. Rose could smell the sea, the distant haze of it drawing ever closer. She felt suddenly free and light-headed, a small kernel of excitement starting up inside.

'I hope you don't object to my intruding on your little jaunt,' Bryce said with a smile.

'Not at all. The carriage is yours, after all.'

Bryce frowned. 'Now that is a strange remark to make, for I believe it actually belongs to that little chap there.'

'Oh, I suppose it does. I hadn't thought.' She really must take more care over the remarks she made. Rosalind would never have made such a silly mistake. But it wasn't easy when inside her head she knew that she really didn't have any right to a single thing, least of all free use of a fine carriage. 'Well, I doubt he'll be driving it any time soon.' Rose couldn't help but giggle at the thought of a baby sitting holding the reins.

Bryce chuckled too, then asked, 'Does he always sleep so well?'

'He's a very good baby. Robbie only wakes when he's hungry.' As if to prove her wrong, he chose that moment to wake with a jolt and start to cry. Laughing, Rose picked him up to rock him against her shoulder. 'He's unused to the bumping of the carriage on the rough ground. Generally, he's an absolute angel.'

'I expect all mothers think the same of their offspring,'

Bryce said, finding himself entranced by the way her otherwise unremarkable features lit up into true beauty when she laughed. 'You should smile more,' he told her, the words out before he'd properly considered them. 'Why don't you?'

For a moment Rose couldn't think of a thing to say by way of reply, all too aware of his scrutiny, and the closeness of his knees almost touching hers. But if he thought to patronise her, he had misjudged his mark. 'Do other widows of your acquaintance laugh more than I do? If so, then perhaps they miss their husbands less.' Oh dear, she was really becoming quite sharp, a veritable virago. Rose waited with bated breath for his response, certain Bryce would view her words as a criticism of Lady Tregowan, which, in effect, they were. But he took her completely by surprise by laughing out loud.

'Touché! Don't expect my mother to weep. She's had four husbands and never grieved for any one of them. Marriage, so far as Lydia is concerned, is little more than a business arrangement, which I suppose makes a certain sense.'

'Does it? Is that how you see marriage too, as a business arrangement?'

'I most certainly avoid making observations upon my mother's marital career,' he said, not quite answering her question. 'At least she will never be disappointed in love, which is not pleasant.'

'You sound as if you speak from experience.'

'I am twenty-three years of age, so not entirely untainted by the charms of the female sex.'

'Yet no one has captured your heart?'

'Not yet, but I live in hope.'

Dark eyes narrowed as he turned his head to gaze unfocused at the passing scenery, a thoughtful expression on his handsome face. Was he already pining for someone? Rose wondered. And was that person Gwenna? And why should it matter to her if he was? She certainly had no intention of pressing him on the subject. 'Perhaps you have someone in mind?' she challenged, instantly quashing this decision.

The corner of his mouth quirked upwards into a wry smile. 'Perhaps I do. But dare I take the risk of pursuing my fancy, that is the question? It could all go horribly wrong and the lady in question rebuff any approaches I make, which can be mortifying for a fellow, do you not think?'

Could the sparkle in his eyes be sending her a certain message, or was that her fevered imagination? 'Nothing ventured, nothing gained. Isn't that what they say?' Rose remarked, rather flippantly, studiously ignoring the fluttering of her heart.

'Ah yes, and better to have loved and lost than never to have loved at all is another old saw. Do you believe in all that nonsense? I don't. Better either to love the right person for life, or leave the whole business well alone, which I fully intend to do.'

'But that could result in rather a lonely life, if you don't ever find the right person, or decide to take a gamble on someone, couldn't it?'

'I leave gambling to my brother,' Bryce snapped, before

adding more calmly, 'A solitary life is surely better than marrying the wrong person?'

'Oh, I would never marry except for love,' Rose agreed with some fervour. Wasn't that the reason she had resisted Joe's advances?

'You already did,' he quietly reminded her, resting his elbows on his knees as he leant closer.

'Did what?' Rose felt mesmerised by the way he was gazing into her eyes, as if he were studying her and rather liked what he saw.

'Married for love.'

Startled by this second blunder, she hastily readjusted her thoughts, sliding smoothly back into dear Rosalind's skin, as she was becoming increasingly adept at doing. 'I did, yes, of course. What I meant was, I would never marry *again*, unless I loved him as much as I loved Robert.'

Bryce let out a sigh. 'But how could you ever do that?'

Rose began to tremble. Was he mocking her, or was he suspicious? Had he guessed that she was an impostor, and really only a young virgin who had never been married at all, didn't even know what it was to be in love?

Bryce sat back in his seat, propping one leg across the other as he did so. His thighs, Rose couldn't help but notice, were well muscled and strong. 'Of course, I may opt to follow my mother's example. Both Jago and I are expected to marry an heiress,' he said, his expression carefully bland. 'Do you know of any suitable candidates?'

He *was* making fun of her, or else he was deadly serious and about to proposition her. Rose could never be certain how to take these droll comments of his. He was a most confusing man to understand. She opted on the side of caution. 'How should I, since I'm new to the area?'

'Ah, of course. But you may be able to recommend someone, once you are settled into society. We are, after all, related, at least by marriage, are we not? But how, I wonder? What are we? Let me see. My mother married the father of your late husband. Correct?'

'Yes,' Rose agreed, in her quietest voice. Was this the moment he would challenge her claim? Her heart began to race.

'But I was my mother's son from a previous marriage and only Sir Ralph's stepson, so half-brother – no, stepbrother – to Robert. Can that be right? I assume one can have stepbrothers? Which makes you and I . . . Goodness, that's far too complicated to work out. In-laws of some sort?'

Despite her fears, Rose began to laugh, perhaps with relief as he seemed to be tying himself into knots. 'Step in-laws?'

'Nothing close anyway, thank goodness,' he said with a grin.

After which enigmatic remark Rose confined their discussion to safer topics such as the weather.

Lydia clipped off a dead rose and tossed it into the rubbish basket, wishing she could as easily rid herself of that chit. 'Our newly appointed Lady Tregowan is a mite too independent, do you not think? She is certainly not the shy, retiring person I first took her for. All that business over those dratted candles for one thing. Would you believe both Quintrell and Rowell approached me on the subject, claiming there had been a spate of accidents recently as the maids couldn't see what they were doing. I was obliged to double the candle ration as a result. What an interfering little madam she is. And have you any notion where she is going today?'

'I've no idea and even less interest,' Jago snapped, pacing restlessly to and fro, still fretting over the way she'd stood up to him so brazenly on the cliff top. They were in the conservatory and Lydia was cutting flowers for the house, and indulging in a little gentle watering with a tiny copper watering can, in the fond belief this ladylike activity could be described as gardening.

'There is an intrinsic stubbornness about her that I find deeply troubling. Too much independence must undoubtedly be curbed. There are limits to my tolerance. She may well have the law on her side, for now, but I will not have my family ousted from our home. Nor will I have my rules flouted, or stand by and do nothing while she takes over. The chit must learn that she cannot simply walk in here and do as she pleases.'

'My thoughts entirely, dearest Mama. A point I attempted to make clear to her only the other day.'

Lydia cast her son a sharp glance. 'Obviously not too successfully.'

'Indeed not. On this occasion. But there will be other opportunities. For the moment we must hold fast to our patience and wait for the right moment to present itself, as it surely will.'

'And if the little madam thinks she can foist that brat on us and take possession of the title, property and entire inheritance, then she is sadly mistaken. As the only son Sir Ralph has known in twelve years, you should be granted your rightful share of the estate. It is only fair and proper, considering the amount of time you have given to it. I would sooner die than see you robbed of your true deserts.'

'And we can't have that, Mama, can we? Better she, or the brat, be the one to suffer such a fate. And babies are so vulnerable, I have always thought. Do you not agree?'

Lydia drew in a sharp breath, setting the watering can down with a clatter. 'Take care what you say, my love. Walls have ears.' She glanced about, as if to give proof to the fear.

'We are all minutes from death, as you and I have discussed before, I seem to recall.'

Lydia's cheeks flushed to a dark pink. 'I cannot think what you mean. I remember no such discussion.'

Jago laughed, and it was not a pleasant sound. 'Can you not? How very surprising, for I recall it all too clearly. I believe you were tending to your dearly departed husband at the time. Not suffering a nudge of conscience, are you, dearest Mama?'

'Enough!' Striding over to her son, Lydia slapped his face with a sharp crack of her hand. 'Sometimes your tongue runs away with you, and I will not have it. I don't want you doing anything rash, do you understand? We'll deal with the brat through the proper channels. Right now, it is more important than ever that you concentrate on diverting some of the estate income to our personal accounts, as I instructed.'

His smirk of satisfaction still in place, and looking

156

far from chastened by his mother's show of temper, Jago inclined his head by way of agreement. 'Have no fears on that score, Mama, everything is in hand. Those who cannot pay their rents will be evicted, their farm or smallholding sold, and the resulting sums will not all slip into the estate coffers, I do assure you. Bryce can please himself but we, that is, you and I, deserve some recompense for our loyalty and patience over the years.'

She smiled at him now, leaning into him, her hands smoothing his chest as she gazed adoringly up into his beloved face. 'Indeed we do, my love. We will finish what we started without let or hinder.'

It was but a short drive to the little town of Fowey. Rose thought it fortunate the carriage was a small, neat equipage, drawn by one chestnut mare, since any larger vehicle would have great difficulty in negotiating the steep, narrow streets. They clattered down Lostwithiel Street and came to a halt on the Town Quay.

'Wait for us here,' Bryce instructed the driver as he lifted the bassinet, then took Rose's hand to help her out of the carriage. His grip felt firm and warm, a hand one could depend on. 'You'll find refreshment at the Ship Inn on Trafalgar Square, John. Have your meal put on my account. But no more than one tankard of ale, mind. We have no wish to be driven home by a tipsy driver.'

'I'm a Methodist, sir, and never touch strong liquor.'

'Excellent, then we are in safe hands.' Turning to Rose while Tilly fussed over the baby, he continued, 'We'll go our separate ways, then, since I have business matters to attend to. For all it is Sunday, I dare say I will find my colleague in his office. Shall we agree to meet back here at, say, three o'clock? Will that be sufficient time for you? There is something I would like to show you, Rose, and it would be a shame not to take advantage of this glorious day.'

Rose's heart seemed to turn over at the prospect of yet more time alone with Bryce Tregowan, not sure whether she welcomed the notion or feared it for some reason. And she really must consider Tilly, whose day off it was. But the arrangement would allow them three hours with her parents as it wasn't quite twelve o'clock, surely ample time for a visit. 'That would be lovely, thank you.'

'Had you any particular excursion in mind?' he asked. 'A walk to Readymoney beach perhaps?'

Rose cast a desperate glance across at Tilly, who quickly came to her rescue. 'I thought we might take the ferry and I'd show milady Polruan, where I was born.'

'Ah, splendid idea. I'm very fond of Polruan. Then if there is no tea shop open, you might try the Lugger.'

'Ma will give us a bite to eat,' Tilly told him. 'And I'll make sure we're back sharp on three.'

Bryce smiled at Rose as he again took her hand, then stunned her by raising it to his lips to kiss it. The touch of his mouth upon her fingertips was light, but sent shivers of emotion rippling down the length of her arm. 'Farewell then, My Lady, till we meet again later,' he teasingly remarked, before sauntering away on his long, easy stride.

Tilly giggled. 'I reckon he's taken quite a shine to you, milady.'

'Don't be ridiculous,' Rose demurred, blushing furiously.

Then as they climbed into the ferry boat, she remembered their conversation earlier in the carriage. More likely it was her inheritance which interested him, and for the first time in her life Rose wished she were still poor.

There was a light offshore breeze and the sky was a cloudless blue as the small ferry tied up on Polruan Quay alongside a few clinker-built rowing boats full of happy families setting out for a picnic on this lovely June day. Several fishing boats stood idle, this being a Sunday. Even so, nets seemed to be hanging everywhere while the men sat mending them, chatting as they worked like gossipy old women. Children were swinging in some of the nets, using them as hammocks, but nobody seemed to object.

'It's a long pull up the hill,' Tilly warned. 'Do you reckon you can manage it?'

'I can if you can.' Rose grinned. She was greatly enjoying herself, loved the feel of the wind in her hair, and would welcome any challenge which stopped her thinking of Bryce Tregowan's enigmatic smile.

It certainly took all her effort to make the long climb, the bassinet carried between them, and Rose was quite out of breath by the time she reached the top, with a stitch in her side. But it was surely worth it as the Carwyn family lived high above the tiny fishing village, from where they enjoyed spectacular views across the river to the cluster of white cottages that comprised Fowey, all seeming to lean together as if for protection against the blustering winds.

'How marvellous to grow up here, Tilly. You were very lucky,' Rose said, thinking of the lodging house on

Fishponds Road in Bristol where she'd spent her own formative years.

'Wonderful views, aye, but you might not think me so fortunate when you see where I actually lived,' laughed Tilly.

It was a simple Cornish cottage with one living kitchen on the ground floor, and a wooden ladder leading up to what was probably one bedroom above, where the entire family no doubt slept. Rose had lived in worse, but kept that fact to herself.

A wood fire burnt in the grate, despite the warmth of the day. Rose suspected it had been lit in her honour to stave off the dankness of the cottage. Several small children sat on the pegged rug before it, or stood about shyly with their thumb in their mouth, regarding their visitor in wide-eyed wonder. She couldn't help noticing how thin and ragged they all looked, reminding her so much of her own younger days.

Rose shook Mr Carwyn's hand, smiling with genuine warmth as she introduced herself. He politely bowed his head while Mrs Carwyn bobbed a curtscy, just as if she were a queen and not plain and simple Rose Belsfield. But then they believed her to be Lady Rosalind Tregowan, she must remember that.

Tilly's mother insisted on making her tea, using a lovely china teapot which no doubt only came out on special occasions. There was mackerel for dinner, running with butter they could probably ill afford to spare, followed by plain scones, which Mrs Carwyn called Cornish splits.

'This is Mother's best home-made blackcurrant jam,' Tilly proudly informed her, as she passed her the stone jar.

'It tastes wonderful,' Rose said, trying not to take too

much as she knew how poor these people were. 'And I can't remember when I tasted mackerel as good, or as fresh.'

'I caught them yesterday,' Ennor Carwyn told her. 'So they don't come much fresher.'

Rose looked surprised. 'You fish as well as farm?'

'I do, milady.' Tilly's father explained how he rose each morning before dawn to go out with the fishing fleet, leaving his wife to see to the milking and mind the animals. 'We keep half a dozen cows, and grow all our own feed: mangels and turnips and the like, to save on the hay. We brings the animals into the barn in winter, d'you see, when it gets cold. Then there's barley which we grinds up for the pigs. They gets the peelings and bits o' cabbage too, whatever we has handy. They sows do like to run around so we has to put rings in their noses to stop them rooting up all the field. Wife gives the chickens a handful of corn each day, and we rears a few geese for Christmas.'

Rose was struggling to take in all this rush of information, not being conversant with country living. 'It sounds like a hard life.'

'I reckon 'tis, but we're used to hard work here. We keep a few long-wool sheep, South Devons crossed with a Suffolk ram. Then when the butcher comes to see to 'em, he pays us what 'ee can but the price keeps on going down, d'you see? Can't blame him, 'ee does his best by us, see. It's the fault of the government and they taxes, 'ee says. We don't spend a penny we don't has to,' he finished, on a note of defiance.

'It must be difficult to make ends meet, Mr Carwyn.'

'It ain't getting no easier, that's for sure. We don't ever

enjoy the meat ourselves, you understand. We depend largely on rabbit.'

'Leastways we did till Mr Jago accused us of poaching,' put in his wife, a bitter tone to her voice. 'Which was a bit of a puzzle to us, rabbits being wild and running everywhere. Proper nuisance they are, and best in a pot.'

Even Rose understood that the countryside was not short of rabbits. 'Jago accused you of poaching? I wonder why he should do such a thing.' She chose her words with care, not wishing to sound disloyal, or for her to seem to criticise him to his tenants. That would never do.

'We used to be allowed the odd pheasant, once over,' Dolly Carwyn said. 'But those days are long gone.'

Rose understood now why the children were so thin, with legs like sticks, their faces pale and washed-out-looking. Their parents didn't appear much healthier. In fact Tilly's mother looked as if one breath of wind might blow her away. 'Do you have enough vegetables for your stock pot?' she asked, thinking of her own mother's valiant efforts to feed her brood over the years, and how she would walk for miles to find a field where a farmer might have missed a few of those tiny potatoes called chats, when he harvested.

'We've cabbage and potatoes in a good year,' Dolly assured her. 'We grow leeks and peas, runner beans when we can get them, and there are plenty of fruit in the hedgerows.'

Rose remembered scouring the hedges too, for blackberries, and coming home with a rim of black juice around her mouth, feeling slightly sick. But she knew that there were many times when the years were not good, when the potatoes caught some blight or other, or the peas

162

and runner beans didn't flourish. So she listened with close attention as Ennor Carwyn outlined their lives in painful detail, his family gathered close about him, offering their silent support. Finally, she asked, 'So tell me what you are being asked to pay in rent for this holding.'

When he told her, she blenched. 'But that is surely far too much? Goodness, it would represent a quarter's pay for some.'

'Aye, it do.' Ennor nodded, his tone of voice low, harsh with unspoken anger. 'It's double what we were paying last year, but Mr Jago claims the rent was uneconomic before because Sir Ralph allowed himself to be taken advantage of, which isn't true. The master was always fair, but Mr Jago—'

His wife nudged him with her elbow and Ennor stopped whatever he'd been about to say, clearly adjusting it slightly before continuing. 'Mr Jago, 'ee says as how prices are rising, jobs are scarce and we're lucky to have a roof over our heads at all.

'We started down this road in my father's day, back thirty year or more. Agriculture went into a depression, and we've hardly come out of it since. We all blamed the weather at first, there being several wet summers, followed by years of drought. The weather didn't help, of course, but then it became clear that imports flooding the market were causing havoc with prices. With no sign of recovery, folks lost heart. They upped sticks and went north to work in the factories, earning more money than they could ever get on the land. It's little better today. Prices may rise in other things, but not in farming, where they're as depressed as ever. Like I say, if I sell a cow or a young lamb, I'm paid a pittance for 'ee. I might as well give it away. The golden years of farming are over.'

'Can't you explain all of this to Jago?' Rose asked, feeling somewhat bemused by this long, heart-rending tale.

The farmer almost laughed. 'There's no shifting the master once 'ee has an idea in his head. All I would say is, even if 'ee turns us out, 'ee'll not find anyone else willing to pay the rent 'ee's asking. There aren't many fool enough to work the hours for what we get in return, not and live as we do, a bucket out back for the necessary. I tell you, milady, we wouldn't eat as well as we do if it weren't for my good wife. We'd be in a worse state if it weren't for her skills.'

Judging by the state of the family, Rose couldn't begin to imagine how much worse that might be, but her mind was made up. These people were tenants on Robbie's land, and she was quite certain that dear Rosalind would have moved heaven and earth to help them.

'I shall certainly have a word with Jago, and put these points to him. I will do the very best I can for you. I'm sure we can resolve this matter to everyone's satisfaction.' But as they made their way back in the ferry to Fowey, Tilly gushing with gratitude, Rose didn't feel anywhere near as confident as she had sounded. But then Jago represented a formidable adversary.

Chapter Eleven

Bryce was waiting for them on the Town Quay as the ferry boat bumped against the harbour steps, and came quickly down to hand her out before the ferryman had the chance.

'Are you agreeable to a short walk, or have you had enough for one day?'

Just the touch of his hand on hers was turning her knees to jelly. What could be wrong with her? Didn't she thoroughly dislike this man?

'What about Tilly? We can't just abandon her.'

'Don't worry about me, milady, I shall call on my aunt and uncle, who have a watchmaker's shop on Fore Street, and visit various friends hereabouts. I could introduce them to Master Robbie, if you'll allow me to mind him for you.'

'That would be most kind, Tilly.'

They agreed to meet back at the Town Quay on the dot of five, then Rose hesitantly accepted the arm Bryce offered, and allowed him to lead her away.

They walked the length of Fore Street, past Albert Quay, named after Victoria's beloved consort, and on through Passage Street, the whitewashed cottages seeming to nod to each other across the narrow street, as if enjoying a pleasant gossip.

They walked for some distance and Rose was about to ask where he was taking her when he stopped outside a large house built close to the Bodinnick Ferry, a small jetty jutting out from the front yard into the river. 'Here we are, my new place of business. Ideally placed for passing traffic, both of the road and river variety. It's not open yet, but would you like to see inside?'

'Very much.'

He led her up the steps of a tall Georgian building and unlocked a blue-painted door. Rose wasn't certain what to expect, having heard of his intention to open a chandler's but not being entirely sure what that might involve. Once inside, it was like an Aladdin's cave. There was everything the boatman might need, from ropes to waterproofs, lanterns and nets, life jackets and whistles, paint and varnish, and all manner of provisions and supplies.

'We'll supply the big ships that come down the River Fowey, not only the simple fisherman, and as it's a busy port, we hope to do well.'

'By "we", do you mean you and Jago?'

His face seemed to darken. 'No, what my brother will ultimately do with his life I have no idea, but I am in partnership with a fine young man who was looking for a backer to loan him the money to start this splendid business. I was only too happy to oblige.'

'For a share in the profit, obviously?' Rose said with a smile.

'But of course. We will be equal partners, and business is business, after all. Don't tell me that you are against making a profit? Every woman likes money, certainly my mother does.'

Rose carefully expressed no opinion on that particular point. 'I personally have never been in the position to open a business, but I'm sure if I were then I'd consider a good profit on my investment to be essential. I applaud your entrepreneurial spirit.'

'Was your husband not in business, in New York?'

Rose looked up into his politely questioning eyes and felt her mind freeze over. Yet again he had caught her off balance, one minute all jovial and friendly, the next catching her unawares with a pointed question. She really had no idea what job, if any, Rosalind's husband had done. She'd rather assumed that as a gentleman he'd had no need to work. Now, she wondered if that were true. Their wedding had been simple and they'd lived in a one-bedroom apartment, so perhaps the couple were not as well off as she'd at first imagined.

'Oh, Robert managed to earn an honest living one way or another,' she said, rather dismissively. So many questions. So many lies. Rose really had no wish to add to them, not just now. 'Goodness, what is this?' she asked, anxious to change the subject.

'It's a flagpole, for a ship. We can provide your own personal flag too.' But he clearly had no intention of letting her off the hook so easily. 'What kind of honest living? Did Robert work in finance, or politics, as gentlemen do? Or did his father provide an allowance for him despite their estrangement?'

'My husband was ever the gentleman. With regard to the allowance, I really couldn't say. I never thought it my place to ask.' She met his curious gaze with defiance in her own, watching his struggle not to press the matter further with some amusement. Yet all Rose could think of was that having removed his hat, the wind had tousled his hair most delightfully. She was wondering how it would feel to brush back those dark curls from his brow.

'Then you were a rare wife indeed.'

'Oh, very rare.'

He said nothing more, as if by his silence he might force her to continue. Feeling rather pleased with herself at having resisted yet another attempt to probe, Rose again turned to examining the stock. 'And what is this, might I ask?'

'It's a tiller, and here are several rather clever compasses that will help you navigate your way around the world. Would you like to travel one day, do you think?'

'Sailing from America to England was quite enough for me.' She almost laughed out loud at the question, wondering what his reaction would be if she told him that she had in fact travelled halfway around the world to America, and back again. 'Particularly since I was alone.'

'You could always come with me.'

Rose quickly turned away, flustered by his teasing, and by that so-familiar glint in his eye. 'This must be the finest set of oars I ever saw,' she said, in desperation. Not that she was any judge on such devices, never having any reason to notice them in the past. They'd certainly had little sight of such items in steerage.

Bryce was chuckling softly in that knowing way he had, which always brought a warmth to her cheeks. It was almost as if he recognised the effect he was having on her, and was really quite enjoying it. 'Perhaps you would simply wish to cruise up and down the river, in which case we could provide mahogany seating for your cabin, with plush crimson cushions. And here is a most beautiful set of crockery to which we can have your own personal crest added. What do you think of that?'

The awkward moment seemed to have passed, and Rose too was laughing, responding to his boyish enthusiasm. 'Quite astonishing. I'm hugely impressed.'

'Would you like to see the offices?'

Then they were clattering up the stairs and Bryce was explaining which would be his office on the days he came in to deal with the accounts. It all looked most efficient and businesslike.

'When do you open?'

'Any day now. Certainly by Midsummer's Day.'

A thoughtful crease marred her brow. 'That's the next quarter day, isn't it? The 24th of June.'

'It is indeed, when our – or rather your – son's estate rents are paid.'

'Who sets the rents?'

'That is Jago's job.'

'I rather thought it might be.' She said nothing about the Carwyn family, not wishing to break Ennor's confidence. Rose was reluctant to embroil them in a dispute. Besides, Rose deemed it more correct to speak to Jago first. 'Does no one else have any say?'

'Not now that Sir Ralph is dead. Why do you ask?'

'No reason, I was curious, that's all.'

'You weren't considering replacing him with someone else, were you? I doubt my brother would be too pleased about that.'

'No, of course not. I'm sure he does a splendid job.' It was as they were walking back along Fore Street that she asked a question very much on her mind. 'I take it then that you have no real regrets about the loss of inheritance you've suffered?'

'None whatsoever. I cannot have lost what I never expected to gain. I always had my heart set on some sort of business, and a chandler's seems the perfect solution.'

'Good, I'm glad to hear it,' Rose said.

They walked for a moment in silence, which might almost have been called companionable. Rose was acutely aware of his closeness, of the heat flowing from his body to hers, the strength of his arm upon which she rested her gloved hand. It felt perfectly right there, as if it belonged. She wondered how it might feel if that arm slipped about her waist, if he pressed her to his broad chest and— Her wandering thoughts were jerked back to attention with his next words.

'My brother, however, is another matter altogether. I would warn you to tread softly around him.'

'None of this was my doing,' Rose protested. 'In fact . . .'
Lulled into a sense of closeness with him, she almost told
Bryce then about the incident on the cliff top, but then
changed her mind at the last moment. Blood ran thicker
than water, and it was such a wild and crazy thing for Jago
to do, Bryce might easily accuse her of making the whole
thing up. Then they'd be at loggerheads again. And for some
reason she had no wish to be at odds with this man.

'You were saying?' He'd paused to look down at her,
patiently waiting for her to continue.

She smiled brightly. 'I forget. Nothing of any
consequence.'

'Everything you say is of consequence, at least to me.
You simply don't say enough, that is the problem.'

'Perhaps I have said too much,' she responded, and for
once was pleased to see that he was the one looking puzzled.

Rose chose to confront Jago around noon the next day
in the estate office. She'd spent a largely sleepless night,
and most of the morning, carefully practising what she
wanted to say. Now, with some trepidation, she tapped
on his door.

'Enter.' His tone was not welcoming.

Rose turned the brass knob and did as she was bid.
Jago glanced up in surprise. 'Well, well, what is this?
Come to apologise for your ill-mannered behaviour the
other morning?'

Rose was taken aback. '*My* ill-behaviour? What reason
have I to apologise to *you*?' She felt quite breathless with
outrage at the thought.

'For not trusting me with my nephew. Most unsettling.'

'Step-nephew.'

'Ah, I can see you are a stickler for the truth.' He leant back in his chair, steepling his hands while he considered her at his leisure.

Rose stifled a shiver of foreboding at his choice of phrase. 'He is but a baby and needs to be with me – his mother.' There was the slightest hesitation before she used this word, and Rose could only hope he hadn't spotted it. 'But Robbie is not the reason I wish to speak to you this morning. May I?' She indicated a chair set before his desk.

'By all means. May I offer you coffee?'

'I have already taken some, with your mother in the parlour.' A silent, chilling affair, as always. 'Forgive me, but since the estate is now my son's inheritance, I feel it behoves me to take a proper interest.'

He let out a bark of laughter. 'And what would a chit like you know about managing an estate?'

'Very little, so I thought I'd better learn,' Rose admitted. 'I thought I might begin by speaking to all the tenants to find out if they have any problems or—'

'What kind of problems could they possibly have, coddled as they are?' Jago said, interrupting her.

'I shan't know unless I ask, shall I?' Rose sweetly told him. Having plucked up the courage to get this far, she doggedly pressed on. 'Yesterday while we were in Fowey, I happened to be with Tilly while she paid a visit to her parents. You may remember them, the Carwyn family, who live in Polruan.'

'I know them well,' Jago growled.

172

'Of course you do. Well, Mr Carwyn, who is such a fine, hard-working man both on land and at sea, was explaining to me the dire straits that farming is in these days. I must confess that it is not something I'd ever thought about until he explained it all to me.'

Keenly aware of the intimidating manner in which Jago was regarding her through narrowed eyes, Rose tightened her resolve and pressed on. Never had she played her role of Rosalind with more care and skill than she was doing now. 'I thought it incumbent upon me to investigate further. I intend to sound out the other tenants in order that we can decide how best to tackle the problem. There is little point, for instance, in burdening them with a rent higher than they can reasonably manage to pay. I'm quite sure that were Sir Ralph still with us, he would agree we must do all we can to help these people through hard times. The last thing we want is to lose even more of our tenants to the factories, do you not think? And it behoves me, as Robbie's mother, to ensure I keep his inheritance safe.'

The silence, when Rose finally ran out of both words and breath, was daunting. Jago got to his feet and moved swiftly to the door. 'I thank you for your suggestion on this issue. I shall certainly give it all due consideration, and should I need anyone to speak to the tenants to gather their opinions, I will certainly let you know. In the meantime, madam, you can safely leave the management of this estate in my capable hands, as did Sir Ralph for many years.'

At which point he pulled the door open, clearly eager to

usher her through it. Rose remained where she was, firmly seated in the chair. Her only response to this apparent dismissal was to smile at him, which quite belied the way her heart was pounding with something between fear and fury in her breast.

'In point of fact I was not making a suggestion. I was informing you, out of courtesy, of what I intend to do.'

'You were *informing* me?' Jago slammed the door shut again, took a step towards her that was almost threatening. Rose clasped her hands tightly in her lap and managed, by dint of willpower, not to flinch.

'I'm sure we both have the interests of the estate, its tenants and the new baronet at heart. And I believe it is vital that we work together in harmony, you and I.'

'Do you indeed? And what if I should disagree with your methods?'

Rose could see that he was fuming. She would not have been surprised had Jago actually started to breathe smoke out of that bony nose of his, so fired up was he. 'That would be most unfortunate. You should be aware that I have spoken with Mr Wrayworth, the solicitor, and he agrees with me that every care must be taken to keep the estate in good order until the baronet comes of age.'

Leaving Robbie in Tilly's excellent care, Rose had walked down the lane into Penver village first thing that morning, where she had managed to discuss the terms of Sir Ralph's will with the very helpful solicitor. She'd told him only a part of her concerns, but had come away satisfied, well primed for this discussion with Jago. 'We have agreed, Mr Wrayworth and I, that there will be no further rise in rents at the present time. And certainly no evictions of good tenants who are struggling to pay through no fault of their own.'

'The fixing of rents is no damned business of Wrayworth!' Jago roared.

'But it is *my* business, as guardian of the young baronet, in order to protect his inheritance. I am told it says as much in Sir Ralph's will.' Rose could hardly believe what she was doing. It was really quite astonishing how new courage seemed to be flowing through her veins like quicksilver.

Now she did get to her feet, and using every scrap of dignity she possessed, which she hoped did dear Rosalind proud, walked calmly to the door. 'I do hope we can deal with this matter without acrimony, although I would politely remind you that if you wish to continue in your role of estate manager, then you really have no choice in the matter.'

'No choice? Damn you to hell!' He spat the words in her face. 'And your brat with you.'

'We aren't going anywhere, Jago,' she quietly informed him. 'Certainly not to hell. And there will be no repeat of that dangerous business on the cliff top. It would be most unpleasant if your brother were to hear of how you risked the young baronet's life in that foolish display of bravado. Do you not agree? I'm sure Mr Wrayworth would also be most interested to hear of it.'

Her eyes held his, reflecting a steady challenge, watching as he absorbed the import of her threat.

'This is blackmail.'

'What a very nasty word. Not one I would ever use. I merely state the facts, as I see them in my role as guardian.' And with a swirl of her full skirts, she spun on her heel and walked from the office, softly closing the door behind her.

Rose kept on walking, shaking too much to even think where she was going. It was only too evident that she had made an enemy this day. But then hadn't she faced worse in her life already, losing her dream of America, and her entire family along with it? Rose absolutely refused to allow herself, and more importantly dear Rosalind's son, to be bullied or threatened by this man. She would have no life at all were it not for the generosity and courage of that child's mother, and if it came to it, she would willingly sacrifice her life for his.

Gwenna was waiting for her out in the hall, arms folded and looking far from happy. 'So what are you up to now, getting all cosy with Jago? I thought we'd agreed that you would keep well away from him.'

Rose sighed. She really didn't have the time, or the patience, for Gwenna's foolish jealousy. 'You need not fear. We were discussing estate business, nothing of a personal nature at all.'

'I've only your word for that. How do I know you aren't lying?'

'Why don't you ask Jago? I'm sure he'll be happy to tell you as he did not at all like what I had to say.'

Doubt now registered on the other girl's face, as obviously the prospect of tackling a less than happy Jago was not something she cared to risk. Instead, she changed tactics. 'I wouldn't recommend you argue with Jago. He's been running this place for years, even when Sir Ralph was alive, so he won't take kindly to you sticking your nose in where it's not wanted.'

Now Rose smiled. 'That was basically the drift of our conversation. Did Sir Ralph ever raise objections to the way Jago ran things, do you know, or was he satisfied?'

'Oh, they were constantly at loggerheads,' Gwenna candidly revealed. 'They'd go at it hammer and tongs some days. But as Sir Ralph wasn't in the best of health he was always grumpy, and in no position to judge.'

Or to do anything about it if he wasn't satisfied, Rose thought, which was interesting. She rather hoped Sir Ralph might have approved of her efforts to provide better living conditions for his servants. In which case she would quietly continue the battle on their behalf. Grasping the other girl's hands, she gave them a little squeeze. 'You should encourage Jago to name the day, or at least present you with a ring, even if you are obliged to keep the engagement secret until the period of mourning is over.'

'Oh, he will give me a ring soon, I know he will,' she said, rather too hastily.

'I'm sure he will. That might stop you worrying so much. But I promise you, I would not dream of encroaching upon your territory. I have no interest in Jago. In the meantime you and I can continue to be friends.' There was little sign of this so far, but Rose lived in hope.

'I'm sure there's no need for me to worry,' Gwenna said.

'But I just need *you* to be aware that I'm watching you.' And under this implied threat, she knocked on the estate office door and, without waiting for an answer, lifted up her skirts and flounced inside. Rose stood watching, a hand pressed to her mouth to stop the laughter that threatened to bubble over.

Jago looked up in surprise from a letter he was writing to his bank manager. The stupid man was objecting to the fact that his personal account was overdrawn, due to a slight disappointment at Newton Abbot racecourse recently. Rose's interruption had not helped his temper; now he sighed in exasperation as he saw Gwenna's mournful expression.

'What's wrong, you look rather out of sorts? Not torn your best gown, have you?' he quipped.

'Don't tease, I'm bored and desperately lonely.' Gwenna flung herself into his lap, wrapping her arms about his neck and giving him a long and passionate kiss. Jago was not against enjoying this unexpected free offering and responded with enthusiasm, slipping his hand down the neck of her gown so that he could fondle those deliciously plump little breasts.

Pushing his hand away, she stuck out her lower lip in a sulk. 'You're so cruel to me, Jago.'

He tickled that delightfully pouting lip with his tongue, curling it around the shape of her mouth, then plundered her mouth, making her gasp. Sliding lower, he licked the bud of her nipple, smiling as he felt it harden under the sensitivity of his tongue. 'Do I not make you the happiest girl in all of Cornwall?'

Gwenna purred, barely able to breathe. 'Oh, you could easily do that, if only you would name the day. Perhaps in the autumn? We could get secretly engaged right away, if you like.'

He was chuckling as he pushed the gown further from her shoulder, still busying himself with her breasts. 'We could certainly consider the possibility. You know how important your happiness is to me.'

'Is it? Oh, but I've been so upset lately as you seem to be ignoring me. You're spending far too much time with that Rose.'

Lifting her from his lap, Jago sat Gwenna on his desk, slipping one hand under her skirts while he continued to nibble at the delightful arch of her throat. 'Now you know there is no one for me but you. I cannot stand the woman, have in fact just sent her packing with a flea in her ear.' He chuckled, not wishing it to be known that he had in fact been the loser in that little contretemps. 'Now how can I make my best girl happy again?'

And pushing her back onto the desk he set about the task with vigour, until Gwenna was squealing with delight and had quite forgotten her sulks.

Chapter Twelve

Rose could hardly believe she was once again on board ship, crossing the Bay of Biscay en route for Biarritz. As this was now autumn 1906, it was more than twelve months since that previous voyage to America. She couldn't help thinking how different her life would have been had she not been suffering from influenza on that occasion. If she hadn't coughed, and her eyes been all inflamed, she would have gone through customs with the rest of her family and even now be enjoying life with them in New York.

The thought always brought heartache as she still desperately missed them. She'd written many letters in recent months to her aunt's home in America, and, to her joy, had eventually received one in return from her mother. Several more letters had been exchanged between them and it felt wonderful to be in touch again, to know that her family was well. Micky had found a job as a shoe boy in a fine hotel, hoping to work his way up the promotional ladder to porter one day. Mary and Clara were attending school and the twins would be following them there very soon. Her mother too had found employment as a seamstress, so they'd all settled in well.

One extra benefit from these letters was that Rose was able to learn more about America. Her mother had described to her the apartment they all occupied in the basement of a brown stone building. She'd learnt of the deli on Forty-Seventh Street where they liked to eat pancakes for breakfast as a special treat on a Sunday, of the milk-cart horse called Bud, and the excitement of Thanksgiving. All of these small details helped Rose to answer the myriad questions which came her way from various members of the Tregowan family, and add credibility to the great deception that now held her in a seemingly unbreakable grip. A string of lies constantly waiting to trip her up.

Sadly, she'd been compelled to lie yet again, to her own *mother* for goodness' sake! Nervous of an envelope arriving addressed to Rose Belsfield, she'd told Annie that her name had been changed to Tregowan to suit the family she was working with. Since this was a fairly common occurrence among domestic servants in society households, it seemed a perfectly reasonable explanation to offer.

Rose had also felt obliged to make up a suitable tale to go with it, all about how she and Joe had managed to find employment at this fine house in lovely Cornwall. She explained that Joe worked in the stables and as a chauffeur, that she herself was a housemaid. And when her mother asked to hear about this new life she was living, Rose would describe the tasks Tilly was engaged in, as if it were herself that was doing them. She made no mention of what had happened on the ship with Rosalind, nor little Robbie.

Her lies were now so legion that Rose would mockingly tell Joe she should really start keeping a record, just to make certain she could remember them all. Not that she would ever be so foolish as to do such a thing, but they tripped off her tongue with practised ease. Rose had almost convinced herself that some of them were actually true. But the sense of guilt never left her.

Yet not for a moment did she regret staying to protect her darling Robbie. Wasn't his safety far more important than any possible threat to herself? Already walking, he was growing into a bright and sturdy little boy. It was hard to credit how far she had come since she'd last ventured overseas, returning rejected from Ellis Island. But despite the stormy weather on this voyage, she didn't feel in the least bit seasick. Quite the opposite, in fact. She was coping much better with the inclement weather than poor Tilly, for instance, who had spent most of the passage shut in her cabin. Robbie too appeared to have developed a good pair of sea legs, although he wasn't terribly steady on them yet.

Tilly was still his nursemaid as Rose had managed to resist all efforts on the part of Lady Tregowan to appoint a nanny in her place.

'Tilly is good with him. Better still, Robbie loves her.'

Several nannies had appeared for interviews, each one reciting their 'rules and requirements'. Fortunately, either Lady Tregowan herself did not approve of them, Rose found some good reason to object, or Robbie just screamed and they went quickly away.

But what a joy the child was to her. There was no question in Rose's heart that he was her son, in every way that mattered. She devoted herself entirely to his care, with Tilly's excellent help. Having this precious boy in her life was one good thing which had come out of the nightmare. And had she stayed in America, she would never have set eyes on the enigmatic Bryce Tregowan.

To her shame, Rose couldn't decide whether that was a good or a bad thing.

She'd spent the last several months deliberately avoiding close contact with him. Fortunately, that hadn't been difficult as he'd been very caught up with his new chandler's business. Bryce might appear quite friendly on the surface, but his thoughts ran deep and any conversation with him nearly always ended with him asking pertinent questions about her past. Did he persist with these interrogations out of genuine friendship and affection, or was he truly suspicious of her? She could never be certain.

Rose didn't care to consider the hours she spent thinking about him, of how many wakeful nights she had lain in her bed recalling his smile, weighing his words as he gently teased her. And the way he would so often catch her eye, making it quite impossible for her to break away, was most confusing. She really had no wish to confront her mixed feelings about him, how one minute she could dislike and distrust him, the next be blushing like a silly schoolgirl simply because his arm had accidentally brushed hers.

Jago, however, had turned into her sworn enemy. There was no question about that. Rose was now a regular visitor to Tilly's family in Polruan. She'd liked them on sight, being genuine, salt-of-the-earth Cornish folk, and they'd become dear friends to her. Thankfully, she had successfully spared them eviction, so the confrontation with Jago had been worth it.

Surprisingly, he had not engaged in reprisals, or none that Rose could quite put her finger on. But there was something about the manner in which his narrowed gaze would watch her, following her every movement as she went about her daily life, that sent a shiver down her spine. It was almost as if he knew her secret, that she was an impostor, and he was simply waiting for the right moment to expose her.

But how could he know?

There had been one occasion when Rose had felt certain that her belongings had been searched. Even if that were true and not simply her own fevered imagination, she had few possessions of her own, most of them being dear Rosalind's, so what would such a search reveal? Rose could think of nothing that would condemn her, save for the document they'd all signed making her Robbie's guardian. And this she kept safely secreted beneath the loose floorboard under the bed, where no one would ever think of looking.

Nevertheless, Rose didn't trust him an inch. For that reason alone she was glad to have Tilly by her side on this trip, as only her friend fully understood this silent battle of wills. Joe was entirely unsympathetic to her concerns, making it very clear that he thought she fussed and fretted too much.

'No one will discover the truth so long as you keep playing your part, which you are doing marvellously,' he would say whenever she expressed her doubts.

Rose would draw some comfort from his faith in her, and from the sight of Robbie thriving and growing into a fine little boy. What possible risks could she be running by telling a few little fibs?

Lydia considered it an essential part of the season that she spend winter away from the cold of England, relaxing in Biarritz, a beautiful and stylish coastal town close to the Spanish border. It was very popular with the British upper classes for its mild climate, stunning beaches, and sense of elegance and style. She always insisted on staying at the Hôtel du Palais, formerly the summer mansion of Napoleon III, which seemed reason enough for choosing it so far as Lydia was concerned. The hotel overlooked the main beaches and the Atlantic Ocean, and was decidedly chic and luxurious, a veritable honeypot for the very best people. Which meant, of course, that it was also the perfect place for society gossip. Lydia very much liked to keep abreast of who among her friends was having an affair, or considering remarriage. She might even keep her eye out for a likely new husband on her own account.

More urgently, Lydia wanted a good marriage for each of her sons. 'Gwenna is a sweet child, and I can see that you are attracted to her,' she remarked to Jago as they enjoyed a quiet nightcap together in her suite on the evening before the ship docked. 'But I do hope you weren't thinking of taking this relationship too far. I shall find her a suitable husband, of course. The dear child deserves to be happy. Sadly she is growing rather plump, which is perhaps the reason she has failed to take on her second season out. Too many comfort sweets, I fear.'

Jago's thin lips twisted into a smile, although it did nothing to warm his features, which remained as cold and bland as ever. 'Point of fact, she's rather keen to marry me, increasingly so of late. Of course, she does have a fortune of her own.'

'Of modest size. You can do better. I strongly recommend you leave the girl alone. I've seen you touching her, and taking her off for quiet little strolls. Be careful such dalliance doesn't lead to expectations you cannot fulfil.'

Jago smirked. 'I do take care, but a man must be permitted a few pleasures.'

'Not with Gwenna. For you, my elder son, I have a far more interesting prospect in mind.'

'And who might that be? Not one of your Bohemian friends?' he asked, a suspicious glint in his pale eyes.

Lydia topped up his glass with a generous splash of whisky. 'A certain person whose son, rightfully or not, has a claim to the title.' Lydia had long ago resigned herself to the inevitable and, outwardly at least, accepted Robbie as the new baronet, albeit with some degree of resentment and deep reservations. But the problem could easily be solved if she could but arrange a match between the girl and her elder son. To Lydia's practical way of thinking, that would be the perfect solution. 'You are fortunately not blood related, and it is vitally important to keep the money within the family.'

Jago laughed out loud. 'And how do you suppose I might persuade her, since she has made it abundantly plain she hates my guts?'

Lydia raised an eyebrow. 'Does she? Then you must change her mind by exercising more charm upon her. I've never thought of you as the modest sort when it comes to chasing women. And surely the end justifies the means.'

This time Jago's smile was almost joyous, if one could so describe an expression which revelled at the prospect of causing misery to another, and this woman in particular. 'It would be my pleasure. I rather think I might enjoy the chase, and the capture.'

Rose stood at the rail watching as the ship docked in Bilbao harbour. Life with the Tregowans was never dull, even exciting at times, but it was also quite terrifying. Rose never knew from one day to the next what new challenge she might have to face. She'd been astonished to find herself even included in this expedition, which had been as unexpected as it was unwanted. Lydia may have grudgingly come to terms with her presence at Penver Court, but hardly seemed to welcome it any more now than she had at the beginning. So why the invitation to join them in Biarritz? It was most puzzling.

The family had stayed quietly at home the previous winter, as they'd officially been in mourning, although the death of Lydia's husband had not prevented her from inviting friends to stay for frequent and decidedly noisy house parties.

Rose had once found herself seated next to a Mrs West at dinner, who seemed a most pleasant lady. But when it transpired that she was no less than the Duchess of Manchester, Rose had frozen, not daring to speak another word all evening, let alone risk eating a morsel of food in case she spilt it, her hand was shaking so much.

Now, as Rose watched people start to disembark, she feared there might be a litany of such terrors ahead, and wished herself back at Penver Court rather than hobnobbing with more of the social elite. A prospect which filled her with trepidation.

The party made their way down the gangplank, Rose carrying Robbie, and Tilly following close behind with the toddler's teddy and bag. Gwenna was fussing over Lady Tregowan, putting up her parasol against the sun even as she draped a shawl about the older woman's shoulders in case of a cool breeze. Jago was already on the quay, standing by the motor he'd hired for them, a beautiful Daimler open tourer, issuing orders to Joe and John on how best to stow the luggage safely on board the Ford which would follow on behind. Tilly, together with Gladys, Lady Tregowan's maid, would travel with Joe in this second vehicle.

Rose gazed about her in wonder, lifting her face to savour the warmth of the sun, marvelling at the huge ships in port, the busy, industrial nature of the scene, which reminded her so much of Bristol that she felt quite homesick.

Bryce came to stand beside her. 'Do you have any plans for how you would like to spend your time while in Biarritz?'

'I haven't really given it much thought,' Rose said, paying particular attention to setting Robbie on his feet while keeping a firm hold of his hand, trying to ignore the way her heartbeat always quickened whenever Bryce came near. 'I shall be perfectly content to sit and watch Robbie play in the sand. He is such a live wire now I can't take my eyes off him for a second.'

'Ah, but there will be plenty of events for grown-ups to enjoy too. Cocktail parties and balls, tea dances and the casino, even sea bathing. You might care to try the latter.'

'I really don't think so,' Rose demurred, panicking slightly at the prospect of being seen in a bathing dress by Bryce Tregowan.

'Would you at least allow me to show you the town, perhaps take you on a short motor tour of the surrounding villages?'

Nothing would induce her to accept an invitation from him, despite his very evident charm. She looked up into his handsome face, ready to fix him with a glare and tell him so. 'That would be lovely.'

'Excellent! I shall look forward to it.'

Then, as he smoothly handed her into the car, Rose could have kicked herself for being all kinds of a soft fool. What a weak and feeble creature she must be. Hadn't she promised herself not to get involved?

Lady Tregowan and Gwenna already being comfortably ensconced, Rose settled herself beside them with Robbie on her knee. Bryce climbed into the front with Jago, which was a relief as she'd dreaded being seated next to him in the close confines of the car. With John at the wheel, the motor drove out through the streets of the busy Spanish town, then on to the coast road that led to Biarritz.

The journey was long and tiring. Robbie would sleep for a while then wake up and grow fractious, and Rose would have her work cut out trying to keep the toddler amused. But if she hoped to enjoy a little nap herself, she was soon disillusioned. Lydia took this opportunity to issue her with yet another stern lecture on how to behave in polite society.

'I've no idea how you deal with such matters in America, but now that you are going out into society it is essential that you behave impeccably at all times.' As if no one beyond the shores of England could have any notion of what good manners might mean.

'Should I decide to hold a small soirée, for instance, you must remember always to introduce those of lower rank to the higher, and not the other way around. You would likewise give preference to a lady of more mature years than yourself whenever you enter a room. At a ball, it is also customary to ask a lady's permission before making an introduction to a gentleman, as it would be hugely embarrassing were she to refuse his request for a dance following it. And do remember to incline your head politely when meeting friends out of doors. Oh, and never put a knife in the marmalade jar.'

An error Rose had never been allowed to forget.

Lydia droned on for some time, till finally, satisfied she'd made her point, she moved on to another of her favourite topics: society gossip. 'I do believe that dear Nancy – Lady Astor, you know – will likewise be wintering in Biarritz. If that proves to be the case then I shall certainly make a point of issuing her with an invitation to one of my musical evenings.'

Lydia did so love to name-drop with careless abandon.

'Anyone would think they were bosom pals to hear her talk,' Tilly had once said. 'Yet to my certain knowledge, Lady Astor has never set foot in Penver Court.'

'Lady Tregowan may visit her in London instead,' Rose had suggested, although she tended to agree that it was all show on Lydia's part, simply in order to increase her own sense of importance. Nancy Astor was a formidable and ambitious woman who was married to one of the richest men in England, and lived in Cliveden, one of its finest houses. From what Rose had heard of the lady in question with regard to her spirited sense of independence, she rather thought the two women might have a great deal in common.

Now, as the Daimler bumped along rough country roads, a whole string of names poured out. Lytton Strachey, René Lalique, the jewellery maker from Paris, Lady Gwendolen Guinness, and Mrs Asquith, the politician's wife, all claimed by Lydia to be among her close acquaintances, and likely to be wintering in Biarritz. Yet Rose hadn't seen any of these notables at Penver Court either.

Is it possible that Lydia is as much a liar as me? Rose wondered with some amusement.

Chapter Thirteen

Within twenty-four hours of settling into the Hôtel du Palais, Bryce repeated his invitation to show her around and Rose found herself accepting. She had fully intended to avoid him, but, confusingly, as they lingered over breakfast Jago too asked if he might escort her. Rose wasn't sure who looked more surprised by the request, herself or Gwenna.

'Oh, but I thought we were going to the casino,' the other girl protested, a tremor in her voice.

It was as if she hadn't spoken for all the notice Jago paid her, and the poor girl looked as if she might burst into tears at any moment.

Rose hastened to decline, saying that it wouldn't be at all seemly by way of an excuse. 'I believe Lady Tregowan would insist that I need a chaperon, and Tilly has already taken Robbie to a sandcastle competition.'

Lydia, who had carefully listened in to this little exchange, laughed out loud. 'Dear me, no need to be precious. You are not some unmarried innocent needing to protect her reputation, as our dear little Gwenna is. You are a widow. Besides, you will be perfectly safe with either one of my sons.'

'That is good to hear,' said Bryce, walking in at precisely that moment, 'as I have already asked Rose if I may conduct her on a tour of the town. We'll see you later, Jago.'

Rose gratefully took his arm and allowed him to lead her from the breakfast room, all too aware of Jago's glowering scowl at being bested by his brother. Although why on earth he should seek her company rather than enjoy Gwenna's she could not imagine. Were they not affianced, or very nearly? It could be for no good reason, that was certain.

They walked along the Quai de La Grande Plage as far as the Casino Municipal, a large white building with awnings over a parade of shops to protect the ladies who browsed in their windows from the sun. Wooden walkways led down to the beach where Rose could see rows of tents set out, no doubt where guests could change into their bathing suits. She could see a crowd of children some way off, hear them shouting and laughing, and was quite sure Robbie would be having a lovely time. She was looking forward to spending precious fun time with him herself this holiday. The sky was blue, the sun was shining and she felt deliciously happy and relaxed.

'You must be quite well travelled, having been to Canada

and America. Have you visited any other countries?' Bryce asked, as he led her to a table and ordered a *café au lait* for them both.

'Never,' Rose said. Nor had she been to those places either, truth to tell.

'This Basque area is lovely, don't you think? Conquered in the sixth century by the Romans, who named the region as Aquitania, or Aquitaine,' he explained, 'because of the tradition for raising horses, the name coming from the Latin word "*equites*" meaning horses. You do ride, I assume? I've never thought to ask.'

'There wasn't much call for it in New York,' Rose excused herself, not knowing whether that were true or not, but fearing he planned a horse ride next, a terrifying prospect.

'Not to worry, there are plenty of other pursuits to amuse us in Biarritz. I shall enjoy showing you the sights. Where shall we begin?'

He was grinning boyishly at her, and Rose couldn't help but respond in kind. 'I am entirely in your hands,' she said, then seeing the mischievous twinkle come into his charcoal-grey eyes, instantly wished the words unspoken. 'What I meant was—'

'I realise what you meant,' he laughed. 'Although I would not be averse to handling you, in the nicest possible way, of course.'

Rose could easily deal with Joe's flirtatious flattery, even his pushy boldness. Somehow it felt different coming from this man, and brought that betraying crimson flush to her cheeks which she so hated. Fortunately, she was saved by

194

the arrival of the waiter who set coffee cups before them both, together with a plate of chocolate croissants.

'Goodness, I couldn't eat another thing, not after that breakfast.'

Bryce broke a piece off one and fed it to her, gently putting it to her lips so that she couldn't avoid taking it from him. His fingers brushed lightly against her mouth, sending a shaft of excitement rippling through her.

'You eat, while I finish your history lesson.' He leant closer, his eyes on her mouth, watching as she chewed.

What it was he said to her Rose could afterwards barely recall. Something to do with Biarritz once having been a small fishing village that had depended largely on whale hunting for its living. Information poured out of him, but she was far too engrossed noting how white his teeth were, how strong the square jut of his chin, and how his dark eyes were surprisingly kind, almost merry.

'And in the last century, Napoleon III and his Empress Eugenie used to come here for their vacation every year. They built a palace in 1855. When it was sold, it was turned into a hotel offering a service second to none, pandering to the rich, and to those who would like to be.'

'It also offers beautiful scenery,' Rose added, gazing out over the vista of golden sands.

'It is certainly beautiful from where I am sitting.'

When she glanced across at him she realised he was staring straight at her, and not at the view at all, which brought yet another flush of crimson to her cheeks. Uncertain how to respond, Rose concentrated her attention on sipping her coffee while Bryce went on to say something about the hotel having suffered from a serious fire a couple of years ago, following which it had only recently reopened.

'Goodness, you'd never think it to see how the place looks now – absolutely perfect, so far as I can see.'

'Ah, but sometimes it is not easy to see beneath the surface, do you not think? There may be dark corners, hidden down in the cellars for instance, where its true history can be seen. Rather like people.'

Rose felt a jolt of fear grip her. What was he suggesting? That she had secrets hidden in dark corners too, which was indeed true.

Some of the milk from her coffee must have strayed on to her upper lip, for, reaching out a finger, he wiped it gently away. Rose could feel herself tremble at his touch, and knew that it would be dangerously easy to fall under this man's spell. He was exciting and charismatic, far too much so for her own safety. Taking out her handkerchief she carefully patted her lips dry. 'I do beg your pardon.'

'Not at all, my pleasure,' Bryce said, with a soft chuckle; and then in that unexpected way he had, swiftly changed the subject. 'I was delighted to note that you are an early riser, and amazed to see Mother at breakfast this morning. I doubt we'll see her there again as she rarely sets foot outside her room before noon. Were you sorry that I stole you from Jago?'

'Not in the least. Your brother and I, we don't . . . we are not . . . I'm sorry, I shouldn't say this but—'

'There is no need to explain, I understand perfectly. He wouldn't be my chosen companion either. But he is, or rather was, the heir to much of Penver Court estate, if not the title. I expect Mama came down to breakfast with the intention of seeing her little plan put into action.'

'Little plan?' Rose stared at him, bemused. 'What can you mean?'

'Be warned, she will be set on a little matchmaking between the pair of you.' His jaw seemed to tighten, the previously benign expression hardening very slightly. 'It would, in her eyes, be the perfect solution. And I shouldn't imagine Jago would be against the notion, not for a second.'

Rose again felt her cheeks start to burn, but with temper this time. 'What notion? You aren't seriously suggesting that Jago and I . . . that he would wish to . . .'

'Oh, but I am. My brother misses no opportunity to improve his own status, and marrying you would elevate him considerably.'

'I'm afraid he is entirely wrong there,' Rose demurred. 'More likely his "status", as you call it, would be reduced considerably, certainly in the eyes of the world.' Dear heaven, she'd said too much, or maybe not enough?

Bryce frowned. 'How so? You are the mother of a baronet, and now a rich woman in your own right.'

'The fact of the matter is . . .' Rose paused to take a breath. She wanted to say that she wasn't at all rich, had no intention of touching this inheritance which had been handed to her. It belonged to a dead woman, to dear Rosalind, and not to her at all. For a terrifying second the urge to come clean was overwhelming. She longed to confess that neither was she the mother of a baronet, but only pretending to be, so that she could stay with darling Robbie to keep him safe. But something stopped her. What? Fear of prison for herself and Joe? Such a confession would also demand further explanations, of the incident on the cliff top, which would damage the agreement she'd made with Jago over the Carwyn family. If she broke her side of the bargain, they'd be evicted. They'd lose their home and livelihood, and Rose really couldn't do that to such lovely people.

Or was it the fear of seeing that disappointment in his eyes which would surely come if he learnt the truth about her?

'Ah, you mean your protests over accepting the inheritance because of the rift between Robert and his father.' Bryce seemed unfazed by her flustered silence. 'You must forget all about that little matter, Rose. It was not, in any case, your fault. Think of your son. Robbie is the only one who matters now.'

She almost sighed with relief. 'You're right, of course. Robbie *is* the only one who matters.' Rose sternly reminded herself of Jago's threat to that darling child.

Smiling, Bryce propped his chin in his hand. 'So, if I have no reason to be jealous of my brother, what about your manservant, Joe? When did you first meet him? Is he in love with you?'

Rose started, once more thrown off her stride by this man, and perplexed how best to answer. 'That is a question you must ask him.'

'I did, and he told me I should ask you.' Bryce had that wicked smile on his face again, but his eyes had narrowed slightly, as if waiting on her answer.

Rose got to her feet. 'You promised to show me the town, not drag up my past, which I confess I still find distressing as it reminds me so much of Robert.'

Bryce was at once all contrite apologies, and, tossing a few coins on to the table to cover the cost of their coffees and croissants, he again offered her his arm. They strolled down the narrow streets, smiling at the ladies and their tiny dogs with jewelled collars, of which there were any number, admiring the little shops, in one of which he bought her a pretty fan.

'There is really no need to buy me a gift,' she protested.

'There is every need. I upset you back there with my insensitive questions, and I beg your forgiveness. Besides, I believe you, about Joe, that there is absolutely nothing between you. Although he is clearly badly smitten, how can I blame him for that?'

This was all becoming rather serious, and again stepping into dangerous territory. 'I think I'd like to go back to the hotel now, if you don't mind. I'm rather tired after the journey.'

'Your word is my command,' he agreed.

But as they walked back along the beach, Bryce insisted they stop for lunch at a small café with a panoramic view of the ocean, and over a delicious salmon salad Rose risked a question of her own. 'So why do you and your brother not get on?'

Bryce toyed with a fragment of lettuce. 'For a start he's only my half-brother. Jago was the progeny of Mama's first marriage, a mad elopement at a ridiculously young age, from which she was swiftly rescued by her parents.

199

The young man was so devastated by the prospect of having to live without her that he took an overdose of laudanum and killed himself.'

'Oh, how very sad.'

'Apparently the marriage would never have worked as he turned out to be poor, and Mama had counted on quite the opposite. She was far from pleased to discover herself pregnant after his death, until Jago was actually born. He has been her favourite ever since.'

'But why, when he is so . . . so difficult?'

Bryce smiled. 'I expect she feels she has to compensate him for losing his father so tragically, before he was even born.'

'And what of your own father?'

'He was number two, a Scottish laird of advanced years. Living with my demanding mother wore the poor old chap out rather quickly, I fear. Then he took a fall from his horse while trying to impress his young wife, which left him crippled and he just faded away. Her third was something of a rogue and the marriage ended in a bitter divorce.'

'After which she married Sir Ralph.'

'Indeed. I can't claim that Jago and I are close. We have very different views about life and duty. Yet he is still my brother, at least on the distaff side.'

Rose judged it wise to change the subject and asked him to tell her more about the kind of things that might be expected of her socially in Biarritz. Bryce proved to be highly entertaining on the subject of the Bohemian set who frequented the town. This group, while claiming to scorn wealth, apparently enjoyed spending, being possessed with a passion for gambling and parties, for cabaret, music and the high life. A way of life which very much appealed to his brother.

'And, of course, they love the new artistic movement, known as "art nouveau", which sees everything in life as "art". Even the legs of furniture must have sinuous curves,' he joked. 'And quite right too. What is wrong with a few sinuous curves, that is what I say?'

Rose was soon holding her sides with laughter as his gossip about the fast set became deliciously more risqué. Paying the bill, they continued talking with barely a pause in their conversation as they set off along the walkway back to the hotel.

'Close your eyes,' she suddenly instructed him.

'Why?'

Seating herself on a low wall hidden from general view behind a pine tree, Rose laughed up at him. 'Because I wish to take off my shoes and walk barefoot on the sands, but that will necessitate peeling off my stockings.'

'Ah!' He quickly sat down beside her. 'Allow me to help.'

As he reached for her foot Rose playfully smacked his hand away. 'I insist you close your eyes, and no peeping.'

The stockings were held up by a garter just above the knee and Rose wasn't even sure she could execute this delicate manoeuvre without disgracing herself. Somehow, she managed it.

Bryce softly groaned. 'What you ladies do to we poor males. I must say the new artistic movement would highly approve of your legs.'

'You peeped!'

'My eyes opened quite of their own volition. I fear I had no control over them at all.'

They were both laughing now, and Rose was attempting to ignore the undercurrent of emotion which warned her of the dangers in this mild flirtation. Yet feeling the sand between her toes really was delightful.

'Perhaps I could tempt you to a swim in the sea next time?'

'You never know,' she laughed. 'Robbie, I'm sure, would love to learn.'

So relaxed was she that Rose opened up a little, describing her own siblings and their little idiosyncrasies when young. 'Clara was the brave one, always curious and asking questions, and the first to jump in the pond we often went to at the park for a swim in summer. While Mary would cautiously hang back.' Oh, how very much she missed them all.

He must have seen the sadness come into her eyes for he gently asked, 'I assume they are still in Canada?'

Rose felt obliged to say that they were, already regretting this need of hers to talk of her brothers and sisters.

'Then you must pay them a visit one day. There is absolutely no reason why you shouldn't.'

By now, the hotel was in sight, and Bryce found a bench for Rose to sit on and replace her shoes, although she refused to put her stockings back on. He even helped her to fasten the laces. 'I've so enjoyed our little excursion, and our talk. Most entertaining.' Then leaning forward, he kissed her. It was no more than a light, brotherly kiss, but entirely unexpected and quite took her breath away.

Rose looked at him, eyes wide with surprise and perhaps some betraying emotion of which she was unaware, one he must have recognised for he kissed her again. This time it was rather longer, and, heart pounding, she felt again the alluring danger of desire. As his mouth moved over hers Rose wanted the kiss to go on for ever, sighing with regret when he finally drew away.

'I would like to say that was merely meant as a thank you for a most pleasant morning, and by way of an apology for my rudeness at times, but I would be lying. You looked so delightful with your feet all covered in sand that I simply couldn't resist. Now I shall escort you safely back to the hotel before I feel obliged to apologise again.'

Still mesmerised by the kiss, Rose thought she'd never felt so happy in all her life.

Tilly and Joe were on their way back to the hotel, having enjoyed a delightful morning building sandcastles for Robbie, when Tilly spotted Bryce and Rose seated on the bench and saw the kiss.

'Well now, will you look at that. And there was me thinking she was sweet on you, Joe Colbert. Although why anyone would fancy a great lump like you, I cannot imagine.' Tilly laughingly turned to look at Joe, hoping to share the joke, but her heart sank as she saw his reaction. He was standing stock-still in the middle of the road, his face ashen. 'Ah, so Mrs Pascoe was right, you do have a crush on Her Ladyship, or else you're head over heels in love with the good lady.'

Seeming to jerk himself out of a trance, Joe glowered. 'Rubbish! I've already stated a thousand times that we are nothing more than employer and manservant. I've been with Rose years, that's all, and I don't want to see her get hurt.'

Tilly lifted one eyebrow in disbelief. 'She doesn't look like she's hurting, not from where I'm standing. And why do you call her by her first name? Doesn't seem quite appropriate, even if you have worked for her a long time.'

Joe's expression was surprisingly fierce as he turned on her, which seemed to confirm Tilly's worst fears. 'Why wouldn't I use her first name when I'm only talking about her to you? Anyway, has she struck you as the stuffy sort?'

'No, not at all. Quite the opposite, in fact,' Tilly conceded, and then putting out a hand, she gently touched his arm. 'Aw, look, it's none of my business, and if you do have a fancy for Her Ladyship, then my heart goes out to you. She'd never look your way, you know that, don't you?'

A bleak look came into his eyes. 'I'll say it one more time then let that be an end of the matter. I don't give a fig for her, all right?' He glanced down at the toddler, fast asleep in his perambulator, quite worn out after the hectic excitement of the day. 'Now, can we get going? I reckon this child needs his dinner,' Joe snapped. So saying, he strode away at such a pace Tilly had to almost run to catch up.

But she'd got the message all right, and didn't know whether to feel more sorry for Joe or for herself.

Chapter Fourteen

In the coming days there were many more trips out with Bryce for Rose. Sometimes it would be with Robbie, which involved happy hours sitting on the beach helping the small boy to make sand pies, or holding his hand while he paddled and splashed in the shallows, giggling with happiness. Bryce seemed to have endless patience with him. One afternoon, they left Robbie safely back at the hotel with Tilly, and just the two of them took a motor ride down the coast, with Joe in the driving seat. When Rose questioned this arrangement, finding Joe's presence slightly embarrassing, Bryce was most insistent.

'But if I have to drive then I can't sit in the back with you and hold your hand.'

Blushing prettily, Rose said no more.

Joe, naturally, had no choice but to obey, but his glum expression spoke volumes, making it perfectly clear to Rose that her old friend strongly disapproved of the amount of time she was spending with Bryce Tregowan. This worried her slightly. If Joe became too jealous she feared he might do something foolish, such as blurt out the truth. No, surely not! He would never do such a thing. Not least because it would hurt himself as much as her. Rose brushed aside these concerns and continued to enjoy the day.

He stopped the motor, when instructed, at various vantage points along the way to allow them to admire the views, or explore small fishing villages. The tour ended at St Jean de Luz where they enjoyed lunch at a delightful fish restaurant close to the picturesque harbour.

The attention Bryce was giving her, his flattering compliments and flirtatious manner were a complete revelation to Rose, totally unexpected, and his behaviour that of the perfect gentleman. He even apologised for the kiss.

She looked shyly up at him through her lashes. 'Apology accepted.'

'Of course, I'm never quite sure whether it is correct for a gentleman to apologise for a kiss which gave him so much pleasure.'

Rose giggled. 'Perhaps a gentleman wouldn't have stolen one in the first place.'

'Ah, but where is the romance in asking permission? My only excuse is that I was overcome by your charm, and by the excitement of seeing your bare foot.'

Rose burst out laughing. 'Do stop teasing, you wicked man.'

She could almost sense Joe's groan of quiet fury.

'I'm so glad I found you,' he said, as later they strolled together arm in arm along the quay, watching the colourful fishing boats come and go. They explored the cobbled streets and charming town squares, admiring the Basque architecture and pretty little cottages with their red-tiled roofs. 'I'm so glad you came into my life.'

Rose said, 'I'm not so sure that's what you were thinking when first you saw me in Bristol. Not a word of welcome, only complaints about the amount of luggage I'd brought. You were really rather horrid. Quite cold and brusque.'

Bryce grinned down at her, giving her arm a little squeeze. 'I had other matters on my mind at the time. Besides, I didn't know you then. Nor did I entirely trust you.'

Her heart gave an extra little beat. 'And do you trust me now?'

'Absolutely.' He lightly brushed her cheek with the back of his knuckles. 'I think you're very sweet. Utterly irresistible. I believe I have been searching for you all my life. How can you not be entirely trustworthy?'

Oh, how could she tell him that he'd been right to distrust her, that she'd told him a whole string of lies? 'I think you like to flatter.'

He paused to slip his arm lightly about her waist as he looked deeply into her eyes, his expression uncharacteristically serious. 'You can be sure I would never say anything I didn't mean, Rose. Honest John, that's me. Did you know that you have the most glorious eyes, such a stunning chocolate brown.'

She felt as if she were drowning in his gaze. Desire was strong in her as she instinctively leant into him, lifting her face in an open invitation for him to kiss her, which he then proceeded to do. A slow, lingering kiss that set her very soul on fire. Rose could no longer deny the truth: she was falling in love with Bryce Tregowan, the man she had cheated and deceived. And were he ever to discover the depth of that deceit, it would be the end of any hope of happiness between them.

'You realise you're making a complete exhibition of yourself? Not to mention putting our safety at risk.'

Rose met Joe's anger with calm dignity. This confrontation was not unexpected, but nor did she welcome his interference. 'I believe I may be allowed to do as I please without asking your permission, Joe Colbert, much as I might value your opinion in other matters. Besides, I thought our safety depends on my "playing the part" as you termed it. Isn't that what I'm doing?'

They were standing in the hotel lobby outside the dining room, speaking in hushed, furious tones. 'No,' he hissed, the green flecks in his grey eyes glinting with anger. 'You're playing with fire. You're taking unnecessary risks by getting too close to Bryce Tregowan. He'll start asking personal questions, if he hasn't already, or grow too curious about your background.' He ran agitated fingers through his hair, now more tidily cut, as decreed by Lady Tregowan. 'Maybe it's time we stopped this lark, and slipped quietly away while we still can.'

Rose gasped. 'And abandon little Robbie? Never! This

charade has gone on too long for us to simply walk away. We're in it too deep now to call a halt.' The thought of slipping away with Joe anywhere filled Rose with fear and horror. How could she bear to leave Robbie, her son in all but name? And a second fear was growing alongside the first. How could she live if she never saw Bryce again?

'Mark my words, this will all end in tears,' Joe warned.

'It's a little too late to realise that now. I believe I said as much right at the start,' Rose yelled back at him, angry that he should blame her.

Slapping one hand over her mouth to silence her, he pushed her back into the shadows. 'Shut up, you silly fool, or someone will come to see why you're shouting.'

'I'm not shouting,' Rose hissed back at him, shoving him off her. 'But who got us into this mess in the first place? Not me.'

'Sucking up to Bryce Tregowan isn't going to help. Anyway, I thought you were my girl. We're a team, you and me.'

All the temper drained out of her, as it always did with Joe. She could never stay angry with him for long, particularly when she saw the depth of his misery. 'Oh, Joe, don't start that again. Look, I'm sorry if you feel a bit jealous, but there's never been anything between you and me. We're just friends. I made that clear when you first expressed a desire to come with us to America. I do understand, and feel sorry for you, but fighting each other isn't going to help.'

'Drat you, Rose, when I want your pity I'll ask for it.' Then slamming her back against the wall, he kissed her.

It was a kiss as far removed from the one Bryce had given her as it could possibly be. His mouth on hers was savage, cruelly taking what he wanted without any consideration for her feelings, nor the slightest finesse.

But even as Rose fought him, a voice rang out. 'What on earth is going on here?'

Managing to free herself, Rose turned at the sound of the familiar voice, her face aflame with embarrassment and anger. Dear heaven, now what should she do? But then she thought, what would dear Rosalind do? 'Gwenna, thank goodness!'

Letting out a snort of rage, Joe stormed off.

Gwenna ran at once to her side. 'What was he doing to you, Rose? Are you all right?'

Rose allowed Gwenna to lead her to a chair, the lounge apparently empty and cast in gloom as most of the lamps were switched off, everyone having gone in to dinner. 'Joe does rather appear to have lost his head, but I'm fine, thank you, Gwenna.' She felt very far from fine. Rose found that her heart was beating with breathless rage against her ribcage. She would like to have smacked Joe's face had she been able. Oh, why did Gwenna have to appear at precisely that moment, although it could have been worse, she supposed. If it had been Jago who'd found them, for instance.

'I'm sorry you had to witness that, but I'm afraid Joe has had rather a crush on me for some time. I hoped that if I ignored it, the problem would go away of its own accord.'

Much as Rose hated to put all the blame on to Joe,

she couldn't think what else to do. He had ever been a wild card, and obstinately determined to mire them in this stupid charade, now caring more for the easy life he'd carved out for himself than any possible repercussions that might come her way. He appeared to have lost all common sense.

'You must dismiss him, of course.'

Rose was devastated, knowing she daren't allow that to happen. If Joe was cast out or ostracised, who knew what he might do. 'There's really no need. I'm sure he'll be full of apologies come morning.'

'There is every need. I shall speak to Jago forthwith.' Gwenna turned on her heel, as if about to go to him that very minute. Rose quickly grasped her arm.

'No, please, I beg you not to do that, for my sake. Jago may dismiss him while we're here, on the Continent, and how would Joe get home?'

'That is surely his problem.'

'But he has no money, no means of paying for his own fare. He has been with me a long time, always a good and loyal servant, I can't simply abandon him. I will speak to him tomorrow, make it clear he has overstepped the mark and that his job hangs in the balance. I'm sure it was merely a momentary aberration. We have been through a great deal together: the death of my husband, the birth of my child on board ship, and he is extremely protective of me. Perhaps it is as much my fault as his, for letting him believe he can take liberties. You can safely leave me to deal with this matter, Gwenna. He is my manservant, after all.' This last was a desperate attempt to cling on to her only weapon, that of her alleged status as Lady Tregowan.

Gwenna had remained silent throughout, looking rather thoughtful as Rose made her case. Had she convinced her? Rose worried. Would the ploy work or would she go straight to Jago and have Joe sent packing?

'Very well, if you insist. I will leave the matter to you and say nothing, for the moment. But I beg you, Rose, do not ever be alone with the fellow again. Who knows what might have happened had I not chanced to pass by.'

Rose managed a tremulous smile, drawing in a steadying breath as she saw that she might have won a stay of execution. 'You are quite right, and I will certainly take heed of your advice. Thank you, Gwenna, for being so understanding.' And to cement their agreement, Rose hugged her. Not that the girl reciprocated the gesture with any degree of enthusiasm or warmth, their so-called friendship being quite shallow and somewhat distant, but nor did she resist. 'Now let us go into dinner, shall we, or they'll be wondering what has happened to us.'

As the two young women strolled off, arm in arm, ostensibly in agreement, an unseen figure, who had been quietly engaged in reading the daily newspaper in a winged chair set with its back to them a few feet away, quietly folded it and set it down on a nearby table. There was a smile on his face, for he realised the importance of what he'd just overheard between the two women. Enough to tell him it might well prove advantageous when he made his own move.

* * *

That evening they were visiting the hotel casino, the gaming tables already busy by the time the party arrived. Boule, roulette anglaise, blackjack and many other games were on offer. Lady Tregowan, looking even more glamorous than usual in a red and black silk gown, was already installed at the roulette table, a pile of chips in front of her. Gwenna was at once eager to join her and excitedly dashed off to purchase some chips for herself. Rose declared she had no interest in taking part and declined Bryce's offer to buy some for her.

'I shall be happy to simply watch others play,' she told him.

'Then stand behind me. You might bring me luck.'

She laughed. 'I very much doubt it. I know nothing about gambling.'

'Nevertheless I would be happier if you were close by,' he told her, and they exchanged a smile which seemed to say everything. Whatever was developing between them brought a pulse of excitement to the pit of her stomach.

A glance passed between Lydia and her elder son. 'Rose, dear, if you aren't playing yourself, would you kindly slip along to my room for my stole? My bare shoulders feel rather chilly and I foolishly left it lying on my bed. It won't take you a moment.'

'Of course. My pleasure.' And Rose set off at once to do as she was asked.

'I rather think the pleasure might be all mine,' Jago murmured in his mother's ear, and as Bryce sauntered away to the blackjack table, he turned on his heel and followed in Rose's wake.

She'd just gathered up the lacy black stole and was about to make her way back to the casino when the door of Lydia's bedroom opened and Jago entered, closing it softly behind him. Fear shot through her like the thrust of a sword. 'Jago, what are you doing here?'

His smile offered little reassurance. 'I came to help.'

'I really don't need any help, thank you. I have your mother's stole right here. Now, if you don't mind, I'll take it to her.' She took a step forward but he blocked the door, barring her exit.

'What's the hurry? I thought you and I could take this opportunity for a little private chat. I've been watching you closely these last months.' Reaching out a hand, he tucked a straying curl behind her ear. Rose shuddered.

'I really can't think why.' In her heart, Rose feared she knew only too well.

'Don't you?'

He was standing so close to her that she could smell the cigar on his breath that he'd enjoyed after dinner. With Bryce such intimacy would not be unpleasant, would in fact kindle desire in her; with Jago it only increased her sense of loathing for this man.

'Why would I? Please, stand aside, you know how Lydia hates to be kept waiting.'

'She won't mind in the least, not on this occasion.' He held up both hands, as if to stay her. 'There's something I need to say first, by way of apology. I know we didn't hit it off too well at the start, what with all that business of my taking little Robbie out without your permission, then the Carwyn family being threatened with eviction. Of course, you didn't properly understand how things are done at Penver Court, how I'm the one to make all the important decisions, with no need to ask permission of anyone. But we'll let that pass for the moment, as I confess you've quite won me over. The fact is I've utterly lost my heart to you, dear girl. You really are quite enchanting.'

Rose stared at him in disbelief. 'What nonsense is this?'

He made as if to touch her cheek, but Rose took a hasty step back, avoiding his hand. His thin lips curled into a parody of a smile, his voice dangerously soft as he continued. 'You and I were meant to be together. Fate has decreed it.'

'I don't understand a word you are saying.' Rose could feel herself start to tremble, fear and anger battling for dominance as she struggled to hold on to her failing control.

'I believe you understand only too well. You enjoy acting the siren to both Bryce and myself. Playing one brother off against the other, eager to safely bed yourself in, one might say.' He laughed at his own wit.

Rose gasped, 'That is a lie. I have done no such thing.'

'Have you not? I wonder. But you are an expert in lies. You cannot deny that. Hasn't there been a whole string of them since you arrived?'

At this charge the blood seemed to drain from her face, leaving her chilled and more frightened than ever. *He must know*, she thought. He has discovered the truth.

He pushed his face down to within inches of her own, almost spitting out his next words. 'All this fantasy about your son being the new baronet. A likely tale. You're a

215

chancer, that's what you are, and your lover is in cahoots with you. I heard you talking to Gwenna before dinner, making excuses for him having kissed you, still insisting he's your manservant when it is perfectly plain to me that the pair of you are complete frauds. You married Sir Ralph's son because you knew he didn't have long to live, and thought you could land a plump inheritance for your bastard child.'

Her heart was pounding so loudly by this time, Rose felt sure Jago must be able to hear it. Yet he didn't have it quite right. This was but a repeat of earlier accusations. He'd learnt nothing new, and certainly not the truth. Gathering her courage about her, she met his gaze unflinching. 'I shall listen to no more of this drivel. If you do not let me pass I shall be obliged to call for assistance.'

'And how will you do that, pray? Why don't you scream? There's no one around to hear.'

Aware of the bell pull by Lady Tregowan's bed, Rose quickly turned to reach for it. But she'd taken no more than a couple of steps when his arms came about her, and pulling her down on to the bed he rolled on top of her. Rose cried out in alarm as he tore at her silk bodice, ripping the sleeve from her shoulder. His hands seemed to be everywhere, fondling her breasts, pulling up her skirts, then attempting to capture her wrists as Rose frantically fought to stop him.

Now she did scream. Long and loud. Jago slapped her hard across the face, which certainly silenced her but only fuelled her anger to new heights. Rage rose in her, hot and livid.

'So what are you going to do now?' she almost spat at him. 'Have your wicked way with me? What then? If I'm the scheming liar you claim me to be, do you imagine for one minute such an assault would persuade me to marry you? Aren't I already a fallen woman in your eyes, so why would I worry about a little tumble among the bed sheets?'

'You'd care enough if it bore fruit.'

'Only if I'm innocent and not the slut you paint me.'

Clearly unused to women who answered back, her blunt challenge momentarily startled him. Even so, he snorted with laughter as he pushed his hand between her legs, fondling that secret place that no one but herself had ever touched. It was too much for Rose. She had been brought up in one of the roughest areas in Bristol, and well knew how to stand up for herself. His other hand was coiling a lock of her hair, and twisting round her head she bit down hard on whatever part of it she could reach, which happened to be his little finger.

His shout of agony was a delight to her ears. Rose held on to the digit for several long seconds before finally letting go, spitting out the blood and wiping her mouth with the back of her hand. As he rolled off her, swearing and cursing, Rose snatched up her bag, and Lydia's stole, and fled, pausing only long enough at the door to issue one last warning.

'Touch me again and I'll make you really sorry.' Then she left him bent double on the floor nursing his stricken finger.

Chapter Fifteen

'You've changed your gown.' Bryce considered her with a curious glance.

'I accidentally caught the sleeve and ripped it on the door handle when I was hurrying to fetch Lydia's stole. Sorry to have kept you all waiting. What game are you playing?' The last thing Rose wanted was to create a fuss. The least said about that unpleasant incident, the better.

'Blackjack, but I assure you I do not consider myself an expert. I leave such claims to my brother. Where is he, by the way? I thought he was at the roulette table with Mama, but I don't see him.'

'I am here, right behind you, come to challenge you at blackjack.'

Bryce frowned, glancing from one to the other of them as Jago strolled to the table, clearly coming from the same direction of the lobby as Rose had only minutes earlier. 'Where have you been?'

'About some personal business, if you must know.' And turning his pale gaze directly upon Rose made his meaning all too clear.

A tide of colour washed over Bryce's throat and his jaw tightened with an iron rigidity as he turned a questioning glare upon Rose. Quelled by the fury in those charcoal eyes, she could find no words to defend herself or explain.

'Very well, I accept the challenge,' Bryce announced, a bitter edge to his tone. 'But I set a limit on my losses.'

'Ever the coward,' Jago caustically remarked.

'Not at all, it's because I've more sense than to risk losing more than I can afford. This is a fool's game in which only the banker is the winner.'

Jago snorted his derision. 'More likely you see yourself as a loser. Whereas I always get what I want, one way or another.'

Again he was gazing at Rose as he said this, and she felt herself go quite cold. But what could she do? She could hardly accuse him of attempted rape before complete strangers gathered here simply to have a good time. The very idea of making such a charge, possibly resulting in the police being called, was more than she could contemplate. And how Bryce might react to such a declaration didn't bear thinking of.

Pretending she had not seen this telling glance, she took up a stance behind Bryce's shoulder, and forced herself to become absorbed in watching the game. It seemed to be one of chance as much as skill, and the tension between the two brothers increased with each new round of cards dealt, Jago constantly challenging Bryce, or jeering at him when he lost.

'Give him another hit, dealer. Oh dear, bust again.'

'Such is the luck of the game.'

'Now what else do I have besides this queen, do you reckon?'

'Why not show us so that we can find out?' Bryce calmly asked.

'What will you give to see them?'

Bryce laughed. 'Nothing more than is already on the table.'

'Coward!' And Jago slammed down his cards to furiously reveal that on this occasion he was the one who was bust, which amused Bryce all the more. Jago was not amused, and the tension between them mounted still further. As did the stakes, for, despite his protests, Bryce found himself driven to raise them more than he would have wished.

'I think that's enough,' he said at last, after a further loss.

'I thought you liked to play the hero in front of the ladies,' Jago said, casting a sideways sneer in Rose's direction.

'Bryce has nothing to prove on my account,' she bravely stated, wishing she could find some way to explain to him that things were not quite as they appeared, that she had not been willingly engaged in an assignation with Jago, as he clearly assumed.

Jago kept his narrowed gaze fixed on his brother. 'But

then she might be more impressed by my performance, rather than yours. Perhaps in other games as well as blackjack.'

Bryce tossed down his cards and got abruptly to his feet as Jago laughed out loud.

'Surely you aren't going to walk away and leave me with all of this?' Jago indicated the pile of chips on the table before him. 'One last game, double or quits. If you've run out of money I could always take something else in its place. Or maybe I've helped myself to it already, as I so like to do.' Again glancing meaningfully at Rose.

'That's not true,' Rose gasped, horrified he should say such things in public. Even Lydia and Gwenna had strolled over by this time to see what all the fuss was about. She had never felt more embarrassed or compromised in her life. Bryce, she could see, was clearly seething.

'Damn you to hell!'

'We'll play again,' Jago instructed the dealer, who dutifully dealt the cards, placing his own first card face up, but not yet playing his second as he waited for the players to make their decisions.

Bryce tapped the table, indicating he wanted a third card, and Rose could see how his jaw tightened as he considered his hand, the silence of the interested spectators about the table heavy with anxiety on his behalf. At length he tapped for another card. It was a two.

'Would you care to double the stakes again?' Jago asked, his voice little more than a purr.

'Don't take the risk,' Rose murmured in Bryce's ear, flustered by this undercurrent of fury building between the brothers. How on earth could she stop it?

Bryce ignored her, doubled the stakes and took another card, much to his brother's amusement.

'So what do you have? Show me.'

'I believe you should go first.'

A long pause as Jago met his brother's gaze with a scathing challenge in his own. 'I don't really care whether I win or lose. I already have everything I need to make your life worthless, brother. Which was ever my ambition. By right of age and status I shall take what was promised me – my rightful inheritance – one way or another. And whatever you have I shall take too, even your women. As I say, maybe I've taken one already, willingly offered.'

Bryce came out of his seat like a Termagant from hell, and launched himself at Jago. Within seconds the pair were wrestling, scattering cards and chips everywhere as first one, then the other brother, was pinned to the table. Then they were rolling on the floor, and the entire room was in uproar. People were crowding around to watch the melee, Gwenna in floods of tears while Rose desperately shouted at them to stop.

It was all over in minutes, of course. The croupiers, being well accustomed to such brawls, were upon them to stop the fight immediately, with reinforcements quickly summoned. Both brothers were ignominiously banished, with orders to cool down before they returned.

As the fascinated spectators reluctantly drifted back to their own gaming tables, gossiping and laughing at the thrill of such a disgraceful incident, Rose put her hands to her hot cheeks in despair. What on earth was going on? Why had Jago suddenly taken it upon himself to attack her, and then challenge his brother with the lie that his advances had been welcomed? What did he hope to gain by such behaviour?

Only then did she notice that throughout the fight between her sons, Lydia had stood silently by, saying nothing. Even as she calmly strolled away to continue with her game of roulette, she said not a word of disapproval towards Rose, which was decidedly odd.

What wouldn't she give to know what was running through that woman's mind right now.

Rose hurried after Bryce as he stormed through the lobby, frantically calling to him, but he ignored her and strode out into the garden. Breathing hard, she pulled to a halt. 'Aren't you even going to ask for my version of what happened?'

He stopped dead but kept his back to her. 'Is it worth hearing?' His words came out clipped and hard.

The moon was high in a midnight-blue sky as Rose calmly went to stand before him. She quailed slightly when she saw the fury in his face, looking as if he might explode at any moment. 'Jago may be your brother but why would you take his word against mine, if, as you've already told me, the pair of you don't get on?'

'I didn't hear you protesting your innocence back there.'

His tone remained cutting but she could see the pain in his eyes, and softened her own as a result. 'And make an even greater spectacle of myself by provoking an argument in public? Matters were deteriorating quickly enough as it was. I'll tell you now, in private, if you're prepared to listen. Your brother followed me to Lydia's room and made advances which I assure you were neither invited nor welcomed.'

His eyes widened in dawning comprehension. 'Dear God, and you changed your gown. You said you'd accidentally torn the sleeve. He did that, didn't he? What the hell did he do to you? Drat him, I'll make him sorry he ever—'

'Please, no!' Rose quickly put out a hand, fearful the fight might be about to start all over again. 'Nothing serious happened. Let it go. I'm sure it was no more than an aberration on his part, a stupid show of macho bravado. I assure you he will not risk it again. I made him pay for his folly.'

'What did you do?'

'I bit his little finger, enough to make him yelp, and put a stop to his ardour.'

Bryce looked at her in stunned silence for a moment, then gently drew her into his arms, chuckling softly. 'You are a treasure beyond words. Most women would weep or faint, but you instantly retaliate and go on the attack. What a woman! Now I know why I love you.' Then he was kissing her, his mouth claiming hers, the sound of the waves rushing on the nearby shore seeming to echo in her ears as riotous emotions flooded through her.

When they drew apart to catch their breath, she softly said, 'You shouldn't say such a thing unless it is true.'

He kissed her nose, his gaze warm and loving. 'You must know that it's true. Haven't you been aware from the first that there's something special between us? Please don't say you feel nothing for me, or I'd have to go away for ever, as I'd never be able to see you every day knowing there was no hope for me.'

'Oh no, don't do that.' Her arms went about his neck, running her fingers through his hair. 'Don't ever go away.' Rose was kissing him now, punctuating dozens of tender kisses with protestations of her love. 'I do feel something for you, very much so. I do, I do.'

He sighed with pleasure. 'That's all right, then.' He led her to a quiet bench beneath a palm where his kisses grew ever more passionate, Rose responding eagerly, desire strong in her. His hand strayed to her breast, caressing the bare flesh that rose above her gown, then suddenly he pulled away on a groan of agony. 'Now it is I who am behaving like a brute.'

She cradled his face between her palms. 'Never. This is altogether different to what Jago did to me. Quite the opposite, as I welcome your embrace.'

He got to his feet, her hand still held gently in his. 'Nevertheless, I want no gossip circulating about you. I will not have your reputation ruined by any of my doing. We'll talk another time. For now, make sure you are never alone with Jago.'

'I promise.'

With his arm about her waist, Bryce escorted her safely back to her room.

Tucked away in the conservatory, two figures were engaged in a heated conversation. 'Was that true what you said in there just now? Have you really "helped yourself" to Rose? Did you take her – seduce her – while you were both out of the room? *Tell me*!' Gwenna was so distressed she was almost spitting with fury, quite unlike her usual giddy, careless self. Jago sat on a wrought iron chair with his head in his hands, nursing his bruised ego as much as anything else.

At length, in his own good time, he raised his head to gaze upon her with contempt. 'And what if I did? What has that to do with you?'

Gwenna slapped his face. Never had she done such a thing in her entire life before, wouldn't have dared to do so now had she not been out of her mind with rage and jealousy. 'You know full well what it has to do with me. Haven't you been bedding me for months now? Taking me in the orchard, on the beach, on your *desk*, wherever you fancy. And aren't I now carrying your child as a result?'

He looked at her, shock registering on his face, although only momentarily before it changed to its usual expression of sneering indifference. 'And what the hell do you expect me to do about that? You surely don't think for a moment that I would marry you?'

Gwenna sank to her knees before him, putting her hands to her mouth in shock. The next instant she flew at him, her small fists beating furiously on his chest. 'But you promised! You promised me most faithfully.'

Taking hold of her wrists he flung her off. 'I never did any such thing. You're a stupid, naive girl, if rather generous with your charms, but I see no ring on your finger. There has been no announcement in *The Times*.

Not that I'm aware of. I'll admit I did consider the possibility of marrying you at one time, as your fortune is not unsatisfactory. The fact is, I can do better, do you see?' He got to his feet, towering over her as he so liked to do. 'I'm sorry, but that's how it is. Whatever you can offer doesn't bear comparison with the fortune I gain by marrying Rose.'

'She'll never agree to marry you,' Gwenna spat.

'I'll make damn sure that she does,' came the cold response. 'I mean to have her, and when have I ever failed to get what I want?'

Gwenna seemed to visibly shrink before him, her voice now a pitiful murmur, hands clasped together almost in supplication. 'Please, I beg you, don't do this to me, Jago. You can't just abandon me. You said you loved me.'

His gaze was mocking, his tone cold as ice. 'Love is one thing, marriage quite another entirely. You must appreciate that I cannot possibly risk losing Penver Court. That would be unthinkable.'

'But my reputation will be destroyed, my dreams shattered. I'll be a fallen woman! No one will marry me now. I shall be ruined!'

Jago gave a careless shrug. 'The choice was yours, darling.'

'I had no choice, you f–forced me. When I said n–no, you just carried on.' She leapt to her feet, clawing at his face, and again Jago heartlessly thrust her away, so that she fell against a huge earthenware pot to fall sobbing on to the tiled floor.

'Control yourself, woman, you're growing hysterical.'

He turned to leave but she made a grab for his ankle, sprawled in a most unladylike fashion at his feet, still begging and pleading through her tears. 'Don't leave me. I love you, Jago. I'll be a good wife to you, I swear you won't ever regret marrying me. You *promised* you would marry me once the period of mourning for Sir Ralph was over.'

He kicked out at her, as if she were no more than an irritating puppy, then pinched one small plump cheek between his fingers and laughed in her face. 'You were a willing – nay, an eager – participant, my sweet, however your addled imagination might pretend otherwise. If your dreams and reputation are shattered as a result of my need to keep Penver Court in the family, then so be it. It can't be helped. There is always a little collateral damage in any war, and that is most definitely what this is.'

Lydia was waiting for him in the lobby, stepping out from behind a palm as he came through the door. 'So, was it true, what you hinted at so boldly to your brother? Did you have your wicked way with dearest Rose? Is the deed done?'

Jago sighed. 'Not exactly, Mama. Sadly, things didn't quite go according to plan.'

'You surprise me. It is not like you to fail in a mission.'

'It was but a temporary setback, and Bryce doesn't know that I failed. Not after that fracas in the casino.'

'That was all rather vulgar, darling,' Lydia declared, kissing him on the cheek. 'Try to do better next time, will you? I would like your engagement announced before we

228

leave Biarritz. And I really don't care how you achieve that. Now I must retire. It has really been rather a tiring evening, one way or another. Apart from anything else, the dice were definitely not rolling my way.' She was about to leave but his next words gave her pause.

'We have a problem.'

'Oh?'

He told her bluntly about Gwenna. 'The girl insists the child is mine.'

The sudden spurt of anger in his mother's pale-blue eyes chilled him to the core. No one could make him quake quite as much as Lydia. 'You fool! Didn't I tell you to leave the girl alone? I'd even found her a likely husband, the second son of an Irish lord, would you believe? Quite a catch. He won't look at her now, of course. What an idiot you are! I will not have Gwenna ruined. She may be somewhat stupid, but she doesn't deserve to have her reputation quite done in. How very annoying. Now I shall have to find some other solution. In future, you'd do well to follow my advice, instead of giving in to the urgent pangs in your breeches.'

The answer came to her as she sipped her morning chocolate, and Lydia wasted no time in sending for her younger son. Bryce came to stand before her, clearly expecting a dressing-down for his behaviour in the casino the previous evening. What his mother had to say, however, left him completely stunned.

'I beg your pardon? Say that again.'

Lydia sighed, and moving to her dressing stool began to smooth cream on to her face. She was ever rigorous in such matters, determined to cling on to her beauty for as long as possible. It had brought her a fortune thus far and may well earn her more in the future. Several gentlemen of means had shown interest in her already during the short time they'd been in Biarritz. 'I'm afraid Gwenna requires a husband, rather urgently, and I can think of no better person for the role than you.'

'You jest, of course. This must be some kind of joke.'

'I was never more serious.' She turned to smile up at him, hairbrush in hand as she teased the dark curls falling upon her shoulders. This was a task usually carried out by her maid, but, with this interview in mind, Lydia had temporarily dismissed the girl. 'I'm aware of the affection you feel for Rose. I've watched it grow between you in recent months, and thought it no bad thing. But on further consideration I have decided that it is only right and proper that your brother should take precedence. He is the elder, after all, and it is essential – vital, in fact – that we keep Penver Court and Sir Ralph's fortune within the family. I'm sure you understand how it is.

'Besides, you're quite fond of Gwenna, so it should be no great hardship being married to her. She's rather pretty, if a little too plump, but enormous fun. And if she lacks excitement in the bed department, you can always take a mistress.' She set down the brush with a sharp click. 'I shall make the announcement before we leave for England.'

'You will do no such thing.'

'I beg your pardon?'

'Mother, I am not a child, no longer some slip of a boy

whose life you can order to suit your bidding. I well recall how you packed me off to boarding school the moment I left the nursery, leaving me there for the long holidays too, on many occasions. Nor were my feelings or needs ever taken into account whenever you took it into your head to remarry for the umpteenth time. As a child I had no choice but to cope with your neglect and selfish lack of consideration, but I'll be damned if you'll organise my life now.'

'I can't believe what I'm hearing.' Tears welled in her eyes as she gazed up at him in stunned disbelief, although whether they were real or of the crocodile variety, Bryce didn't care to judge.

'Then allow me to repeat myself, Mama. I'm sorry to hear about Gwenna's little problem, but I can do nothing to assist her to resolve it.'

'*Little problem!* Is that what you call it? It's far more than that.'

'But it is not *my* problem. I suggest you place the blame for her condition squarely in the correct quarter. You certainly have no right to demand that I mop up my brother's leavings.'

'Jago will marry Rose, for the sake of the family and his inheritance.' Her tone now was unyielding, hissing the words at him, the tears quite dried up. 'So what is poor Gwenna to do then? The poor girl will be ruined.'

'Tell that to Jago, not me.'

At that moment the bedroom door burst open and Jago himself strode in. 'Do you know what the dratted girl has done now? She's only gone and drowned herself.'

Gwenna, it seemed, had resolved the problem.

Chapter Sixteen

The Tregowans were back home at Penver Court, their winter holiday cut short as they attempted to come to terms with Gwenna's shocking fate, still analysing what had gone so terribly wrong. It had become clear that she'd walked right out as far as the headland and thrown herself off the rocks.

'Why on earth would she do such a thing?' Rose asked, not for the first time.

'Because she had ruined herself.' Lydia let out an irritable sigh as she poured tea for the two of them in the small parlour, clearly bored with the subject. The absence of Gwenna from this daily ceremony was, to Rose at least, quite distressing. But, as with her own husband's death, Lydia showed not a trace of grief or regret for the loss of a girl for whom she had acted as mother. 'Her reputation was in ribbons. With no hope of an offer of marriage, she had nothing left to live for.'

Rose was outraged. 'That can't be right. This isn't the eighteenth century, or even the nineteenth. Surely in today's modern world people wouldn't cast a girl off simply because she makes one mistake.'

Lydia calmly selected a petit four. 'Not everyone possesses morals as lax as yourself, child.'

Rose stifled an irritated sigh. 'Maybe I have greater faith in the goodness of people than Gwenna. Besides, she could have gone away to have the child in secret, isn't that how things are done? She could have had it adopted.'

'You are familiar with such matters, I dare say.' Pale eyes glittered at her from above the rim of her cup.

'Of course not, but there are always solutions.'

'You resolved your own dilemma, of course, by finding yourself a rich husband, and in the nick of time. Most girls are not so fortunate, and these situations are not always easy to hush up.'

Furious that Lydia took every opportunity to attack her, Rose steeled herself not to react or rush to her own defence. She had learnt to her cost that this was always a bad mistake, as Bryce had once explained. 'What about the man responsible for her fall from grace? Why should he get off scot-free?'

'Men are weak creatures, ruled by their passions. It is the role of women to set the moral tone. Something you would do well to consider with care.'

'But why would he not marry her? Gwenna was pretty, and not without a dowry. Do you know who he was? Was it Jago? Gwenna told me they were about to become engaged.' Rose persisted, and then wished she hadn't as

Lydia slammed down her cup, nearly cracking it by the force with which it met the saucer.

'They were not. Absolute nonsense! You shouldn't believe everything that silly girl told you. Now I really must go as I have a funeral to arrange.' And off she strode in a lather of fury, as if Gwenna had killed herself simply in order to deliberately inconvenience Lydia.

'It's the way of the world,' Tilly said, when Rose asked her the same question. 'Don't men always get away with it?'

'But who do you think he was, the father of her child?' There was just the smallest worry at the back of Rose's mind that it might be Bryce. He'd always seemed rather fond of Gwenna, had enjoyed a close relationship with his cousin. She didn't dare risk asking him such a question outright, as he would no doubt be angry with her for not trusting him. And she did trust him, really she did, Rose told herself, not too convincingly.

The problem was that the feelings between them had blossomed only in the last few weeks, in the heady atmosphere of Biarritz, his declaration of love even more recent, and not repeated. She wasn't even certain he'd meant it, or that she'd heard correctly. What if Bryce had learnt of the girl's condition, and that was the reason he had suddenly turned to her, perhaps by way of escape. A horrible thought!

'It was most likely Jago,' Tilly calmly remarked as she handed over little Robbie, all newly changed and sweet-smelling, to Rose. 'He chases every bit of skirt he sees.'

Rose rocked the baby in her lap, letting out a small sigh of relief. 'That's true.' She was about to say that he'd once chased after her, but changed her mind, instead asking Tilly if she too had suffered at Jago's hand.

'Goodness, yes,' Tilly answered in a matter-of-fact way as she tidied away towels and dirty napkins. 'There isn't a maid in the house who hasn't been propositioned, or worse, by Jago. Not that anyone dares complain. He's the master, after all.'

'Not anymore, he isn't,' Rose said, kissing the baby's head. 'I wish I could find some way to get that important fact across to him.'

The funeral was a small private affair, for close family only, as Gwenna was too young to have made many acquaintances in the world. Far too young to be having a funeral at all. They should by rights be celebrating her wedding, but her two unsuccessful seasons in London had not brought forth the necessary proposal to answer her dreams, and now never would.

'It is so very sad,' Rose kept murmuring as the mournful little ceremony dragged on.

'A tragedy,' Bryce agreed. 'She was such a happy girl as a child. Pretty, and friendly, and always great fun, if a bit scatterbrained. Jago would tease her mercilessly, but she never complained. She absolutely adored him, then and now, and see what it has cost her.'

'Do you think he was responsible, and then rejected her?' Rose tentatively asked.

'I'm quite certain of it.' Bryce glanced at her, gently lowering her prayer book so that he could see her face properly. 'You surely didn't think for one moment it was me.'

'No, of course not,' Rose lied, her cheeks growing pink with guilt.

'Hmm, I rather hoped you'd have a better opinion of me than that.'

'Are you saying you would have offered to marry her, if it had been you?'

'I'm saying I would never ruin a young girl's reputation. A widow's neither,' he finished with a wicked smile. 'Much as I might be tempted to try.' For a moment Rose was at a loss to understand who he was referring to, before it dawned on her that the widow in question was herself, which flustered her for an entirely different reason.

The day following the service and interment, they took a walk together up to the headland, breathing in the thin warmth of winter sunshine. Bright-red berries clustered the holly bushes as they climbed the path through the copse, making Rose think of Christmas, which was almost upon them.

When they finally reached the top, they strolled along the cliff path, the sea like a sheet of chilled glass below, devoid of summer blue today, reflecting a bright, wintry sky. It still brought a shiver to her spine as Rose recalled the day Jago had risked little Robbie's life, as if he were of no account. A man without any morals, or sensitivity, so unlike his brother.

'Are you cold?' Noticing her shudder, he pulled her into his arms, wrapping her within the folds of his jacket. Pressed against his chest she felt warm and secure, safe from all her fears and worries.

'No, I was thinking how besotted Gwenna was with

Jago.' Rose resolutely pushed the memory of that day from her mind, as she had no wish to tell Bryce about the incident, thereby risking further friction between the two brothers. 'I always thought Jago was fond of her too. So why would he refuse to marry her, if they were so close?'

She felt the tension in his body, and glancing up saw how his jaw tightened in that familiar way Bryce had, yet he didn't answer her question. Instead he issued a warning. 'Do not attempt to challenge my brother on this matter. Don't ever ask him outright if he was the one responsible, or why he refused to make an honest woman of her.'

She turned in his arms to look at him askance. 'I would never dream of doing so.'

'Good. He's not a man who likes to be questioned on his actions. Nor does he take kindly to criticism.'

'I've learnt that lesson already when I crossed him over the eviction notice for the Carwyn family.'

'On that occasion you won. It wouldn't always be the case, and certainly not on an issue as sensitive as this one. As a matter of fact, I'd recommend you let the matter drop completely. My mother won't take kindly to being reminded of the scandal either, which does nothing for the Tregowan family reputation.'

'Scandal? Tregowan family reputation? Is that all she cares about?' Rose never ceased to be amazed by the woman. 'Isn't the loss of a young woman's life far more important?'

'Of course it is.' He tenderly hooked a curl behind her ear. 'But you have to understand that my mother views things rather differently. Family honour is all important to her, as are possessions. The same goes for my brother, whereas I much prefer people.' He stroked her cheek with one finger, slipping it under her chin to tilt up her face for a kiss.

'Is that people in general, or one in particular?' she teased, feeling weak at the knees as she always did when Bryce kissed her.

Taking her by the hand he led her over to sit on a fallen tree. Seated beside her he caught her hand in his, thoughtfully smoothing it with his thumb as he talked. 'What happened to Gwenna is a lesson to us all. Life is short and shouldn't be wasted. You know how I feel about you, Rose, or should do by now. I believe we became quite close while in Biarritz, and I flatter myself that you might care for me in the same way.'

She started to speak, anxious to assure him that she did indeed, but he stopped her words with the press of one finger to her lips. 'Pray allow me to finish, or I may lose courage altogether. Quite against a lifetime's determination to tread a solitary path through life, I now find that I am only truly happy when I'm with you. Would you, dearest Rose, do me the honour of becoming my wife, because I rather think I love you to distraction.'

'Oh!' was all she could manage.

Bryce waited for more, his expression growing anxious. 'Does that mean I misread your response entirely? Because if so then—'

'Oh, no, I just . . . I can't say how I . . . can't quite . . .'

He let out an exaggerated sigh, eyes glinting with merry humour. 'Is that a no or a yes?'

'No, I mean yes.' Laughing, she started again. 'I love

you so much I can't quite believe you truly feel the same.'

Now his eyes were alight with love, and something that could only be desire. 'Oh, I mean it all right. But I have no intention of jumping the gun, as Jago did. I shall make an honest woman of you first.'

Rose felt the sweetness of his touch run through her like fire as he kissed her, the beat of her heart escalating to match his. Her response was instinctive, born of the love she felt for him as she arched her body to meet his. She felt the persuasive gentling of his hand as it moved to slide the gown from her shoulder and softly cup her breast, leaving a burning desire in its wake. She was straining ever closer, kissing him with a kind of fevered desperation, her whole body trembling so violently she had little control over it. Nor did she wish to have. He took her lips with softly biting kisses and their mutual need flared to fresh heights, Rose wanting only for these beautiful sensations to go on and on and never stop.

At length he paused to smile down at her. 'The only thing I insist upon is that it be the shortest engagement in history, as I really can't hold myself in check for much longer.'

And judging by the kisses which followed, Rose rather thought she might have a similar problem.

It was an hour later when they strolled back into the courtyard, Rose's cheeks aglow, very much a match for her name, brown hair tumbling loose from the pins which held it. She caught sight of Joe lingering by the stable door and her heart plummeted. Oh dear, he would not take kindly to this news, but she would have to tell him herself. She couldn't have him finding out on the servant grapevine.

Bryce paused, his hand on her arm. 'There's just one thing I should have mentioned – warned you of – but, what with Gwenna's death, we've been rather preoccupied.'

'Can it wait a moment? I need to speak to Joe, let him down gently, you understand.'

'Ah, yes, I see. Of course, I understand perfectly. I'll speak to you later, then, my love. But don't be too soft with him. You have warned him many times in the past not to grow too fond of you.'

'I know, but he's my friend.'

Bryce frowned. 'He's your manservant.'

She kissed him on the nose. 'Can't he be both?'

'What a very singular woman you are,' and he strolled away chuckling.

Joe was in a less benign mood. 'Kissing him in public now, I see.'

'Joe, please don't start your bullying, not now. I've come to tell you something important.'

Folding his arms across his broad chest, he stood legs astride before her, an expression of obstinate disapproval on his round face. 'And what might that be?'

Ignoring the harshness of his tone, and the awkward stiffness of his body, Rose linked her arm in his and drew him into the warmth of the stable. The soft snicker of the horses was a comforting sound in the background, the smell of the saddle and harness he'd been polishing quite intoxicating. He'd left them lying in the straw, carelessly abandoned as he'd obviously rushed out into the yard at her arrival. Did he watch for her all the time? she wondered. Rose worried how best to approach what would undoubtedly be bad news, so far as Joe was concerned. The last thing she wanted was to alarm him, or spark a fresh bout of jealousy which might result in reprisals or a need for revenge. Rose felt far too enmeshed in her new life now to have Joe destroy it.

There was no place to sit, and stifling a nervous sigh, she turned to him with an anxious smile. 'There's no easy way to say this, so I'll come straight to the point. You will be aware that Bryce and I have grown close in recent months. Well, he has asked me to marry him, and I have accepted. I wanted you to be the first to know.'

Joe stared at her, unmoving, saying nothing . 'Are you mad?' he said at last.

'Only with love for Bryce. He is so sweet to me, you really wouldn't believe.' Her hands on his arms, still stubbornly folded across his chest, she gave them an affectionate squeeze. 'Please be happy for me, Joe. I know you're fond of me, but I did make it clear, even when we were still on Ellis Island, that I don't feel the same way. I know things are different now, that all of this business has changed our friendship somewhat, but I haven't changed my mind. You are a good and true friend, sadly that's all you are to me. I'm afraid I could never love you, not as I love Bryce.'

Joe absorbed this before snarling, 'You know why he's so sweet to you, don't you? Why he's asked to marry you? It's the only way he can get his scheming hands on the land and property.'

Rose froze, a spurt of anger starting up inside. This was even worse than she'd feared. 'I think you're confusing him with Jago. Bryce isn't like that. He's started his own business, a chandler's in Fowey.'

Joe made a scoffing sound in his throat. 'Fowey is a small town.'

'It has a very busy river.'

'Even if the business ever makes a profit, it would be nothing compared with an estate of a thousand acres and a dozen or more farms. Don't be naive, Rosie, he's a fortune-hunter after your inheritance.'

Had anyone else made this remark to her, she would have slapped his face. But this was Joe, her old friend feeling bitter over losing her, and the person who held her safety in his two hands. Rose's reply, however, was chilling.

'You're wrong. He loves me, and I love him. He is entirely trustworthy.'

'But does he know that you aren't?'

Rose flinched, but chose to ignore the remark. 'I do hope you can be happy for us, Joe. In any case, I thought you were rather sweet on Tilly these days. She certainly talks a lot about you. I do want you to be happy too.'

'I can't ever be that, Rosie, while you behave so recklessly, that's asking too much. And what about this situation we're in?'

'What about it?'

'Have you confessed, have you told him that you aren't who you claim to be, *My Lady*?'

A familiar sick feeling came into her stomach. 'Joe, don't

ever speak of that. We agreed we'd never refer to it again. It was you who got us into this mess in the first place, and I, like a fool and for the sake of Robbie, went along with it. Now it's far too late to start revealing the truth.'

'Aye, that would be most uncomfortable for you, wouldn't it, Rosie love?'

Fear was growing in her, one she was having trouble suppressing. 'What are you saying? Is this meant to be some sort of threat?'

His mouth twisted into a most unpleasant smile that reminded her more of Jago than the Joe she'd known all her life. 'And if it were?'

'Then I'd warn you that you'd be putting yourself in as much danger as me, were you to come clean. A confession now would result in both of us being thrown in clink. How would you like that?'

'It might be worth it, to deprive Bryce of taking you to his bed.'

'Stop this, Joe!' Anger coursed through her, banishing the fear. 'You don't mean any of this. You're just upset. I can understand you must be disappointed, and I am so very sorry to have hurt you. But I promise you there will always be a good job for you here, for as long as you want it.'

'Oh, well, that's all right then, *My Lady*. Everything's fine, isn't it? I'd best be about my work then, if'n you please, ma'am.' And giving a mocking tug to his forelock, he strode away to tend to the horses, which weren't in need of any attention at all. Rose took the hint and marched off in something of a huff.

Out in the courtyard the front door suddenly opened.

'Ah, Rose, there you are. I've been searching for you everywhere,' Lydia called with some impatience. 'Might I have a word? Now, if you please.'

With a weary sigh, Rose followed her into the house.

They were again sitting in the small parlour as they did every afternoon, except that this time instead of tea and petits fours, there was a bottle of champagne and three glasses set out on the small round table before them. Rose stared at these for a moment, perplexed, as she knew of no celebration due, not when yet again the family had been thrust into mourning. But then Lydia started talking and she forgot all about them.

'May I begin by saying that you seem now to quite belong here at Penver Court, settling in far better than I initially anticipated.'

Rose was pleased by this compliment, if rather surprised by it. This woman was to become her mother-in-law, after all, so it was important that they get along. 'It's most kind of you to say so. It was somewhat overwhelming at first, but I do feel more at home now. And I've come to love the place as much as you.'

Lydia glanced at her with a scathing expression on her face, eyebrows raised. 'Hardly; you are still a newcomer, still a stranger here, but behaving better than expected.'

The woman had such a gift for turning flattery into an insult.

'Obviously it hasn't been easy for us,' she continued. 'We are Sir Ralph's new family, after all, his own having let him down badly.'

Rose bit back an instinctive urge to defend Rosalind's husband which naturally sprang to her lips. But perhaps Robert had let his father down in some way, although such behaviour didn't entirely fit the picture Rosalind had given of him. However, it was all in the past now, and she didn't know the whole story. Nor was it any of her business. Rose clasped her hands in her lap and put a polite smile on her face, wishing she'd been allowed a moment to tidy herself before this unexpected interview.

'The fact of the matter is, that as a family we have no wish to involve ourselves in long drawn-out disputes over that ridiculous will. There is a much better way in which to resolve the problem.'

'Oh, and what problem would that be, exactly?'

'Please don't try to be clever, dear. You know full well.'

Genuinely mystified, Rose protested. 'I'm afraid I don't. I believed all that business of the will was settled last year, by the family solicitor. What more is there to say?'

Lydia primmed her mouth, and then forced it into a stiff smile. 'Everything. You can't imagine we would welcome being passed over for a child that may not even be legitimate. Wrayworth may have accepted young Robbie without the necessary documentary evidence of his birth, but the rest of us are less easily satisfied. But as I say, we have no wish to resort to law as only the lawyers would benefit, and the inheritance, such as it is, would rapidly vanish into their pockets.'

Now she stood up, and walking over to the bell pull that hung by the fireplace, gave it a sharp tug. 'It is in your own best interests that we do not pursue the case, for in the end we'd be sure to win, albeit at considerable cost. I'm sure you have no wish to see your son turned away without a penny, or yourself accused of fraud. Who knows where you might end up?'

A numbness had come over Rose as she listened, a terror growing in her. Had Jago been snooping among her things? Was she about to be unmasked?

'My elder son has undoubtedly been usurped from his rightful inheritance, yet ousting your child would destroy the very inheritance we are trying to protect. Therefore, the solution is obvious. You and Jago must marry. He is willing to accept your child, bastard or no, as the new baronet, if he may maintain his rightful position as master of the estate until the child comes of age, and thereafter is granted not only a proper allowance but several of the farms and holdings by way of compensation. There, is that not the perfect solution for us all?'

While Rose sat in stunned silence, too shocked to think of any immediate response, Lydia moved briskly to the small table and indicated a pile of papers which Rose hadn't noticed before.

'I have had the necessary documents drawn up for you to sign. I think a matrimonial agreement of vital importance where property is concerned. Marriage is a matter of business, after all. Jago will be here at any moment. All you have to do is sign, and the engagement will be announced.' She was already reaching for the champagne bottle. 'Normally one would not contemplate celebrating a wedding while in mourning, but Gwenna's death was rather different, so I'm sure we can ignore such rules for once.'

Rose was thinking that there had been no unmasking, as she had feared, no revelation of the truth. Although Lydia questioned her authenticity, she hadn't a clue why. Even so, Rose was quite certain that had she opened her mouth at this point, nothing but a squeak of horror would have come from it.

The door opened and Jago entered, an air of triumph evident in the way he swaggered over to his mother, took the champagne bottle from her hand and easily popped the cork with which she'd been struggling. Pouring out three glasses, he handed one to Rose.

'To a successful alliance.' Raising the glass to his lips, he drank half of its contents in one gulp. Rose, having finally come to grips with the shock, calmly set her glass down on the table untouched.

'I'm afraid there's been some mistake. It isn't Jago I intend to marry, but your other son, Bryce. He has already asked me, and I have accepted.'

Chapter Seventeen

With one furious flick of his hand, Jago swept the champagne bottle and Rose's goblet from the table, shattering splinters of glass all over the Persian carpet. 'If you think you can cast me off, marry my brother *and* deprive me of my rightful inheritance, then you are very much mistaken.'

'You expect my son to stand by and say nothing while he is effectively robbed?' Lydia snapped, her face quite purple with rage.

Rose was desperately hanging on to her rapidly failing courage, heartily wishing she'd kept her mouth shut and left it to Bryce to make the announcement. She had not expected the news to be welcomed with unalloyed rapture, but not for a moment had she reckoned on this reaction. But despite the delicacy of her situation, she had no intention of allowing herself to be bullied.

'I've done nothing to encourage such a proposal from Jago. Nor have *I* robbed him of anything.' This much at least was true. 'The decision over who should inherit Penver Court was made by Sir Ralph, not by me. I had absolutely no say in the matter, or influence over him. And you are absolutely wrong about Robbie, he is most definitely Sir Ralph's grandson and the rightful heir.'

'We have only your word for that,' snarled Jago.

'Which is no recommendation,' his mother added. 'You haven't even provided us with the necessary documentary proof.'

Rose had had enough for one day, and quickly got to her feet, experiencing an urge to run away somewhere safe, far from Penver Court, with just herself, Robbie and Bryce. If only that were possible. 'I'm sorry you feel that way, Lydia, but I have no control over the legalities of that will, and if you have any complaints to make on the question of my marriage to your younger son, you must take that up with him.'

Jago grabbed her by the arms as she would have walked away, and shook her, quite violently. 'You damn well won't marry him. You are going to marry *me*, like it or not.'

'Don't be ridiculous! This isn't the Middle Ages, or some silly Victorian melodrama. You can't *force* me to marry you.' Rose laughed, which proved to be a bad mistake.

Jago knocked her flying onto the Persian rug, his greedy hands wrenching at her skirts as he attempted to thrust himself upon her. Rose screamed, but if she'd hoped for any help from Lady Tregowan, she was quickly disenchanted. The expression of rapacious excitement in the older woman's face told her she would do nothing to check her son's lust and greed, and the click of the door as she exited seemed to seal Rose's fate.

'I mean to have you one way or another,' Jago panted. 'If not in marriage, then I shall at least enjoy you before Bryce does.'

'I think not.'

The voice, coming out of nowhere, was balm to her heart. Jago instantly released her, stepping away to face his brother with something like murder in his eyes. Rose was filled with terror of a different sort now. 'Stop this,' she cried, scrambling to her feet and quickly smoothing down her gown. 'Stop this at once.'

If either heard her plea they gave no sign of it. Bryce stood, legs apart, before his brother. He was taller, broader, stronger, and with an iron determination in his face. His voice, when he finally spoke, seemed to hum with the depth of his rage despite an outward appearance of calm. 'I will not allow you to treat Rose with the same callousness you used on Gwenna. Sadly, our foolish cousin succumbed to your lust because she loved you. Rose, however, loves me, and she is to be *my* wife, not *yours*. Touch her again, and I'll kill you, brother or no.'

As softly as this threat was uttered, the tension in the room was palpable as Jago said nothing, neither man moving a muscle, and yet each bristling with hatred.

Taking a breath Rose stepped forward, hoping to ease the stand-off with calm reason. 'This has gone quite far enough. In case either of you have forgotten, I am a living, breathing person with a will of my own, not a piece of chattel to be disposed of at the behest of some man. Or your mother, for that matter. I will make my own decisions in life, thank you very much. The choice will be entirely mine! Do you understand that, the pair of you? So even if you brawl and fight and make an exhibition of yourself, as you did in Biarritz, or take out your broadswords and fight a duel at dawn, *I* will make the decision whom I love and marry. And right now, with the way you are each behaving, it may well be neither of you.'

Only after Jago had left, storming from the room and swearing they would live to regret crossing him, did Rose fall into Bryce's arms, knowing she was safe.

'My brave girl,' he said, kissing her.

'Only so long as I have you.'

The wedding took place in the new year, Bryce oblivious to his mother's continued and furious disapproval. 'Rant as much as you like, Mama, I shall marry the woman I love with or without your blessing.'

'Don't imagine this marriage will make one scrap of difference to our opinion of her. The chit will never drive us out of Penver Court, nor oust me from my position as mistress of it.'

'You are overdramatising, as always, Mother. I don't believe Rose has asked you to leave. Nor will she. Can you not simply be pleased for me, just for once? I am a contented man.'

'You're a fool!' Jago told him.

Following the confrontation in the parlour, the two brothers had rarely spoken a word to each other. Jago, in

251

fact, had been notable by his absence, spending much of his time out of doors, riding or hunting.

'And you are jealous.'

'She's tricked us all out of that inheritance. Now you've given her credibility by accepting that bastard of hers.'

'I believe you were willing to do the same, if for a different reason.'

Rose was at last content, never happier. Bryce Tregowan was the love of her life and she could not envisage that life without him. Even more delicious, it was clear that he loved her too.

And if Lydia was seeking a solution to a problem she'd largely created herself, what was wrong with this one? Jago didn't deserve to take control of Penver Court. He had no more rights to it than his brother, elder son or not. The estate belonged to Rosalind's fine young son, Robbie Tregowan, who would one day take up his proper position. Until then, it was Rose's task in life to protect that inheritance from those who would steal it. But unlike his greedy, selfish brother, Bryce, her darling husband-to-be, would never do such a thing.

The ceremony was held in the Tregowan chapel on a sunny day in late March with a scattering of snow frosting the lawns, and a pale sun bathing them in warmth and new hope. Rose looked stunning in a gown of pearl-white satin, with a veil of old lace. The entire ensemble belonged to Lydia, no doubt one of several she owned.

'Let's hope it brings you better luck than it did me,' she'd caustically remarked as Rose had delightedly accepted the offer.

Rose chose not to wear the satin gloves as she did not relish the fuss of having to remove them when the moment came for Bryce to slip the wedding ring on to her finger. The final touch was a small bouquet of cherry blossom picked out with snowdrops and lily of the valley.

'You have never looked more beautiful,' he told her, as he took her hand at the altar.

Then the familiar words were being recited to her and she was repeating them in the time-honoured way, sounding far more confident than she felt inside. Now she stood beside her husband in the ballroom, feeling suddenly shy as a hundred or so guests queued to shake her hand and congratulate her. The whole event seemed magical, surreal, that it should be she standing beside Bryce, and not one of these lovely young women.

'I'm astonished you'd even consider me as a possible bride when you could have your pick of beautiful and rich heiresses across the land,' she whispered to him, as yet another notable beauty pecked him a kiss on each cheek.

Bryce chuckled. 'It's you that I love, my darling.'

'Yet arranged marriages among the rich are still very much the norm.'

'Not for me. Didn't I tell you right from the start, on the day we first visited Fowey, I seem to recall, that I would marry for love or remain obstinately single? I had no intention of following my mother's example, and I never sought riches, although I've certainly found myself a beauty.'

Remembering Joe's more forthright opinion on the subject, Rose secretly hoped this to be true.

Taking her hand Bryce brought it to his lips to press a

kiss into her palm. 'It's rather late in the day to be having second thoughts. Don't you trust me?'

She smiled up at him. 'With my life.'

'Be assured, my love, there is but one girl for me, and she is right here beside me, where she will always be.'

Rose sighed with contentment. Only one worry remained on her mind now. Her new husband thought her to be a widow, a woman of experience, when in reality Rose was still a virgin. Would he, she worried, be able to tell?

Later, as Tilly helped her to disrobe, Rose's nervousness increased and she dragged out these last few moments with her maid for as long as possible, watching as Tilly carefully folded the gown preparatory to putting it back in Lady Tregowan's press.

'You never know, it might come in again, should she marry husband number five.' And both girls fell into a fit of giggles.

'One husband is enough for me, Tilly. I am the luckiest girl alive.'

'Indeed you are, milady. Now let's take off your petticoats, then I'll help you into your nightgown and brush out your hair.'

Moments later, or so it seemed, Tilly set down the brush. 'There we are, you're ready, and still as beautiful as ever, if I might say so, milady.' Bobbing a curtsey, Tilly turned to go.

'Need you leave quite so soon? Bryce isn't here yet.'

Pausing at the door, Tilly frowned, then took a step or two back into the room. 'Are you all right, milady?

It is quite normal to feel a bit nervous, on your wedding night,' she said kindly. 'But I'm sure you'll be fine. He's a gent is Mr Bryce, and it's not like it's your first time, begging your pardon, milady, is it?'

A short pause before Rose managed a bright smile. 'Quite. Well, goodnight, Tilly, and thank you.'

'You're welcome, milady. God bless.'

When the door had closed leaving Rose alone, she turned her gaze upon the pale oval face in the mirror, a somewhat bleak image of herself, and not, to Rose's mind, beautiful at all. What had she done? What on earth was she, common Rosie Belsfield, doing pretending to be a part of the aristocracy? What on earth would happen were her new husband to discover that she wasn't at all who she claimed to be? She'd told lie after lie, and now it had come to the biggest lie of all. Whatever Joe had set in motion with his scheming, it was never meant to go this far. Could he be right, had she gone quite mad to take such a risk? Had love addled her brain, and she'd now set foot on a course that would lead to her own destruction?

The door opened and she started with alarm.

Bryce hurried towards her. 'My darling, what is it? You look as if you've seen a ghost. Were you thinking of Robert, your first husband? No, it's all right, no need to apologise, I'm sure there was much to remind you of him today, and I have no reason to be jealous. He loved you and made you happy, as I intend to do from now on.'

'I think I'm just tired,' she protested. 'I'm not sure I shall be quite myself – quite what you might be expecting – tonight.'

He laughed softly, then sitting beside her on the dressing

stool pulled her into his arms to kiss her, most tenderly. Perhaps too tenderly, for at the touch of his lips on hers the fire of desire lit inside her and she wanted more. Soon he was teasing open her mouth to allow his tongue to caress hers, and later she made no protest at all as he led her to the bed. Between the sheets that night, Rose discovered that making love to her beloved husband was the most natural thing in the world, even if it was her first time.

'How should a good wife behave?' she sleepily asked her husband the next morning as they lay entwined, having made love at dawn and several times since.

'Exactly as you are doing, my love. I have no complaints.' He rubbed a thumb over her breasts and her nipples peaked deliciously, the sensation making her gasp.

Rose smoothed her hands over his chest and shoulders, loving the strength of him, the hardness of his stomach and muscled length of his thighs. Filled with a sudden burst of shyness, she studied his nakedness from beneath her lashes. 'I do so want to make you happy.'

Spreading her arms out against the pillows, he set about trailing kisses over her throat and breasts, settling himself between her legs. 'In that, you are succeeding wonderfully.'

Giggling, Rose playfully tapped his nose. 'I don't mean in bed, that's the fun part, I mean in more important matters.'

He looked at her, wide-eyed. 'What could possibly be more important than this?' And as he proceeded to slide his hands beneath her bottom and lift her to him so that he could enter her once more, Rose couldn't possibly imagine anything which could come remotely close in importance. She was having considerable difficulty even thinking as her senses flared at his lightest touch, and, as she felt him move inside her, spin out of control entirely.

Some time later, as she lay with her head on his chest listening to the beloved beat of his heart, she attempted the question again, in a slightly different way. 'Your mother is mistress of this house, and has made it plain that she has no intention of surrendering that role, so what is mine, do you think?'

'That, my darling, is of no consequence whatsoever. If Mama wishes to run the house, let her. Why worry your head about housekeeping?'

'I would like to do something for the servants,' Rose persisted. 'They seem to have little time off, and I saw the maids' room once. It was not only very stark but freezing cold, with no heat at all in that part of the house. They didn't even have enough candles.'

Bryce was frowning, looking concerned. 'I can understand your concern, but I suggest you tread warily. Mama has her own way of going about things, and she won't take kindly to interference. Don't look so serious,' he teased, gently pinching her nose, then kissing it. 'I'm not suggesting that you shouldn't assert your authority a little, as this is your house too, I'm simply saying go slowly – that way you're more likely to succeed.'

'Your advice is no doubt sound, and I will do my utmost to heed it, I promise. Can we get up now? I believe it must be almost lunchtime. Everyone will wonder what we are about.'

Bryce chortled with delight. 'They will know exactly what we are about. In fact,' he murmured, sliding a hand to that secret private part of her with a touch that had proved to be a revelation the previous night, 'we might well delay rising for a few more minutes.'

'Indeed, we won't,' Rose vehemently protested. She was beginning to feel rather sore from such sustained loving, but to admit as much would invite awkward questions. She had supposedly been married for years, after all. Leaping briskly out of bed, she teasingly tugged at his arm and Bryce groaned as he reluctantly got to his feet.

'Very well, if you are determined. But we might decide to take a small siesta after lunch.'

'You are very wicked.'

He grinned at her. 'Aren't I just?'

It was a week later when Rose approached Lydia on the subject, only to discover that Bryce was absolutely correct. Her new mother-in-law had no intention of relinquishing the reins, and did not take kindly to having Rose intrude on her duties. Being obliged to provide extra candles for the servants was bad enough, allowing the chit to take more control was quite beyond the pale. 'Being mistress of Penver Court has been my role for almost fifteen years, I see no reason why I should surrender it now to some slip of a girl.'

Rose cleared her throat, feeling entirely inadequate for the battle which clearly lay ahead. 'I would not, for a moment, wish to deprive you of that role entirely. But I wondered if, with your agreement, I might relieve you of some of it. Surely you would welcome being rid of the more tedious chores? I am aware of your expertise in planning menus and organising the many soirées and dinners that you hold, and wouldn't dream of intruding upon those. But perhaps I might take a little more responsibility for the servants' welfare.'

'Good heavens, weren't the candles enough? Why on earth bother your silly head with such matters?'

Rose took a breath. 'I once had occasion to visit the maids' room, for example, and found there was no heating and not many blankets on their beds. Surely we can afford to make some improvements, so that the staff are at least comfortable and warm.'

'Fiddlesticks! If we make things too easy for them we'd never get any work out of them at all. They'd be lying in bed all day. No indeed, leave well alone.'

'But—'

Lydia gave that all too familiar cool smile, which turned those pale eyes of hers to ice. 'As I said, running a house of this size is no task for an ignorant slip of a girl. Pray don't interfere in something you know nothing about.'

Rose realised she had perhaps been a mite hasty, but she'd return to the problem later, at a more appropriate juncture.

The weeks and months slipped by in blissful contentment, the newly-weds rarely out of each other's company for more than a few hours. Often Rose would accompany Bryce to Fowey on business. When his work was done they would spend time together on Readymoney beach helping Robbie build sandcastles or holding his hand while the little boy paddled in the sea, as he so loved to do. He would laugh with delight as the waves rippled over his bare feet. Then Bryce would carry him a little way out, holding him afloat while the little boy kicked his legs and arms like a little frog.

'No child should live near the sea and not be able to swim,' Bryce said, and thinking of Jago and his earlier threats towards her precious child, Rose could only agree.

Bryce bought a puppy for Robbie, which delighted the small boy, and the pair would happily play for hours. He even wanted Sam, as the Labrador pup was duly named, to sleep with him, but Rose was adamant that beds were for small boys, not dogs.

When the year began to die, and cold winds blew over the land, the rest of the family packed up and left for Biarritz, as usual. Bryce and Rose chose to spend Christmas alone at Penver Court. They put up a tree with candles, looped paper chains around the banisters, and brought in holly and mistletoe from the woods to decorate the house. They would light a log fire in the small parlour to make it warm and cosy, cuddling up together on the sofa as Robbie played with his bricks on the Persian rug. It was the most perfect time, with no one to interfere, no Lydia to constantly chide Rose whenever she failed to do anything correctly. No Jago to constantly watch and be wary of. They even took breakfast in bed and nobody minded.

'How deliciously decadent,' Bryce murmured, nibbling her ear and making her giggle.

'Will we always be this happy?' she asked him, eyes alight with love.

'Always and for ever, my love.'

They were almost sorry when spring arrived, and with the first snowdrops, Lydia and Jago returned.

* * *

It was Robbie's third birthday and the family had gathered to celebrate with tea and chocolate cake, and to watch him open his presents, of which there was quite a pile. Nothing from Lydia or Jago, sadly, but the servants had been surprisingly generous. Rose had bought him a rocking horse. Someone in the village had made it for her, a local man found by Joe. The little boy was so excited when he saw it that he at once tried to climb aboard. 'Me want a ride.'

'He's a natural, this boy,' laughed Bryce, and lifting him up, placed him in the saddle. 'Go on, gee up, Neddy.'

'Gee up, Dobbin,' corrected Robbie as he grasped the reins and tried to set the horse rocking, which made everyone laugh all the more.

'He clearly has a mind of his own, our young baronet. Just like his mother,' Bryce said, casting a warm glance across at Rose where she sat on the sofa, watching the fun with a happy smile on her face.

'Of course, but we mustn't let him become spoilt.'

'You cannot spoil a child with love. Is that not so, Mama?'

Lydia gave no more than a grunt by way of response, aware her son was surreptitiously criticising her. Jago came over and began to push the horse, making it rock a little faster. 'Go on, boy, ride good old Dobbin. But you should be on a real horse, not a wooden one.'

'He's only three,' Rose protested. 'Far too young.'

'Poppycock! If you mollycoddle the child he'll turn into a namby-pamby, which is no good to any of us. He needs toughening up, make a man of him, and the sooner the better.'

'I've said all along that the boy should go away to school at five,' intervened Lydia, idly cutting herself a second slice of chocolate cake. This time Rose was wise enough not to respond. She'd learnt that the more she protested, the more difficult Lydia made life for her, and she really had no wish for a battle, not on this special day.

No one quite knew how it happened. One minute the horse was rocking back and forth, neither too fast nor too slow, then suddenly there was a loud crack and Robbie was pitched forward from his seat right over the horse's head. Had Bryce not been standing in front of it and therefore able to catch him, the little boy might well have landed on his head, with terrifying consequences.

Rose was at his side in seconds, his screams throwing her into a panic.

'It's all right,' Bryce assured her, as he gently relinquished the screaming child into her arms. 'I don't think he's hurt. He's just frightened.' Then as Rose gathered him close to check his little arms and legs, Bryce turned on his brother in fury. 'Was this your doing? Did you push him too hard?'

'Damn it, I was only rocking the thing. If you look, one of the front legs is broken.'

Bryce was already examining that possibility. 'You're right, and it looks as if the two front legs were partly sawn through, then gave way as pressure came to bear on them when the horse rocked.'

'Nonsense, but if that is the case, I declare myself not guilty of that either.'

Not for a moment did Rose believe him.

Chapter Eighteen

Rose voiced these suspicions to her husband as they lay in bed together that night, the one person she felt she could turn to for support. 'I'm quite convinced Jago was the culprit.'

Bryce was dismissive as he stroked her hair. 'I think your imagination is running away with you. Why would he do such a thing? I agree, Jago has ever been wild, but I doubt even he would go so far as to hurt a child.'

'Not even one who stands in the way of his inheritance?'

His expression was surprisingly stern. 'Not even then. My brother is not completely without common sense.'

'But he does like things all his own way, believes he can do as he pleases on the estate. He buys and sells land, puts up rents, evicts tenants for no reason, all without discussions with anyone. I had to speak to him most firmly about his threat to evict Tilly's family. Why does your mother not exercise more control over him?' Rose seethed, quite unable to settle in her distress.

'Sadly, Mama *does* exercise rather too much control over her elder son. And she is more likely the source of the problem.'

Rose looked at him in stunned disbelief. 'Are you saying that *Lydia* would go so far as to hurt Robbie in order to satisfy her greed? She may be a difficult woman, but I find that hard to believe.'

Bryce flung himself back against the pillows, letting out a heavy sigh. 'I do so wish I could share your confidence. Yet I look at the misfortune which befell all her previous husbands, and I can't help but wonder . . .'

Before Rose had time to even begin to absorb the implications of this remark, he pulled her into his arms on a short laugh. 'No doubt my imagination is running riot now. I do tend to expect the worst where my mother and brother are concerned. It's a fault in me, as much as them. I'm sure you're worrying unduly about the horse, but I'll do some snooping, ask a few questions here and there. And I agree, Jago does behave at times as if he were some sort of despot. If you saved the Carwyn family from eviction, then I'm glad to hear it. They did not deserve to be turned out of their home. You are wise to keep a close eye on everything Jago does on the estate. You have that right, as Robbie's mother. Speak to Wrayworth about the possibility of putting in a manager to replace him, if that would make you easier in your mind. As for Robbie, he will come to no harm. Isn't he thoroughly spoilt at every turn?'

He kissed her then, making her heart sing as his loving always did. 'Let us always remember that no matter what difficulties Jago may present with his selfish, grasping ways, underneath all of that bravado he is an embittered, lonely soul. While we have our love, and each other to trust and rely upon. Does that not make us rich, and strong?'

Nestling close, Rose could only smile. 'Of course we are; my strength comes from your love.'

The following morning Rose took a walk into the village to call again upon the solicitor. This time Mr Wrayworth was less amenable to her concerns. 'I am dismayed to hear of this accident, and thankful the boy is safe, but what exactly are you suggesting? I cannot believe that Master Jago would go so far as to attempt to hurt the boy in order to gain an inheritance which isn't even rightly his.'

'Who else would gain by cutting through the legs?' Rose persisted.

'My dear lady, that is only surmise on your part. Without evidence it would be impossible to make any charge against Master Jago stick.'

Proof was not something she'd considered. Rose's heart seemed to plummet. 'There must be something I can do. I have to protect my child's future, and his life too, it seems.'

'Are you sure you aren't seeing problems where none, in fact, exist?' the solicitor asked, as kindly as he could.

There was a silence, one in which Rose attempted to look at the situation more objectively. Mr Wrayworth was taking very much the same attitude as Bryce, and it may be that they could be right and she was entirely wrong. But Rose very much doubted that was the case. Yet how could she prove Jago culpable without explaining what happened on that cliff top soon after she'd arrived. And if she told them about that incident now, what reason could she give for not reporting it at the time? Rose doubted it would be wise to admit she'd used the threat as a means to blackmail Jago into allowing tenants to be spared from eviction. Wouldn't that only make herself appear as guilty as he? Or that her fear of Jago had a deeper source.

And were she to call the police now, like Mr Wrayworth and her own husband they would assume her to be simply a hysterical mother. If the authorities were to put the blame on anyone, rather than class it as an unfortunate accident, it would be the carpenter in the village who had made the toy in all good faith. And she mustn't allow that to happen to an honest man. So what other options did she have?

'I believe the threat to be real, but, as you say, I cannot prove it. Is it a possibility that I could insist Jago steps down from his post as estate manager? I really do not like the way he runs things.'

The solicitor steepled his fingers, leaning back in his chair while he considered the question. 'I'm not sure that would be a good idea. He is not, I will concede, an easy man to deal with; nevertheless, the estate remains sound under his management, if you take into consideration the difficult economic climate under which farming is suffering at the moment. You must also remember that Sir

Ralph's will states Penver Court must continue to provide a home for his two stepsons and widow for as long as they need one. Of course, if you wished Master Bryce to take over, now that you are married, the question could be discussed further. But even as your husband he has few rights. Have you considered that they could perhaps share the work?'

'Bryce is partner in a chandler's in Fowey. He has no wish to be involved in the running of Penver Court. What about me?'

'Dear lady, I am quite certain that you are a very capable person, but even so, managing an estate of that size is a monumental task, which I politely suggest would be quite beyond your scope.'

He softened the harshness of this comment with a warm smile, and Rose had to agree with him. She wouldn't have the first idea where to begin. 'But I can continue to keep a watching brief, ask questions, talk to tenants, all of that?'

'Of course, and quite right too. Take the child with you on your visits, as I'm sure they would love to meet their new baronet.'

Rose's face lit up. 'That's an excellent idea. I will do that.'

'But until your son is old enough to take up the reins himself, I see no reason for change. Not unless there were proof of mismanagement or an attempt on Jago's part to defraud the estate of money, which is highly unlikely.'

Rose wasn't too sure about that. According to Ennor Carwyn, one or two farms and smallholdings had been sold off. But when she mentioned this point, without naming names, to the solicitor, he dismissed it as unimportant.

'Holdings are bought and sold all the time, the least profitable disposed of. Jago is planning to buy other land and property to replace the ones for which he could no longer find a tenant, or are no longer profitable.'

'But what if he doesn't – buy more land, I mean? What if he spends the money on other things? Perhaps he's squirrelled the money away for his own personal use in the future?'

He gave Rose what she could only describe as an old-fashioned look. 'I see no evidence of profligate living.' Mr Wrayworth half glanced at the clock, reminding Rose that she was taking up his valuable time. And since she had no proof to back up these accusations, any more than she had over the rocking horse incident, there was clearly no possibility of ousting Jago from his power. Not yet, anyway.

Bryce began his search in the stables. If there were any evidence to be found of his brother's culpability, perhaps in the form of a tool used, it would surely be here. He sincerely hoped he didn't find any. Although he was fully aware there was nothing his brother would like more than to banish Rose from Penver Court and have it all to himself, to accuse him of attempted murder was a considerable leap. Even so, Jago must realise that his days in charge of the estate were numbered, that in just a few years' time young Robbie would be old enough to take over for himself. In the meantime, the boy had a mother, and also a father now, to protect both him and his inheritance.

He decided to speak to Joe, who was grooming one of the horses. Bryce sauntered over, not wishing to appear too eager or curious. He began by admiring the horse and checking his feet.

'I remember his dam, terrific little mare she was. This son of hers would do well on Newton Abbot racetrack, I reckon.'

'Aye, you're right there,' Joe said with a chuckle. 'Godolphin does like to be in front. Were you wanting a ride, sir? I could tack him up for you.'

'Good idea. I could do with some fresh air and exercise.' And as Joe reached for the saddle, he idly asked, 'Has anyone ever been in here who shouldn't, or in the barn working on something? Or asked to borrow a tool?'

Joe regarded him with a steady gaze. 'Such as a saw, you mean?'

'Well, yes, anything of that nature.'

'Not to my knowledge, but then I'm not here all the time. There would be ample opportunity while I'm driving Lady Tregowan out for someone to make use of the workshops. John isn't always around either; like me he has other duties. Are you looking for whoever did for the young master's toy?' Joe was no fool.

'I'm quite sure it must have been an accident, but one must consider all possibilities.' There was no pretence over the reason for his questions.

'Do you have anyone in mind, sir?'

'I really couldn't say. Do you have any ideas yourself?'

There was a long pause while Joe fastened the girth straps, then fitted the head collar. 'Begging your pardon, sir, but since you ask, I'd say that if you were to suspect that your brother, for instance, might have damaged the little chap's rocking horse, then I'd agree he's the most likely candidate.'

Bryce considered the fellow with a narrowed gaze. 'Why do you say that?'

'Because he's the one with the motive.'

'And what would that be, exactly? I ask because I would welcome a less prejudiced viewpoint upon my brother.'

Joe rubbed a hand over his face, then through his hair, as long and tousled as ever as he so hated going to the barber. 'He doesn't believe the child is the true baronet, does he?'

'No, I don't believe he does.'

'Well, happen he's right to have doubts.'

Bryce drew in a sharp breath. 'Are you seriously telling me that there is good reason to doubt the veracity of Robbie's claim to the title? How can you suggest such a thing? Were you not employed by my wife from before the boy's birth?'

'Happen that's why I can say it with some conviction. Master Jago is right – the boy is illegitimate and his mother is a fraud, exactly as your brother suspects.'

The cold fury that raged through Bryce at these words almost robbed him of breath, but he managed, at last, to speak. 'So I was right, you were her lover.'

Joe shook his head, fervently denying the charge. 'Nay, it weren't me, more's the pity.'

'I'm not sure I can believe you, but whether that's the

truth or not, you realise you are accusing my wife of a crime, of passing off her son as the baronet when he isn't. Is that what you intended to say? And take care how you answer.'

Joe looked at the man who had stolen his beloved Rose. 'Aye,' he said, after a long moment. 'That's what I intended to say.' And crossing his fingers against the lie, he continued, 'She's deceived you all.'

Disappointed over not being allowed to oust Jago from his position, Rose decided to grasp the nettle so far as the house was concerned and devote herself to improving the living conditions of the servants, despite being warned off by Lydia. Perhaps if she concentrated on this it would take her mind off these other worries. 'Tilly, will you show me again, please, the rooms where the maids sleep.'

'Ooh, milady, it's more than my job's worth, and it's vital I don't lose that. Mam and Dad might have been given a stay of execution, as it were, thanks to your efforts on their behalf, but how long that will last is anybody's guess.'

Rose frowned. 'Jago hasn't made any more threats, has he?'

'Oh no, milady, but Dad is afeared he might decide to put the rents up next quarter day. We can't be sure how long his patience will last.'

Rose agreed. 'Nevertheless, I mean to investigate the maids' living quarters, and the menservants' rooms too. But in view of your concerns I shall not involve you.'

She sent for the butler. Where was the point in being

the young Lady Tregowan if she could not wield even the smallest amount of power? Rose offered him her most winning smile. 'Mr Rowell, I hope you are well?'

Unused to receiving enquiries about the state of his health the butler mumbled that he was very well, thank you kindly. 'May I be of service in any way, milady?'

'Yes, indeed. I should like to take a tour of the servants' quarters. Spare me nothing, I wish to see everything, every bedroom, bathroom, dormitory, lavatory, every nook and cranny.'

The butler could not have appeared more shocked had she asked to view his unmentionables. 'My Lady, far be it for me to question this decision, but—'

'Then don't. I have quite made up my mind. Nothing you say will dissuade me.' Rowell opened his mouth as if about to protest further, but again Rose forestalled him. 'I have notebook in hand, so that I can jot down whatever improvements I feel are necessary.' She waved it at him with a little flirtatious smile. 'Lead on, Macduff, if you please.'

He seemed to soften a little at her joke. 'If you insist, milady.'

They began the inspection with the menservants' quarters, whose rooms were even worse than the maids, with less space between beds, threadbare covers, and fewer hooks on the walls. There were no chairs, save for one under the window upon which a jug and basin stood, no rugs on the floor, and cobwebs laced every corner as if the place hadn't been cleaned in months, or even years.

'This is quite dreadful!' Rose said, genuinely shocked. 'I've seen hovels for the poor that were better than this.'

He glanced at her in surprise. 'Have you indeed, milady?' Rose realised she'd made a silly mistake, yet again, and could only hope he would assume she meant she'd seen such places while undergoing charity work. The butler insisted on calling the housekeeper to show her around the maids' quarters. 'Gentlemen are not allowed in that area, milady.'

Mrs Quintrell came, lips tightly buttoned and a challenging look in her eye. 'I've never had no complaints before about accommodation, so if any of the maids have been speaking out of turn, I should like to know who it is, milady.'

'None of the maids have said a word, let alone complained,' Rose assured her. 'This decision to investigate is mine entirely, although I admire their fortitude. It must be freezing cold in these dormitories at night, and fairly comfortless preparing for bed with only the stub of a candle, if you're lucky, to light you.'

'The Dowager Lady Tregowan increased the ration for candles, milady,' Mrs Quintrell remarked, rather tartly.

'Excellent! And what about blankets?'

'One is provided for each occupant. They are free to bring another from home so long as they wash it themselves.'

'And do they take advantage of this?'

'Very few, so I assume they are quite warm enough.'

'Mightn't the reason be that they don't have any blankets to spare which they can bring from home, or else they don't have the time in their daily duties to wash them? Would you say that is more likely the case?'

'It may well be, milady, I really couldn't say.' The woman was giving nothing away, merely folded her arms across her considerable chest and glowered.

Rose battled on, politely enquiring why the beds were so close together, why there were no cupboards or drawers for clothes. 'Why cannot they at least bring their own box with them?' The reason, of course, was lack of space. 'But why are there so many beds in each room?' Rose asked on a sigh of exasperation. 'There would be more space if they weren't so overcrowded.'

No answer came, so Rose was obliged to repeat it. 'Are there too many servants employed here, or too few rooms? Which is it?'

'You would need to ask the Dowager Lady Tregowan as to why more rooms are not made available, milady. I really couldn't say.'

Rose opened her eyes wide. 'Are you saying that there *are* suitable rooms not currently being used? Empty rooms?'

'I believe that might be the case.'

'Either it is the case or it isn't. Don't try my patience too much, Mrs Quintrell, I am rapidly running out of it. Are there empty rooms available in the house or not?'

The older woman's cheeks had grown quite pink, so that Rose almost felt sorry for her. She was but the messenger, after all, not the policy maker. 'I believe so,' she mumbled.

'I would appreciate it if you showed them to me.'

'But milady—'

'At once.'

* * *

274

A full inspection revealed that there were any number of empty rooms, most lacking in beds or any other sort of furniture, let alone curtains or rugs, and all needing a good clean. But that was easily rectified. When they were done, Rose turned to her guide, the housekeeper's face by now very red. 'I take it that the reason for these rooms standing empty is the lack of furniture, along with their filthy state?'

'I really couldn't say. The Dowager Lady Tregowan thinks that it is neither wise nor necessary to pander to—'

Rose had heard enough of what the Dowager Lady Tregowan thought. 'We can move beds, quite easily, but is there any other furniture stored elsewhere? If so, then I would like to know, if you please.'

The answer to this was a visit to the cellars, reluctantly conducted, where Rose found stored any number of iron bedsteads, cupboards and chests of drawers, not to mention chairs, boxes, pictures, mirrors and coat stands, among other detritus.

Rose beamed at the housekeeper. 'A veritable treasure trove. Well now, our first task is to scrub out the empty rooms. You can put the maids onto that job, Mrs Quintrell. Perhaps a lick of paint would not come amiss. I'll speak to Mr Rowell and get him to organise the menservants to do that. They can then bring up the furniture we need. I shall put a chalk mark on each piece in advance so they will know which to take. The maids can then give everything a good polish. Are we agreed?'

Mrs Quintrell was looking rather as if she'd been asked to re-equip Buckingham Palace. 'I would respectfully suggest that you speak to the Dowager Lady Tregowan first, milady. I doubt she'd welcome—'

'You can safely leave that to me. I shall also look into the matter of more blankets. Ah, we should first check what bedding and curtains we have in the linen room. Would you do that for me, Mrs Quintrell?' Rose politely asked, with her friendliest smile. 'No point in buying new if there's a treasure trove of linen too hidden away somewhere.' She received no answering smile in response.

Following a second visit to Mr Rowell, and having put all arrangements in hand, Rose sighed with pleasure, a happiness which soon faded as she contemplated her final task: that of informing Lydia of her plans. Rose surmised that the housekeeper would by now have fully acquainted her mistress, her beloved Dowager Lady Tregowan, of everything that had gone on that morning. Even as this thought occurred to her, Rose received a summons to the small parlour, brought by a trembling maid the moment she'd finished speaking to the butler.

'Thank you, Mr Rowell, I'm most grateful for your help in this matter. I appreciate it.'

'The servants will likewise appreciate your efforts on their behalf, milady. You do, after all, have the right to make such decisions,' he told her kindly, all sign of his earlier frostiness now melted under the warmth of her charm and compassion. 'Let no one tell you otherwise.'

She smiled at him. 'I hope you and I can work well together on this project, thus making life more comfortable for everyone. But if you meet with any problems, please do let me know.'

The two exchanged a look, almost as if they were conspirators in a plot. But if the butler's change of heart lifted her own, Rose was soon cast down the moment she saw Lydia's expression: one of white-faced fury. Even as she felt her heart sink, Rose told herself to hold fast to her courage. The servants in this great house needed a little more comfort and consideration, and not for a moment did she intend to give in to Lydia's bullying. She'd come a long way from the shy young girl evicted from Ellis Island.

'Lydia, I hope you are well?' Rose said, her own cheerful words seeming to echo in the chilling silence. Her mother-in-law did not offer her a seat, but Rose took one all the same, thereby letting it be known that they were equals now.

'Can I have heard correctly? Is what Mrs Quintrell tells me really true?'

'That depends what it is she's told you,' Rose brightly remarked. 'If she says we are in the process of opening up some of the unused attic rooms and giving them a lick of paint and a good scrub, then that is absolutely correct. I hadn't realised we had so much space up there, enough to provide the servants with decent accommodation for them to sleep and store their clothes and belongings, effectively to live in much greater comfort. As I believe I remarked in an earlier conversation we had on this issue, I quite see that you do not have the time to deal with such matters, Lydia, and I did promise to help. It is all rather exciting.'

'It is an absolute outrage! Good heavens, you'll be putting their wages up next.'

'Ah, indeed I may well do that as many don't appear

to have enjoyed a rise in some years. I don't suppose Sir Ralph, poor man, was well enough to notice what his staff were being paid. But I mustn't trouble you with such boring matters. Staff wages are something I can discuss with Jago at a later date.'

Lydia sat up very straight in her chair, her face now turning a dull shade of purple. 'You will do no such thing. I will not have my wishes flouted, or any interference in the running of this house, as I think I made very clear when you first brought this idea to my attention. Servants are just that, here to serve, to wait upon us, not to live a life of ease and comfort. That would be quite against the order of things.'

'But they are human beings too, and deserve proper respect and welfare,' Rose sweetly reminded her.

'They are housed and fed, what more do they need?'

'A little care and attention, that is all, and we have the wherewithal to provide it without going to any extra expense. The cellar is stuffed with furniture. Isn't that marvellous? So you can safely set aside any fears you might have on cost, Lydia, as there will be none. At least, very little,' Rose assured her, getting to her feet as if the interview were over. 'Now I really must help Mrs Quintrell to check out the linen room. I'm quite certain that too will yield further treasures. I'll let you know how I get on.'

Lydia was left speechless, her mouth hanging open. The chit had not even the grace to ask her permission.

Chapter Nineteen

For no reason Rose could fathom, Bryce's attitude slowly began to change towards her in the days and weeks following. Relations between them became oddly cool. He would go so far as to avoid her company during the day, come late to bed and then declare himself exhausted and lie with his back to her, not even touching her let alone loving her. Rose was bewildered.

If he did ever make love to her, driven perhaps by frustration or need, or else because she had pressed him into it, it would be a most matter-of-fact sort of coupling. No longer did Rose hear the loving words he'd used in the early months of their marriage, there were no more tender kisses or exciting caresses. It was all very brisk and speedy, over in minutes, then he would turn from her and fall instantly asleep, or give every impression of such.

'Is something wrong?' she queried one night, heart-sore with worry. 'Are you sick?'

'Do I appear sick?'

'N-no, but you seem somehow rather distant. Have I done something wrong, Bryce? I can only assume you are disappointed in me for some reason. That I have failed you.'

'Why should you have?' he grunted, head buried in his pillow.

'Perhaps you've decided that I'm really rather unsuitable as a wife, too low class, or entirely inadequate as chatelaine of Penver Court?'

He didn't even look at her as he answered, keeping his back firmly turned away, and an acre of bed between them. 'Don't be foolish, I told you to leave the housekeeping to Mama. It really isn't important who does it.'

'It is to me because I wish to be useful. If that is your reason for turning from me, perhaps because of your mother's complaints, then it is quite unfair. The fact is . . .' Rose was longing to tell him of the progress she was making opening up the abandoned rooms in the attic. She'd tried on numerous occasions but he never seemed interested.

'Mama has made no complaints. Go to sleep, it's all in your imagination – clearly a rich one that serves you well.'

'I don't think she's very happy with what I'm doing,' Rose responded, not picking up on his sarcasm. Whatever the reason for his apparent disappointment in her, Rose loved him, therefore she persisted, desperate to put things right between them. 'I am trying to fit in, really I am. But your mother does everything. She liaises with Mrs Pascoe over the meals, organises the lunches, parties, soirées and such. She scolds the maids if they don't do their job to her satisfaction, and is entirely responsible for hiring and firing them. She instructs the gardeners on what needs to be done in the gardens, and even does the flowers for the house herself. So if I am idle, of which she often accuses me, it is because there is nothing for me to do. Therefore, much against Lydia's wishes, I've started to take an active interest in servant welfare. I feel it right for me to do so.'

'If it makes you happy, why not? So long as it doesn't offend Mama,' he mumbled, pulling the sheet over his head as if to block out the sound of her voice.

Rose experienced a jolt of pain deep in her heart. Why was he ignoring her? She had the urge to shake him, to laugh him out of this gloom he'd sunk into for some reason, to tease and flirt as they used to. But she was far too miserable to risk it, afraid he might be angry, or reject her. Girding her patience, she maintained her calm and gentle approach. She smoothed a hand over his hair, leant over to kiss his head, or what she could see of it peeping above the sheets.

'My love, I want only for us to be happy, as we were until recently. I know the rich have rules of their own, which I do not always understand, but I love you so much. Will you not tell me in what way I have upset you? I agree that your mama as the Dowager Lady Tregowan is still very much mistress here, even though the house now belongs to Robbie – my son.' Rose always felt a little tremor inside at this lie. Yet she could not have loved the child more had he truly been so.

Flinging back the covers as if she had said something which annoyed him, Bryce glared at her, his eyes cold and shrewdly assessing. 'Is that right? Penver Court now belongs to *your son*, does it? How very fortunate.'

Rose sat up, in some distress, but his stern expression in the light of the bedside lamp offered little reassurance. 'Bryce, what is it? You know this to be true. Are you jealous or something? I did speak to Mr Wrayworth, as you suggested, but he can see no reason to ask Jago to step down. Were you wanting to take his place, because if so, I could ask again? Just tell me what you want.'

'I want you to stop lying to me.'

Rose stared at him, numb with shock. 'I don't know what you mean.'

'Yes, you do.' He almost spat the words at her. 'I know that you were a widow when we married, but little else about you, save that you lived in Toronto and come from a middle-class background, or even poorer for all I know. No doubt you considered your marriage with Robert an excellent way of lifting yourself higher up the social ladder, and providing a good future for the child you were expecting. After he died, you then decided to seek out Sir Ralph as a means of ensuring that fortune was secure.'

Rose sighed, feeling a strange sort of relief. 'Not that old chestnut again. Are you still doubting my word, after all we've been to each other? Why, for goodness sake? What has changed?'

Bryce's expression now was heartbreakingly sad, his disappointment at her alleged betrayal only too apparent. 'Who was your lover – was it Joe, as I once suggested? He claims to be innocent of that charge but can I believe him? Can I trust either of you?'

Tears sprang to her eyes, unable to believe what she

was hearing. 'You're playing the same cruel game as Jago. What are you suggesting?'

His expression was chilling, very much resembling that of his brother. 'I am saying, Rose, that if you find yourself obliged to share your newly won fortune with us, Sir Ralph's second family, you have no right to complain. I've learnt your little secret, you see. You can stop this pretence now, I've had the truth confirmed.'

Rose was devastated. He knew! He had learnt her 'little secret'. What else could he mean but that he knew her true identity? Who had told him? Surely not Joe, who was equally concerned for his own skin. But then, if that were the case, why did Bryce not confront her with the whole story? Why did he not reveal the full extent of this new knowledge instead of dragging out all that old nonsense about Robbie being the child of her lover?

Before she could gather her wits sufficiently to find an answer, he blithely continued, 'I have learnt that your child is in fact illegitimate, *that you are indeed a fortune-hunter*! You have made a fool of me, and my mother and brother were right all along. Except that I may well have married you for the same reason. Should I choose to expose your lies, we could both be the losers. That is almost funny, in the circumstances.'

If he made this remark out of bravado, or to save his injured pride, Rose did not recognise it as such. She felt as if she'd been punched in the face. Bryce, her lovely husband of only twelve months, appeared to be suggesting their marriage was nothing more than a sham, that he had never loved her. As much a rogue as Jago, he must have duped her completely, and merely married her for the money. Never, despite everything she'd been through and suffered, had she felt more wounded, more betrayed. How could he think so little of her? How could he treat her with such cruel contempt?

'Get out! If that's what you believe, I don't want you anywhere near me.'

Deeply hurt by this rejection of their love, Rose rather dramatically ordered Bryce from her bed. Worse, he did indeed leave it, storming off to sleep in his dressing room. Rose spent the rest of that night sobbing her heart out.

First thing the next morning Rose ran straight to Joe. 'Have you been talking to Bryce? He says he knows my "little secret". Did you spill the beans and tell him everything?'

Quickly putting a hand to her mouth, he glanced about the barn where he was cleaning the Ford motor. 'Shut up,' he hissed, as Rose furiously struggled to be free. Finally satisfied they were alone, he released her and turned back to his polishing. 'So what are you accusing me of now?'

'Bryce has been behaving oddly over these last few weeks, barely speaking to me.'

Joe snorted his disdain. 'Married life not turning out quite as much fun as you'd hoped, is that it?'

'I've realised that this strangeness started around the time he started to look for proof over the damaged rocking horse. Did he speak to you then? What did you tell him?'

Joe kept on rubbing the windscreen with the wash leather, as if he really wasn't interested in what she had to say. 'That's right, blame me for everything, as usual.

Your best friend if you need me to do something for you, otherwise you treat me with complete contempt.'

'Is it any wonder with this silly jealousy of yours? I thought I knew you, Joe Colbert, but ever since I met dear Rosalind you've changed. You've become obsessed with money.'

'I was obsessed with surviving!' he snapped right back at her, flinging the leather back into the bucket so that it sprayed water everywhere. 'I don't recall you being too keen to sell your charms on the waterfront, so don't look down your nose at me now you've joined the ranks of the high and mighty, Rosie Belsfield.'

'That's unfair!'

'It's the truth. We did what we did because we had no choice.'

'We had every choice! And there have been a thousand chances for us to come clean since. But you never intended this to be a short-term plan, did you? You always meant to keep the deceit going because you had an eye to the main chance. That's why you wouldn't let me speak out. I can see that now.'

'And I was right.'

'No, you were wrong, Joe. You've got us into this mess, and there's no way out of it. Oh, what's the use, you never listen, and I'm in far too deep now to even try. Like it or not, we have to keep silent, for ever if necessary. Our lives depend upon it.'

Rosie Belsfield, was that the name? And what, exactly, had Joe got her into, and why must they keep silent? Jago, out in the courtyard, hidden behind the barn door, had listened avidly to every word. Whatever the mystery might be, it was clear the pair were in it together, up to their stupid necks. It looked like a bit of snooping was most definitely called for.

Keeping a close eye on Rose for the rest of that morning, Jago patiently waited until lunch was over and she'd taken the child out for his afternoon walk, then slipped up to the nursery wing. No doors were ever locked so he had no difficulty in letting himself in, where he began a systematic search, taking great care not to disturb anything as he had no wish to alert her. He carefully rummaged through every drawer, riffled through her wardrobe, dipping his fingers into every pocket and bag. When he found the writing slope, Jago painstakingly slid letters from envelopes to quickly scan them and fold them as carefully away again.

He'd been searching for over twenty minutes and found nothing to prove the child a bastard, as there surely must be somewhere, nor any evidence of this new name: Rosie Belsfield.

Going over to the bed he ran his hands under the pillows, then under the mattress. Nothing. Yet still Jago kept on looking, convinced that if he searched long and hard enough, he would find something eventually.

He took a step back to look about him. A floorboard creaked beneath his foot, and upon the instant he knew. Going down on his knees, he easily prised it up and brought out the tin box from under the bed. Somewhere outside in the courtyard he heard laughter. Chattering voices, the clop of horses' hooves and the giggle of a child. No doubt the devoted mother was letting young Robbie feed carrots to the horses, but she'd be here any minute to put him down for his nap. As these thoughts raced through his head, Jago found what he was looking for. Scarcely glancing at the documents, he slipped them into his pocket, quickly returned the box to its hiding place, replaced the floorboard and let himself quietly out.

Safely back in the peace and privacy of his own room, Jago was stunned by what he read, not at all what he'd been expecting. He'd always suspected that Rose had deliberately withheld her marriage certificate, now he could guess why. The dates were all wrong, which was a puzzle. The second document was even more disturbing. For some time after he'd finished studying them both he sat staring into space, thinking through the implications. Then he pulled out pen and paper and began to write at once to the shipping company for more details. Someone must know more about this tale, and when he'd finally unearthed all the answers, then he would make his move.

In the days and weeks following, relations between husband and wife remained outwardly cool. Deep inside, Bryce couldn't help but admire her stoic courage, the way she persisted with the improvements in the servants' quarters, defiantly standing up to his mother whenever Lydia criticised the project.

'Why would servants need more space?' she'd ask when Rose arrived late and flustered for dinner, with dust in her hair and paint on her chin looking very like a daub of cream. If only it was, then he could take her up to bed and lick it off. He could smooth his hands over her soft skin, caress her lovely breasts, and make love to her as he had in those wonderful early days of their marriage. Bryce was jerked out of these nostalgic yearnings by his mother's voice rising in pitch. 'They should know their place and not demand curtains and rugs, and goodness knows what else. This is a complete waste of *your* time and *my* money.'

Rose's response was to smile sweetly. 'Now there, I'm afraid, we must agree to differ, Lydia. Even the lowest kitchen skivvy, in my view, deserves respect and decent living conditions. And as I've nothing else to do with my time, I'm more than happy to help with the cleaning and painting. It's fun, as a matter of fact, and so far has cost nothing. The house seems to have stocks of everything, if one only knows where to look.'

Again, Bryce was filled with admiration for her courage. How she had changed!

'But those things belong to the estate, not to *you*, madam,' Lydia scolded.

Rose started on her soup, making no reply to this. Nevertheless, Bryce could see the hurt in her eyes, the pain it cost her to always be looked upon as an outsider with no rights. No wonder she was championing the staff.

Nothing more had been said between them about the lies and deceit she'd practised upon them, the fraud she must have perpetrated. Bryce still hadn't made up his mind how to deal with what he'd discovered. It wasn't that he didn't believe Joe's confession, it was simply that he couldn't bear the thought of losing her. And when he revealed the truth to the rest of the family, announced that what they'd suspected was absolutely correct, she would surely leave.

But was that what he wanted, or did she deserve a second chance?

Right now Bryce felt too deeply injured by her trickery to be tempted by the sorrowful expression in her eyes whenever she looked his way. There were occasions still when he would find himself filled with regret, his love for her impossible to deny. Only to see the sadness in her lovely face, the tremor of her lower lip, made him want her all the more. The way she moved, the sweet scent of her, the tenderness of her touch stroking his back as she lay beside him in bed was like a constant knife in his heart, his need for her was so great. However much he might resist the urge to turn and take her, he could never dispel that longing.

But he must ever remember that she had deceived them all. She was a liar and a cheat. Jago had been right all along.

'May I join you on your ride this morning, brother?' Jago asked. 'There's something I wish to discuss with you.' Bryce paused as he was about to mount Godolphin, surprised by this request. His brother was no rider, had never been particularly fond of the sport, not unless he was chasing a fox.

'If you feel so inclined.'

It was a bright summer's day, the sun dappling the leaves as they guided their horses at a gentle trot through the woods. As they reached the headland, Bryce urged Godolphin into a canter, a soft sea breeze whistling in his ears as the two brothers rode unspeaking across the open pasture. He loved Cornwall, had dreamt of living contentedly here with his wife to the end of his days. Now, Bryce was seriously contemplating an alternative future, perhaps going away to sea, anything to avoid seeing Rose every day, knowing their marriage was effectively in all but name.

'I'll race you,' Jago called.

'You're on,' and kicking his heels in the horse's flanks, Bryce urged the young stallion to a gallop, riding it hard, testing it to the limit. He and Jago had often raced each other as boys, and, just as then, it was no different now, with Bryce easily beating his brother.

'My horse is lame, so I was forced to take this much quieter mare,' Jago complained by way of excuse as they reined their horses back into a steady trot and then to a quiet walk to allow them to gently cool down.

Bryce laughed. 'And you do so hate to lose. So, what is it you wished to say to me that couldn't be said in the house?'

'Can we dismount and walk for a bit?'

'Curiouser and curiouser,' Bryce quipped, but obediently dismounted. Leaving Godolphin, along with Jago's mare, tied to a nearby tree where he could happily crop the grass, they set off in a parody of companionship along the coastal path. Bryce was wondering why it was the pair of them had never been bosom pals but always at odds, his brother fiercely competitive, as if needing to prove himself the whole time.

Now, having brought him out here for some private conversation or other, Jago was taking an unconscionable time in coming to the point, walking along sunk in deep thought. Determined not to make it easy over whatever was troubling him, Bryce remained silent, and concentrated on admiring the view. He watched the waves crashing upon the rocks below, then being sucked out again taking broken branches and other flotsam and jetsam with them. He felt rather like those bits of wood, as if he was being tossed about by a huge ocean with no control over his life, least of all his own happiness.

Jago had started to speak. 'I'm aware things are not going as well as you'd hoped in your marriage at the present time.'

Despite the distance which had sprung up between himself and Rose of late, Bryce was at once on the defensive. He knew that he would resent it greatly if his brother became involved in their marital dispute, perhaps by naming Rose's lover, or claiming she was again engaged in an affair. 'That is none of your business.'

'I believe it is. I've discovered something about your wife that I think you should know.'

Bryce felt himself bridle. 'And what that might be? Take care what you say.'

'What I have to say cannot be avoided. I'm sorry to have to tell you, brother, that she is a fraud.'

Bryce stifled a sigh, inwardly furious. So now it would all come out, how Jago had been right to distrust Rose and her alleged son. And he would have to listen to his crowing, as if he hadn't already heard enough of the sorry tale from Joe. 'I'm sure you will enjoy telling me what you mean by that.' His tone was cautious, bored even, yet Bryce felt deeply nervous of what must follow, let alone what his own reaction would be. Was he prepared to forgive Rose, if only for the love he still felt for her, or would that love soon turn to hate when he contemplated the depth of her deceit? Perhaps it rather depended upon her motive. Was she greedy and avaricious like his brother, or had she merely been needy and foolish with a child to protect? Had it been a planned crime or an opportunistic folly?

As it turned out, the crime, as described to him by Jago, was far worse than Bryce could ever have dreamt possible.

'Rosalind Tregowan, or Rose as we now know her, is not who she claims to be. Her real name is Rosie Belsfield. I was always doubtful about whether the child was legitimate, and that point remains uncertain. Unfortunately the real Rosalind tragically died on board ship, allegedly while giving birth, although we have no proof that this child is hers. Rose either stole the boy, or Rosalind's child died and she put her own bastard in its place, presumably in order to make herself a fortune.'

Bryce had stopped dead in his tracks, was staring in stunned disbelief at his brother. 'I don't believe a word of this.'

'I'm afraid you must. And there's worse to come.'

By the time Bryce had heard the rest of Jago's garbled version of the tale he was striding as fast as he could back to the tethered horses. 'If this is some damned plot of yours to rid yourself of Rose and that boy, some lie you've made up, then I'll see you in hell before I—'

'It's no lie, I assure you,' Jago shouted, hurrying to catch up as Bryce flung himself into the saddle and set off at a tearing gallop across the grass towards the woodland. But by the time Bryce reached the house he saw at once that he was too late. A large horse-drawn Black Maria was at the door, and Rose was already being led out into the courtyard by two policemen, an expression of bewildered disbelief on her lovely face.

'I'm sorry to have to inform you, sir,' said the sergeant, 'that we've just charged your wife with murder.'

Chapter Twenty

'I've told the police sergeant that she's innocent. Rosie would never murder anyone, she's far too sweet and nice. But he won't listen.' Joe was sitting with his head in his hands at the kitchen table, almost sobbing with fear. He'd never felt so dreadful in all his life. This was not at all how things were meant to work out when he'd first come up with the notion. His plan had been to keep them comfortable and safe, and set them up with a bit of cash before they slipped away to marry with a nice little nest egg in their pockets. Now his lovely Rose was facing a murder charge. 'How has this come about? Why won't he believe me?'

Tilly put her arms about him. 'Because the police don't work that way. Your word isn't good enough, Joe, not if they think they have evidence against her.'

'What evidence could they possibly have when she

didn't do it?' His cheeks were wet as he looked up at Tilly in desperation. 'This is all my fault. I told the sergeant that it was my idea for her to pretend to be Lady Rosalind, but once he'd questioned me and learnt that I wasn't actually present at the lady's death, he said I could go. He'll contact me if he has any more questions, he says, otherwise I'm off the hook. But Rosie is still on it. I can't bear it! They might hang her! Oh Lordy, what have I done?'

'A good question, what have you done, Joe?' Bryce stood before him, his face ashen. 'I'm willing to listen to the whole sorry tale, so long as you swear to tell the truth this time.'

Joe eagerly nodded, anxious to rid himself of the guilt that was weighing him down, hoping that a confession might somehow make it all come right. 'I'll tell you everything, I swear, exactly as it was. But it ain't a pretty tale.'

'I don't suppose it is. Tilly, put the kettle on, I think we're all going to need a strong cup of tea. And get rid of those gawking maids. I'd rather have this conversation here, in the kitchen, than up in the parlour where Mama is having the vapours and my brother is preening himself like a peacock.'

Tilly rushed to do his bidding while Joe wiped his nose on his sleeve and began at once to talk, gabbling so fast that Bryce put out a hand to stop him.

'Slow down, Joe. I'm listening, but it's essential you don't panic and tell the tale properly.'

Joe took a breath to calm himself, wishing his heart would also slow down instead of pounding like a tom-

tom in his head. 'I've known Rosie since we were nippers together in Bristol. She lived in a flea-ridden cellar, and my lot at that time were all crowded in a miserable room next door. Neither of us knew where our next meal was coming from but Rosie was my best friend, always good fun, and I loved her. Still do. Though happen not in quite the same way, not anymore.'

He glanced up at Tilly when he said this, but she turned away, not seeing the pleading in his gaze. Joe struggled on. 'When my family did another of their moonlight flits, I stayed and moved in with the Belsfields. They were lovely, treating me as one of their own.'

He sniffed and rubbed at his moist eyes with his sleeve, and Bryce handed over his own clean handkerchief. Joe stared at the perfectly embroidered monogram in the corner of the folded linen, then set it down on the table without using it, feeling himself unworthy of such pristine beauty.

'After her dad died in the Boer War, and her mam's sister sent the money for them to go to America, I asked if I could go with them and they said I could. 'Course, Rosie kept on telling me she didn't feel the same way about me as I did about her, so I wasn't to read anything special into this. We were just friends, no more. But I was certain I'd win her round in the end. And I might have done, had it not been for you.' Joe looked at Bryce, yet there was neither anger nor jealousy in his eyes now, only a terrible fear for his dearest friend. 'Maybe the better man won. I'm not fit to clean her shoes, not anymore. Seeing as how she's grown into such a fine lady.'

'So what happened on that ship to America? How did you meet Rosalind?'

Joe shook his head. 'It didn't happen on the way to America, it happened on the way back. It was after Rose had been rejected by Ellis Island and was to be shipped off home without a soul in the world to care for her.'

Tilly brought the tea at this point, pouring them each a cup from the large brown earthenware teapot. As the two men helped themselves to sugar and milk, Tilly silently took her own cup and went to sit beside Joe. He smiled down at her, grateful for her support, clutching hold of her hand beneath the table and loving the gentle warmth of it in his.

'Tell me about Ellis Island, and why Rose was rejected.'

The story took a long time as Joe felt the need to fill in all the details, to describe the horror of the place, and compare the poverty and starvation they'd left behind in Bristol with their hopes for a better life in the new world. Then he explained about the eye test and how it had all gone terribly wrong. He lingered over the story of Rose's sickness on the return journey, unable to resist painting himself as something of a hero. The part concerning Rosalind took no time at all, since he knew little of the relationship between the two women, or what had been agreed between them.

'I didn't even know the lady was dead until we docked at Bristol and I met up with Rose again. I couldn't believe me eyes. There she was looking all posh in milady's best gown, and carrying a pink parasol, apparently so she'd be recognised by whoever came to collect Miss Rosalind.'

'That would be where I came in.'

'Aye, and just before you arrived, sir, was when I made my big mistake.' Joe freely confessed that the deception had been all his idea, how they'd argued fiercely as Rose vehemently objected. 'So you see, it were all my fault. Rose never approved, and refused to go along with it. Then I dropped her right into it by telling you that I was her manservant. Did she give me an earful on that train going down to Cornwall.'

Bryce had largely listened in silence to a recital of this tale, now he almost smiled. 'She can be quite formidable. Ask my mother. So tell me, Joe, given that you'd "dropped her in it" as you say, why did she not speak up and tell the truth? She had countless opportunities. You both did.'

'She had to protect little Robbie, didn't she?'

Bryce got impatiently to his feet. 'Stuff and nonsense! Robbie was in no danger at all. I've listened to these excuses long enough. Quite frankly, it's a pity she didn't manage to knock any sense into that bone head of yours. But then perhaps the pair of you deserve each other. Mama was right, neither of you possesses a moral bone in your body. But all of that aside, what of this charge? Did she tell you how Rosalind died?'

Joe looked bleak. 'She blamed the doctor, said the poor lady had bled to death.'

'Hmm, well, we'll just have to hope she can prove that, along with the rest of this unlikely tale.'

Bryce glared at him so fiercely, clearly struggling to control his temper, that Joe half expected him to lash out and sock him one. He would not have resisted, or attempted to fight back if he had, rather believing that he deserved a good thumping, in view of what was happening to Rose. Instead, Bryce calmly concluded, 'Now I suppose I must visit my wife in jail and see what she has to say about all of this. Then face the reality of whatever happens next.'

What happened next so far as Joe was concerned was that they were interrupted at that moment by Gladys rushing in, cheeks aflame and quite out of breath. 'The police are back, and this time they've come for Joe. He's to be charged as an accomplice, and with fraud.'

Rose didn't have any tears left to shed. She'd cried herself dry that first night, wrung every last tear from her body till there was nothing left, and still she hadn't slept a wink. But then the hard, biscuit-like mattress that passed for a bed was not meant to offer much in the way of comfort. Nor was there any warmth in the cell as the damp ran down the walls, cockroaches and mice scuttled about in the darkness, and the whole place stank of urine, filth and stale sweat. The warden had told her she was fortunate to be given a cell of her own, but she didn't feel fortunate, not in the least. Rose felt as if her life was over.

All the second day she'd waited and waited, hoping against hope that Bryce would come and rescue her, that someone would tell her it had all been a terrible mistake and she wasn't to be tried for murder after all.

No such miracle had occurred, and she'd faced a second night all alone, locked in her prison cell. How many more lonely nights would follow?

On the third morning she was brought before the

magistrates and remanded in custody to await trial.

'When will that be?' she'd asked the warden as he'd locked her back in her cell.

'When the judge has time to hear your case. Could be months.'

'Months! But I'm innocent,' she cried as he clanged shut the door.

'Aye,' he laughed. 'That's what they all say.'

So now Rose sat in stunned disbelief, a feeling of dread growing inside her over how long she would have to spend locked up in this cell, and what would happen if the judge didn't believe her version of events. How could she prove her innocence without word from the doctor? But then no one had been with her when Rosalind had actually passed away early in the morning, not even the steward. What if they presumed her to be guilty and she was told that she'd be hanged by the neck until dead?

A voice inside of Rose's head was screaming, even as outwardly she remained silent and frozen, paralysed by fear.

And why hadn't Bryce come?

On the fourth morning she was told there was a visitor to see her. Her heart gave a leap of hope. He was here, he hadn't forgotten her after all. She quickly smoothed down her hair, straightened the grey prison gown in which she was now dressed, both looking somewhat grubby and unkempt. She pinched her cheeks to bring some colour into them, desperately wanting to look her best when she saw Bryce, for didn't he love her and would never let her down, which was surely what he'd come to say?

He probably regretted their quarrel now, and all that nonsense about his marrying her for money.

Waiting for her in the visitors' room was Mr Wrayworth. Disappointment flooded through her, coupled with a terrible grief for the love she had once believed in and which seemed to have been entirely false. The old solicitor grasped her hands, and giving them a little squeeze gently steered her to a chair, clucking softly like the proverbial mother hen.

'Dear, dear, what a pretty pickle this is. But let us come directly to the point—'

'Before you do that,' Rose interrupted. 'What of Bryce? Why didn't he come himself?'

Mr Wrayworth cleared his throat, looking oddly embarrassed. 'Master Bryce is otherwise engaged at the present time. In addition, he considers that your best chance of release is to have proper legal representation, which is why he has sent me in his place.'

Rose saw no reason why Bryce couldn't have come as well, but didn't say as much. She had no wish to appear ungrateful. 'I certainly do need help, Mr Wrayworth.'

'And you shall most certainly be given it. Not for a moment, dear lady, do I believe a word of this charge. I've already made my views upon the matter very clear to the sergeant, although as you will appreciate there appears to be a slight question of integrity. You have apparently been less than honest with all of us, and are not in fact Lady Rosalind Tregowan.' He looked at her in his kindly fashion, one bushy eyebrow raised, as if she were a naughty schoolgirl.

'No, I'm sorry to have deceived you all, but it's true, I'm not Rosalind. No doubt you've been told the whole sorry tale by this time.' Shame brought a blush to her cheeks. 'I deeply regret what we did, Joe and I, but it was for little Robbie, do you see? I couldn't just hand him over to complete strangers without checking the Tregowans out first. Nor did I think they'd allow me to do that if they knew I was nothing more than some bit of rubbish rejected from Ellis Island.'

Mr Wrayworth frowned. 'Don't speak of yourself in such a derogatory way, dear. I'm quite sure you acted with the best will in the world; unfortunately your friend perhaps had less altruistic motives.'

She could hardly deny it. 'How is Joe?'

The solicitor swiftly explained that he too was in jail, although facing a lesser charge. 'I will do what I can for Joe too, but it is your own situation which concerns me the most. Tell me the whole story, please. I'd like to hear it in your own words.'

It was only when she actually explained out loud how it all came about that Rose truly saw the depth of her own stupidity. She should never have allowed this to happen. If she'd spoken up and been honest from the first, she would not now be in this dreadful situation.

When she was done, and Mr Wrayworth had finished writing his notes, he invited Rose to ask any questions of her own. But instead of querying what the outcome might be, as the solicitor clearly expected, ready to answer as diplomatically as possible, she instead asked how the truth had been revealed.

'Do you know who discovered our secret, who told the police?'

The solicitor started to gather up his papers, as if suddenly anxious to be on his way. It appeared to be a question he was unable, or unwilling, to answer. 'Do not worry your head about such things, my dear. I shall call again next week, and keep you fully informed of any progress I make on your behalf.'

'You must find the doctor, or the steward. They will speak up for me, I'm sure,' she cried, desperation making her voice crack.

Mr Wrayworth sighed, even as he patted her hand in sympathy. 'Unfortunately, my dear, such peripatetic persons are rarely in one place long enough to locate, let alone ask them the necessary questions. But you can be sure that I will do everything in my power to secure your acquittal.'

Rose looked into the face of this elderly man of whom she had grown quite fond, and believed that he would keep his word to do his very best for her. But she could also see in the way he failed to meet her gaze that he held little hope of success.

'Please give my love to my husband, and tell him . . . tell him . . . that I never meant to deceive him . . . and that I'm sorry.'

Rose had so badly wanted it to be Bryce who came, instead of Mr Wrayworth, for then she could have told Bryce to his face how she had done this out of love, not out of greed – love for Robbie – and then later she had kept quiet for fear of losing him.

After the solicitor had gone Rose was silently escorted back to her cell, the door clanged shut and the huge key turned in the lock. It was only then, as the bitterness of her disappointment struck, that the tears started again, and she knew she faced yet another sleepless night.

'The first thing to be done, Mama, is to rid ourselves of that child.'

'Oh, I do so agree! How very clever of you to have exposed his cheat of a mother. Well done, darling. The thought of that brat walking off with our inheritance gives me the shudders. Deal with it at once, will you, dear? I won't enquire where you send him, but I'm quite sure you'll find somewhere suitable for an illegitimate orphan.'

Jago's thin lips quirked with pleasure at the prospect. 'I shall set about the task immediately.'

'Excellent! My first job this morning is to revert all those ridiculous sops of comfort that interfering madam put in place for the servants,' Lydia said, giving the bell pull a sharp tug. 'Goodness me, the woman was a complete liability. How dare she walk in, steal our money and then lord it over us! What a relief to be rid of the silly chit's interference at last. Now do start making the necessary arrangements without delay, before Bryce discovers what we are about. We don't want him creating difficulties.'

'You can leave the matter safely in my hands.'

'I know, darling,' and Lydia kissed her son, full on the lips, as she so loved to do.

Mrs Quintrell entered just as Jago was hurrying away, anxious to put their agreed plan into effect.

'Was there something you wanted, milady?' the housekeeper politely enquired.

'Yes, Mrs Quintrell, you can tell everyone to move back into their original rooms.' This order was met by a strangely blank look. Paying no heed to the housekeeper's frowning silence, Lydia blithely continued with her instructions. 'And make sure that all fripperies such as curtains, rugs and personal items be removed. This is not a hotel for layabouts, the servants are here to work, and should carry out their duties without distractions. Please see to it at once.'

The housekeeper cleared her throat, finally finding her voice. 'I'm sorry to have to say this, milady, but I very much doubt they'll agree to that.'

Lydia stared at the woman askance, eyes wide with shock that anyone should dare to cross her. 'I beg your pardon?'

'The fact is, milady, being cold in your bed with not enough covers on, nor even the comfort of a hot-water bottle, is more distracting. A person can't sleep, so starts work tired every morning. Now everyone is warm and cosy they sleep well and come to their duties properly refreshed. The staff also like to have enough light so's they can write home to family, or read quietly for a few minutes before falling asleep.'

'I will *not* have my maids reading twopenny novels.'

'They're more likely to read letters from loved ones, or the beauty pages from the *Woman At Home* magazine, although some do like to read their Bible, milady. It's worth remembering that. And they're all nicely settled in now. The rooms have been cleaned and decorated, they have more space for their belongings and more pride in themselves as a result. Even the menservants are happy to keep their rooms clean now. I wouldn't like to comment on Miss Rose's present situation, milady, but what she did for the servants was a good thing. I see that now.'

'It is not your place, Mrs Quintrell, to comment on anything. I cannot believe I'm even hearing this.'

'I could ask them, if you like, see what they have to say on the matter.'

Now Lydia put a hand to her head, which had suddenly started to ache, her shock was so profound. 'I have never, in my entire life, *asked* a servant what they have to say about anything, and have certainly no intention of starting now.'

'Begging your pardon, milady, but times are changing and I'm only suggesting that mebbe it might be wise. A happy staff is an efficient one, wouldn't you agree?'

Lydia almost laughed. 'I'm not interested in whether or not they are happy. They are here to work, not to enjoy themselves. Pray do exactly as I say, woman. If they do not like it you can tell them they have no choice in the matter. Either they move back to their original rooms as they were before that chit interfered, or they can collect their wages and leave forthwith. And that goes for you too, Mrs Quintrell.'

The housekeeper's eyes glittered, but, bobbing a curtsey, all she said was, 'Thank you, milady.' At which point she was dismissed and sent about her business.

Later that afternoon Lydia was comfortably drowsing on her favourite sofa when she woke with a start to hear the clock chime five. 'Goodness gracious, it surely can't be that time already?' She was quite alone, Bryce about some business matter or other in Fowey, and Jago presumably making the necessary arrangements. 'Why wasn't I brought tea at four o'clock, as usual?' Lydia muttered to herself as she angrily tugged on the bell pull.

No one came. For once Mrs Quintrell did not instantly obey the summons, as she normally did, not even a housemaid came running. Furious at being ignored, and desperate for her tea, Lydia tugged the rope again. No response.

'What on earth is happening?'

Snatching open the door, she marched out into the hall. Nothing would induce her to go down the backstairs to the kitchen. Heaven forfend, it was not her place to go chasing after servants. Instead, she stood at the head of the stairs and shouted.

'Mrs Quintrell? Gladys? Where is everyone? I require tea in the small parlour, if you please. This minute!'

Returning to the sofa, she waited. By half past five when still no tea or delicious scones had arrived, Lydia decided no one could have heard her, and the bell must be faulty. She went across to the library and pulled the bell pull there instead. Waiting with barely constrained patience, foot tapping, arms folded, her cheeks had grown quite scarlet by the time Lydia realised no one intended to answer that one either. She next tried the drawing room, and the dining room, where the same thing happened. No one was responding to any of her calls. It was as if the house were deserted, suddenly devoid of servants.

Only then did Lydia notice that no fires had been lit.

They had all been laid that morning, as usual, by the parlourmaid, who should by rights have come to light them by now so that the rooms had time to warm up before dinner. It was already beginning to go dark and not even the lamps had been lit or curtains drawn. Both the dining and drawing rooms felt cold, barren and decidedly gloomy.

Back in the hall, and having abandoned all hope of afternoon tea, Lydia stamped off upstairs to change, calling her maid as she usually did at this time. Gladys did not arrive.

'That stupid girl surely does not expect me to struggle into my dinner gown by myself? Where is she?'

When there was still no sign of Gladys by half past six, and no answer to her increasingly frantic tugs of the bell pull, Lydia was obliged to don the simplest gown she could find. She was raging by the time she returned to the library, where she would normally expect to find Rowell serving drinks. Jago was helping himself to a whisky but there was no sign of the butler. At least the fire was lit now, and she gave a small sigh of relief.

'Thank goodness, these housemaids must be half asleep today. No afternoon tea and not even Gladys to assist me to dress for dinner. I shall have something to say about that. Oh, do pour me a gin and it, darling, I feel quite fraught.' Sinking into the comfiest chair, she asked, 'Where is Bryce?'

'Gone out. I was just thinking of doing the same, probably to my club in town,' Jago remarked, swallowing his whisky in one gulp. 'I very much doubt there will be any dinner tonight.'

'Good gracious me, what are you talking about?'

'I am reliably informed that the staff are on strike.'

Lydia laughed out loud. 'Don't be ridiculous!'

'I'm perfectly serious.' Jago shrugged on his coat, which he'd left draped across the back of a chair. 'I think you'll find they are objecting to being sent back to those squalid little dormitories like naughty schoolchildren. I think you may have to back down on that one, Mama. Best of luck, anyway. Oh, there are a few nuts and raisins in the cocktail cabinet. Those might keep you going for a while.'

Lydia treated her son's remarks with the disdain she considered they deserved, and quietly sipped her gin after he'd gone. But later, when she wanted her glass refilled, when eight o'clock came and still no dinner gong had sounded, she was grateful for the nuts and raisins. She realised then that Jago must have been speaking the truth. By ten o'clock the fire had fallen to ashes, and still no one had answered her frequent and increasingly furious tugs of the bell. Lydia decided she had no alternative but to retire to her bed, cold and hungry and very angry. She might very well dismiss the lot of them come morning.

By breakfast time, however, when she found no warming dishes filled with bacon, sausage and scrambled egg waiting on the sideboard, no toast or hot coffee set ready, she had second thoughts. This time the housekeeper did come when called, perhaps scenting victory.

'I may have been somewhat hasty in making a decision, Mrs Quintrell, but I've been giving that little matter we discussed yesterday more thought. You may inform the servants that they can stay in the newly decorated rooms.'

'Thank you, milady,' the housekeeper politely remarked. 'And would milady care to order breakfast now?'

'Oh, yes please. That would be lovely.' Lydia knew when she was beaten. Her personal comforts were everything to her.

Mrs Quintrell only just managed not to smile as she bobbed a curtsey and hurried to inform the staff of their success. Later that same morning, having suffered yet another sleepless night and skipped breakfast entirely as he had no appetite, Bryce was sitting in a sheltered arbour in the rose garden. It seemed somehow appropriate as he again gloomily contemplated the horror of Rose's situation. He kept going over and over in his mind the story Joe had told him. He was also filled with guilt for not having been to see Rose yet, but then he was desperately trying to sort out his true feelings. Did he still love her? He could not deny it, although a part of him hated her too for having brought this catastrophe upon them. Did he believe her guilty of such a crime? Surely not. Rose was the gentlest, sweetest soul, so loving and caring, both of himself and the child.

Then what exactly had happened to Rosalind? Whose was this child? How had this whole stupid charade come about? If he went to the prison and asked Rose to explain her version of the story, could he trust her answer? Did he even want his marriage to continue?

His thoughts were interrupted as Tilly came running to him, quite out of breath. 'Oh, thank goodness, I've found you at last, sir. I've been searching for you an hour or more. Master Jago has taken Robbie.'

Chapter Twenty-One

Bryce stared at Tilly in dismay. 'Taken Robbie where?'

'I really don't know, sir, but Master Jago just walked into the nursery first thing this morning, picked Robbie up and carried him away. Screaming and kicking like a banshee, he was, poor lamb. I ran after them, of course, asked where he was taking the child. I was told it was none of my business but that my services as nursemaid would no longer be required as he was to be sent to a home for orphans forthwith, which was where he belonged.'

Bryce was on his feet in a second. 'But that's entirely wrong. He can't do that. The boy isn't an orphan. It would appear that we have no proof he is even illegitimate as he could very well still be Rosalind's child. Where the hell has my brother taken the boy? I must put a stop to this at once.'

He strode off at a cracking pace back to the house,

Tilly scurrying along behind, but Jago was nowhere to be found. Lydia calmly informed her younger son that he'd left in the motor at first light, with John driving, destination unknown.

'Did he have Robbie with him?' Bryce barked out the question, making his mother flinch.

'Of course. The child cannot possibly stay here.'

'Why can't he?' Bryce repeated what he had already said to Tilly, who was even now standing behind him, her face a picture of distress with tears running down her cheeks. 'Rose may have tricked us all with this silly charade but that child could still be Rosalind's son, the young baronet.'

Lydia snorted her derision. 'If you believe that then you are a greater fool than I took you for, and you have most certainly behaved like one. I do not believe a word that girl says, nor that lover of hers, Joe whatever-his-name-is. I said from the start it was a mistake to take the pair in, and I've been proved right, as always. They've made us look utterly ridiculous to be taken in by such charlatans. I have absolutely no reason to believe in the authenticity of that child. He is undoubtedly their bastard.'

'For once in your life, Mother, you could be wrong. In which case you will have dispatched the next baronet of Penver, the grandson Sir Ralph would have adored, had he been fortunate enough to live a little longer, to some penurious orphanage.'

If he had hoped for any sign of regret or guilt, he was disappointed. Fervently wishing that he had indeed visited Bodmin prison and insisted on Rose telling him the whole sordid story in her own words, Bryce rapidly came to a decision. 'Until we know for certain that the boy is not who Rose claims him to be, then he belongs here, at Penver Court, whether you like it not, Mother. Have you any idea where Jago may have taken him? If you know anything at all, please speak now, for I will not stand silently by and see that child punished for a deceit practised by another.'

Holding fast to his temper, Bryce felt as if he might explode as he waited in vain for her reply.

Lydia simply looked at him, lips curled with contempt. 'You always were far too soft for your own good, Bryce. It's a pity you don't have more of your brother's backbone.'

'I have never lacked backbone, Mother,' Bryce told her through gritted teeth. 'What is missing in me, thank goodness, is my brother's callous ruthlessness, a trait he no doubt inherited from you. Make no mistake, I shall find little Robbie, and bring him home where he belongs, and no one will stop me.' Wasting no time, Bryce hastened to his room where he stuffed a few clothes into an overnight bag. He was in the stables saddling up Godolphin when again Tilly came running, as hot and flushed as ever.

'I've asked a few questions among the staff and the general opinion is that John said something about being asked to drive Master Jago to Bristol. It does seem the most likely place he'd choose, sir.'

'Since that was where Joe and Rose came from, you mean. You may well be right, Tilly. Well done! I'll certainly try there first. In which case I shall take the Electric Phaeton. For all it has a tendency to break down

312

from time to time, it will be faster than even Godolphin. And goodness knows when the next train is, even if there were someone to drive me to the station.'

'Everyone wishes you well in your quest, sir, and hopes you bring Master Robbie home safe and sound.'

'I will do my very best, Tilly. None of this is any fault of that child, whoever he may be.'

'Nor is it the fault of your wife. As if she would murder anyone, lovely lady like her. Begging your pardon, sir, but these charges are wicked, and if I were you I'd be questioning where they originated from in the first place.'

Bryce stared at her for a long moment, then without another word, climbed into the motor and drove away. But Tilly's words hung in his mind, refusing to budge. He wished, with all his heart and soul, that he could share her faith.

Bryce was tireless in his search. He not only drove in his motor for hours on end each day, but also walked for miles around the city, visiting missions and churches, speaking to nuns and priests, to vicars and teachers, doctors and midwives, and whatever charity officials he could find who might direct him to any orphanage or children's home. And in case Jago had changed the boy's name, whenever he visited one he would refuse to simply inspect the admissions book but insisted on viewing all likely children of Robbie's age.

But his search proved fruitless. By the end of the week there were no more places left to try, he'd run out of ideas and contacts, and still hadn't located the boy. However much Bryce might tell himself that there was no proof that this child was Rosalind's son, and therefore the baronet, he still felt as if he had failed.

But who had he failed, exactly? Surely not Rose, since her entire story had been built on lies. None of this would have happened if she hadn't perpetrated this deceit. If she was not the woman he thought her to be, was she also capable of killing Rosalind in order to steal her inheritance?

Surely not. How could he even doubt Rose's innocence? She was his own darling wife and he loved her, had believed that she loved him as deeply. Wrayworth still believed in her. The old solicitor had urged him to investigate further, to find some evidence, some witness perhaps, who could speak in her favour. Yet Bryce had found none. He'd painstakingly gone through her belongings and found nothing to prove her identity, or that of the boy. The woman was a complete mystery to him, and he hated the fact that she'd deliberately deceived him.

Bryce felt himself torn in two, desperately wanting to trust Rose, yet quite unable to do so. He could hardly stand before the judge and insist his wife could not be guilty of this heinous charge because he still loved her. But was that even true? Did he still love her, or did he hate her?

As he drove back down to Cornwall, Bryce thought of the state of some of the institutions that he'd viewed, of the stern-faced wardens, the bleakness and cold that had permeated every stark room, the endless regimentation, the lessons and chores and rules. None of it softened by the love of a mother, as Robbie had received in abundance from Rose. Row upon row of children, from babies to adolescents, some looking up at him with bright hope in their small eager faces, still anticipating rescue, while others were blank, as if long resigned to their loveless fate.

Most of all, Bryce realised, he'd failed the child. Whether or not Robbie was Sir Ralph's grandson, or Rose guilty or innocent, Robbie did not deserve to be shunted off to one of these dismal establishments where he was no more than a numbered label on his pinafore.

Yet what more could be done?

Speak to Rose, urged the voice in his head. Perhaps if he went to see her, this allegedly wicked woman who happened to be his own wife, he could resolve some of this inner turmoil.

They sat at a table opposite each other, not touching, not speaking, but Rose could see by the cool detachment in those enigmatic dark eyes that she had little hope of winning him over. Her husband's belief in her guilt was written plain on his face. Whatever she said in her own defence, Rose doubted Bryce would accept it as the truth. She had deceived him for far too long, hurt him too deeply.

'Why have you come?' she asked. She might have added, why now, after all this time? But pride held her silent. Rose was determined to hang on to her dignity, even as she ached to fling herself into his arms and beg him to love her, to believe in her.

'Perhaps I wanted to ask you why?' Bryce felt a nudge of cruel satisfaction as he saw the shock of this blunt question register on her face, the way she blinked as if he'd physically struck her. But then why should he be the only one hurting?

Her voice, when she answered, was astonishingly devoid of emotion. 'Why I killed Rosalind, do you mean? Is that what you think I did?'

'Did you?'

The pain caused by this seemingly simple question was so bad that Rose felt as if her heart might break in two. Perhaps it already had and was now bleeding, draining away the last of her strength, the final remnants of hope. She had no fight left in her. 'Would you believe me, were I to attempt to answer your question by telling you what really happened?'

He paused very slightly before answering. 'I'm not sure. You do seem to find difficulty with the truth.' Bryce was thinking how pale she looked, how thin and ill. He wanted to take her home and make her well again, feed her one of Mrs Pascoe's best pasties, then make love to her till the roses came back into her cheeks.

'I went along with the plan out of love, not greed.'

'You *lied* out of pure selfishness, for your own gain, and that of Joe, your alleged lover!' Bryce almost spat the words at her, hating himself for wanting to pull her on to his lap and kiss her even as fury raged through him like fire. If the prison guard hadn't been standing directly behind her, he might well have done so.

'No!' she cried. 'That's not true. I wanted to tell you, to confess, oh so many times.'

'Then why didn't you?'

'Because I was afraid for Robbie, and later of losing you.'

He almost laughed. 'Why on earth would you be afraid for Robbie? He was never in any danger, except that created by yourself.'

'He *was*! Jago threatened him out on the headland one day, shortly after I arrived.'

'And you never thought to mention this before? I wonder why? Perhaps because it's yet another of your lies. Stop making excuses and blaming other people. First Joe, whether he be friend or lover, now Jago, even my own mother. It really is time you took some responsibility for your own actions, Rose, or whatever your name is. You brought this upon yourself.'

Rose sat before him in her shapeless prison dress, soiled from the floors she'd been scrubbing all morning, as, white-faced, she fought back tears. If only he would allow her to properly explain then he might understand. But he was too filled with anger and bitterness to listen.

He leant closer, so that the guards couldn't hear, so close that Rose could see the way his eyes twitched with anger. 'My faith in women had been badly damaged by the matrimonial shenanigans of my own mother, by her cupidity and malice. Finding you changed all of that. You healed me, like a fresh sea breeze blowing away all the cobwebs of bitterness. I loved you. It's as simple as that. Now I see that I was duped yet again. Your greed is even greater than hers.'

Again the pain kicked in and Rose winced, as if physically wounded by the arrows of his words. 'And *I* love *you*.' She did indeed love this man, would give her life for him, but he saw her as a merciless killer who cared only for her own needs. If she had lost Bryce, her one true love, then she'd lost everything that was good in her life.

How many times must she face loss and drag herself back from the brink? First her father to the war, then their home following his death. She'd been rejected and separated from her mother and siblings and lost her dreams of a new life in America with them. But Rose had believed she'd found true happiness at last. Now she'd lost that too.

But what was the use of complaining? As Bryce said, she'd brought this upon herself. And what did it matter anymore? During the seemingly endless days and weeks of her confinement Rose had learnt acceptance. She'd made a bad mistake, practised a wicked deceit, created a whole web of lies, and now she must pay the price. The charge might be wrong, the punishment more harsh than she rightly deserved, but there was nothing to be done about that.

Only one person mattered now. At least she'd ensured that he was safe. 'How is Robbie?' she asked, her voice softening with a mother's love.

Now it was Bryce's turn to be filled with despair. He dropped his gaze, tearing his eyes from her at last as he worried what her reaction would be when she learnt that Robbie was gone. Jago had already been back at Penver Court almost two weeks by the time Bryce had returned from his search of the Bristol institutions, and they'd had the most almighty row. Unusually, Bryce had lost his temper, and, gripping his brother by the collar, he'd shaken him hard, only just managing to restrain himself sufficiently not to punch the life out of him. 'Where have you taken him?'

'Where you won't find him,' came the caustic response. 'And where the brat deserves to be.'

'Is this your doing? Are you the one responsible for my wife being held on this ridiculous charge?'

Jago had smirked. 'She's the one who committed a crime, not me. She, Rosie Belsfield, was the one who killed Rosalind in order to inherit a fortune, then lied and cheated and tricked us all. I have no doubt that she should be hanged.'

'Damn you to hell! What proof do you have of her guilt?'

'What proof do you have that she's innocent?'

They'd argued, they'd sworn and rampaged and roared, and flung furious insults at each other. And when ultimately it had indeed come to blows, the noise of the fight had brought John and Tilly and other concerned servants running to forcibly pull the pair apart, worried Bryce might actually kill his brother. Nevertheless, Jago had remained obstinately silent about Robbie's whereabouts.

'And quite right too,' Lydia said, as always taking her elder son's side.

Resolving not to admit defeat, Bryce had turned his attention to searching other towns nearby: Bodmin, Newquay, Liskeard, even as far as Truro in one direction, and Exeter in the other. Bone-weary from travelling, of the constant bumping over unmade roads, mending punctured tyres, and spending a small fortune on petroleum, still he searched. Bryce knew that the longer he left it, the less likelihood there was of ever finding Robbie, as children grew and changed so quickly. But he had failed. Now he must face Rose with this unpalatable truth.

'I'm not sure how he is, or where, for that matter. I'm sorry to have to tell you but Robbie is no longer at Penver Court.'

Rose stared at him, bemused. 'What do you mean, no longer at Penver Court?'

'He's gone.'

'Gone where?'

'Jago sent him away, put him in an institution, an orphanage or some such. I've no idea which one.' Bryce could hardly bear to witness the agony in her lovely face. Yet could he be certain the pain and shock were because she actually loved the child? More likely, if the boy was indeed lost, it would mean that all her efforts in procuring a fortune for him had been for naught.

Rose was on her feet, staring at him wild-eyed, a roaring in her head as the shock slowly ebbed away and the implications of what he'd just told her began to sink in. 'What are you saying? *You've lost Robbie?* Then why are you even here? Why aren't you out looking for him? Have you no heart, no feelings of any kind? Ignore me if you like, treat me with utter contempt if you must. I deserve it for deceiving you, but don't take it out on Robbie! How can you do such a thing to dear Rosalind's precious boy!'

Then, quite beside herself with grief, Rose began to slap him, raining blows upon his head with such fury that two prison guards leapt forward to grab her and half carried her away, still screaming.

Bryce left the prison in a daze. He was not greatly bruised by her attack, or particularly shocked by her reaction. Of course she loved the child. How could he have doubted it for a second? But the only words now ringing in his head were, '*How can you do such a thing to dear Rosalind's precious boy!*' Bryce went twice more to the prison, neither visit proving any easier for either of them. On the third occasion, when he admitted that he still hadn't found Robbie, Rose told him not to come again.

'If you can't be bothered to look for him properly, I really don't want you here.'

'But I *have* been looking for him, night and day.'

'Not nearly hard enough.'

'Why did you call him dear Rosalind's precious son?'

'Because that's what he is. Why won't you believe me?'

'I no longer know what to believe.'

'Then go away!' she shouted, and asked the guards to take her back to her cell. Rose couldn't even bear to look at him, the very sight of his dear face reminding her all too clearly of what she had lost.

The court was in session. The prosecution and the barrister for the defence appointed for Rose by Mr Wrayworth seemed to be engaged in some legal argument, speaking about her as if she weren't sitting right before them, calling her 'the accused' as if she wasn't a real person at all. Fear was sharp in her, making her feel sick, yet Rose had a great desire to shout at them both to speak in common

321

English so that she could understand, and for somebody to explain to her what was going on. Instead, she bit her lip and sent up a silent prayer that she would maintain control, even when it came to the part where the judge slipped that square of black cloth on to his head and . . .

Rose shuddered, blocking off the thought before it went any further.

Turning her attention to the rest of the courtroom she noticed a growing audience, no doubt all come to gawp and salivate over seeing someone charged with murder. She looked for Bryce, searching every row, but could see no sign of him. She was aware that he'd called several more times at the prison to see her, but she'd always refused. And then he'd stopped coming and perversely she'd felt mortified, deserted and abandoned, needing him more than ever. Yet surely he would come on this most important day?

The panelled room was dark and gloomy, smelt of polish and something rancid, rather like vomit. The seat in the dock was hard and already making her back ache after only an hour and a half. But the proceedings had hardly begun, with only the jury sworn in and one or two points of law dealt with, whatever they might be.

Right at the last moment, just as the judge addressed the prosecution, telling him to call his first witness, Bryce slipped in to take a seat at the back. He immediately looked across at her and, heart pounding, Rose managed a little smile. He did not respond, merely looked down at his hands for a moment, then at the prosecutor.

Jago was the first to enter the witness box and Rose started to tremble, as much with fury as fear, as she looked with loathing upon this man who she was convinced had ruined her life. What had he discovered about her? How would he twist it to suit his own desire to deprive Robbie of his true heritage?

He was asked to give his name and explain his relationship with the defendant, plus a few other fairly innocuous questions. Then the prosecution came to the meat of his evidence.

'When were you first suspicious that this supposed Rosalind Tregowan was not in fact who she claimed to be?'

'Almost from the start,' Jago said, looking extremely pleased with himself.

'Can you tell us why that was.'

'She was a woman without a history. She told us nothing about her childhood, where she'd lived in Canada, nothing. Simply claimed to have married Robert in New York a few years ago. She wasn't even specific about the date of their marriage.'

'Did she provide any documentary evidence of this alleged marriage?'

'No, but I later discovered the certificate myself, hidden under a floorboard in her room. I dare say that was an intrusion, but I was so suspicious by this time that I had to find some answers.'

As the certificate was passed forward as evidence, Rose gasped. So that was how this had all come about. But if he'd found the tin box, he must also have found the letter signed by Rosalind, with the steward acting as witness, granting her custody of the boy. Yet throughout the questioning that followed, no mention was made of this. When the judge declared they break for lunch, Rose asked to speak to her counsel and asked him why.

'Is this letter important?'

'Of course it is important!' Was nobody listening to her? 'It proves that Rosalind knew she was dying and asked me to take care of Robbie for her, and deliver the baby safely to his grandfather. She didn't know Sir Ralph himself was sick and close to death – had never even met her father-in-law – but she was deeply concerned that her precious son be brought up in the bosom of his father's family. I told Mr Wrayworth about that letter, mentioned it several times.'

'Do you have any other copy of it?'

'No, why would I?'

'I agree it could be valuable evidence, but it is only your word against Jago's that the document even exists.' The barrister asked her more questions in the short time they were allowed, and Rose waited with hope in her heart for him to bring the matter up in court. But when Jago was finally asked if he'd found anything else in the tin box other than the marriage certificate, he shook his head. 'No, nothing.'

'Did you find any letters among Rosalind's papers?'

'Only a bundle of love letters, which I ignored, having no wish to pry,' Jago said, somewhat sanctimoniously.

'Is it not true that you found a copy of an agreement between the accused and Rosalind?'

'No.'

'That is a lie!' Rose called out, trembling with rage.

'Miss Belsfield, I must ask you to remain silent. This is a court of law, not the cheap seats at the music hall.'

The defence barrister shot her a warning look before continuing with his line of questioning. 'Is it not true that you did in fact find and read this agreement and then destroyed it, as it revealed that Rosalind, aware she was dying, asked the defendant to care for her baby, and would therefore prove my client innocent?'

'No.'

At this point the judge interrupted to impatiently ask the defence counsel if he possessed any evidence that such a document existed. The barrister was forced to admit that he did not.

'Then let us move on. Next witness, please.'

Rose sat in stunned disbelief, appalled that this, the most vital piece of evidence in her favour, had not been found nor even proved to exist.

Various members of the household were called by the prosecution. Lydia, of course, who was more than happy to paint the worst possible picture of Rose. The servants came next including Mrs Pascoe, Tilly and finally Joe. Bryce was not called, probably because as her husband his word would not be considered reliable. The questions continued over the following days. On the third morning Rose felt a spurt of hope as the ship's doctor appeared for the defence and confirmed that Rosalind had indeed given birth to a fine healthy son. But he spoke with some condescension of Rose's efforts.

'She was but a ragamuffin from the slums without the first notion of how to care for a lady of class and distinction.'

'That's not true!' Rose shouted, unable to help herself.

'Quiet!' roared the judge, glowering at her most sternly.

'Did you expect Rosalind, Lady Tregowan, to make a full recovery, or did you experience some doubts, possibly due to the storm and difficult conditions on board?' asked the defence.

'There was absolutely no reason for her not to survive the birth.'

'There was,' Rose shouted again. 'She was bleeding to death, and you went off to see to the other passengers who were only seasick.'

'Counsel, if you cannot keep your client quiet I must ask for her to be removed from the court. I will not tell you again, Miss Belsfield.'

Rose hated the judge for calling her that. This must be the second or third time. She glanced across at Bryce sitting ashen-faced and silent on the back row. Why didn't he say something? But then she saw him write a note and pass it down, and her defence counsel said, 'My Lord, the accused is in fact a married lady. Her correct title is still Mrs Tregowan.'

'We can at least be sure of that, can we?' grumbled His Honour.

'We can indeed, My Lord. That is one document we do have.'

The doctor had been no help, the letter written by Rosalind that she most needed could not be found, and the more Rose listened to the case against her, the more convinced she became that all was lost.

On the fifth day of the trial, following the judge's summing-up, the jury retired to consider their verdict. They were out for less than an hour. It was then that Rose came face to face with her fate.

Chapter Twenty-Two

Bryce was waiting for Rose as she came from the courtroom, her face ashen and her hesitant steps that of an old woman. A guard tried to usher him away, but he stood his ground. He had no idea what he intended to say to her, what he could do to help, or even what he was feeling right now. Bryce felt numb, yet fiercely determined to do something. 'I must see my wife. She is in a dreadful state. Let me at least speak to her.'

They were allowed a few precious moments together before Rose was to be boarded into the Black Maria and transported back to Bodmin prison for the last time. Her next outing would be to visit the hangman, just one short week from now. The judge didn't intend wasting any time in ridding the world of this wicked woman.

Hearing that one word – guilty – had left him paralysed with shock. Bryce felt almost as if he were standing outside of himself, watching, observing, not really a part of this terrible catastrophe. How could this be happening, his entire world falling apart around him? He could hardly bear to look into Rose's lovely face and think what she was about to suffer. Far too dreadful to contemplate!

They sat holding hands, saying nothing but drawing strength each from the other. He could feel her shaking but she wasn't crying, or in hysterics, as he'd feared she might be. He was filled with admiration for her courage and strength. Perhaps, like him, she was still in shock and hadn't quite taken it all in. Unable to resist, Bryce kissed her brow, ignoring a grunted reprimand from the guard. 'I love you, Rose. I want you to know that I believe in you absolutely. I will never give up on you. I'll get you released, I swear it.'

Rose put her fingers to his lips, tears spilling from eyes filled with love. 'It is enough that you believe in my innocence. I shall die content.'

'I will not allow you to die, my love. I'll move heaven and earth if need be, but I'll never give up fighting for you.'

'That's enough. Time to go now.' The guard was grasping her arm, pulling her away, clipping handcuffs to her wrists. 'You can see her at normal visiting times next week, before the sentence is carried out,' he told Bryce with stark disinterest, then Rose was being marched away, surrounded by guards on every side.

'I'll never give up,' he called after her. 'I love you.'

'Do you realise what you've done?' Bryce roared at his brother. Hot anger soared through his veins as he thought of her bravery, her stoic courage, her innocence. How could he ever have doubted it? 'My wife is to lose her life because of your spiteful interference. Your vengeful greed will result in her being hanged for a crime she did not commit.'

Jago made a scoffing sound deep in his throat. 'This is none of my doing. Blame the jury, or that doctor. Blame Rosie Belsfield herself for the lies she's told.'

'Don't call her that. Her name is Rose Tregowan. She is still my wife and I'll have you treat her with proper respect.'

Eyes glittering with amused disbelief, Jago gave a bark of laughter. 'Respect? That's almost funny. She deserves all that's coming to her.'

'Indeed she does, the grasping little madam,' put in Lydia.

Bryce could hardly speak let alone concentrate, his thoughts and feelings were a confused jumble in his head. He'd never quite believed this would happen, certain everyone would realise what a terrible mistake they were making and she'd be acquitted. He'd already ordered Wrayworth to start work on an appeal, but the solicitor said that unless they could come up with some new evidence, there was little hope of success.

But there was still Robbie. Bryce snatched on this thought rather as a drowning man might grasp on a twig.

'This is all because you refused to accept Robbie as the legitimate heir. You've given away the child who was indeed Sir Ralph's grandson, the genuine heir to the title and this estate, as the doctor has surely proved. You must bring him back at once.'

'Why should I?'

'How can you live with yourself if you don't?'

'Very easily, brother, and in increased comfort.' As if to emphasise his point, Jago tugged on the bell pull to call for a servant to pour him a shot of whisky from a decanter standing on a table less than a few feet away.

Bryce gritted his teeth in an effort to control his temper. He'd hoped that concentrating on the child's predicament might help him to feel he was doing something positive, as well as occupying his mind from more morbid speculation. He felt this desperate need to do something for Robbie, and for Rose. 'Which godforsaken orphanage did you put him in? Tell me before I—'

'Before you what? Kill me? Is murder to become a family trait, then?'

'Speak to him, Mama, make him see sense.'

Lydia considered her younger son from the comfort of her sofa where she kept dipping her fingers into a box of chocolate truffles as she listened, unmoved, to this familiar squabble. It had been going on for weeks, as well as throughout the trial, and she was thoroughly bored with it. Taking another chocolate, she held it delicately between finger and thumb while she nibbled. 'He seems to be making perfect sense from where I am sitting. We really do not want that brat of a child robbing us of what is rightfully ours.'

'Didn't you hear what that doctor said? He delivered the baby. Nor is there any proof that Rose also had a child, which just happened to be the same age. Robbie is not a brat, I truly believe he is Rosalind and Robert's son.' Bryce was simmering with outrage.

Her response to this argument was a dismissive shrug. 'Sir Ralph and his son were estranged years ago, now they are both dead, let that be an end to them.'

A footman appeared. 'Did you call, sir?'

Jago smiled at his mother. 'Time for a small celebration on that verdict, don't you think?'

'Oh, what a good idea. Order a bottle of champagne, Jago darling.' And ignoring the cold rage emanating from her younger son, she spat out her next words with a pitiless venom. 'That boy should have died at birth.'

Bryce turned on his heel and stormed from the room, otherwise he might have committed the ultimate sin of slapping his own mother.

Without thinking where he was going, Bryce found himself in the kitchen. As he burst in, his rage still bubbling, Mrs Pascoe, Tilly, Gladys and the rest of the servants looked up surprised from where they were all sitting around the big pine table. They appeared to be sipping a glass of sherry each, looking very serious.

Mrs Quintrell, the housekeeper, came quickly to his side. 'Were you wanting something, sir?'

Bryce looked like a man who'd been poleaxed, as if he'd aged ten years in as many hours. 'Yes please, get me one of those, whatever it is you're having.'

'I think a spot of brandy would be more in order,' said Rowell, and seconds later Bryce was seated beside Tilly at the kitchen table, and the butler was handing him a tumbler half full of the stuff. Bryce took a large slug and felt the warmth of the liquid ease its way down to his vitals.

Tilly gently touched his arm. 'It won't happen, sir. They won't really hang her. They can't. She's innocent.'

'I think she is too, Tilly. I've instructed Wrayworth to lodge an appeal, plead for a reprieve, whatever he can do for her. The trouble is we can't find that dratted agreement to prove her innocence. I believe my brother destroyed it.'

Gladys turned to John, Jago's valet and driver. 'Didn't you say there were a stack of papers in Master Jago's room?'

'Aye, but I wouldn't know what they were, would I? I don't go rummaging through the master's stuff.'

Bryce was instantly on the alert. 'Where does he keep them?'

'In a shoebox on top of his wardrobe; not the most original place in the world, but I doubt anyone would dare to pry into Master Jago's stuff.'

Bryce was careful to say nothing more, but he'd made a mental note. He took a second swallow, and the servants glumly followed suit, seeking what comfort they could in their sips of sherry. 'If only my poor darling wife hadn't kept up the charade for so long, or told so many lies.'

Mrs Pascoe gave a scornful snort. 'She ain't the only one can tell lies. Your dear Mama, begging your pardon, sir, is an expert in that department.'

'What do you mean, Mrs Pascoe?'

Leaning closer, the old cook dropped her voice in that conspiratorial way she had, and with her tongue sufficiently loosened by the sherry, began her tale. 'It happened years ago when they had that family bust-up. That was all down to a lie. Your ma told Sir Ralph that his son Robert had made a pass at her, followed her to her bedroom one evening and wanted her to . . . you know. That's why father and son fell out, because Sir Ralph, still besotted with his new wife at that time, believed the tale. But t'weren't true, not a word of it. I know because I were there. I served Master Robert with a late supper and chatted with him, as he liked to do, then he went to his own room. He never went near her.'

'So that was all a scheme to rid herself of Robert?'

'And I'm sorry to say it succeeded. Robert went off to America, met Rosalind and never saw his father again, which is why we're where we are today.'

Bryce shook his head in despair, then let out a heavy sigh. 'The awful thing is that I can believe my mother and brother perfectly capable of such calumny. Not that it helps us much with the problem we have today. If only Rose had confessed to her mistake in going along with Joe's stupid scheme, it could all have been so different.'

'She could never do that, sir,' Tilly said. 'She was afraid you'd send her packing, and Her Ladyship – er . . . Miss Rose – would never risk leaving little Robbie unprotected.'

'Unprotected?' Bryce slammed the glass down hard on the table, sending a shower of brandy flying. 'Not that nonsense again. Protect him from Jago, you mean? I'm aware my brother was devastated at losing what he believed to be rightfully his, but he would never seriously hurt a child.' Even as Bryce said these words a doubt formed in his mind. Had Jago not already done so by packing Robbie off to some unknown institution?

Tilly remained firm. 'Ah, but he did. I know that for

a fact as I was there when it happened. Did milady never tell you?'

'She did hint at something of the sort, but I didn't take her seriously. I wouldn't listen.' His eyes were suddenly bleak.

'Oh, it's true, right enough.' Tilly bluntly related the incident on the cliff top, making her audience gasp in horror. 'He dangled that child over a sixty-foot drop, talking about what would happen if his foot slipped, how a baby was no more important than a rabbit or a rat. "Babies are easy to come by and even easier to dispose of." Those were his exact words, then he tossed him to Rose. Thank God she caught him safely. That was the moment when she made up her mind to put Robbie's life before her own. We both did. We made a pact,' Tilly finished, in a rather matter-of-fact tone, but then her eyes flooded with tears. 'Except that I failed him. I let Master Jago walk away with him. What has happened to the little chap? Where is he?'

Bryce handed her a handkerchief to mop up her tears. 'Don't blame yourself, Tilly. You could never have stopped Jago. It's up to us to find the boy, and to remain strong for Rose's sake. We must all think hard on how we can help her. There are only days left, so time is desperately short. John, tell me again, where did you drive Jago when he took Robbie away that day?'

Tilly interrupted. 'I've already asked him that question a hundred times, sir. It didn't help.'

'It was only to the station,' John said, looking mournful. 'Not Bristol at all. I can't tell you any more than that.'

Bryce narrowed his eyes as he thought about this for a moment. 'Was this from Bodmin?'

'St Austell, sir.'

'Which platform? Did you notice what train he took?'

'The one that goes upcountry of course, sir.'

'To Plymouth?'

'Aye, and beyond.'

Again Tilly cut in. 'Haven't you already searched Plymouth?'

Bryce slumped. 'Yes, Tilly, I've searched everywhere I can think of.'

'So where else might he be?'

They all sat in abject misery as they tried to think of a likely place. Then John suddenly brightened. 'Newton Abbot. Jago loves the races, and there was a meeting on that day. Is there an orphanage at Newton Abbot, or nearby?'

'I don't know, John, but I mean to find out.'

Bryce fully intended to visit Newton Abbot and make a thorough search of the surrounding area, but there was one other important matter to attend to first. He waited until the next morning when Jago was safely closeted in the estate office. As this was quarter day, hopefully he'd be kept fully occupied collecting rents for some hours.

Wasting no time, he went to his brother's room, grabbed a chair to stand on, and easily located the shoebox tucked right at the back on top of the big mahogany wardrobe. Only Jago's supreme arrogance would convince him that no one would intrude upon his private space or investigate his personal possessions.

Bryce took the box over to the window to riffle through the contents, which largely seemed to comprise various receipts and an alarming number of unpaid bills. Rosalind's marriage certificate was not there, of course, having been presented as evidence, but neither was there any sign of the letter of agreement written by the dying Rosalind to hand over the care of her son to Rose.

Despair engulfed Bryce yet again. He hadn't realised how much he'd banked on finding it here, until he felt the bitter taste of disappointment. But he'd been right in his surmise. Jago had indeed destroyed the evidence. And there were only six days left.

Why had he wasted so much time immediately after her arrest in worrying over his confused feelings, trying to decide whether or not she was guilty? He could instead have been searching for the necessary evidence. Bryce awarded himself no accolades for his indefatigable search for Robbie, but then he hadn't found the boy, had he? Why hadn't he believed in her innocence implicitly from the start? What kind of a husband was he to be swayed by Joe's tale rather than listen to his own wife?

It was as he was attempting to put the papers back in the correct order that one slipped out. It was a single folded sheet of blue writing paper which he hadn't noticed before. Now he opened it, his heart quickening as he read the contents.

He took the letter straight to Wrayworth. 'It's from the steward. Jago must have found him, and the man has written back to give his version of events on the night Rosalind died. It states quite plainly that he did indeed witness such a document, written by Rosalind's own hand, even though "the poor lady was clearly nearing her end", as she wanted to make provision for her son. There it is in black and white, exactly the evidence we need.'

The solicitor looked pleased with his find, but less excited than Bryce had hoped. 'It's a step nearer, certainly.'

'What do you mean, "a step nearer"?'

'We need the man himself. The prosecution could claim that this letter was a forgery, produced to save your wife at the eleventh hour. We need the steward in person to swear that this is his writing, his own words, that he did indeed sign that paper.'

'And how do we go about finding him?'

'We write to the ship's company.'

'We don't have time for letters. We could telephone. We're living in the twentieth century, after all. Surely the company will possess a telephone?' Bryce reached for the solicitor's own phone, but Wrayworth's next words stopped him in his tracks.

'I doubt that is our main problem. This man's job is to act as steward on the great liners. He could be anywhere in the world. What hope do we have of getting him here in time?'

Rose sat in her cell with the calmness of a woman who had long since accepted her fate. Where was the point in grieving for a life she might have lived? There was nothing more to be done now. Somewhere in this gloomy building the hangman would be making the necessary preparations. She could only hope that he was good at his job, that he would be efficient, and the end quick and painless.

Mr Wrayworth and the defence counsel had tried their best. It was no fault of theirs that she'd been found guilty.

Nor did she blame those twelve gentlemen and true who had issued the verdict. The fault lay entirely with Jago who had undoubtedly destroyed the agreement they'd all signed. Without that, and with no one else present at the time of Rosalind's death, there was no way of proving that she hadn't hastened her end. As if she would do such a thing to such a dear, kind, lovely lady.

Rose knew that she herself must also bear a fair part of the blame. Had she not agreed to go along with Joe's plan of checking out the Tregowan family before handing Robbie over, she would not now be in this situation. He'd been working on his own little scheme, and she'd been too stupid to notice. What an idiot she'd been, what a naive fool. As time had gone by, she'd become fearful for Robbie's safety, then fallen hopelessly in love with Bryce, thereby becoming ever more deeply enmeshed. Yet the punishment for this folly was somewhat excessive.

Poor Joe had been charged as an accessory to murder and attempted fraud. He'd been sent down for twenty-five years. That too seemed an exceptionally cruel punishment to pay for one foolish lie. Although, as with all lies, it hadn't stopped at one but unfortunately gathered momentum and grown into a veritable web of lies, with unforeseen consequences.

What hurt Rose most was the way Bryce had seemingly abandoned her. Following their last meeting when she'd still been in shock over the verdict, he'd sent her a note telling her to keep faith, promising he would do what he could, and that he'd visit. All week she'd waited, but still he hadn't come.

Nor was there any further news from Mr Wrayworth. The solicitor had come to see her once, a few days ago, telling her how an appeal had been lodged, albeit with precious little conviction in his voice. She'd hardly listened to his explanation regarding the problems they were having over lack of evidence. He'd even spoken of his hopes for a reprieve, but she'd taken no notice. Rose was no longer a fool. She had no intention of allowing herself any false hopes. Acceptance of her fate was undoubtedly her safest plan. It would be far too painful to face again the bitter gall of disappointment.

Right now she was struggling to write to her mother. How did one begin to explain the terrible fate that was about to befall her beloved daughter? Rose had left this task until the last possible moment, thinking that the longer Annie could enjoy life without the burden of knowing her fate, the better. When it was done, she folded the letter carefully, kissed it, then slipped it into the envelope and sealed it.

What dreams they had had when first they'd set sail for America. Micky, Mary, Clara and the twins had been so excited. So had she, certain it was the right thing for the family to have a fresh start in a new country. But all her dreams had come to nothing, and she would never see them again. The pain swelling her heart threatened to burst it wide open, but she didn't shed a single tear. It was too late for weeping. Now such things as dreams no longer mattered.

Rose could not eat the last meal they brought her, but she knelt and said her final prayers with the priest, handing him the letter to post. 'And this one is for my husband,' she told him. 'Will you please see that he gets it safely?'

'Of course, my dear.'

They led her along a passage, dark and dank, and smelling strangely of cats. Then a woman was tying up her hair with a ribbon.

'Why a green one?' Rose asked, giving the woman a little smile.

'Because it's a lucky colour. Have they not told you there might still be a reprieve?'

Rose looked at her but said nothing.

'We don't need to go into the next room for ten more minutes. Is there anything more you would like me to do for you?' the woman asked.

'I have the love of my husband, and his faith in my innocence. What more do I need?'

The minutes clicked by like hours, but then, just as the woman moved to conduct her into the next chamber, there came the sound of loud voices in the corridor outside. 'Let this man through,' someone shouted. The door burst open and a police officer appeared. Beside him was Mr Wrayworth, a paper in his hand and a huge grin on his round face. 'It is here. It's come through in time. You are to be reprieved, dear Rose, pending an appeal. We have found the steward and there's no reason to suppose you won't soon be a free woman.'

At which point Rose fell to the floor in a dead faint.

Chapter Twenty-Three

'I will not have that woman in this house!' Lydia was white to the lips. Since hearing the news she had stormed back and forth in the small parlour, spitting and hissing like a wild cat, volubly expressing her anger.

'Rose has been found innocent, Mother,' Bryce sternly reminded her, watching this performance in disbelief. 'You know full well that we managed to track the steward down, as by great good fortune his ship happens to be docked in Liverpool. Wrayworth has persuaded the fellow to appear in court to present this new evidence at the appeal. We have every reason to believe that she will then be allowed to walk free. Rose is innocent. Rosalind bled to death, most likely as a result of a botched childbirth. By the sound of it, the doctor should be the one in the dock. When Rose comes home, you will receive her with good grace.'

'I will not!' Lydia grabbed a small Chinese vase that happened to be standing on a nearby table and flung it to the floor with a scream of fury. With exemplary patience, Bryce picked up the pieces and tossed them into the waste basket.

Jago took a step forward. 'You ask too much, brother. If you must continue with this unfortunate union, then live with the woman somewhere else. I agree with Mama, we will not have her here at Penver Court. She has caused too much trouble.'

'You cannot prevent her from living here.'

'I most certainly can. It is my right, as master!'

Yet again the two brothers faced each other like combatants in a duel, although fortunately with no weapons beyond their fists. Bryce firmly clenched his, in an effort to retain control of himself. 'You are not, strictly speaking, master here and never were, as no doubt Wrayworth will inform you. You ran the place by default, that is all. You have no rights. Neither do I. Sir Ralph very generously made provision for us to continue to call this our home, *but we have no rights to it*. Get that into your head once and for all. The trouble with you, Jago, is that you're weak and selfish and greedy. Incapable of making a success of your life by your own efforts, you expect everything to be handed to you on a plate.' Bryce prodded his brother in the chest with one jabbing finger. '*You* were the one to cause Rose all this trouble. I also know that you deliberately destroyed the evidence, and that you hid a letter you received from the steward which proved the original document to be genuine. A letter which

342

could have proved her innocence. Then you disposed of the boy. What of him, eh? Would you deny Rosalind's son the right to live here too? Too late, I've beaten you on that one too. He is home.'

To his great relief and delight, Bryce had finally found Robbie. He inwardly smiled at the memory of how he'd walked into one orphanage not far from Newton Abbot, rapidly losing hope that he would ever find him. The sister in charge had led him directly to her office, but on the way they'd crossed the hall where Bryce could see scores of children sitting at their desks in regimented rows.

A voice had suddenly piped up. 'Uncle Bryce, Uncle Bryce.' And one small boy had cannoned straight into his arms like a bullet. 'I *knew* you'd come. I *knew* you would.'

Bryce had lifted Robbie high in his arms to give him a great big hug, and the children had cheered and laughed, delighted that one of their number, at least, had found happiness. Perhaps it gave them hope that the same might happen to them one day.

Young as he was, Robbie was quite old enough to understand what had happened. He explained to Bryce how Jago had said he would leave him there just for a few days, but had never come back for him. 'I waited and waited. The sisters keep calling me Robert Blight. I've told them I'm a Tregowan, but they won't listen.'

'You were a brave boy.' Bryce looked at the sister's flushed face. 'Robert Blight? No doubt a reference to the fact he was considered by some to be a blight on the family. Did my brother make a donation to your charity, Sister?'

The crimson hue deepened. 'He did, as a matter of fact, but we believed the child to be unwanted, and we were willing to care for him.'

'I dare say you were, at a price.' No doubt Jago made it worth their while to keep the child tucked away and persist with this new name until such time as he forgot his own, or everyone had stopped looking for him.

Now Bryce faced that brother with cold hatred in his heart. 'Thank God he is safe, even now with his adoring Tilly. You are the one who is a blight upon this family, not that child.'

Lydia, in her distress, had turned to food, as was her way, helping herself to a slice of shortcake and a cup of tea while her two sons argued. Bryce addressed her with barely concealed contempt in his tone. 'Do you see what you have done to this son of yours, Mama, by teaching him your own grasping and heartless tricks?'

Lydia calmly sipped her tea, little finger poised. 'If you lack ambition, Bryce, the fault lies with you, not with your dear brother.'

Bryce let out an exasperated sigh. Disagreeing with these two always had a bad effect upon his temper. 'You should take care, Mother, that you too aren't investigated by the courts.'

Lydia actually jerked, slopping the tea into her saucer. 'What on earth do you mean by that?'

'I am referring to the fact that you also nursed a dying man, your much lamented husband. Did you, I wonder, help him on his way just a little?'

There was an appalled silence, one that seemed to

344

stretch endlessly before Lydia set down the cup and saucer and gathered her wits sufficiently to respond. 'How dare you speak to me in that manner! I'll have you know that I devoted years of my life to my beloved husband.'

Bryce actually laughed out loud at that. 'You devoted years of your life to nurturing your husband's fortune, and he was never your beloved. Nor did you shed a single tear at his death. And what of your previous husbands?'

Two little lines puckered her brow, despite the fact Lydia made a policy of never frowning, as it was bad for her complexion. Yet there was a nervous glitter in her eye. 'What about them?'

'I was wondering how it is that all of them suffered some sort of tragedy at the end.'

'Such things happen all too frequently in life,' Lydia snapped, a wildness now creeping into her glare which might almost be described as fear.

'With surprising regularity, it seems, in your case.' Bryce leant against the mantelpiece, thoughtfully rubbing his chin as he recalled the details. 'Let's see, allegedly your first husband took an overdose of laudanum, because he couldn't bear to live without you. But then he'd turned out not to be rich, so he was no great loss, was he? Then there was my father, the old Scottish laird, who you wore out rather quickly. How did you manage that, I wonder: by overexercise, too much food and whisky? Ah yes, then he rode his horse too hard in the hunt to impress you, took a tumble, and the poor old soul never recovered. The third, admittedly, lived to tell the tale after a bitter divorce. Perhaps you'd met your match and decided to cut your losses. And then we come to the enigma of Sir Ralph. Yet another ancient, invalid husband under your care. It was becoming quite a habit. Who is to know for sure what happened while you were nursing him? The press of a pillow might have seemed preferable to endless months or years of living with a man in a coma.'

Bryce saw at once that his words had struck home. His mother had sat frozen throughout this lengthy speech, eyes wide, rather like a startled rabbit caught in the glare of a poacher's lamp, but at mention of the pillow her face contorted with a furious terror.

'This is all lies!' she screamed. 'I did no such thing.'

From the corner of his eye Bryce noticed Jago slip quietly away, clearly distancing himself from this charge. Looking about her in a blind panic, his mother too realised that she had lost her stalwart supporter, and finding herself deserted by this adored favourite son, began to cry, ever her last resort.

'Cut the waterworks, Mama, my fund of sympathy is at a particularly low ebb right now.'

'How can you malign your own mother so?' she sobbed, dabbing at eyes surprisingly dry, considering the noise she was making.

'I'll admit this may be rather a harsh judgement on my part, and perhaps I'm reading too much into perfectly innocent and unfortunate incidents. On the other hand it could be terrifyingly accurate. Which is it? Never mind, I would rather not know.' Bryce came to sit beside her, stroking her hand as it gripped her skirts in distress. 'If the former is the case and you are innocent, then you should find more sympathy for Rose, not less. If the latter, then you were fortunate no one chose to investigate these personal tragedies. Or else you didn't have Jago as your enemy. But take care, Mama, Rose is my wife, and I will not see her wronged. Is that clear?'

'You expect me to—'

'I expect you to treat my wife with proper respect, particularly in view of the fact that you have suffered similar misfortunes. It would be most *unfortunate* were the police to hear there is some doubt over Sir Ralph's demise and decide to investigate further, would it not?'

She stared at him in complete horror. 'You would never do that to me, your own mother.'

Her lovely face, with its alabaster skin, round childlike eyes and Cupid's bow mouth, remained amazingly unmarked by the passage of time, and had been the downfall of many men over the years. Bryce, as her son, damped down the surge of pity which automatically rose in his throat at the sight of his mother's distress. But together with Jago, she had made Rose's life a complete misery, and almost robbed her of it in the end. Somehow he had to make it very clear he would stand for no more of these plots against her.

'I have also recently learnt, dearest Mama, that the reason for Sir Ralph's estrangement with his only son all those years ago was because you had informed your husband that Robert had propositioned you. That was a lie, wasn't it? He did no such thing. Rather, you planned the whole thing to put the young man in the worst possible light in order to create dissension between father and son.'

'Who told you such a thing?'

He smiled at her, rather wickedly. 'Would you believe that I have been gossiping with the servants? They are not so blind, deaf and dumb as you might imagine. I suppose you simply decided that you wanted rid of him, that you needed a clear field for your own purpose in bleeding his poor father dry. Was that not the case, Mama?'

She fell silent at this, all the bluster draining out of her, the shocked expression on her ashen face speaking volumes.

Patting her hand one last time, Bryce got to his feet. 'Good, I'm glad we understand each other at last. I'm sure Mrs Pascoe will be only too happy to arrange some form of celebration for Rose, once the appeal is behind us, and my wife is set free.'

The first question Rose asked when she saw him, was of Robbie.

'Do not fret he is safe.'

'Thank God.'

'But before I tell you that tale, let me first apologise. I was wrong to mistrust you, my darling. I should have had more faith. Can you ever forgive me?'

'Can you forgive *me* for getting into this mess in the first place?'

Bryce laughed. 'Then let us agree to set all this unpleasantness behind us and look to a new future together.'

Rose glanced up at him through her lashes with a return of her old shyness. 'Are you sure you still want me as your wife?'

'More than ever, for I have discovered how very much I love you, even more than before.' He kissed her then and Rose melted in his arms, unable to believe her good fortune.

The last few weeks in prison awaiting her appeal had not been easy, but now she could put all of that behind her. The steward, a most pleasant man, exactly as she'd remembered him, had clearly stated the facts of the case, relating how they'd each signed the document, and how poor dear Rosalind had been determined to see her son safe as her own life ebbed away.

The papers for her release had been properly processed, her clothes and belongings returned to her, and now she was sitting in the Electric Phaeton, her husband's lips on hers, and her heart was pounding with happiness. Just to feel the warm strength of him as he held her, as if he might never let her go, was like falling into paradise.

'Now tell me how you found Robbie?'

Bryce told his tale, a delighted grin on his face. 'John's guess was right. He was in an orphanage near Newton Abbot, under a different name, but the moment he saw me he came running into my arms.'

There were tears in her eyes now. 'Then all is well. I can't wait to see him. But there's just one thing that is still troubling me.'

He kissed her nose. 'And what is that, my darling? Because whatever you want you shall have, if it is in my power to provide it.'

'I'm not certain that either Lydia or Jago will wish me to return to Penver Court. They made it very clear from the start that I was unwanted, and their resentment against me now must be a thousand times worse.'

There was a familiar tightening of muscles in Bryce's jaw, but then he gave her his warm, lazy smile. 'You can be quite certain, my darling, that there will be no problems from them.'

They were all waiting for her. This time, as the motor drove Rose down the long drive to Penver Court, she was astonished to see a veritable crowd of people, all apparently waiting for her. She couldn't help but remember that first occasion when she'd been quaking with nerves, worrying what the Tregowan family would be like, what she could say to explain the impossible position Joe had put her in. She recalled their freezing glances at the funeral, the way they'd cold-shouldered her, then interrogated and publicly humiliated her. They were clearly determined from the start not to accept this stranger into their home, let alone the unwanted young rival for the title. Lydia and her son would have sought any excuse to reject her.

But today, by the time the car drew up and John opened the door for her to step out, Rose saw that the entire staff were now standing in line, broad smiles on all their friendly faces.

'Welcome home, milady,' said Mrs Quintrell, bobbing a little curtsey.

'Oh, but I'm not—'

'You are as far as we are concerned,' Mr Rowell said, the butler bearing a huge grin on his kindly face. 'And always will be.'

One by one she shook their hands: Mrs Pascoe, who promised her a veritable feast later; Gladys and all the other maids; Thomas the footman and the rest of the menservants; John, and best of all, Joe, who had likewise been released, all charges of fraud dropped by the family.

Rose hugged him. 'Don't ever do such a thing to me again.'

'Don't worry, Rosie, I've learnt my lesson. Tilly and me are going to be wed, and I shall become a pillar of the community.'

She laughed. 'That'll be the day. 'But where is Tilly, and . . . ?' She was itching to see Robbie, but her old friend stepped forward and Rose hugged her too.

'Bless you, Tilly, and thank you for being such a good friend, for always believing in me, and always caring for Robbie.'

It was then that a small voice cried out. 'Mummy, Mummy, you're home!' And a small boy came running. Sweeping him up into her arms, Rose could not stop the tears now as they rolled unchecked down her cheeks. But they were tears of happiness, and Bryce came to put his arms about them both. To hear this precious child accept her as his mother overwhelmed Rose with joy, but there was more to come.

'I have another treat in store for you, my darling.' I have a passage booked for the three of us with the White Star Line to visit your family in New York. We sail at the end of the month, only this time you will travel first class.'